071732

808.831   Sherlock Holmes through
S   time and space.

SHERLOCK HOLMES
THROUGH
TIME AND SPACE

SHERLOCK HOLMES THROUGH TIME AND SPACE

edited by

Issac Asimov, Martin Harry Greenberg, and Charles G. Waugh

Bluejay Books Inc.

The publisher wishes to acknowledge the special editorial contributions made to this book by Stuart Shiffman and Larry Carmody. Furthermore, the artists wish to acknowledge Stuart Shiffman's contributions without which this book would have not have looked truly Sherlockian.

Contents

"Watson! The game is afoot."
—Sherlock Holmes

Sherlock Holmes

by

Isaac Asimov

It can easily be argued that Sherlock Holmes is the most successful fictional character of all time. It has been a century since he was created in the mind of Arthur Conan Doyle, and in all that time he has delighted countless millions of readers with an intensity that has not diminished with time. A substantial fraction of those readers refused to accept Holmes as fictional, but thought (and some think so even today, I'm sure) that he was real and alive and sent him letters, addressed to 221B Baker Street, outlining their problems.

This very success, which gave pleasure to the reading public generally, was the source of great annoyance to Conan Doyle. Sherlock Holmes obscured all his other literary endeavors, which dwindled and died in the vast Sherlockian shade. It even obscured Conan Doyle as an individual, for he became nothing but an intermediary between the detective and the public.

Conan Doyle knew this and resented it bitterly. He tried to end his enslavement by demanding a higher price with each story he wrote. It didn't work; the price was always met. He resorted to

1

more drastic measures and wrote a story in which he ruthlessly killed his detective. It didn't work; outraged public demand forced him to resurrect Holmes.

I have often thought that Conan Doyle turned to spiritualism and other follies in later life in an (unconscious?) effort to dissociate himself from Holmes and to achieve some sort of fame that would adhere to himself alone. The extremities of irrationality to which he descended (he believed in fairies and let himself be fooled by obviously faked photographs) may well have been a wild attempt to rebel against Holmes's supreme rationality. If so, that didn't work either. Conan Doyle was laughed at, but Holmes was still revered.

Holmes's success added him quickly to the notable roster of people (both real and fictional) who are "undefined." What I mean by this is simple:

When Holmes describes James Moriarty, that master criminal, as "the Napoleon of crime," he doesn't bother to pause and explain who Napoleon was. He takes it for granted that Watson knows who Napoleon was and Conan Doyle can safely take it for granted that virtually anyone capable of reading him knows who Napoleon was.

In the same way, when anyone describes someone as being "a regular Sherlock Holmes," he never pauses to explain what he means. The name is part of the English language. Each of us assumes that all others know exactly who Sherlock Holmes is.

Holmes set the fashion for detectives, or at least for the most unfailingly fascinating ones, for all times. To be sure, there were fictional detectives before Holmes; and some who must undoubtedly have inspired Conan Doyle's creative effort (notably, Edgar Allan Poe's detective, Dupin), but the overwhelming success and popularity of Sherlock Holmes wiped out all that had gone before as though they had never been. It was Holmes who became the model.

Holmes was a gifted amateur who could see clearly through a fog that kept the professional police (Scotland Yard bunglers) hopelessly puzzled.

This sounds like an inversion of the natural order of things. How can amateurs be superior to professionals? Actually, it's a reflection of Victorian superstition and the English acceptance of their caste system. The Scotland Yard bunglers were, at best, middle class; perhaps even lower class in origin. The gifted amateur, however, was a gentleman who had been to Eton (or Harrow) and Oxford (or Cambridge). Naturally, an English gentleman would be born far superior to tradesmen and others who were beyond the pale.

And so the tradition of the gentleman detective came into being and was particularly beloved by a century of superb mystery writers, particularly those who were English, with Peter Wimsey being perhaps the most extreme case. Even when the detectives were professionals, they were often gentlemen who became policemen out of some quirk (Roderick Alleyn and John Appleby, for instance).

Nor did those mystery writers who followed Conan Doyle attempt to hide their indebtedness, for they could not. Consider the very first mystery written by Agatha Christie (the most successful of all the post-Doyle writers), *The Mysterious Affair at Styles*. The narrator, Captain Hastings, confesses his ambition to become a detective himself. He is asked "The real thing— Scotland Yard? Or Sherlock Holmes?" And Hastings replies, "Oh, Sherlock Holmes by all means."

The stage is set, in this way, for the appearance of Hercule Poirot, the best of all fictional detectives in the Sherlockian tradition.

To step down several notches, I have frequently described my own creation, the waiter Henry, in the stories that feature him, as "the Sherlock Holmes of the Black Widowers." Since it is useless to deny the debt, mystery writers refer to it brazenly and thus disarm, in advance, those who might otherwise sneer.

Sherlock Holmes invited imitation, of course, both worshipful and mocking. Mark Twain was one of the mockers, and did a very poor job of it, unfortunately. More successful was Robert Fish in his Schlock Homes stories. While Conan Doyle's copyrights were in force writers could only approach Holmes obliquely, of course, but they managed to write pastiches, often humorous ones, in a variety of ways. After the stories passed into the public domain, "new" Sherlock Holmes stories, as identical to the original in all respects as the writer could manage, began to be written in surprising numbers.

In fact, so numerous are the Sherlock Holmes continuations, parodies, and pastiches, that they can be divided into subgroups. The particular subgroup we deal with in this book are stories in which the Sherlockian style of fiction is treated in terms of science fiction or fantasy, and it is surprising (as you will see) how well the legend survives the transition.

This book contains fifteen stories that in one way or another deal with Sherlock Holmes. The first story is by Conan Doyle himself; an authentic Holmes story entitled "The Adventure of the Devil's Foot," one of two that, in all the canon, are most nearly science fiction.* It is very good science fiction, too, and you will be amazed how neatly Conan Doyle anticipated a phenomenon that was to be commonplace a generation after his death.

The last story is one of my Black Widowers, one in which an aspect of the Holmes stories is analyzed in the true spirit of the Baker Street Irregulars (see the story itself for some details on this organization), and a legitimate conclusion is reached.

In between are thirteen stories in which you will meet the spirit of Sherlock Holmes in the form of animals, robots, extraterrestrials, and so on. There is no limit to authors' imaginations in this respect—or to the pleasure they will give to all true Sherlockians (the American phrase), or Holmesians (the British).

*The other, "The Adventure of the Creeping Man," can be found in *The Best Science Fiction of Arthur Conan Doyle* (Carbondale, Ill.: Southern Illinois University Press, 1981), edited by Charles G. Waugh and Martin H. Greenberg.

The Adventure of the Devil's Foot
by
Sir Arthur Conan Doyle

As a matter of fact, Conan Doyle wrote science fiction, too, and very good science fiction. My personal feeling is—and I hope the Baker Street Irregulars don't hear me—that his science fiction is better than his mysteries.

The Adventure of the Devil's Foot

by Sir Arthur Conan Doyle

In recording from time to time some of the curious experiences and interesting recollections which I associate with my long and intimate friendship with Mr. Sherlock Holmes, I have continually been faced by difficulties caused by his own aversion to publicity. To his somber and cynical spirit all popular applause was always abhorrent, and nothing amused him more at the end of a successful case than to hand over the actual exposure to some orthodox official, and to listen with a mocking smile to the general chorus of misplaced congratulation. It was indeed this attitude upon the part of my friend and certainly not any lack of interesting material which has caused me of late years to lay very few of my records before the public. My participation in some of his adventures was always a privilege which entailed discretion and reticence upon me.

It was, then, with considerable surprise that I received a telegram from Holmes last Tuesday—he has never been known to write where a telegram would serve—in the following terms:

Why not tell them of the Cornish horror—strangest case I have handled.

I have no idea what backward sweep of memory had brought the matter fresh to his mind, or what freak had caused him to desire that I should recount it; but I hasten, before another canceling telegram may arrive, to hunt out the notes which give me the exact details of the case and to lay the narrative before my readers.

It was, then, in the spring of the year 1897 that Holmes's iron constitution showed some symptoms of giving way in the face of constant hard work of a most exacting kind, aggravated, perhaps, by occasional indiscretions of his own. In March of that year Dr. Moore Agar, of Harley Street, whose dramatic introduction to Holmes I may some day recount, gave positive injunctions that the famous private agent lay aside all his cases and surrender himself to complete rest if he wished to avert an absolute breakdown. The state of his health was not a matter in which he himself took the faintest interest, for his mental detachment was absolute, but he was induced at least, on the threat of being permanently disqualified from work, to give himself a complete change of scene and air. Thus it was that in the early spring of that year we found ourselves together in a small cottage near Poldhu Bay, at the further extremity of the Cornish peninsula.

It was a singular spot, and one peculiarly well suited to the grim humor of my patient. From the windows of our little whitewashed house, which stood high upon a grassy headland, we looked down upon the whole sinister semicircle of Mounts Bay, that old death trap of sailing vessels, with its fringe of black cliffs and surge-swept reefs on which innumerable seamen have met their end. With a northerly breeze it lies placid and sheltered, inviting the storm-tossed craft to tack into it for rest and protection.

Then come the sudden swirl round of the wind, the blustering gale from the southwest, the dragging anchor, the lee shore, and the last battle in the creaming breakers. The wise mariner stands far out from that evil place.

On the land side our surroundings were as somber as on the sea. It was a country of rolling moors, lonely and dun-colored, with an occasional church tower to mark the site of some old-world village. In every direction upon these moors there were traces of some vanished race which had passed utterly away, and left as its sole record strange monuments of stone, irregular mounds which contained the burned ashes of the dead, and curious earthworks which hinted at prehistoric strife. The glamour and mystery of the place, with its sinister atmosphere of forgotten nations, appealed to the imagination of my friend, and he spent much of his time in long walks and solitary meditations upon the moor. The ancient Cornish language had also arrested his attention, and he had, I remember, conceived the idea that it was akin to the Chaldean, and had been largely derived from the Phoenician traders in tin. He had received a consignment of books upon philology and was settling down to develop this thesis when suddenly, to my sorrow and to his unfeigned delight, we found ourselves, even in that land of dreams, plunged into a problem at our very doors which was more intense, more engrossing, and infinitely more mysterious than any of those which had driven us from London. Our simple life and peaceful, healthy routine were violently interrupted, and we were precipitated into the midst of a series of events which caused the utmost excitement not only in Cornwall but throughout the whole west of England. Many of my readers may retain some recollection of what was called at the time "The Cornish Horror," though a most imperfect account of the matter reached the London press. Now, after thirteen years, I will give the true details of this inconceivable affair to the public.

I have said that scattered towers marked the villages which dotted this part of Cornwall. The nearest of these was the hamlet of Tredannick Wollas, where the cottages of a couple of hundred inhabitants clustered round an ancient, moss-grown church. The vicar of the parish, Mr. Roundhay, was something of an archaeologist, and as such Holmes had made his acquaintance. He was a middle-aged man, portly and affable, with a considerable fund of local lore. At his invitation we had taken tea at the vicarage and had come to know, also, Mr. Mortimer Tregennis, an independent gentleman, who increased the clergyman's scant resources by taking rooms in his large, straggling house. The vicar, being a bachelor, was glad to come to such an arrangement, though he had little in common with his lodger, who was a thin, dark, spectacled man, with a stoop which gave the impression of actual, physical deformity. I remember that during our short visit we found the vicar garrulous, but his lodger strangely reticent, a sad-faced, introspective man, sitting with averted eyes, brooding apparently upon his own affairs.

These were the two men who entered abruptly into our little sitting-room on Tuesday, March the 16th, shortly after our breakfast hour, as we were smoking together, preparatory to our daily excursion upon the moors.

"Mr. Holmes," said the vicar in an agitated voice, "the most extraordinary and tragic affair has occurred during the night. It is the most unheard-of business. We can only regard it as a special Providence that you should chance to be here at the time, for in all England you are the one man we need."

I glared at the intrusive vicar with no very friendly eyes; but Holmes took his pipe from his lips and sat up in his chair like an old hound who hears the view-halloo. He waved his hand to the sofa, and our palpitating visitor with his agitated companion sat side by side upon it. Mr. Mortimer Tregennis was more self-contained than the clergyman, but the twitching of his thin hands and the brightness of his dark eyes showed that they shared a common emotion.

"Shall I speak or you?" he asked of the vicar.

"Well, as you seem to have made the discovery, whatever it may be, and the vicar to have had it second-hand, perhaps you had better do the speaking," said Holmes.

I glanced at the hastily clad clergyman, with the formally dressed lodger seated beside him, and was amused at the surprise which Holmes's simple deduction had brought to their faces.

"Perhaps I had best say a few words first," said the vicar, "and then you can judge if you will listen to the details from Mr. Tregennis, or whether we should not hasten at once to the scene of this mysterious affair. I may explain, then, that our friend here spent last evening in the company of his two brothers, Owen and George, and of his sister Brenda, at their house of Tredannick Wartha, which is near the old stone cross upon the moor. He left them shortly after ten o'clock, playing cards round the dining-room table, in excellent health and spirits. This morning, being an early riser, he walked in that direction before breakfast and was overtaken by the carriage of Dr. Richards, who explained that he had just been sent for on a most urgent call to Tredannick Wartha. Mr. Mortimer Tregennis naturally went with him. When he arrived at Tredannick Wartha he found an extraordinary state of things. His two brothers and his sister were seated round the table exactly as he had left them, the cards still spread in front of them and the candles burned down to their sockets. The sister lay back stone-dead in her chair, while the two brothers sat on each side of her laughing, shouting, and singing, the senses stricken out of them. All three of them, the dead woman and the two demented men, retained upon their faces an expression of the utmost horror—a convulsion of terror which was dreadful to look upon. There was no sign of the presence of anyone in the house, except, Mrs. Porter, the old cook and housekeeper, who declared that she had slept deeply and heard no sound during the night. Nothing had been stolen or disarranged, and there is absolutely no explanation of what the horror can be which has frightened a woman to death and two strong men out of their senses. There is the situation, Mr. Holmes, in a nutshell, and if you can help us to clear it up you will have done a great work."

I had hoped that in some way I could coax my companion back into the quiet which had been the object of our journey; but one glance at his intense face and contracted eyebrows told me how vain was now the expectation. He sat for some little time in silence, absorbed in the strange drama which had broken in upon our peace.

"I will look into this matter," he said at last. "On the face of it, it would appear to be a case of a very exceptional nature. Have you been there yourself, Mr. Roundhay?"

"No, Mr. Holmes. Mr. Tregennis brought back the account to the vicarage, and I at once hurried over with him to consult you."

"How far is it to the house where this singular tragedy occurred?"

"About a mile inland."

"Then we shall walk over together. But before we start I must ask you a few questions, Mr. Mortimer Tregennis."

The other had been silent all this time, but I had observed that his more controlled excitement was even greater than the obtrusive emotion of the clergyman. He sat with a pale, drawn face, his anxious gaze fixed upon Holmes, and his thin hands clasped convulsively together. His pale lips quivered as he listened to the dreadful experience which had befallen his family, and his dark eyes seemed to reflect something of the horror of the scene.

"Ask what you like, Mr. Holmes," said he eagerly. "It is a bad thing to speak of, but I will answer you the truth."

"Tell me about last night."

"Well, Mr. Holmes, I supped there, as the vicar has said, and my elder brother George proposed a game of whist afterwards. We sat down about nine o'clock. It was a quarter-past ten when I moved to go. I left them all round the table, as merry as could be."

"Who let you out?"

"Mrs. Porter had gone to bed, so I let myself out. I shut the hall door behind me. The window of the room in which they sat was closed, but the blind was not drawn down. There was no change in door or window this morning, nor any reason to think that any stranger had been to the house. Yet there they sat, driven clean mad with terror, and Brenda lying dead of fright, with her head hanging over the arm of the chair. I'll never get the sight of that room out of my mind so long as I live."

"The facts, as you state them, are certainly most remarkable," said Holmes. "I take it that you have no theory yourself which can in any way account for them?"

"It's devilish, Mr. Holmes, devilish!'" cried Mortimer Tregennis. "It is not of this world. Something has come into that room which has dashed the light of reason from their minds. What human contrivance could do that?"

"I fear," said Holmes, "that if the matter is beyond humanity it is certainly beyond me. Yet we must exhaust all natural explanations before we fall back upon such a theory as this. As to yourself, Mr. Tregennis, I take it you were divided in some way from your family, since they lived together and you had rooms apart?"

"That is so, Mr. Holmes, though the matter is past and done with. We were a family of tin-miners at Redruth, but we sold out our venture to a company, and so retired with enough to keep us. I won't deny that there was some feeling about the division of the money and it stood between us for a time, but it was all forgiven and forgotten, and we were the best of friends together."

"Looking back at the evening which you spent together, does anything stand out in your memory as throwing any possible light upon the tragedy? Think carefully, Mr. Tregennis, for any clue which can help me."

"There is nothing at all, sir."

"Your people were in their usual spirits?"

"Never better."

"Were they nervous people? Did they ever show any apprehension of coming danger?"

"Nothing of the kind."

"You have nothing to add then, which could assist me?"

Mortimer Tregennis considered earnestly for a moment.

"There is one thing occurs to me," said he at last. "As we sat at the table my back was to the window, and my brother George, he being my partner at cards, was facing it. I saw him once look hard over my shoulder, so I turned round and looked also. The blind was up and the window shut, but I could just make out the bushes on the lawn, and it seemed to me for a moment that I saw something moving among them. I couldn't even say if it was man or animal, but I just thought there was something there. When I asked him what he was looking at, he told me that he had the same feeling. That is all that I can say."

"Did you not investigate?"

"No; the matter passed as unimportant."

"You left them, then, without any premonition of evil?"

"None at all."

"I am not clear how you came to hear the news so early this morning."

"I am an early riser and generally take a walk before breakfast. This morning I had hardly started when the doctor in his carriage overtook me. He told me that old Mrs. Porter had sent a boy down with an urgent message. I sprang in beside him and we drove on. When we got there we looked into that dreadful room. The candles and the fire must have burned out hours before, and they had been sitting there in the dark until dawn had broken. The doctor said Brenda must have been dead at lest six hours. There were no signs of violence. She just lay across the arm of the chair with that look on her face. George and Owen were singing snatches of songs and gibbering like two great apes. Oh, it was awful to see! I couldn't stand it, and the doctor was as white as a sheet. Indeed, he fell into a chair in a sort of faint, and we nearly had him on our hands as well."

"Remarkable—most remarkable!" said Holmes, rising and taking his hat. "I think, perhaps, we had better go down to Tredannick Wartha without further delay. I confess that I have seldom known a case which at first sight presented a more singular problem."

Our proceedings of that first morning did little to advance the investigation. It was marked, however, at the outset by an incident which left the most sinister impression upon my mind. The approach to the spot at which the tragedy occurred is down a narrow, winding, country lane. While we made our way along it we heard the rattle of a carriage coming towards us and stood aside to let it pass. As it drove by us I caught a glimpse through the closed window of a horribly contorted, grinning face glaring out at us. Those staring eyes and gnashing teeth flashed past us like a dreadful vision.

"My brothers!" cried Mortimer Tregennis, white to his lips. "They are taking them to Helston."

We looked with horror after the black carriage, lumbering upon its way. Then we turned our steps towards this ill-omened house in which they had met their strange fate.

It was a large and bright dwelling, rather a villa than a cottage, with a considerable garden which was already, in that Cornish air, well filled with spring flowers. Towards this garden the window of the sitting-room fronted, and from it, according to Mortimer Tregennis, must have come that thing of evil which had by sheer horror in a single instant blasted their minds. Holmes walked slowly and thoughtfully among the flower-plots and along the path before we entered the porch. So absorbed was he in his thoughts, I remember, that he stumbled over the watering-pot, upset its contents, and deluged both our feet and the garden path. Inside the house we were met by the elderly Cornish housekeeper, Mrs. Porter, who, with the aid of a young girl, looked after the wants of the family. She readily answered all Holmes's questions. She had heard nothing in the night. Her employers had all been in excellent spirits lately, and she had never known them more cheerful and prosperous. She had fainted with horror upon entering the room in the morning and seeing that dreadful company round the table. She had, when she recovered, thrown open the window to let the morning air in, and had run down to the lane, whence she sent a farm-lad for the doctor. The lady was on her bed upstairs if we cared to see her. It took four strong men to get the brothers into the asylum carriage. She would not herself stay in the house another day and was starting that very afternoon to rejoin her family at St. Ives.

We ascended the stairs and viewed the body. Miss Brenda Tregennis had been a very beautiful girl, though now verging upon middle age. Her dark, clear-cut face was handsome, even in death, but there still lingered upon it something of that convulsion of horror which had been her last human emotion. From her bedroom we descended to the sitting-room, where this strange tragedy had actually occurred. The charred ashes of the overnight fire lay in the grate. On the table were the four guttered and burned-out candles, with the cards scattered over its surface. The chairs had been moved back against the walls, but all else was as it had been the night before. Holmes paced with light, swift steps about the room; he sat in the various chairs, drawing them up and reconstructing their positions. He tested how much of the garden was visible; he examined the floor, the ceiling, and the fireplace; but never once did I see that sudden brightening of his eyes and tightening of his lips which would have told me that he saw some gleam of light in this utter darkness.

"Why a fire?" he asked once. "Had they always a fire in this small room on a spring evening?"

Mortimer Tregennis explained that the night was cold and damp. For that reason, after his arrival, the fire was lit. "What are you going to do now, Mr. Holmes?" he asked.

My friend smiled and laid his hand upon my arm. "I think, Watson, that I shall resume that course of tobacco-poisoning which you have so often and so justly condemned," said he. "With your permission, gentlemen, we will now return to our cottage, for I am not aware that any new factor is likely to come to our notice here. I will turn the facts over in my mind, Mr. Tregennis, and should anything occur to me I will certainly communicate with you and the vicar. In the meantime I wish you both good-morning."

It was not until long after we were back in Poldhu Cottage that Holmes broke his complete and absorbed silence. He sat coiled in his armchair, his haggard and ascetic face hardly visible amid the blue swirl of his tobacco smoke, his black brows drawn down, his forehead contracted, his eyes vacant and far away. Finally he laid down his pipe and sprang to his feet.

"It won't do, Watson!" said he with a laugh. "Let us walk along the cliffs together and search for flint arrows. We are more likely to find them than clues to this problem. To let the brain work without sufficient material is like racing an engine. It racks itself to pieces. The sea air, sunshine, and patience, Watson—all else will come.

"Now, let us calmly define our position, Watson," he continued as we skirted the cliffs together. "Let us get a firm grip of the very little which we *do* know, so that when fresh facts arise we may be ready to fit them into their places. I take it, in the first place, that neither of us is prepared to admit diabolical intrusions into the affairs of men. Let us begin by ruling that entirely out of our minds. Very good. There remain three persons who have been grievously stricken by some conscious or unconscious human agency. That is firm ground. Now, when did this occur? Evidently, assuming his narrative to be true, it was immediately after Mr. Mortimer Tregennis had left the room. That is a very important point. The presumption is that it was within a few minutes afterwards. The cards still lay upon the table. It was already past their usual hour for bed. Yet they had not changed their position or pushed back their chairs. I repeat, then, that the occurrence was immediately after his departure, and not later than eleven o'clock last night.

"Our next obvious step is to check, so far as we can, the movements of Mortimer Tregennis after he left the room. In this there is no difficulty, and they seem to be above suspicion. Knowing my methods as you do, you were, of course, conscious of the somewhat clumsy water-pot expedient by which I obtained a clearer impress of his foot than might otherwise have been possible. The wet, sandy path took it admirably. Last night was also wet, you will remember, and it was not difficult—having obtained a sample print—to pick out his track among others and to follow his movements. He appears to have walked away swiftly in the direction of the vicarage.

"If, then, Mortimer Tregennis disappeared from the scene, and yet some outside person affected the cardplayers, how can we reconstruct that person, and how was such an impression of horror conveyed? Mrs. Porter may be eliminated. She is evidently harmless. Is there any evidence that someone crept up to the garden window and in some manner produced so terrific an effect that he drove those who saw it out of their senses? The only suggestion in this direction comes from Mortimer Tregennis himself, who says that his brother spoke about some movement in the garden. That is certainly remarkable, as the night was rainy, cloudy, and dark. Anyone who had the design to alarm these people would be compelled to place his very face against the glass before he could be seen. There is a three-foot flower-border outside this window, but no indication of a footmark. It is difficult to imagine, then, how an outsider could have made so terrible an impression upon the company, nor have we found any possible motive for so strange and elaborate an attempt. You perceive our difficulties, Watson?"

"They are only too clear," I answered with conviction.

"And yet, with a little more material, we may prove that they are not insurmountable," said Holmes. "I fancy that among your extensive archives, Watson, you may find some which were nearly as obscure. Meanwhile, we shall put the case aside until more accurate data are available, and devote the rest of our morning to the pursuit of neolithic man."

I may have commented upon my friend's power of mental detachment, but never have I wondered at it more than upon that spring morning in Cornwall when for two hours he discoursed upon celts, arrowheads, and shards, as lightly as if no sinister mystery were waiting for his solution. It was not until we had returned in the afternoon to our cottage that we found a visitor awaiting us, who soon brought our minds back to the matter in hand. Neither of us needed to be told who that visitor was. The huge body, the craggy and deeply seamed face with the fierce eyes and hawklike nose, the grizzled hair which nearly brushed our cottage ceiling, the beard—golden at the fringes and white near the lips, save for the nicotine stain from his perpetual cigar—all these were as well known in London as in Africa, and could only be associated with the tremendous personality of Dr. Leon Sterndale, the great lion-hunter and explorer.

We had heard of his presence in the district and had once or twice caught sight of his tall figure upon the moorland paths. He made no advances to us, however, nor would we have dreamed of doing so to him, as it was well known that it was his love of seclusion which caused him to spend the greater part of the intervals between his journeys in a small bungalow buried in the lonely wood of Beauchamp Arriance. Here, amid his books and his maps, he lived an absolutely lonely life, attending to his own simple wants and paying little apparent heed to the affairs of his neighbors. It was a surprise to me, therefore, to hear him asking Holmes in an eager voice whether he had made any advance in his reconstruction of this mysterious episode. "The county police are utterly at fault," said he, "but perhaps your wider experience has suggested some conceivable explanation. My only claim to being taken into your confidence is that during my many residences here I have come to know this family of Tregennis very well—indeed, upon my Cornish mother's side I could call them cousins—and their strange fate has naturally been a great shock to me. I may tell you that I had got as far as Plymouth upon my way to Africa, but the news reached me this morning, and I came straight back again to help in the inquiry."

Holmes raised his eyebrows.

"Did you lose your boat through it?"

"I will take the next."

"Dear me! that is friendship indeed."

"I tell you they were relatives."

"Quite so—cousins of your mother. Was your baggage aboard the ship?"

"Some of it, but the main part at the hotel."

"I see. But surely this event could not have found its way into the Plymouth morning papers."

"No, sir; I had a telegram."

"Might I ask from whom?"

A shadow passed over the gaunt face of the explorer.

"You are very inquisitive, Mr. Holmes."

"It is my business."

With an effort Dr. Sterndale recovered his ruffled composure.

"I have no objection to telling you," he said. "It was Mr. Roundhay, the vicar, who sent me the telegram which recalled me."

"Thank you," said Holmes. "I may say in answer to your original question that I have not cleared my mind entirely on the subject of this case, but that I have every hope of reaching some conclusion. It would be premature to say more."

"Perhaps you would not mind telling me if your suspicions point in any particular direction?"

"No, I can hardly answer that."

"Then I have wasted my time and need not prolong my visit." The famous doctor strode out of our cottage in considerable ill-humor, and within five minutes Holmes had followed him. I saw him no more until the evening, when he returned with a slow step and haggard face which assured me that he had made no great progress with his investigation. He glanced at a telegram which awaited him and threw it into the grate.

"From the Plymouth hotel, Watson," he said. "I learned the name of it from the vicar, and I wired to made certain that Dr. Leon Sterndale's account was true. It appears that he did indeed spend last night there, and that he has actually allowed some of his baggage to go on to Africa, while he returned to be present at this investigation. What do you make of that, Watson?"

"He is deeply interested."

"Deeply interested—yes. There is a thread here which we have not yet grasped and which might lead us through the tangle. Cheer up, Watson, for I am very sure that our material has not yet all come to hand. When it does we may soon leave our difficulties behind us."

Little did I think how soon the words of Holmes would be realized, or how strange and sinister would be that new development which opened up an entirely fresh line of investigation. I was shaving at my window in the morning when I heard the rattle of hoofs and, looking up, saw a dog-cart coming at a gallop down the road. It pulled up at our door, and our friend, the vicar, sprang from it and rushed up our garden path. Holmes was already dressed, and we hastened down to meet him.

Our visitor was so excited that he could hardly articulate, but at last in gasps and bursts his tragic story came out of him.

"We are devil-ridden, Mr. Holmes! My poor parish is devil-ridden!" he cried. "Satan himself is loose in it! We are given over into his hands!" He danced about in his agitation, a ludicrous object if it were not for his ashy face and startled eyes. Finally he shot out his terrible news.

"Mr. Mortimer Tregennis died during the night, and with exactly the same symptoms as the rest of his family."

Holmes sprang to his feet, all energy in an instant.

"Can you fit us both into your dog-cart?"

"Yes, I can."

"Then, Watson, we will postpone our breakfast. Mr. Roundhay, we are entirely at your disposal. Hurry—hurry, before things get disarranged."

The lodger occupied two rooms at the vicarage, which were in an angle by themselves, the one above the other. Below was a large sitting-room; above, his bedroom. They looked out upon a croquet lawn which came up to the windows. We had arrived before the doctor or the police, so that everything was absolutely undisturbed. Let me describe exactly the scene as we saw it upon that misty March morning. It has left an impression which can never be effaced from my mind.

The atmosphere of the room was of a horrible and depressing stuffiness. The servant who had first entered had thrown up the window, or it would have been even more intolerable. This might partly be due to the fact that a lamp stood flaring and smoking on the center table. Beside it sat the dead man, leaning back in his chair, his thin beard projecting, his spectacles pushed up on to his forehead, and his lean dark face turned towards the window and twisted into the same distortion of terror which had marked the features of his dead sister. His limbs were convulsed and his fingers contorted as though he had died in a very paroxysm of fear. He was fully clothed, though there were signs that his dressing had been done in a hurry. We had already learned that his bed had been slept in, and that the tragic end had come to him in the early morning.

One realized the red-hot energy which underlay Holmes's phlegmatic exterior when one saw the sudden change which came over him from the moment that he entered the fatal apartment. In an instant he was tense and alert, his eyes shining, his face set, his limbs quivering with eager activity. He was out on the lawn, in through the window, round the room, and up into the bedroom, for all the world like a dashing foxhound drawing a cover. In the bedroom he made a rapid cast around and ended by throwing open the window, which appeared to give him some fresh cause for excitement, for he leaned out of it with loud ejaculations of interest and delight. Then he rushed down the stair, out through the open window, threw himself upon his face on the lawn, sprang up and into the room once more, all with the energy of the hunter who is at the heels of his quarry. The lamp, which was an ordinary standard, he examined with minute care, making certain measurements upon its bowl. He carefully scrutinized with his lens the talc shield which covered the top of the chimney and scraped off some ashes which adhered to its upper surface, putting some of them into an envelope, which he placed in his pocketbook. Finally, just as the doctor and the official police put in an appearance, he beckoned to the vicar and we all three went upon the lawn.

"I am glad to say that my investigation has not been entirely barren," he remarked. "I cannot remain to discuss the matter with the police, but I should be exceedingly obliged, Mr. Roundhay, if you would give the inspector my compliments and direct his attention to the bedroom window and to the sitting-room lamp. Each is suggestive, and together they are almost conclusive. If the police would desire further information I shall be happy to see any of them at the cottage. And now, Watson, I think that, perhaps, we shall be better employed elsewhere."

It may be that the police resented the intrusion of an amateur, or that they imagined themselves to be upon some hopeful line of investigation; but it is certain that we heard nothing from them for the next two days. During this time Holmes spent some of his time smoking and dreaming in the cottage; but a greater portion in country walks which he undertook alone, returning after many hours without remark as to where he had been. One experiment served to show me the line of his investigation. He had bought a lamp which was the duplicate of the one which had burned in the room of Mortimer Tregennis on the morning of the tragedy. This he filled with the same oil as that used at the vicarage, and he carefully timed the period which it would take to be exhausted. Another experiment which he made was of a more unpleasant nature, and one which I am not likely ever to forget.

"You will remember, Watson," he remarked one afternoon, "that there is a single common point of resemblance in the varying reports which have reached us. This concerns the effect of the atmosphere of the room in each case upon those who had first entered it. You will recollect that Mortimer Tregennis, in describing the episode of his last visit to his brother's house, remarked that the doctor on entering the room fell into a chair? You had forgotten? Well, I can answer for it that it was so. Now, you will remember also that Mrs. Porter, the housekeeper, told us that she herself fainted upon entering the room and had afterwards opened the window. In the second case—that of Mortimer Tregennis himself—you cannot have forgotten the horrible stuffiness of the room when we arrived, though the servant had thrown open the window. That servant, I found upon inquiry, was so ill that she had gone to her bed. You will admit, Watson, that these facts are very suggestive. In each case there is evidence of a poisonous atmosphere. In each case, also, there is combustion going on in the room—in the one case a fire, in the other a lamp. The fire was needed, but the lamp was lit—as a comparison of the oil consumed will show—long after it was broad daylight. Why? Surely because there is some connection between three things—the burning, the stuffy atmosphere, and, finally, the madness or death of those unfortunate people. That is clear, is it not?"

"It would appear so."

"At least we may accept it as a working hypothesis. We will suppose, then, that something was burned in each case which produced an atmosphere causing strange toxic effects. Very good. In the first instance—that of the Tregennis family—this substance was placed in the fire. Now the window was shut, but the fire would naturally carry fumes to some extent up the chimney. Hence one would expect the effects of the poison to be less than in the second case, where there was less escape for the vapor. The result seems to indicate that it was so, since in the first case only the woman, who had presumably the more sensitive organism, was killed, the others exhibiting that temporary or permanent lunacy which is evidently the first effect of the drug. In the second case the result was complete. The facts, therefore, seem to bear out the theory of a poison which worked by combustion.

"With this train of reasoning in my head I naturally looked about in Mortimer Tregennis's room to find some remains of this substance. The obvious place to look was the talc shield or smoke-guard of the lamp. There, sure enough, I perceived a number of flaky ashes, and round the edges a fringe of brownish powder, which had not yet been consumed. Half of this I took, as you saw, and I placed it in an envelope."

"Why half, Holmes?"

"It is not for me, my dear Watson, to stand in the way of the official police force. I leave them all the evidence which I found. The poison still remained upon the talc had they the wit to find it. Now, Watson, we will light our lamp; we will, however, take the precaution to open our window to avoid the premature decease of two deserving members of society, and you will seat yourself near that open window in an armchair unless, like a sensible man, you determine to have nothing to do with the affair. Oh, you will see it out, will you? I thought I knew my Watson. This chair I will place opposite yours, so that we may be the same distance from the poison and face to face. The door we will leave ajar. Each is now in a position to watch the other and to bring the experiment to an end should the symptoms seem alarming. Is that all clear? Well, then, I take our powder—or what remains of it— from the envelope, and I lay it above the burning lamp. So! Now, Watson, let us sit down and await developments."

They were not long in coming. I had hardly settled in my chair before I was conscious of a thick, musky odor, subtle and nauseous. At the very first whiff of it my brain and my imagination were beyond all control. A thick, black cloud swirled before my eyes, and my mind told me that in this cloud, unseen as yet, but about to spring out upon my appalled senses, lurked all that was vaguely horrible, all that was monstrous and inconceivably wicked in the universe. Vague shapes swirled and swam amid the dark cloud-bank, each a menace and a warning of something coming, the advent of some unspeakable dweller upon the threshold, whose very shadow would blast my soul. A freezing horror took possession of me. I felt that my hair was rising, that my eyes were protruding, that my mouth was opened, and my tongue like leather. The turmoil within my brain was such that something must surely snap. I tried to scream and was vaguely aware of some hoarse croak which was my own voice, but distant and detached from myself. At the same moment, in some effort of escape, I broke through that cloud of despair and had a glimpse of Holmes's face, white, rigid, and drawn with horror—the very look which I had seen upon the features of the dead. It was that vision which gave me an instant of sanity and of strength. I dashed from my chair, threw my arms round Holmes, and together we lurched through the door, and an instant afterwards had thrown ourselves down upon the grass plot and were lying side by side, conscious only of the glorious sunshine which was bursting its way through the hellish cloud of terror which had girt us in. Slowly it rose from our souls like the mists from a landscape until peace and reason had returned, and we were sitting upon the grass, wiping our clammy foreheads, and looking with apprehension at each other to mark the last traces of that terrific experience which we had undergone.

"Upon my word, Watson!" said Holmes at last with an unsteady voice. "I owe you both my thanks and an apology. It was an unjustifiable experiment even for one's self, and doubly so for a friend. I am really very sorry."

"You know," I answered with some emotion, for I had never seen so much of Holmes's heart before, "that it is my greatest joy and privilege to help you."

He relapsed at once into the half-humorous, half-cynical vein which was his habitual attitude to those about him. "It would be superfluous to drive us mad, my dear Watson," said he. "A candid observer would certainly declare that we were so already before we embarked upon so wild an experiment. I confess that I never imagined that the effect could be so sudden and so severe." He dashed into the cottage, and, reappearing with the burning lamp held at full arm's length, he threw it among a bank of brambles. "We must give the room a little time to clear. I take it, Watson, that you have no longer a shadow of doubt as to how these tragedies were produced?"

"None whatever."

"But the cause remains as obscure as before. Come into the arbor here and let us discuss it together. That villainous stuff seems still to linger round my throat. I think we must admit that all the evidence points to this man, Mortimer Tregennis, having been the criminal in the first tragedy, though he was the victim in the second one. We must remember, in the first place, that there is some story of a family quarrel, followed by a reconciliation. How bitter that quarrel may have been, or how hollow the reconciliation we cannot tell. When I think of Mortimer Tregennis, with the foxy face and the small shrewd, beady eyes behind the spectacles, he is not a man whom I should judge to be of a particularly forgiving disposition. Well, in the next place, you will remember that this idea of someone moving in the garden, which took our attention for a moment from the real cause of the tragedy, emanated from him. He had a motive in misleading us. Finally, if he did not throw this substance into the fire at the moment of leaving the room, who did do so? The affair happened immediately after his departure. Had anyone else come in, the family would certainly have risen from the table. Besides, in peaceful Cornwall, visitors do not arrive at ten o'clock at night. We may take it, then, that all the evidence points to Mortimer Tregennis as the culprit."

"Then his own death was suicide!"

"Well, Watson, it is on the face of it a not impossible supposition. The man who had the guilt upon his soul of having brought such a fate upon his own family might well be driven by remorse to inflict it upon himself. There are, however, some cogent reasons against it. Fortunately, there is one man in England who knows all about it, and I have made arrangements by which we shall hear the facts this afternoon from his own lips. Ah! he is a little before his time. Perhaps you would kindly step this way, Dr. Leon Sterndale. We have been conducting a chemical experiment indoors which has left our little room hardly fit for the reception of so distinguished a visitor."

I had heard the click of the garden gate, and now the majestic figure of the great African explorer appeared upon the path. He turned in some surprise towards the rustic arbor in which we sat.

"You sent for me, Mr. Holmes. I had your note about an hour

ago, and I have come, though I really do not know why I should obey your summons."

"Perhaps we can clear the point up before we separate," said Holmes. "Meanwhile, I am much obliged to you for your courteous acquiescence. You will excuse this informal reception in the open air, but my friend Watson and I have nearly furnished an additional chapter to what the papers call the Cornish Horror, and we prefer a clear atmosphere for the present. Perhaps, since the matters which we have to discuss will affect you personally in a very intimate fashion, it is as well that we should talk where there can be no eavesdropping."

The explorer took his cigar from his lips and gazed sternly at my companion.

"I am at a loss to know, sir," he said, "what you can have to speak about which affects me personally in a very intimate fashion."

"The killing of Mortimer Tregennis," said Holmes.

For a moment I wished that I were armed. Sterndale's fierce face turned to a dusky red, his eyes glared, and the knotted, passionate veins started out in his forehead, while he sprang forward with clenched hands towards my companion. Then he stopped, and with a violent effort he resumed a cold, rigid calmness, which was, perhaps, more suggestive of danger than his hot-headed outburst.

"I have lived so long among savages and beyond the law," said he, "that I have got into the way of being a law to myself. You would do well, Mr. Holmes, not to forget it, for I have no desire to do you an injury."

"Nor have I any desire to do you an injury, Dr. Sterndale. Surely the clearest proof of it is that, knowing what I know, I have sent for you and not for the police."

Sterndale sat down with a gasp, overawed for, perhaps, the first time in his adventurous life. There was a calm assurance of power in Holmes's manner which could not be withstood. Our visitor stammered for a moment, his great hands opening and shutting in his agitation.

"What do you mean?" he asked at last. "If this is bluff upon your part, Mr. Holmes, you have chosen a bad man for your experiment. Let us have no more beating about the bush. What *do* you mean?"

"I will tell you," said Holmes, "and the reason why I tell you is that I hope frankness may beget frankness. What my next step may be will depend entirely upon the nature of your own defense."

"My defense?"

"Yes, sir."

"My defense against what?"

"Against the charge of killing Mortimer Tregennis."

Sterndale mopped his forehead with his handkerchief. "Upon my word, you are getting on," said he. "Do all your successes depend upon this prodigious power of bluff?"

"The bluff," said Holmes sternly, "is on your side, Dr. Leon Sterndale, and not upon mine. As a proof I will tell you some of the facts upon which my conclusions are based. Of your return from Plymouth, allowing much of your property to go on to Africa, I will say nothing save that it first informed me that you were one of the factors which had to be taken into account in reconstructing this drama—"

"I came back—"

"I have heard your reasons and regard them as unconvincing and inadequate. We will pass that. You came down here to ask me whom I suspected. I refused to answer you. You then went to the vicarage, waited outside it for some time, and finally returned to your cottage."

"How do you know that?"

"I followed you."

"I saw no one."

"That is what you may expect to see when I follow you. You spent a restless night at your cottage, and you formed certain plans, which in the early morning you proceeded to put into execution. Leaving your door just as day was breaking, you filled your pocket with some reddish gravel that was lying heaped beside your gate."

Sterndale gave a violent start and looked at Holmes in amazement.

"You then walked swiftly for the mile which separated you from the vicarage. You were wearing, I may remark, the same pair of ribbed tennis shoes which are at the present moment upon your feet. At the vicarage you passed through the orchard and the side hedge, coming out under the window of the lodger Tregennis. It was now daylight, but the household was not yet stirring. You drew some of the gravel from your pocket, and you threw it up at the window above you."

Sterndale sprang to his feet.

"I believe that you are the devil himself!" he cried.

Holmes smiled at the compliment. "It took two, or possibly three, handfuls before the lodger came to the window. You beckoned him to come down. He dressed hurriedly and descended to his sitting-room. You entered by the window. There was an interview—a short one—during which you walked up and down the room. Then you passed out and closed the window, standing on the lawn outside smoking a cigar and watching what occurred. Finally, after the death of Tregennis, you withdrew as you had come. Now, Dr. Sterndale, how do you justify such conduct, and what were the motives for your actions? If you prevaricate or trifle with me, I give you my assurance that the matter will pass out of my hands forever."

Our visitor's face had turned ashen gray as he listened to the words of his accuser. Now he sat for some time in thought with his face sunk in his hands. Then with a sudden impulsive gesture he plucked a photograph from his breast-pocket and threw it on the rustic table before us.

"That is why I have done it," said he.

It showed the bust and face of a very beautiful woman. Holmes stooped over it.

"Brenda Tregennis," said he.

"Yes, Brenda Tregennis," repeated our visitor. "For years I have loved her. For years she has loved me. There is the secret of that Cornish seclusion which people have marveled at. It has brought me close to the one thing on earth that was dear to me. I could not marry her, for I have a wife who has left me for years and yet whom, by the deplorable laws of England, I could not divorce. For years Brenda waited. For years I waited. And this is what we have waited for." A terrible sob shook his great frame, and he clutched his throat under his brindled beard. Then with an effort he mastered himself and spoke on:

"The vicar knew. He was in our confidence. He would tell you that she was an angel upon earth. That was why he telegraphed to me and I returned. What was my baggage or Africa to me when I learned that such a fate had come upon my darling? There you have the missing clue to my action, Mr. Holmes."

"Proceed," said my friend.

Dr. Sterndale drew from his pocket a paper packet and laid it upon the table. On the outside was written *"Radix pedis diaboli"* with a red poison label beneath it. He pushed it towards me. "I understand that you are a doctor, sir. Have you ever heard of this preparation?"

"Devil's-foot root! No, I have never heard of it."

"It is no reflection upon your professional knowledge," said he, "for I believe that, save for one sample in a laboratory in Buda, there is no other specimen in Europe. It has not yet found its way either into the pharmacopoeia or into the literature of toxicology. The root is shaped like a foot, half human, half goatlike; hence the fanciful name given by a botanical missionary. It is used as an ordeal poison by the medicine-men in certain districts of West Africa and is kept as a secret among them. This particular specimen I obtained under very extraordinary circumstances in the Ubangi country." He opened the paper as he spoke and disclosed a heap of reddish-brown, snufflike powder.

"Well, sir?" asked Holmes sternly.

I am about to tell you, Mr. Holmes, all that actually occurred, for you already know so much that it is clearly to my interest that you should know all. I have already explained the relationship in which I stood to the Tregennis family. For the sake of the sister I was friendly with the brothers. There was a family quarrel about money which estranged this man Mortimer, but it was supposed to be made up, and I afterwards met him as I did the others. He was a sly, subtle, scheming man, and several things arose which gave me a suspicion of him, but I had no cause for any positive quarrel.

"One day, only a couple of weeks ago, he came down to my cottage and I showed him some of my African curiosities. Among other things I exhibited this powder, and I told him of its strange properties, how it stimulates those brain centers which control the emotion of fear, and how either madness or death is the fate of the unhappy native who is subjected to the ordeal by the priest of his tribe. I told him also how powerless European science would be to detect it. How he took it I cannot say, for I never left the room, but there is no doubt that it was then, while I was opening cabinets and stooping to boxes, that he managed to abstract some of the devil's-foot root. I well remember how he plied me with questions as to the amount and the time that was needed for its effect, but I little dreamed that he could have a personal reason for asking.

"I thought no more of the matter until the vicar's telegram reached me at Plymouth. This villain had thought that I would be at sea before the news could reach me, and that I should be lost for years in Africa. But I returned at once. Of course, I could not listen to the details without feeling assured that my poison had been used. I came round to see you on the chance that some other explanation had suggested itself to you. But there could be none. I was convinced that Mortimer Tregennis was the murderer; that for the sake of money, and with the idea, perhaps, that if the other members of his family were all insane he would be the sole guardian of their joint property, he had used the devil's-foot powder upon them, driven two of them out of their senses, and killed his sister Brenda, the one human being whom I have ever loved or who has ever loved me. There was his crime; what was to be his punishment?

"Should I appeal to the law? Where were my proofs? I knew that the facts were true, but could I help to make a jury of countrymen believe so fantastic a story? I might or I might not. But I could not afford to fail. My soul cried out for revenge. I have said to you once before, Mr. Holmes, that I have spent much of my life outside the law, and that I have come at last to be a law to myself. So it was now. I determined that the fate which he had given to others should be shared by himself. Either that or I would do justice upon him with my own hand. In all England there can be no man who sets less value upon his own life than I do at the present moment.

"Now I have told you all. You have yourself supplied the rest. I did, as you say, after a restless night, set off early from my cottage. I foresaw the difficulty of arousing him, so I gathered some gravel from the pile which you have mentioned, and I used it to throw up to his window. He came down and admitted me through the window of the sitting-room. I laid his offense before him. I told him that I had come both as judge and executioner. The wretch sank into a chair, paralyzed at the sight of my revolver. I lit the lamp, put the powder above it, and stood outside the window, ready to carry out my threat to shoot him should he try to leave the room. In five minutes he died. My God! how he died! But my heart was flint, for he endured nothing which my innocent darling had not felt before him. There is my story, Mr. Holmes. Perhaps, if you loved a woman, you would have done as much yourself. At any rate, I am in your hands. You can take what steps you like. As I have already said, there is no man living who can fear death less than I do."

Holmes sat for some little time in silence.

"What were your plans?" he asked at last.

"I had intended to bury myself in central Africa. My work there is but half finished."

"Go and do the other half," said Holmes. "I, at least, am not prepared to prevent you."

Dr. Sterndale raised his giant figure, bowed gravely, and walked from the arbor. Holmes lit his pipe and handed me his pouch.

"Some fumes which are not poisonous would be a welcome change," said he. "I think you must agree, Watson, that it is not a case in which we are called upon to interfere. Our investigation has been independent, and our action shall be so also. You would not denounce the man?"

"Certainly not," I answered.

"I have never loved, Watson, but if I did and if the woman I loved had met such an end, I might act even as our lawless lion-hunter has done. Who knows? Well, Watson, I will not offend your intelligence by explaining what is obvious. The gravel upon the window-sill was, of course, the starting-point of my research. It was unlike anything in the vicarage garden. Only when my attention had been drawn to Dr. Sterndale and his cottage did I find its counterpart. The lamp shining in broad daylight and the remains of powder upon the shield were successive links in a fairly obvious chain. And now, my dear Watson, I think we may dismiss the matter from our mind and go back with a clear conscience to the study of those Chaldean roots which are surely to be traced in the Cornish branch of the great Celtic speech."

The Problem of the Sore Bridge—Among Others

by

Philip José Farmer

(writing as Harry Manders)

Every notable Baker Street Irregular gets an "investiture," a title of sorts drawn from some passage in the sacred writings. My own investiture is that of "the remarkable worm unknown to science." Why that was chosen I don't know, but it increases my interest in this story.

The Problem of the Sore
Bridge—Among Others

by Harry Manders
(Philip José Farmer)

(Editor's Preface): Harry "Bunny" Manders was an English writer whose other profession was that of gentleman burglar, circa 1890–1900. Manders' adored senior partner and mentor, Arthur J. Raffles, was a cricket player rated on a par with Lord Peter Wimsey or W. G. Grace. Privately, he was a second-story man, a cracksman, a quick-change artist and confidence man whose only peer was Arsène Lupin. Manders' narratives have appeared in four volumes titled (in America) *The Amateur Cracksman, Raffles, A Thief in the Night,* and *Mr. Justice Raffles.* "Raffles" has become incorporated in the English language (and a number of others) as a term for a gentleman burglar or dashing upper-crust Jimmy Valentine. Mystery story aficionados, of course, are thoroughly acquainted with the incomparable, though tragically flawed, Raffles and his sidekick Manders.

After Raffles' death in the Boer War, Harry Manders gave up crime and became a respectable journalist and author. He married, had children, and died in 1924. His earliest works were agented by E. W. Hornung, Arthur Conan Doyle's brother-in-law. A number of Manders' posthumous works have been agented by Barry Perowne. One of his tales, however, was forbidden by his will to be printed until fifty years after his death. The stipulated time has passed, and now the public may learn how the world was saved without knowing that it was in the gravest peril. It will also discover that the paths of the great Raffles and the great Holmes did cross at least once.

I.

The Boer bullet that pierced my thigh in 1900 lamed me for the rest of my life, but I was quite able to cope with its effects. However, at the age of sixty-one, I suddenly find that a killer that has felled far more men than bullets has lodged within me. The doctor, my kinsman, gives me six months at the most, six months which he frankly says will be very painful. He knows of my crimes, of course, and it may be that he thinks that my suffering will be poetic justice. I'm not sure. But I'll swear that this is the meaning of the slight smile which accompanied his declaration of my doom.

Be that as it may, I have little time left. But I have determined to write down that adventure of which Raffles and I once swore we would never breathe a word. It happened; it really happened. But the world would not have believed it then. It would have been convinced that I was a liar or insane.

I am writing this, nevertheless, because fifty years from now the world may have progressed to the stage where such things as I tell of are credible. Man may even have landed on the moon by then, if he has perfected a propeller which works in the ether as well as in the air. Or if he discovers the same sort of drive that brought . . . well, I anticipate.

I must hope that the world of 1974 will believe this adventure. Then the world will know that, whatever crimes Raffles and I committed, we paid for them a thousandfold by what we did that week in the May of 1895. And in fact, the world is and always will be immeasurably in our debt. Yes, my dear doctor, my scornful kinsman, who hopes that I will suffer pain as punishment, I long ago paid off my debt. I only wish that you could be alive to read these words. And, who knows, you may live to be a hundred and may read this account of what you owe me. I hope so.

II.

I was nodding in my chair in my room at Mount Street when the clanging of the lift gates in the yard startled me. A moment later, a familiar tattoo sounded on my door. I opened it to find, as I expected, A. J. Raffles himself. He slipped in, his bright blue eyes merry, and he removed his Sullivan from his lips to point with it at my whisky and soda.

"Bored, Bunny?"

"Rather," I replied. "It's been almost a year since we stirred our stumps. The voyage around the world after the Levy affair was stimulating. But that ended four months ago. And since then . . ."

"Ennui and bile!" Raffles cried. "Well, Bunny, that's all over! Tonight we make the blood run hot and cold and burn up all green biliousness!"

"And the swag?" I said.

"Jewels, Bunny! To be exact, star sapphires, or blue corundum, cut *en cabochon*. That is, round with a flat underside. And large, Bunny, vulgarly large, almost the size of a hen's egg, if my informant was not exaggerating. There's a mystery about them, Bunny, a mystery my fence has been whispering with his Cockney speech into my ear for some time. They're dispensed by a Mr. James Phillimore of Kensal Rise. But where he gets them, from whom he lifts them, no one knows. My fence has hinted that they may not come from manorial strongboxes or milady's throat but are smuggled from Southeast Asia or South Africa or Brazil, directly from the mine. In any event, we are going to do some reconnoitering tonight, and if the opportunity should arise . . ."

"Come now, A. J.," I said bitterly. "You *have* done all the needed reconnoitering. Be honest! Tonight we suddenly find that the moment is propitious, and we strike? Right?"

I had always been somewhat piqued that Raffles chose to do all the preliminary work, the casing, as the underworld says, himself. For some reason, he did not trust me to scout the layout.

Raffles blew a huge and perfect smoke ring from his Sullivan, and he clapped me on the shoulder. "You see through me, Bunny! Yes, I've examined the grounds and checked out Mr. Phillimore's schedule."

I was unable to say anything to the most masterful man I have ever met. I meekly donned dark clothes, downed the rest of the whisky, and left with Raffles. We strolled for some distance, making sure that no policemen were shadowing us, though we had no reason to believe they would be. We then took the last train to Willesden at 11:21. On the way I said, "Does Phillimore live near old Baird's house?"

I was referring to the money lender killed by Jack Rutter, the details of which case are written in *Wilful Murder*.

"As a matter of fact," Raffles said, watching me with his keen steel-gray eyes, "it's the *same* house. Phillimore took it when Baird's estate was finally settled and it became available to renters. It's a curious coincidence, Bunny, but then all coincidences are curious. To man, that is. Nature is indifferent."

(Yes, I know I stated before that his eyes were blue. And so they were. I've been criticized for saying in one story that his eyes were blue and in another that they were gray. But he has, as any idiot should have guessed, gray-blue eyes which are one color in one light and another in another.)

"That was in January, 1895," Raffles said. "We are in deep waters, Bunny. My investigations have unearthed no evidence that Mr. Phillimore existed before November, 1894. Until he took the lodgings in the East End, no one seems to have heard of or even seen him. He came out of nowhere, rented his third-story lodgings—a terrible place, Bunny—until January. Then he rented the house where bad old Baird gave up the ghost. Since then he's been living a quiet-enough life, excepting the visits he makes once a month to several East End fences. He has a cook and a housekeeper, but these do not live in with him."

At this late hour, the train went no farther than Willesden Junction. We walked from there toward Kensal Rise. Once more, I was dependent on Raffles to lead me through unfamiliar country. However, this time the moon was up, and the country was not quite as open as it had been the last time I was here. A number of cottages and small villas, some only partially built, occupied the empty fields I had passed through that fateful night. We walked down a footpath between a woods and a field, and we came out on the tarred woodblock road that had been laid only four years before. It now had the curb that had been lacking then, but there was still only one pale lamppost across the road from the house.

Before us rose the corner of a high wall with the moonlight shining on the broken glass on top of the wall. It also outlined the sharp spikes on top of the tall green gate. We slipped on our masks. As before, Raffles reached up and placed champagne corks on the spikes. He then put his covert-coat over the corks. We slipped over quietly, Raffles removed the corks, and we stood by the wall in a bed of laurels. I admit I felt apprehensive, even more so than the last time. Old Baird's ghost seemed to hover about the place. The shadows were thicker than they should have been.

I started toward the gravel path leading to the house, which was unlit. Raffles seized my coattails. "Quiet!" he said. "I see somebody—something, anyway—in the bushes at the far end of the garden. Down there, at the angle of the wall."

I could see nothing, but I trusted Raffles, whose eyesight was as keen as a Red Indian's. We moved slowly alongside the wall, stopping frequently to peer into the darkness of the bushes at the angle of the wall. About twenty yards from it, I saw something shapeless move in the shrubbery. I was all for clearing out then, but Raffles fiercely whispered that we could not permit a competitor to scare us away. After a quick conference, we moved in very slowly but surely, slightly more solid shadows in the shadow of the wall. And in a few very long and perspiration-drenched minutes, the stranger fell with one blow from Raffles' fist upon his jaw.

Raffles dragged the snoring man out from the bushes so we could get a look at him by moonlight. "What have we here, Bunny?" he said. "Those long curly locks, that high arching nose, the overly thick eyebrows, and the odor of expensive Parisian perfume? Don't you recognize him?"

I had to confess that I did not.

"What, that is the famous journalist and infamous duelist, Isadora Persano!" he said. "Now tell me you have never heard of him, or her, as the case may be?"

"Of course!" I said. "The reporter for the *Daily Telegraph!*"

"No more," Raffles said. "He's a free-lancer now. But what the devil is he doing here?"

"Do you suppose," I said slowly, "that he, too, is one thing by day and quite another by night?"

"Perhaps," Raffles said. "But he may be here in his capacity of journalist. He's also heard things about Mr. James Phillimore. The devil take it! If the press is here, you may be sure that the Yard is not far behind!"

Mr. Persano's features curiously combined a rugged masculinity with an offensive effeminacy. Yet the latter characteristic was not really his fault. His father, an Italian diplomat, had died before he was born. His English mother had longed for a girl, been bitterly disappointed when her only-born was a boy, and, unhindered by a husband or conscience, had named him Isadora and raised him as a girl. Until he entered a public school, he wore dresses. In school, his long hair and certain feminine actions made him the object of an especially vicious persecution by the boys. It was there that he developed his abilities to defend himself with his fists. When he became an adult, he lived on the continent for several years. During this time, he earned a reputation as a dangerous man to insult. It was said that he had wounded half a dozen men with sword or pistol.

From the little bag in which he carried the tools of the trade, Raffles brought a length of rope and a gag. After tying and gagging Persano, Raffles went through his pockets. The only object that aroused his curiosity was a very large matchbox in an inner pocket of his cloak. Opening this, he brought out something that shone in the moonlight.

"By all that's holy!" he said. "It's one of the sapphires!"

"Is Persano a rich man?" I said.

"He doesn't have to work for a living, Bunny. And since he hasn't been in the house yet, I assume he got this from a fence. I also assume that he put the sapphire in the matchbox because a pickpocket isn't likely to steal a box of matches. As it was, *I* was about to ignore it!"

"Let's get out of here," I said. But he crouched staring down at the journalist with an occasional glance at the jewel. This, by the way, was only about a quarter of the size of a hen's egg. Presently, Persano stirred, and he moaned under the gag. Raffles whispered into his ear, and he nodded. Raffles, saying to me, "Cosh him if he looks like he's going to yell," undid the gag.

Persano, as requested, kept his voice low. He confessed that he had heard rumors from his underworld contacts about the precious stones. Having tracked down our fence, he had contrived easily enough to buy one of Mr. Phillimore's jewels. In fact, he said, it was the first one that Mr. Phillimore had brought in to fence. Curious, wondering where the stones came from, since there were no reported thefts of these, he had come here to spy on Phillimore.

"There's a great story here," he said. "But just what, I haven't the foggiest. However, I must warn you that . . ."

His warning was not heeded. Both Raffles and I heard the low voices outside the gate and the scraping of shoes against gravel.

"Don't leave me tied up here, boys," Persano said. "I might have a little trouble explaining satisfactorily just what I'm doing here. And then there's the jewel . . ."

Raffles slipped the stone back into the matchbox and put it into Persano's pocket. If we were to be caught, we would not have the gem on us. He untied the journalist's wrists and ankles and said, "Good luck!"

A moment later, after throwing our coats over the broken glass, Raffles and I went over the rear rail. We ran crouching into a dense woods about twenty yards back of the house. At the other side at some distance was a newly built house and a newly laid road. A moment later, we saw Persano come over the wall. He ran by, not seeing us, and disappeared down the road, trailing a heavy cloud of perfume.

"We must visit him at his quarters," said Raffles. He put his hand on my shoulder to warn me, but there was no need. I too had seen the three men come around the corner of the wall. One took a position at the angle of the wall; the other two started toward our woods. We retreated as quietly as possible. Since there was no train available at this late hour, we walked to Maida Vale and took a hansom from there to home. Raffles went to his rooms at the Albany and I to mine on Mount Street.

III.

When we saw the evening papers, we knew that the affair had taken on even more bizarre aspects. But we still had no inkling of the horrifying metamorphosis yet to come.

I doubt if there is a literate person in the West—or in the Orient, for that matter—who has not read about the strange case of Mr. James Phillimore. At eight in the morning, a hansom cab from Maida Vale pulled up before the gates to his estate. The housekeeper and the cook and Mr. Phillimore were the only occupants of the house. The area outside the walls was being surveilled by eight men from the Metropolitan Police Department. The cab driver rang the electrically operated bell at the gate. Mr. Phillimore walked out of the house and down the gravel path to the gate. Here he was observed by the cab driver, a policeman near the gate, and another in a tree. The latter could see clearly the entire front yard and house, and another man in a tree could clearly see the entire back yard and the back of the house.

Mr. Phillimore opened the gate but did not step through it. Commenting to the cabbie that it looked like rain, he added that he would return to the house to get his umbrella. The cabbie, the policemen, and the housekeeper saw him reenter the house. The housekeeper was at that moment in the room which occupied the front part of the ground floor of the house. She went into the kitchen as Mr. Phillimore entered the house. She did, however, hear his footsteps on the stairs from the hallway which led up to the first floor.

She was the last one to see Mr. Phillimore. He did not come back out of the house. After half an hour Mr. Mackenzie, the Scotland Yard inspector in charge, decided that Mr. Phillimore had somehow become aware that he was under surveillance. Mackenzie gave the signal, and he with three men entered the gate, another four retaining their positions outside. At no time was any part of the area outside the walls unobserved. Nor was the area inside the walls unscrutinized at any time.

The warrant duly shown to the housekeeper, the policemen entered the house and made a thorough search. To their astonishment, they could find no trace of Mr. Phillimore. The six-foot-six, twenty-stone* gentleman had utterly disappeared.

*Two hundred and eighty pounds.

For the next two days, the house—and the yard around it—was the subject of the most intense investigation. This established that the house contained no secret tunnels or hideaways. Every cubic inch was accounted for. It was impossible for him not to have left the house; yet he clearly had not done so.

"Another minute's delay, and we would have been cornered," Raffles said, taking another Sullivan from his silver cigarette case. "But, Lord, what's going on there, what mysterious forces are working there? Notice that no jewels were found in the house. At least, the police reported none. Now, did Phillimore actually go back to get his umbrella? Of course not. The umbrella was in the stand by the entrance; yet he went right by it and on upstairs. So, he observed the foxes outside the gate and bolted into his briar bush like the good little rabbit he was."

"And where is the briar bush?" I said.

"Ah! That's the question," Raffles breathed. "What kind of a rabbit is it which pulls the briar bush in after it? That is the sort of mystery which has attracted even the Great Detective himself. He has condescended to look into it."

"Then let us stay away from the whole affair!" I cried. "We have been singularly fortunate that none of our victims have called in your relative!"

Raffles was a third or fourth cousin to Holmes, though neither had, to my knowledge, ever seen the other. I doubt that the sleuth had even gone to Lord's, or anywhere else, to see a cricket match.

"I wouldn't mind matching wits with him," Raffles said. "Perhaps he might then change his mind about who's the most dangerous man in London."

"We have more than enough money," I said. "Let's drop the whole business."

"It was only yesterday that you were complaining of boredom, Bunny," he said. "No, I think we should pay a visit to our journalist. He may know something that we, and possibly the police, don't know. However, if you prefer," he added contemptuously, "you may stay home."

That stung me, of course, and I insisted that I accompany him.

A few minutes later, we got into a hansom, and Raffles told the driver to take us to Praed Street.

IV.

Persano's apartment was at the end of two flights of Carrara marble steps and a carved mahogany banister. The porter conducted us to 10-C but left when Raffles tipped him handsomely. Raffles knocked on the door. After receiving no answer within a minute, he picked the lock. A moment later, we were inside a suite of extravagantly furnished rooms. A heavy odor of incense hung in the air.

I entered the bedroom and halted aghast. Persano, clad only in underwear, lay on the floor. The underwear, I regret to say, was the sheer black lace of the *demi-mondaine*. I suppose that if brassieres had existed at that time he would have been wearing one. I did not pay his dress much attention, however, because of his horrible expression. His face was cast into a mask of unutterable terror.

Near the tips of his outstretched fingers lay the large matchbox. It was open, and in it writhed *some thing*.

I drew back, but Raffles, after one soughing of intaken breath, felt the man's forehead and pulse and looked into the rigid eyes.

"Stark staring mad," he said. "Frozen with the horror that comes from the deepest of abysses."

Emboldened by his example, I drew near the box. Its contents looked somewhat like a worm, a thick tubular worm, with a dozen slim tentacles projecting from one end. This could be presumed to be its head, since the area just above the roots of the tentacles was ringed with small pale-blue eyes. These had pupils like a cat's. There was no nose or nasal openings or mouth.

"God!" I said shuddering. "What is it?"

"Only God knows," Raffles said. He lifted Persano's right hand and looked at the tips of the fingers. "Note the fleck of blood on each," he said. "They look as if pins have been stuck into them."

He bent over closer to the thing in the box and said, "The tips of the tentacles bear needlelike points, Bunny. Perhaps Persano is not so much paralyzed from horror as from venom."

"Don't get any closer, for Heaven's sake!" I said.

"Look, Bunny!" he said. "Doesn't that thing have a tiny shining object in one of its tentacles?"

Despite my nausea, I got down by him and looked straight at the monster. "It seems to be a very thin and slightly curving piece of glass," I said. "What of it?"

Even as I spoke, the end of the tentacle which held the object opened, and the object disappeared within it.

"That *glass*," Raffles said, "is what's left of the *sapphire*. It's eaten it. That piece seems to have been the last of it."

"Eaten a sapphire?" I said, stunned. "Hard metal, blue corundum?"

"I think, Bunny," he said slowly, "the sapphire may only have looked like a sapphire. Perhaps it was not aluminum oxide but something hard enough to fool an expert. The interior may have been filled with something softer than the shell. Perhaps the shell held an embryo."

"What?" I said.

"I mean, Bunny, is it inconceivable, but nevertheless true, that that thing might have *hatched* from the jewel?"

V.

We left hurriedly a moment later. Raffles had decided against taking the monster—for which I was very grateful—because he wanted the police to have all the clues available.

"There's something very wrong here, Bunny," he said. "Very sinister." He lit a Sullivan and added in a drawl, "Very *alien!*"

"You mean un-British?" I said.

"I mean . . . un-Earthly."

A little later, we got out of the cab at St. James's Park and walked across it to the Albany. In Raffles' room, smoking cigars and drinking scotch whisky and soda, we discussed the significance of all we had seen but could come to no explanation, reasonable or otherwise. The next morning, reading the *Times*, the *Pall Mall Gazette*, and the *Daily Telegraph*, we learned how narrowly we had escaped. According to the papers, Inspectors Hopkins and Mackenzie and the private detective Holmes had entered Persano's rooms two minutes after we had left. Persano had died while on the way to the hospital.

"Not a word about the worm in the box," Raffles said. "The

police are keeping it a secret. No doubt, they fear to alarm the public."

There would be, in fact, no official reference to the creature. Nor was it until 1922 that Dr. Watson made a passing reference to it in a published adventure of his colleague. I do not know what happened to the thing, but I suppose that it must have been placed in a jar of alcohol. There it must have quickly perished. No doubt the jar is collecting dust on some shelf in the backroom of some police museum. Whatever happened to it, it must have been disposed of. Otherwise, the world would not be what it is today.

"Strike me, there's only one thing to do, Bunny!" Raffles said after he'd put the last paper down. "We must get into Phillimore's house and look for ourselves!"

I did not protest. I was more afraid of his scorn than of the police. However, we did not launch our little expedition that evening. Raffles went out to do some reconnoitering on his own, both among the East End fences and around the house in Kensal Rise. The evening of the second day, he appeared at my rooms. I had not been idle, however. I had gathered a supply of more corks for the gatetop spikes by drinking a number of bottles of champagne.

"The police guard has been withdrawn from the estate itself," he said. "I didn't see any men in the woods nearby. So, we break into the late Mr. Phillimore's house tonight. If he is late, that is," he added enigmatically.

As the midnight chimes struck, we went over the gate once more. A minute later, Raffles was taking out the pane from the glass door. This he did with his diamond, a pot of treacle, and a sheet of brown paper, as he had done the night we broke in and found our would-be blackmailer dead with his head crushed by a poker.

He inserted his hand through the opening, turned the key in the lock, and drew the bolt at the bottom of the door open. This had been shot by a policeman who had then left by the kitchen door, or so we presumed. We went through the door, closed it behind us, and made sure that all the drapes of the front room were pulled tight. Then Raffles, as he did that evil night long ago, lit a match and with it a gas light. The flaring illumination showed us a room little changed. Apparently, Mr. Phillimore had not been interested in redecorating. We went out into the hallway and upstairs, where three doors opened onto the first-floor hallway.

The first door led to the bedroom. It contained a huge canopied bed, a midcentury monster Baird had bought secondhand in some East End shop, a cheap maple tallboy, a rocking chair, a thunder mug, and two large overstuffed leather armchairs.

"There was only one armchair the last time we were here," Raffles said.

The second room was unchanged, being as empty as the first time we'd seen it. The room at the rear was the bathroom, also unchanged.

We went downstairs and through the hallway to the kitchen, and then we descended into the coal cellar. This also contained a small wine pantry. As I expected, we had found nothing. After all, the men from the Yard were thorough, and what they might have missed, Holmes would have found. I was about to suggest to Raffles that we should admit failure and leave before somebody saw the lights in the house. But a sound from upstairs stopped me.

Raffles had heard it, too. Those ears missed little. He held up a hand for silence, though none was needed. He said, a moment later, "Softly, Bunny! It may be a policeman. But I think it is probably our quarry!"

We stole up the wooden steps, which insisted on creaking under our weight. Thence we crept into the kitchen and from there into the hallway and then into the front room. Seeing nobody, we went up the steps to the first floor once more and gingerly opened the door of each room and looked within.

While we were poking our heads into the bathroom, we heard a noise again. It came from somewhere in the front of the house, though whether it was upstairs or down we could not tell.

Raffles beckoned to me, and I followed, also on tiptoe, down the hall. He stopped at the door of the middle room, looked within, then led me to the door of the bedroom. On looking in (remember, we had not turned out the gaslights yet), he started. And he said, "Lord! One of the armchairs! It's gone!"

"But—but . . . who'd want to take a chair?" I said.

"Who, indeed!" he said, and ran down the steps with no attempt to keep quiet. I gathered my wits enough to order my feet to get moving. Just as I reached the door, I heard Raffles outside shouting, "There he goes!" I ran out onto the little tiled veranda. Raffles was halfway down the gravel path, and a dim figure was plunging through the open gate. Whoever he was, he had had a key to the gate.

I remember thinking, irrelevantly, how cool the air had become in the short time we'd been in the house. Actually, it was not such an irrelevant thought since the advent of the cold air had caused a heavy mist. It hung over the road and coiled through the woods. And, of course, it helped the man we were chasing.

Raffles was as keen as a bill-collector chasing a debtor, and he kept his eyes on the vague figure until it plunged into a grove. When I came out its other side, breathing hard, I found Raffles standing on the edge of a narrow but rather deeply sunk brook. Nearby, half shrouded by the mist, was a short and narrow footbridge. Down the path that started from its other end was another of the half-built houses.

He didn't cross that bridge," Raffles said. "I'd have heard him. If he went through the brook, he'd have done some splashing, and I'd have heard it. But he didn't have time to double back. Let's cross the bridge and see if he's left any footprints in the mud."

We walked Indian file across the very narrow bridge. It bent a little under our weight, giving us an uneasy feeling. Raffles said, "The contractor must be using as cheap materials as he can get away with. I hope he's putting better stuff into the houses. Otherwise, the first strong wind will blow them away."

"It does seem rather fragile," I said. "The builder must be a fly-by-night. But nobody builds anything as they used to do."

Raffles crouched down at the other end of the bridge, lit a match, and examined the ground on both sides of the path. "There are any number of prints," he said disgustedly. "They undoubtedly are those of the workmen, though the prints of the man we want could be among them. But I doubt it. They're all made by heavy workingmen's boots."

He sent me down the steep muddy bank to look for prints on the south side of the bridge. He went along the bank north of the bridge. Our matches flared and died while we called out the results of our inspections to each other. The only tracks we saw were ours. We scrambled back up the bank and walked a little way onto the bridge. Side by side, we leaned over the excessively thin railing to stare down into the brook. Raffles lit a Sullivan, and the pleasant odor drove me to light one up too.

"There's something uncanny here, Bunny. Don't you feel it?"

I was about to reply when he put his hand on my shoulder. Softly, he said, "Did you hear a groan?"

"No," I replied, the hairs on the back of my neck rising like the dead from the grave.

Suddenly, he stamped the heel of his boot hard upon the plank. And then I heard a very low moan.

Before I could say anything to him, he was over the railing. He landed with a squish of mud on the bank. A match flared under the bridge, and for the first time I comprehended how thin the wood of the bridge was. I could see the flame through the planks.

Raffles yelled with horror. The match went out. I shouted, "What is it?" Suddenly, I was falling. I grabbed at the railing, felt it *dwindle* out of my grip, struck the cold water of the brook, felt the planks beneath me, felt them sliding away, and shouted once more. Raffles, who had been knocked down and buried for a minute by the collapsed bridge, rose unsteadily. Another match flared, and he cursed. I said, somewhat stupidly, "Where's the bridge?"

"Taken flight," he groaned. "Like the chair!"

He leaped past me and scrambled up the bank. At its top he stood for a minute, staring into the moonlight and the darkness beyond. I crawled shivering out of the brook, rose even more unsteadily, and clawed up the greasy cold mud of the steep bank. A minute later, breathing harshly, and feeling dizzy with unreality, I was standing by Raffles. He was breathing almost as hard as I.

"What *is* it?" I said.

"*What* is it, Bunny?" he said slowly. "It's something that can change its shape to resemble almost anything. As of now, however, it is not what it is but *where* it is that we must determine. We must find it and kill it, even if it should take the shape of a beautiful woman or a child."

"What are you talking about?" I cried.

"Bunny, as God is my witness, when I lit that match under the bridge, I saw one brown eye staring at me. It was embedded in a part of the planking that was thicker than the rest. And it was not far from what looked like a pair of lips and one malformed ear. Apparently, it had not had time to complete its transformation. Or, more likely, it retained organs of sight and hearing so that it would know what was happening in its neighborhood. If it sealed off all its organs of detection, it would not have the slightest idea when it would be safe to change shape again."

"Are you insane?" I said.

"Not unless you share my insanity, since you saw the same things I did. Bunny, that thing can somehow alter its flesh and bones. It has such control over its cells, its organs, its bones— which somehow can switch from rigidity to extreme flexibility— that it can look like other human beings. It can also metamorphose to look like objects. Such as the armchair in the bedroom, which looked exactly like the original. No wonder that Hopkins and Mackenzie and even the redoubtable Holmes failed to find Mr. James Phillimore. Perhaps they may even have sat on him while resting from the search. It's too bad that they did not rip into the chair with a knife in their quest for the jewels. I think that they would have been more than surprised.

"I wonder who the original Phillimore was? There is no record of anybody who could have been the model. But perhaps it based itself on somebody with a different name but took the name of James Phillimore from a tombstone or a newspaper account of an American. Whatever it did on that account, it was also the bridge that you and I crossed. A rather sensitive bridge, a sore bridge, which could not keep from groaning a little when our hard boots pained it."

I could not believe him. Yet I could *not* not believe him.

VI.

Raffles predicted that the thing would be running or walking to Maida Vale. "And there it will take a cab to the nearest station and be on its way into the labyrinth of London. The devil of it is that we won't know what, or whom, to look for. It could be in the shape of a woman, or a small horse, for all I know. Or maybe a tree, though that's not a very mobile refuge.

"You know," he continued after some thought, "there must be

definite limitations on what it can do. It has demonstrated that it can stretch its mass out to almost paper-thin length. But it is, after all, subject to the same physical laws we are subject to as far as its mass goes. It has only so much substance, and so it can get only so big. And I imagine that it can compress itself only so much. So, when I said that it might be the shape of a child, I could have been wrong. It can probably extend itself considerably but cannot contract much."

As it turned out, Raffles was right. But he was also wrong. The thing had means of becoming smaller, though at a price.

"Where could it have come from, A.J.?"

"That's a mystery that might better be laid in the lap of Holmes," he said. "Or perhaps in the hands of the astronomers. I would guess that the thing is not autochthonous. I would say that it arrived here recently, perhaps from Mars, perhaps from a more distant planet, during the month of October, 1894. Do you remember, Bunny, when all the papers were ablaze with accounts of the large falling star that fell into the Straits of Dover, not five miles from Dover itself? Could it have been some sort of ship which could carry a passenger through the ether? From some heavenly body where life exists, intelligent life, though not life as we Terrestrials know it? Could it perhaps have crashed, its propulsive power having failed it? Hence, the friction of its too-swift descent burned away part of the hull? Or were the flames merely the outward expression of its propulsion, which might be huge rockets?"

Even now, as I write this in 1924, I marvel at Raffles' superb imagination and deductive powers. That was 1895, three years before Mr. Wells' *War of the Worlds* was published. It was true that Mr. Verne had been writing his wonderful tales of scientific inventions and extraordinary voyages for many years. But in none of them had he proposed life on other planets or the possibility of infiltration or invasion by alien sapients from far-off planets. The concept was, to me, absolutely staggering. Yet Raffles plucked it from what to others would be a complex of complete irrelevancies. And I was supposed to be the writer of fiction in this partnership!

"I connect the events of the falling star and Mr. Phillimore because it was not too long after the star fell that Mr. Phillimore suddenly appeared from nowhere. In January of this year Mr. Phillimore sold his first jewel to a fence. Since then, once a month, Mr. Phillimore has sold a jewel, four in all. These look like star sapphires. But we may suppose that they are not such because of our experience with the monsterlet in Persano's matchbox. Those pseudo jewels, Bunny, are eggs!"

"Surely you do not mean that?" I said.

"My cousin has a maxim which has been rather widely quoted. He says that, after you've eliminated the impossible, whatever remains, however improbable, is the truth. Yes, Bunny, the race to which Mr. Phillimore belongs lays eggs. These are in their initial form, anyway, something resembling star sapphires. The star shape inside them may be the first outlines of the embryo. I would guess that shortly before hatching, the embryo becomes opaque. The material inside, the yolk, is absorbed or eaten by the embryo. Then the shell is broken and the fragments are eaten by the little beast.

"And then, sometime after hatching, a short time, I'd say, the beastie must become mobile, it wriggles away, it takes refuge in a hole, a mouse hole, perhaps. And there it feeds upon cockroaches, mice, and, when it gets larger, rats. And then, Bunny? Dogs? Babies? And then?"

"Stop," I cried. "It's too horrible to contemplate!"

"Nothing is too horrible to contemplate, Bunny, if one can do something about the thing contemplated. In any event, if I am right, and I pray that I am, only one egg has so far hatched. This was the first one laid, the one that Persano somehow obtained. Within thirty days, another egg will hatch. And this time the thing might get away. We must track down all the eggs and destroy them. But first we must catch the thing that is laying the eggs.

"That won't be easy. It has an amazing intelligence and adaptability. Or, at least, it has amazing mimetic abilities. In one month it learned to speak English perfectly and to become well acquainted with British customs. That is no easy feat, Bunny. There are thousands of Frenchmen and Americans who have been here for some time who have not yet comprehended the British language, temperament, or customs. And these are human beings, though there are, of course, some Englishmen who are uncertain about this."

"Really, A.J.!" I said. "We're not all that snobbish!"

"Aren't we? It takes one to know one, my dear colleague, and I am unashamedly snobbish. After all, if one is an Englishman, it's no crime to be a snob, is it? Somebody has to be superior, and we know who that someone is, don't we?"

"You were speaking of the thing," I said testily.

"Yes. It must be in a panic. It knows it's been found out, and it must think that by now the entire human race will be howling for its blood. At least, I hope so. If it truly knows us, it will realize that we would be extremely reluctant to report it to the authorities. We would not want to be certified. Nor does it know that we cannot stand an investigation into our own lives.

"But it will, I hope, be ignorant of this and so will be trying to escape the country. To do so, it will take the closest and fastest means of transportation, and to do that it must buy a ticket to a definite destination. That destination, I guess, would be Dover. But perhaps not."

At the Maida Vale cab station, Raffles made inquiries of various drivers. We were lucky. One driver had observed another pick up a woman who might be the person—or thing—we were chasing. Encouraged by Raffles' pound note, the cabbie described her. She was a giantess, he said, she seemed to be about fifty years old, and, for some reason, she looked familiar. To his knowledge, he had never seen her before.

Raffles had him describe her face feature by feature. He said, "Thank you," and turned away with a wink at me. When we were alone, I asked him to explain the wink.

"She—it—had familiar features because they were Phillimore's own, though somewhat feminized," Raffles said. "We are on the right track."

On the way into London in our own cab, I said, "I don't understand how the thing gets rid of its clothes when it changes shape. And where did it get its woman's clothes and the purse? And its money to buy the ticket?"

"Its clothes must be part of its body. It must have superb control; it's a sentient chameleon, a superchameleon."

"But its money?" I said. "I understand that it had been selling its eggs in order to support itself. Also, I assume, to disseminate its young. But from where did the thing, when it became a woman, get the money with which to buy a ticket? And was the purse a part of its body before the metamorphosis? If it was, then it must be able to detach parts of its body."

"I rather imagine it has caches of money here and there," Raffles said.

We got out of the cab near St. James's Park, walked to Raffles' rooms at the Albany, quickly ate a breakfast brought in by the porter, donned false beards and plain-glass spectacles and fresh clothes, and then packed a Gladstone bag and rolled up a traveling rug. Raffles also put on a finger a vulgar large ring. This concealed in its hollow interior a spring-operated knife, tiny but very sharp. Raffles had purchased it after his escape from the Camorra deathtrap (described in *The Last Laugh*). He said that if he had had such a device then, he might have been able to cut himself loose instead of depending upon someone else to rescue him from Count Corbucci's devilish automatic executioner. And now a hunch told him to wear the ring during this particular exploit.

We boarded a hansom a few minutes later and soon were on the Charing Cross platform waiting for the train to Dover. And then we were off, comfortably ensconced in a private compartment, smoking cigars and sipping brandy from a flask carried by Raffles.

"I am leaving deduction and induction behind in favor of intuition, Bunny," Raffles said. "Though I could be wrong, intuition tells me that the thing is on the train ahead of us, headed for Dover."

"There are others who think as you do," I said, looking through the glass of the door. "But it must be inference, not intuition, that brings them here." Raffles glanced up in time to see the handsome aquiline features of his cousin and the beefy but genial features of his cousin's medical colleague go by. A moment later, Mackenzie's craggy features followed.

"Somehow," Raffles said, "that human bloodhound, my cousin, has sniffed out the thing's trail. Has he guessed any of the truth? If he has, he'll keep it to himself. The hardheads of the Yard would believe that he'd gone insane, if he imparted even a fraction of the reality behind the case."

VII.

Just before the train arrived at the Dover station, Raffles straightened up and snapped his fingers, a vulgar gesture I'd never known him to make before.

"Today's the day!" he cried. "Or it should be! Bunny, it's a matter of unofficial record that Phillimore came into the East End every thirty-first day to sell a jewel. Does this suggest that it lays an egg every thirty days? If so, then it lays another *today!* Does it do it as easily as the barnyard hen? Or does it experience some pain, some weakness, some tribulation and trouble analogous to that of human women? Is the passage of the egg a minor event, yet one which renders the layer prostrate for an hour or two? Can one lay a large and hard star sapphire with only a trivial difficulty, with only a pleased cackle?"

On getting off the train, he immediately began questioning porters and other train and station personnel. He was fortunate enough to discover a man who'd been on the train on which we suspected the thing had been. Yes, he had noticed something disturbing. A woman had occupied a compartment by herself, a very large woman, a Mrs. Brownstone. But when the train had pulled into the station, a huge man had left her compartment. She was nowhere to be seen. He had, however, been too busy to do anything about it even if there had been anything to do.

Raffles spoke to me afterward. "Could it have taken a hotel room so it could have the privacy needed to lay its egg?"

We ran out of the station and hired a cab to take us to the nearest hotel. As we pulled away, I saw Holmes and Watson talking to the very man we'd just been talking to.

The first hotel we visited was the Lord Warden, which was near the railway station and had a fine view of the harbor. We had no luck there, nor at the Burlington, which was on Liverpool Street, nor the Dover Castle, on Clearence Place. But at the King's Head, also on Clearence Place, we found that he—it—had recently been there. The desk clerk informed us that a man answering our description had checked in. He had left exactly five minutes ago. He had looked pale and shaky, as though he'd had too much to drink the night before.

As we left the hotel, Holmes, Watson, and Mackenzie entered. Holmes gave us a glance that poked chills through me. I was sure that he must have noted us in the train, at the station, and now at this hotel. Possibly, the clerks in the other hotels had told him that he had been preceded by two men asking questions about the same man.

Raffles hailed another cab and ordered the driver to take us along the waterfront, starting near Promenade Pier. As we rattled along, he said, "I may be wrong, Bunny, but I feel that Mr. Phillimore is going home."

"To Mars?" I said, startled. "Or wherever his home planet may be?"

"I rather think that his destination is no farther than the vessel that brought him here. It may still be under the waves, lying on the bottom of the straits, which is nowhere deeper than twenty-five fathoms. Since it must be airtight, it could be like Mr. Campbell's and Ash's all-electric submarine. Mr. Phillimore could be heading toward it, intending to hide out for some time. To lie low, literally, while affairs cool off in England."

"And how would he endure the pressure and the cold of twenty-five fathoms of sea water while on his way down to the vessel?" I said.

"Perhaps he turns into a fish," Raffles said irritatedly.

I pointed out the window. "Could that be he?"

"It might well be *it*," he replied. He shouted for the cabbie to slow down. The very tall, broad-shouldered, and huge-paunched man with the great rough face and the nose like a red pickle looked like the man described by the agent and the clerk. Moreover, he carried the purplish Gladstone bag which they had also described.

Our hansom swerved toward him; he looked at us; he turned pale; he began running. How had he recognized us? I do not know. We were still wearing the beards and spectacles, and he had seen us only briefly by moonlight and matchlight when we were wearing black masks. Perhaps he had a keen sense of odor, though how he could have picked up our scent from among the tar, spices, sweating men and horses, and the rotting garbage floating on the water, I do not know.

Whatever his means of detection, he recognized us. And the chase was on.

It did not last long on land. He ran down a pier for private craft, untied a rowboat, leaped into it, and began rowing as if he were training for the Henley Royal Regatta. I stood for a moment on the edge of the pier; I was stunned and horrified. His left foot was in contact with the Gladstone bag, and it was melting, flowing *into* his foot. In sixty seconds, it had disappeared except for a velvet bag it contained. This, I surmised, held the egg that the thing had laid in the hotel room.

A minute later, we were rowing after him in another boat while its owner shouted and shook an impotent fist at us. Presently, other shouts joined us. Looking back, I saw Mackenzie, Watson, and Holmes standing by the owner. But they did not talk long to him. They ran back to their cab and raced away.

Raffles said, "They'll be boarding a police boat, a steam driven paddlewheeler or screwship. But I doubt that it can catch up with *that*, if there's a good wind and a fair head start."

That was Phillimore's destination, a small single-masted sailing ship riding at anchor about fifty yards out. Raffles said that she was a cutter. It was about thirty-five feet long, was fore-and-aft rigged, and carried a jib, forestaysail, and mainsail— according to Raffles. I thanked him for the information, since I knew nothing and cared as much about anything that moves on water. Give me a good solid horse on good solid ground any time.

Phillimore was a good rower, as he should have been with that great body. But we gained slowly on him. By the time he was boarding the cutter *Alicia*, we were only a few yards behind him. He was just going over the railing when the bow of our boat crashed into the stern of his. Raffles and I went head over heels, oars flying. But we were up and swarming up the rope ladder within a few seconds. Raffles was first, and I fully expected him to be knocked in the head with a belaying pin or whatever it is that sailors use to knock people in the head. Later, he confessed that he expected to have his skull crushed in, too. But Phillimore was too busy recruiting a crew to bother with us at the moment.

When I say he was recruiting, I mean that he was splitting himself into three sailors. At that moment, he lay on the foredeck and was melting, clothes and all.

We should have charged him then and seized him while he was helpless. But we were too horrified. I, in fact, became nauseated, and I vomited over the railing. While I was engaged in this,

Raffles got control of himself. He advanced swiftly toward the three-lobed monstrosity on the deck. He had gotten only a few feet, however, when a voice rang out.

"Put up yore dooks, you swells! Reach for the blue!"

Raffles froze, I raised my head and saw through teary eyes an old grizzled salt. He must have come from the cabin on the poopdeck, or whatever they call it, because he had not been visible when we came aboard. He was aiming a huge Colt revolver at us.

Meanwhile, the schizophrenic transformation was completed. Three little sailors, none higher than my waist, stood before us. They were identically featured, and they looked exactly like the old salt except for their size. They had beards and wore white-and-blue striped stocking caps, large earrings in the left ear, red-and-black-striped jerseys, blue calf-length baggy pants, and they were barefooted. They began scurrying around, up came the anchor, the sails were set, and we were moving at a slant past the great Promenade Pier.

The old sailor had taken over the wheel after giving one of the midgets his pistol. Meanwhile, behind us, a small steamer, its smokestack belching black, tried vainly to catch up with us.

After about ten minutes, one of the tiny sailors took over the wheel. The old salt and one of his duplicates herded us into the cabin. The little fellow held the gun on us while the old sailor tied our wrists behind us and our legs to the upright pole of a bunk with a rope.

"You filthy traitor!" I snarled at the old sailor. "You are betraying the entire human race! Where is your common humanity?"

The old tar cackled and rubbed his gray wirelike whiskers.

"Me humanity? It's where the lords in Parliament and the fat bankers and church-going factory owners of Manchester keep theirs, me fine young gentlemen! In me pocket! Money talks louder than common humanity any day, as any of your landed lords or great cotton spinners will admit when they're drunk in the privacies of their mansion! What did common humanity ever do for me but give me parents the galloping consumption and make me sisters into drunken whores?"

I said nothing more. There was no reasoning with such a

beastly wretch. He looked us over to make sure we were secure, and he and the tiny sailor left. Raffles said, "As long as Phillimore remains—like Gaul—in three parts, we have a chance. Surely, each of the trio's brain must have only a third of the intelligence of the original Phillimore, I hope. And this little knife concealed in my ring will be the key to our liberty. I hope."

Fifteen minutes later, he had released himself and me. We went into the tiny galley, which was next to the cabin and part of the same structure. There we each took a large butcher knife and a large iron cooking pan. And when, after a long wait, one of the midgets came down into the cabin, Raffles hit him alongside the head with a pan before he could yell out. To my horror, Raffles then squeezed the thin throat between his two hands, and he did not let loose until the thing was dead.

"No time for niceties, Bunny," he said, grinning ghastily as he extracted the jewel-egg from the corpse's pocket. "Phillimore's a type of Boojum. If he succeeds in spawning many young, mankind will disappear softly and quietly, one by one. If it becomes necessary to blow up this ship and us with it, I'll not hesitate a moment. Still, we've reduced its forces by one-third. Now let's see if we can't make it one hundred percent."

He put the egg in his own pocket. A moment later, cautiously, we stuck our heads from the structure and looked out. We were in the forepart, facing the foredeck, and thus the old salt at the wheel couldn't see us. The other two midgets were working in the rigging at the orders of the steersman. I suppose that the thing actually knew little of sailsmanship and had to be instructed.

"Look at that, dead ahead," Raffles said. "This is a bright clear day, Bunny. Yet there's a patch of mist there that has no business being there. And we're sailing directly into it."

One of the midgets was holding a device which looked much like Raffles' silver cigarette case except that it had two rotatable knobs on it and a long thick wire sticking up from its top. Later, Raffles said that he thought that it was a machine which somehow sent vibrations through the ether to the spaceship on the bottom of the straits. These vibrations, coded, of course, signaled the automatic machinery on the ship to extend a tube to the surface. And an artificial fog was expelled from the tube.

His explanation was unbelievable, but it was the only one

extant. Of course, at that time neither of us had heard of wireless, although some scientists knew of Hertz's experiments with oscillations. And Marconi was to patent the wireless telegraph the following year. But Phillimore's wireless must have been far advanced over anything we have in 1924.

"As soon as we're in the mist, we attack," Raffles said.

A few minutes later, wreaths of gray fell about us, and our faces felt cold and wet. We could barely see the two midgets working furiously to let down the sails. We crept out onto the deck and looked around the cabin's corner at the wheel. The old tar was no longer in sight. Nor was there any reason for him to be at the wheel. The ship was almost stopped. It obviously must be over the space vessel resting on the mud twenty fathoms below.

Raffles went back into the cabin after telling me to keep an eye on the two midgets. A few minutes later, just as I was beginning to feel panicky about his long absence, he popped out of the cabin.

"The old man was opening the petcocks," he said. "This ship will sink soon with all that water pouring in."

"Where is he?" I said.

"I hit him over the head with the pan," Raffles said. "I suppose he's drowning now."

At that moment, the two little sailors called out for the old sailor and the third member of the trio to come running. They were lowering the cutter's boat and apparently thought there wasn't much time before the ship went down. We ran out at them through the fog just as the boat struck the water. They squawked like chickens suddenly seeing a fox, and they leaped down into the boat. They didn't have far to go since the cutter's deck was now only about two feet above the waves. We jumped down into the boat and sprawled on our faces. Just as we scrambled up, the cutter rolled over, fortunately away from us, and bottomed up. The lines attached to the davit had been loosed, and so our boat was not dragged down some minutes later when the ship sank.

A huge round form, like the back of a Brobdingnagian turtle, broke water beside us. Our boat rocked, and water shipped in, soaking us. Even as we advanced on the two tiny men, who jabbed at us with their knives, a port opened in the side of the great metal craft. Its lower part was below the surface of the sea, and suddenly water rushed into it, carrying our boat along with it. The ship was swallowing our boat and us along with it.

Then the port had closed behind us, but we were in a metallic and well-lit chamber. While the fight raged, with Raffles and me swinging our pans and thrusting our knives at the very agile and speedy midgets, the water was pumped out. As we were to find out, the vessel was sinking back to the mud of the bottom.

The two midgets finally leaped from the boat onto a metal platform. One pressed a stud in the wall, and another port opened. We jumped after them, because we knew that if they got away and got their hands on their weapons, and these might be fearsome indeed, we'd be lost. Raffles knocked one off the platform with a swipe of the pan, and I slashed at the other with my knife.

The thing below the platform cried out in a strange language, and the other one jumped down beside him. He sprawled on top of his fellow, and within a few seconds they were melting together.

It was an act of sheer desperation. If they had had more than one-third of their normal intelligence, they probably would have taken a better course of action. Fusion took time, and this time we did not stand there paralyzed with horror. We leaped down and caught the thing halfway between its shape as two men and its normal, or natural, shape. Even so, tentacles with the poisoned claws on their ends sprouted, and the blue eyes began to form. It looked like a giant version of the thing in Persano's matchbox. But it was only two-thirds as large as it would have been if we'd not slain the detached part of it on the cutter. Its tentacles also were not as long as they would have been, but even so we could not get past them to its body. We danced around just outside their reach, cutting the tips with knives or batting them with the pans. The thing was bleeding, and two of its claws had been knocked off, but it was keeping us off while completing its metamorphosis. Once the thing was able to get to its feet, or I should say, its pseudopods, we'd be at an awful disadvantage.

Raffles yelled at me and ran toward the boat. I looked at him stupidly, and he said, "Help me, Bunny!"

I ran to him, and he said, "Slide the boat onto the thing, Bunny!"

"It's too heavy," I yelled, but I grabbed the side while he pushed on its stern; and somehow, though I felt my intestines would spurt out, we slid it over the watery floor. We did not go very fast, and the thing, seeing its peril, started to stand up. Raffles stopped pushing and threw his frying pan at it. It struck the thing at its head end, and down it went. It lay there a moment as if stunned, which I suppose it was.

Raffles came around to the side opposite mine, and when we were almost upon the thing, but still out of reach of its vigorously waving tentacles, we lifted the bow of the boat. We didn't raise it very far, since it was very heavy. But when we let it fall, it crushed six of the tentacles beneath it. We had planned to drop it squarely on the middle of the thing's loathsome body, but the tentacles kept us from getting any closer.

Nevertheless, it was partially immobilized. We jumped into the boat and, using its sides as a bulwark, slashed at the tips of the tentacles that were still free. As the ends came over the side, we cut them off or smashed them with the pans. Then we climbed out, while it was screaming through the openings at the ends of the tentacles, and we stabbed it again and again. Greenish blood flowed from its wounds until the tentacles suddenly ceased writhing. The eyes became lightless; the greenish ichor turned black-red and congealed. A sickening odor, that of its death, rose from the wounds.

VIII.

It took several days to study the controls on the panel in the vessel's bridge. Each was marked with a strange writing which we would never be able to decipher. But Raffles, the ever redoubtable Raffles, discovered the control that would move the vessel from the bottom to the surface, and he found out how to open the port to the outside. That was all we needed to know.

Meantime, we ate and drank from the ship's stores which had been laid in to feed the old tar. The other food looked nauseating, and even if it had been attractive, we'd not have dared to try it. Three days later, after rowing the boat out onto the sea—the mist was gone—we watched the vessel, its port still open, sink back under the waters. And it is still there on the bottom, for all I know.

We decided against telling the authorities about the thing and its ship. We had no desire to spend time in prison, no matter how patriotic we were. We might have been pardoned because of our great service. But then again we might, according to Raffles, be shut up for life because the authorities would want to keep the whole affair a secret.

Raffles also said that the vessel probably contained devices which, in Great Britian's hands, would ensure her supremacy. But she was already the most powerful nation on Earth, and who knew what Pandora's box we'd be opening? We did not know, of course, that in twenty-three years the Great War would slaughter the majority of our best young men and would start our nation toward second-classdom.

Once ashore, we took passage back to London. There we launched the month's campaign that resulted in stealing and destroying every one of the sapphire-eggs. One had hatched, and the thing had taken refuge inside the walls, but Raffles burned the house down, though not until after rousing its human occupants. It broke our hearts to steal jewels worth in the neighborhood of a million pounds and then destroy them. But we did it, and so the world was saved.

Did Holmes guess some of the truth? Little escaped those gray hawk's eyes and the keen gray brain behind them. I suspect that he knew far more than he told even Watson. That is why Watson, in writing *The Problem of Thor Bridge,* stated that there were three cases in which Holmes had completely failed.

There was the case of James Phillimore, who returned into his house to get an umbrella and was never seen again. There was the case of Isadora Persano, who was found stark mad, staring at a worm in a match box, a worm unknown to science. And there was the case of the cutter *Alicia,* which sailed on a bright spring morning into a small patch of mist and never emerged, neither she nor her crew ever being seen again.

The Adventure of the Global Traveler

by

Anne Lear

Next to Holmes and Watson the most notable character in the canon is Professor James Moriarty, as consummate a villain as Holmes is a hero. He actually appears in only one story, but that is enough, and any story that deals with him is a candidate for this anthology.

The Adventure of
The Global Traveler

by Anne Lear

All I wanted was to find out who the Third Murderer in *Macbeth* really was. Well, I know now. I also know the secret identity and the fate of one famous personage, that the death of another occurred many years before it was reported to have done, and a hitherto unknown detail of Wm. Shakespeare's acting career.

Which just goes to show what a marvelous place to do research is the Folger Shakespeare Library in Washington, DC. In the crowded shelves and vaults of that great storehouse are treasures in such number and variety that even their passionately devoted caretakers do not know the whole.

In my quest for the Third Murderer I started at the logical place. I looked in the card catalogue under M for Murderer. I didn't find the one I had in mind; but I found plenty of others and, being of the happy vampire breed; switched gleefully onto the sidetrack offered.

Here was gore to slake a noble thirst: murders of apprentices by their masters; murders of masters by apprentices; murders of

67

husbands by wives, wives by husbands, children by both. Oh, it was a bustling time, the Age of Elizabeth! Broadsides there were and pamphlets, each juicier than the last.

The titles were the best of it perhaps. Yellow journalism is a mere lily in these declining days. Consider:

A true discourse. Declaring the damnable life and death of one Stubbe Peeter, a most wicked Sorcerer, who in the likeness of a Woolf, committed many murders . . . Who for the same fact was taken and executed . . .

or

Newes from Perin in Cornwall:
Of a most Bloody and unexampled Murther very lately committed by a Father on his own Sonne . . . at the Instigation of a merciless Step-mother . . .

or the truly spectacular

Newes out of Germanie. A most wonderful and true discourse of a cruell murderer, who had kylled in his life tyme, nine hundred, threescore and odde persons, among which six of them were his owne children begotten on a young woman which he forceablie kept in a caue seven yeeres . . .

(This particular murtherer is on record as having planned, with true Teutonic neatness of mind, to do in precisely one thousand people and then retire.)

Eventually I found myself calling for *The moft horrible and tragicall murther, of the right Honorable, the vertuous and valerous gentleman, John Lord Bourgh, Baron of Caftell Connell, committed by Arnold Cosby, the foureteenth of Ianuarie. Togeather with the forrofull fighes of a fadde foule, vppon his funeral: written by W.R., a feruant of the faid Lord Bourgh.*

The pamphlet was sent up promptly to the muffled, gorgeously Tudor reading room, where I signed for it and carried it off to one of the vast mahogany tables that stand about the room and intimidate researchers.

As I worked my way through the blackletter, I found the promising title to be a snare and a delusion. The story turned out to be a mediocre one about a social-climbing coward who provoked a duel and then, unable to get out of it, stabbed his opponent on the sly. Pooh. I was about to send it back, when I noticed an inappropriate thickness. A few pages beyond where I had stopped (at the beginning of the forrofull fighes) the center of the pamphlet seemed thicker than the edges. 'Tis some other reader's notes, I muttered, only this and nothing more.

So, it appeared when I turned to them, they were. There were four thin sheets, small enough to fit into the octavo pamphlet with more than an inch of margin on every side. The paper was of a good quality, much stronger than the crumbling pulp which had concealed it.

I hadn't a clue as to how long ago the sheets had been put there. They might have gone unnoticed for years, as the librarians and users of the ultra-scholarly Folger are not much given to murder as recreation, even horrible and tragicall murthers of the vertuous and valerous, and therefore they don't often ask for the bloody pulps.

Further, the descriptive endorsement on the envelope made no mention of the extra sheets, as it surely would have done had they been any part of the collection.

I hesitated briefly. People tend to be touchy about their notes, academicians more than most, as plagiarism romps about universities more vigorously than anyone likes to admit. The writing was difficult in any case, a tiny, crabbed scribble. It had been done with a steel pen, and the spellings and style were for the most part those of *fin de siècle* England, with a salting of unexpected Jacobean usages. The paper was clearly well aged, darkened from a probable white to a pale brown, uniformly because of its protected position, and the ink cannot have been new, having faded to a medium brown.

My scruples were, after all, academic, as I had inevitably read part of the first page while I examined it. And anyway, who was I kidding?

"On this bleak last night of the year I take up my pen, my anachronistic steel pen which I value highly among the few relics I have of my former—or is it my future?—life, to set down a record which stands but little chance of ever being seen by any who can comprehend it.

"The political situation is becoming dangerous even for me, for all that I am arranging to profit by my foreknowledge of events as well as from the opportunities civil confusion offers to those who know how to use it. However, my prescience does not in this or any other way extend to my own fate, and I would fain leave some trace of myself for those who were my friends, perhaps even more for one who was my enemy. Or will be.

"To settle this point at once: those events which are my past are the distant future for all around me. I do not know what they may be for you who read this, as I cannot guess at what date my message will come to light. For my immediate purpose, therefore, I shall ignore greater realities and refer only to my own lifeline, calling my present *the* present and my past *the* past, regardless of 'actual' dates.

"To begin at approximately the beginning, then, I found it necessary in the spring of 1891 to abandon a thriving business in London. As head of most of Britain's criminal activities—my arch-enemy, Mr. Sherlock Holmes, once complimented me with the title 'The Napoleon of Crime.'"

At this point my eyes seemed to fix themselves immovably. They began to glaze over. I shook myself back to full consciousness, and my hand continued to shake slightly as I slipped the pamphlet back into its envelope and the strange papers, oh so casually, into my own notes. After an experimental husk or two I decided my voice was functional and proceeded to return the pamphlet and thank the librarian. Then I headed for the nearest bar, in search of a quiet booth and beer to wash the dryness of astonishment and the dust of centuries from my throat.

The afternoon was warm, a golden harbinger in a gray March, and the interior of the Hawk and Dove, that sturdy Capitol Hill saloon, was invitingly dark. It was also nearly empty, which was soothing to electrified nerves. I spoke vaguely to a waitress, and by the time I had settled onto a wooden bench polished by buttocks innumerable, beer had materialized before me, cold and gold in a mug.

The waitress had scarcely completed her turn away from my table before I had the little pages out of my portfolio and angled to catch the light filtering dustily in through the mock-Victorian colored window on my left.

*   *   *

". . . I had wealth and power in abundance. However, Holmes moved against me more effectively than I had anticipated, and I was forced to leave for the Continent on very short notice. I had, of course, made provision abroad against such exigency, and, with the help of Colonel Moran, my ablest lieutenant, led Holmes into a trap at the Reichenbach Falls.

"Regrettably, the trap proved unsuccessful. By means of a Japanese wrestling trick I was forced to admire even as it precipitated me over the edge, Holmes escaped me at the last possible moment. He believed he had seen me fall to my death, but this time it was he who had underestimated his opponent.

"A net previously stretched over the gulf, concealed by an aberration of the falls' spray and controlled by Moran, lay ready to catch me if I fell. Had it been Holmes who went over the edge, Moran would have retracted the net to permit his passage down into the maelstrom at the cliff's foot. A spring-fastened dummy was released from the underside of the net by the impact of my weight, completing the illusion.

"I returned to England in the character of an experimental mathematician, a *persona* I had been some years in developing, as at my Richmond residence I carried out the mathematical researches which had been my first vocation. I had always entertained there men who were at the head of various academic, scientific, and literary professions, and my reputation as an erudite, generous host was well established. It was an ideal concealment for me throughout the next year, while my agents, led by the redoubtable Colonel, tracked Mr. Holmes on his travels, and I began to rebuild my shadowy empire.

"During this time I beguiled my untoward leisure with concentrated research into the nature of Time and various paradoxes attendant thereon. My work led me eventually to construct a machine which would permit me to travel into the past and future.

"I could not resist showing the Time Machine to a few of my friends, most of whom inclined to believe it a hoax. One of the more imaginative of them, a writer named Wells, seemed to think there might be something in it, but even he was not fully convinced. No matter. They were right to doubt the rigmarole I spun out for them about what I saw on my travels. Mightily noble it sounded, not to say luridly romantic—Weena indeed!—although, as a matter of fact, some few parts were even true.

"Obviously, the real use to which I put the Machine during the 'week' between its completion and my final trip on it was the furtherance of my professional interests. It was especially convenient for such matters as observing, and introducing judicious flaws into, the construction of bank vaults and for gathering materials for blackmail. Indeed, I used 'my' time well and compiled quite an extensive file for eventual conversion into gold.

"As I could always return to the same time I had left, if not an earlier one, the only limit to the amount of such travelling I could do lay in my own constitution, and that has always been strong.

"My great mistake was my failure to notice the wearing effect all this use was having on the Time Machine. To this day I do not know what part of the delicate mechanism was damaged, but the ultimate results were anything but subtle.

"I come at last to the nature of my arrival at this place and time. Having learned early of the dangers attendant upon being unable to move the Time Machine, I had added to its structure a set of wheels and a driving chain attached to the pedals originally meant simply as foot rests. In short, I converted it into a Time Velocipede.

"It was necessary to exercise caution in order to avoid being seen trundling this odd vehicle through the streets of London during my business forays, but there was nothing to prevent my riding about to my heart's content in the very remote past, providing always that I left careful markings at my site of arrival.

"Thus did I rest from my labors by touring on occasion through the quiet early days of this sceptered isle—a thief's privilege to steal, especially from a friend—ere ever sceptre came to it. Most interesting it was, albeit somewhat empty for one of my contriving temperament.

"It was, then, as I was riding one very long ago day beside a river I found it difficult to realize from its unfamiliar contours would one day be the Thames, that the Velocipede struck a hidden root and was thrown suddenly off balance. I flung out a hand to stabilize myself and, in doing so, threw over the controls, sending myself rapidly forward in time.

"Days and nights passed in accelerating succession, with the concomitant dizziness and nausea I had come to expect but never to enjoy, and this time I had no control of my speed. I regretted even more bitterly than usual the absences of gauges to indicate temporal progress. I had never been able to solve the problem of their design; and now, travelling in this haphazard fashion, I had not the least idea when I might be.

"I could only hope with my usual fervency and more that I should somehow escape the ultimate hazard of merging with a solid object—or a living creature—standing in the same place as I at the time of my halt. Landing in a time-fostered meander of the Thames would be infinitely preferable.

"The swift march of the seasons slowed, as I eased the control lever back, and soon I could perceive the phases of the moon, then once again the alternating light and dark of the sun's diurnal progression.

"Then all of a sudden the unperceived worn part gave way. The Machine disintegrated under me, blasted into virtual nothingness, and I landed without a sound, a bit off balance, on a wooden floor.

"A swift glance around me told me my doom. Whenever I was, it was in no age of machines nor of the delicate tools I required to enable my escape.

"Reeling for a moment with the horror of my position, I felt a firm nudge in the ribs. A clear, powerful voice was asking loudly, 'But who did bid thee join with us?'

"The speaker was a handsome man of middle age, with large, dark eyes, a widow's peak above an extraordinary brow with a frontal development nearly as great as my own, a neat moustache, and a small, equally neat beard. He was muffled in a dark cloak and hood, but his one visible ear was adorned with a gold ring. As I stood dumbly wondering, he nudged me again, and I looked in haste beyond him for enlightenment.

"The wooden floor was a platform, in fact a stage. Below on one side and above on three sides beyond were crowds of people dressed in a style I recognized as that of the early seventeenth century.

"Another nudge, fierce and impatient: 'But who did bid thee join with us?'

"The line was familiar, from a play I knew well. The place,

this wooden stage all but surrounded by its audience—could it possibly be the Globe? In that case, the play . . . the play must be . . . 'MACBETH!' I all but shouted, so startled was I at the sudden apprehension.

"The man next to me expelled a small sigh of relief. A second man, heretofore unnoticed by me, spoke up quickly from my other side. 'He needs not our mistrust, since he delivers our offices and what we have to do, to the direction just.'

" 'Then stand with us,' said the first man, who I now realized must be First Murderer. A suspicion was beginning to grow in my mind as to his offstage identity as well, but it seemed unlikely. We are told that the Bard only played two roles in his own plays: old Adam in As you Like it, and King Hamlet's ghost. Surely . . . but my reflections were cut off short, as I felt myself being covertly turned by Second Murderer to face upstage.

"First Murderer's sunset speech was ended, and I had a line to speak. I knew it already, having been an eager Thespian in my university days. Of course, to my companions and others I could see watching from the wings most of the lines we were speaking were spontaneous. 'Hark!' said I. 'I hear horses.'

"Banquo called for a light 'within,' within being the little curtained alcove at the rear of the stage. Second Murderer consulted a list he carried and averred that it must be Banquo we heard, as all the other expected guests were already gone into the court. First Murderer proffered me a line in which he worried about the horses' moving away; and I reassured him to the effect that they were being led off by servants to the stables, so that Banquo and Fleance could walk the short way in. 'So all men do,' I said, 'From hence to th' Palace Gate make it their walk.'

"Banquo and Fleance entered. Second Murderer saw them coming by the light that Fleance carried, and I identified Banquo for them, assisted in the murder—carefully, for fear habit might make me strike inconveniently hard—and complained about the light's having been knocked out and about our having failed to kill Fleance.

"And then we were in the wings, and I had to face my new acquaintances. Second Murderer was no serious concern, as he was a minor person in the company. First Murderer was a different matter altogether, however, for my conjecture had proved to be the truth, and I was in very fact face to face with William Shakespeare.

"I am a facile, in fact a professional, liar and had no trouble in persuading them that I was a man in flight and had hidden from my pursuers in the 'within' alcove, to appear among them thus unexpectedly. That Shakespeare had been so quick of wit to save his own play from my disruption was no marvel; that the young player had followed suit was matter for congratulation from his fellows; that I had found appropriate lines amazed them all. I explained that I had trod the boards at one time in my life and, in answer to puzzled queries about my strange garb, murmured some words about having spent time of late amongst the sledded Polack, which I supposed would be mysterious enough and did elicit a flattered smile from the playwright.

"As to my reasons for being pursued, I had only to assure my new friends that my troubles were of an amatory nature in order to gain their full sympathy. They could not afford openly to harbor a fugitive from justice, although players of that time, as of most times, tended to the shady side of the law, and these would gladly have helped me to any concealment that did not bring them into immediate jeopardy. As I was but newly arrived in the country from my travels abroad, lacked employment, and could perform, they offered me a place in the company, which I accepted gladly.

"I did not need the pay, as I had observed my customary precaution of wearing a waistcoat whose lining was sewn full of jewels, the universal currency. However, the playhouse afforded me an ideal *locus* from which to begin making the contacts that have since established me in my old position as 'the Napoleon of crime,' ludicrous title in a time more than a century before Napoleon will be born.

"As to how my lines came to be part of the play's text, Will himself inserted them just as the three of us spoke them on the day. He had been filling the First Murderer part that afternoon by sheer good luck, the regular player being ill, and he found vastly amusing the idea of adding an unexplained character to create a mystery for the audience. He had no thought for future audiences and readers, certainly not for recondite scholarship, but only sought to entertain those for whom he wrote: the patrons of the Globe and Blackfriars and the great folk at Court.

"I am an old man now, and, in view of the civil strife soon to burst its festering sores throughout the country, I may not live to be a much older one. I have good hopes, however. Knowing the outcome is helpful, and I have taken care to cultivate the right men. Roundheads, I may say, purchase as many vices as Cavaliers, for all they do it secretly and with a tighter clasp on their purses.

"Still, I shall leave this partial record now, not waiting until I have liberty to set down a more complete one. If you who read it do so at any time during the last eight years of the nineteenth century, or perhaps even for some years thereafter, I beg that you will do me the great favor to take or send it to Mr. Sherlock Holmes at 221B Baker Street, London.

"Thus, in the hope that he may read this, I send my compliments and the following poser:

"The first time the Third Murderer's lines were ever spoken, *they were delivered from memory.*

"Pray, Mr. Holmes, who wrote them?

"Moriarty
"London
"31st December 1640"

The Great Dormitory Mystery
by
S. N. Farber

Time to catch your breath with a quicky. I presume you will recognize the correct version of the phrase with which this miniature ends. Incidentally, Holmes *never* says, anywhere in the canon, "Quick, Watson, the needle."

The Great Dormitory
Mystery

by S. N. Farber

After the third murder in as many months of residents on the fourth floor of the dormitory, the Great Detective was called in on the case.

In each death the body of a student had been discovered the next morning crushed and covered with tire marks. "The halls are wide enough for a small car, but the elevator and stairwells are not," the baffled campus security chief said. "But how did the car get to the fourth floor?"

"Have you observed," the Great Detective replied, "that the tragic events coincided with a full moon? I believe we are dealing with that unhappy curse of modern technological society—the descendant of the werewolf, the weremobile."

On the next night that the moon was full, the Great Detective took action. Every student who lived on the fourth floor was locked in a separate room, along with an electrically monitored five-gallon can of gasoline.

Toward the middle of the night the instruments reported the disappearance of five gallons of gas in Room 440,

78

which was occupied by a Japanese-American youth named Nagawa.

"He must be pouring the gasoline out," the security chief said.

"Or drinking it!" said the Great Detective. He led the security chief to Room 440, where they peered through the keyhole. Nagawa was no longer there, and in his place was a shiny compact car.

The next morning the Great Detective confronted Nagawa. "When the moon is full, you become an automobile, and you ran over your fellow students on the fourth floor."

"But how did you know?" gasped Nagawa.

"Alimentary, my were-Datsun."

The Adventure of the Misplaced Hound
by
Poul Anderson and Gordon R. Dickson

Anderson and Dickson wrote a series of stories about the Hokas, in each of which some form of fictional society was pastiched—if the word can be used as a verb. In my opinion this one is the best of the series—and it was a good series.

The Adventure of the Misplaced Hound

by Poul Anderson and Gordon R. Dickson

Whitcomb Geoffrey was the very model of a modern major operative. Medium tall, stockily muscular, with cold gray eyes in a massively chiseled, expressionless face, he was quietly dressed in purple breeches and a crimson tunic whose slight bulge showed that he carried a Holman raythrower. His voice was crisp and hard as he said: "Under the laws of the Interbeing League, you are required to give every assistance to a field agent of the Interstellar Bureau of Investigation. Me."

Alexander Jones settled his lean length more comfortably behind the desk. His office seemed to crackle with Geoffrey's dynamic personality; he felt sure that the agent was inwardly scorning its easy-going sloppiness. "All right," he said. "But what brings you to Toka? This is still a backward planet, you know. Hasn't got very much to do with spatial traffic." Remembering the Space Patrol episode, he shuddered slightly and crossed his fingers.

"That's what you think!" snapped Geoffrey. "Let me explain."

"Certainly, if you wish," said Alex blandly.

"Thanks, I will," said the other man. He caught himself, bit his lip, and glared. It was plain that he thought Alex much too young for the exalted position of plenipotentiary. And in fact Alex's age was still, after nearly ten years in this job, well below the average for a ranking CDS official.

After a moment, Geoffrey went on: "The largest problem the IBI faces is interstellar dope smuggling, and the most dangerous gang in that business is—or was—operated by a group of renegade ppussjans from Ximba. Ever seen one, or a picture? They're small, slim fellows, cyno-centauroid type: four legs and two arms, muzzled doglike faces. A Class A species, very gifted, and extremely vicious when they go bad. The IBI has spent years trying to track down this particular bunch of dream peddlers. We finally located their headquarters and got most of them. It was on a planet of Yamatsu's Star, about six light-years from here. But the leader, known as Number Ten—"

"Why not Number One?" asked Alex.

"Ppussjans count rank from the bottom up. Ten escaped, and has since been resuming his activities on a smaller scale, building up the ring again. We've *got* to catch him, or we'll soon be right back where we started.

"Casting around in this neighborhood with tracer beams, we caught a spaceship with a ppussjan and a load of nixl weed. The ppussjan confessed what he knew, which wasn't much, but still important. Ten himself is hiding out alone here on Toka—he picked it because it's backward and thinly populated. He's growing the weed and giving it to his confederates, who land here secretly at night. When the hunt for him has died down, he'll leave Toka, and space is so big that we might never catch him again."

"Well," said Alex, "didn't your prisoner tell you just where Ten is hiding?"

"No. He never saw his boss. He merely landed at a certain desolate spot on a large island and picked up the weed, which had been left there for him. Ten could be anywhere on the island. He doesn't have a boat of his own, so we can't track him down with metal detectors; and he's much too canny to come near a spaceship, if we should go to the rendezvous and wait for him."

"I see," said Alex. "And nixl is deadly stuff, isn't it? Hmm-m. You have the coordinates of this rendezvous?"

He pushed a buzzer. A Hoka servant entered, in white robes, a turban, and a crimson cummerbund, to bow low and ask: "What does the sahib wish?"

"Bring me the big map of Toka, Rajat Singh," said Alex.

"At once, sahib." The servant bowed again and disappeared. Geoffrey looked his surprise.

"He's been reading Kipling," said Alex apologetically. It did not seem to clear away his guest's puzzlement.

The coordinates intersected on a large island off the main continent. "Hm," said Alex, "England. Devonshire, to be precise."

"Huh?" Geoffrey pulled his jaw up with a click. An IBI agent is never surprised. "You and I will go there at once," he said firmly.

"But—my wife—" began Alex.

"Remember your duty, Jones!"

"Oh, all right. I'll go. But you understand," added the younger man diffidently, "there may be a little trouble with the Hokas themselves."

Geoffrey was amused. "We're used to that in the IBI," he said. "We're well-trained not to step on native toes."

Alex coughed, embarrassed. "Well, it's not exactly that—" he stumbled. "You see . . . well, it may be the other way around."

A frown darkened Geoffrey's brow. "They may hamper us, you mean?" he clipped. "Your function is to keep the natives non-hostile, Jones."

"No," said Alex unhappily. "What I'm afraid of is that the Hokas may try to help us. Believe me, Geoffrey, you've no idea of what can happen when Hokas take it into their heads to be helpful."

Geoffrey cleared his throat. He was obviously wondering whether or not to report Alex as incompetent. "All right," he said. "We'll divide up the work between us. I'll let you do all the native handling, and you let me do the detecting."

"Good enough," said Alex, but he still looked doubtful.

The green land swept away beneath them as they flew toward England in the plenipotentiary's runabout. Geoffrey was scowling. "It's urgent," he said. "When the spaceship we captured fails to show up with its cargo, the gang will know something's gone wrong and send a boat to pick up Ten. At least one of them must know exactly where on the island he's hiding. They'll have an excellent chance of sneaking him past any blockade we can set up." He took out a cigarette and puffed nervously. "Tell me, why is the place called England?"

"Well—" Alex drew a long breath. "Out of maybe a quarter million known intelligent species, the Hokas are unique. Only in the last few years have we really begun to probe their psychology. They're highly intelligent, unbelievably quick to learn, ebullient by nature . . . and fantastically literal-minded. They have difficulty distinguishing fact from fiction, and since fiction is so much more colorful, they don't usually bother. Oh, my servant back at the office doesn't *consciously* believe he's a mysterious East Indian; but his subconscious has gone overboard for the role, and he can easily rationalize anything that conflicts with his wacky assumptions." Alex frowned, in search of words. "The closest analogy I can make is that the Hokas are somewhat like small human children, plus having the physical and intellectual capabilities of human adults. It's a formidable combination."

"All right," said Geoffrey. "What's this got to do with England?"

"Well, we're still not sure just what is the best starting point for the development of civilization among the Hokas. How big a forward step should the present generation be asked to take? More important, what socio-economic forms are best adapted to their temperaments and so on? Among other experiments, about ten years ago the cultural mission decided to try a Victorian English setup, and chose this island for the scene of it. Our robofacs quickly produced steam engines, machine tools, and so on for them . . . of course, we omitted the more brutal features of the actual Victorian world. The Hokas quickly carried on from the start we'd given them. They consumed mountains of Victorian literature—"

"I see," nodded Geoffrey.

"You begin to see," said Alex a little grimly. "It's more complicated than that. When a Hoka starts out to imitate something, there are no half measures about it. For instance, the first place we're going, to get the hunt organized, is called London, and the office we'll contact is called Scotland Yard, and—well, I hope you can understand a nineteenth-century English accent, because that's all you'll hear."

Geoffrey gave a low whistle. "They're that serious about it, eh?"

"If not more so," said Alex. "Actually, the society in question has, as far as I know, succeeded very well—so well that, being busy elsewhere, I haven't had a chance to keep up with events in England. I've no idea what that Hoka logic will have done to the original concepts by now. Frankly, I'm scared!"

Geoffrey looked at him curiously and wondered whether the plenipotentiary might not perhaps be a little off-balance on the subject of his wards.

From the air, London was a large collection of peak-roofed buildings, split by winding cobbled streets, on the estuary of a broad river that could only be the Thames. Alex noticed that it was being remodeled to a Victorian pattern: Buckingham Palace, Parliament, and the Tower were already erected, and St. Paul's was halfway finished. An appropriate fog was darkening the streets, so that gas lamps had to be lit. He found Scotland Yard on his map and landed in the court, between big stone buildings. As he and Geoffrey climbed out, a Hoka bobby complete with blue uniform and bulging helmet saluted them with great deference.

" 'Umans!" he exclaimed. "H'I sye, sir, this must be a right big case, eh what? Are you working for 'Er Majesty, h'if h'I might myke so bold as ter awsk?"

"Well," said Alex, "not exactly." The thought of a Hoka Queen Victoria was somewhat appalling. "We want to see the chief inspector."

"Yes, sir!" said the teddy bear. "H'Inspector Lestrade is right down the 'all, sir, first door to yer left."

"Lestrade," murmured Geoffrey. "Where've I heard that name before?"

They mounted the steps and went down a gloomy corridor lit by flaring gas jets. The office door indicated had a sign on it in large letters:

FIRST BUNGLER

"Oh, no!" said Alex under his breath.

He opened the door. A small Hoka in a wing-collared suit and ridiculously large horn-rimmed spectacles got up from behind the desk.

"The plenipotentiary!" he exclaimed in delight. "And another human! What is it, gentlemen? Has—" He paused, looked in sudden fright around the office, and lowered his voice to a whisper. "Has Professor Moriarty broken loose again?"

Alex introduced Geoffrey. They sat down and explained the situation. Geoffrey wound up with: "So I want you to organize your—CID, I imagine you call it—and help me track down this alien."

Lestrade shook his head sadly. "Sorry, gentlemen," he said. "We can't do that."

"Can't do it?" echoed Alex, shocked. "Why not?"

"It wouldn't do any good," said Lestrade, gloomily. "We wouldn't find anything. No, sir, in a case as serious as this, there's only one man who can lay such an arch-criminal by the heels. I refer, of course, to Mr. Sherlock Holmes."

"Oh, NO!" said Alex.

"I beg your pardon?" asked Lestrade.

"Nothing," said Alex, feverishly wiping his brow. "Look here—Lestrade—Mr. Geoffrey here is a representative of the most effective police force in the Galaxy. He—"

"Come now, sir," said Lestrade, with a pitying smile. "You surely don't pretend that he is the equal of Sherlock Holmes. Come, come, now!"

Geoffrey cleared his throat angrily, but Alex kicked his foot. It was highly illegal to interfere with an established cultural pattern, except by subtler means than argument. Geoffrey caught on and nodded as if it hurt him. "Of course," he said in a strangled voice. "I would be the last to compare myself with Mr. Holmes."

"Fine," said Lestrade, rubbing his stubby hands together. "Fine. I'll take you around to his apartments, gentlemen, and we can lay the problem before him. I trust he will find it interesting."

"So do I," said Alex, hollowly.

* * *

A hansom cab was clopping down the foggy streets and Lestrade hailed it. They got in, though Geoffrey cast a dubious look at the beaked, dinosaurian reptile which the Hokas called a horse, and went rapidly through the tangled lanes. Hokas were abroad on foot, the males mostly in frock coats and top hats, carrying tightly rolled umbrellas, the females in long dresses; but now and then a bobby, a red-coated soldier, or a kilted member of a Highland regiment could be seen. Geoffrey's lips moved silently.

Alex was beginning to catch on. Naturally, the literature given these Englishmen must have included the works of A. Conan Doyle, and he could see where the romantic Hoka nature would have gone wild over Sherlock Holmes. So they had to interpret everything literally; but who had they picked to be Holmes?

"It isn't easy being in the CID, gentlemen," said Lestrade. "We haven't much of a name hereabouts, y'know. Of course, Mr. Holmes always gives us the credit, but somehow word gets around." A tear trickled down his furry cheek.

They stopped before an apartment building in Baker Street and entered the hallway. A plump elderly female met them. "Good afternoon, Mrs. Hudson," said Lestrade. "Is Mr. Holmes in?"

"Indeed he is, sir," said Mrs. Hudson. "Go right up." Her awed eyes followed the humans as they mounted the stairs.

Through the door of 221B came a horrible wail. Alex froze, ice running along his spine, and Geoffrey cursed and pulled out his raythrower. The scream sawed up an incredible scale, swooped down again, and died in a choked quivering. Geoffrey burst into the room, halted, and glared around.

The place was a mess. By the light of a fire burning in the hearth, Alex could see papers heaped to the ceiling, a dagger stuck in the mantel, a rack of test tubes and bottles, and a "V.R." punched in the wall with bullets. It was hard to say whether the chemical reek or the tobacco smoke was worse. A Hoka in dressing gown and slippers put down his violin and looked at them in surprise. Then he beamed and came forward to extend his hand.

"Mr. Jones!" he said. "This is a real pleasure. Do come in."

"Uh—that noise—" Geoffrey looked nervously around the room.

"Oh, that," said the Hoka, modestly. "I was just trying out a little piece of my own. Concerto in Very Flat for violin and cymbals. Somewhat experimental, don't y'know."

Alex studied the great detective. Holmes looked about like any other Hoka—perhaps he was a trifle leaner, though still portly by human standards. "Ah, Lestrade," he said. "And Watson—do you mind if I call you Watson, Mr. Jones? It seems more natural."

"Oh, not at all," said Alex, weakly. He thought the real Watson—no, dammit, the Hoka Watson!—must be somewhere else; and the natives' one-track minds—

"But we are ignoring our guest here, whom I perceive to be in Mr. Lestrade's branch of the profession," said Holmes, laying down his violin and taking out a big-bowled pipe.

IBI men do not start; but Geoffrey came as close to it as one of his bureau's operatives had ever done. He had no particular intention of maintaining an incognito, but no officer of the law likes to feel that his profession is written large upon him. "How do you know that?" he demanded.

Holmes' black nose bobbed. "Very simple, my dear sir," he said. "Humans are a great rarity here in London. When one arrives, thus, with the estimable Lestrade for company, the conclusion that the problem is one for the police and that you yourself, my dear sir, are in some way connected with the detection of criminals, becomes a very probable one. I am thinking of writing another little monograph— But sit down, gentlemen, sit down, and let me hear what this is all about."

Recovering what dignity they could, Alex and Geoffrey took the indicated chairs. Holmes himself dropped into an armchair so overstuffed that he almost disappeared from sight. The two humans found themselves confronting a short pair of legs beyond which a button nose twinkled and a pipe fumed.

"First," said Alex, pulling himself together, "let me introduce Mr.—"

"Tut-tut, Watson," said Holmes. "No need. I know the estimable Mr. Gregson by reputation, if not by sight."

"Geoffrey, dammit!" shouted the IBI man.

Holmes smiled gently. "Well, sir, if you wish to use an alias, there is no harm done. But between us, we may as well relax, eh?"

"H-h-how," stammered Alex, "do you know that he's named Gregson?"

"My dear Watson," said Holmes, "since he is a police officer, and Lestrade is already well known to me, who else could he be? I have heard excellent things of you, Mr. Gregson. If you continue to apply my methods, you will go far."

"Thank you," snarled Geoffrey.

Holmes made a bridge of his fingers. "Well, Mr. Gregson," he said, "let me hear your problem. And you, Watson, will no doubt want to take notes. You will find pencil and paper on the mantel."

Gritting his teeth, Alex got them while Geoffrey launched into the story, interrupted only briefly by Holmes's "Are you getting all this down, Watson?" or occasions when the great detective paused to repeat slowly some thing he himself had interjected so that Alex could copy it word for word.

When Geoffrey had finished, Holmes sat silent for a while, puffing on his pipe. "I must admit," he said finally, "that the case has its interesting aspects. I confess to being puzzled by the curious matter of the Hound."

"But I didn't mention any hound," said Geoffrey numbly.

"That is the curious matter," replied Holmes. "The area in which you believe this criminal to be hiding is Baskerville territory, and you didn't mention a Hound once." He sighed and turned to the Scotland Yard Hoka. "Well, Lestrade," he went on, "I imagine we'd all better go down to Devonshire and you can arrange there for the search Gregson desires. I believe we can catch the 8:05 out of Paddington tomorrow morning."

"Oh, no," said Geoffrey, recovering some of his briskness. "We can fly down tonight."

Lestrade was shocked. "But I say," he exclaimed. "That just isn't done."

"Nonsense, Lestrade," said Holmes.

"Yes, Mr. Holmes," said Lestrade, meekly.

The village of St. Vitus-Where-He-Danced was a dozen

thatch-roofed houses and shops, a church, and a tavern, set down in the middle of rolling gray-green moors. Not far away, Alex could see a clump of trees which he was told surrounded Baskerville Hall. The inn had a big signboard announcing "The George and Dragon," with a picture of a Hoka in armor spearing some obscure monster. Entering the low-ceilinged tap-room, Alex's party were met by an overawed landlord and shown to clean, quiet rooms whose only drawback was the fact that the beds were built for one-meter Hokas.

By then it was night. Holmes was outside somewhere, bustling around and talking to the villagers, and Lestrade went directly to bed; but Alex and Geoffrey came back downstairs to the tap-room. It was full of a noisy crowd of Hoka farmers and tradesmen, some talking in their squeaky voices, some playing darts, some clustering around the two humans. A square, elderly native introduced as Farmer Toowey joined them at their table.

"Ah, lad," he said, "it be turrible what yeou zee on the moor o' nights." And he buried his nose in the pint mug which should have held beer but, true to an older tradition, brimmed with the fiery liquor this high-capacity race had drunk from time immemorial. Alex, warned by past experience, sipped more cautiously at his pint; but Geoffrey was sitting with a half-empty mug and a somewhat wild look in his eyes.

"You mean the Hound?" asked Alex.

"I du," said Farmer Toowey. "Black, 'tis, an' bigger nor any bullock. And they girt teeth! One chomp and yeou'm gone."

"Is that what happened to Sir Henry Baskerville?" queried Alex. "Nobody seems to know where he's been for a long time."

"Swall'd um whole," said Toowey, darkly, finishing his pint and calling for another one. "Ah, poor Sir Henry! He was a good man, he was. When we were giving out new names, like the human book taught us, he screamed and fought, for he knew there was a curse on the Baskervilles, but—"

"Tha dialect's slipping, Toowey," said another Hoka.

"I be zorry," said Toowey. "I be oold, and times I forget masel'."

Privately, Alex wondered what the real Devonshire had been like. The Hokas must have made this one up out of whole cloth.

Sherlock Holmes entered in high spirits and sat down with

them. His beady black eyes glittered. "The game is afoot, Watson!" he said. "The Hound has been doing business as usual. Strange forms seen on the moors of late— I daresay it's our criminal, and we shall soon lay him by the heels."

"Ridic'lous," mumbled Geoffrey. "Ain't—isn't any Hound. We're affer dope smuggler, not some son of—YOWP!" A badly thrown dart whizzed by his ear.

"Do you have to do that?" he quavered.

"Ah, they William," chuckled Toowey. "Ee's a fair killer, un is."

Another dart zoomed over Geoffrey's head and stuck in the wall. The IBI man choked and slid under the table   whether for refuge or sleep, Alex didn't know.

"Tomorrow," said Holmes, "I shall measure this tavern. I always measure," he added in explanation. "Even when there seems to be no point in it."

The landlord's voice boomed over the racket. "Closing time, gentlemen. It is time!"

The door flew open and banged to again. A Hoka stood there, breathing hard. He was unusually fat, and completely muffled in a long black coat; his face seemed curiously expressionless, though his voice was shrill with panic.

"Sir Henry!" cried the landlord. "Yeou'm back, squire!"

"The Hound," wailed Baskerville. "The Hound is after me!"

"Yeou've na cause tu fee-ar naow, Sir Henry," said Farmer Toowey. " 'Tis Sheerlock Holmes unself coom down to track yan brute."

Baskerville shrank against the wall. "Holmes?" he whispered.

"And a man from the IBI," said Alex. "But we're really after a criminal lurking on the moors—"

Geoffrey lifted a tousled head over the table. "Isn't no Hound," he said. "I'm affer uh dirty ppussjan, I am. Isn't no Hound nowheres."

Baskerville leaped. "It's at the door!" he shrieked, wildly. Plunging across the room, he went through the window in a crash of glass.

"Quick, Watson!" Holmes sprang up, pulling out his archaic revolver. "We'll see if there is a Hound or not!" He shoved through the panicky crowd and flung the door open.

The thing that crouched there, dimly seen by the firelight spilling out into darkness, was long and low and black, the body a vague shadow, a fearsome head dripping cold fire and snarling stiffly. It growled and took a step forward.

"Here naow!" The landlord plunged ahead, too outraged to be frightened. "Yeou can't coom in here. 'Tis closing time!" He thrust the Hound back with his foot and slammed the door.

"After him, Watson!" yelled Holmes. "Quick, Gregson!"

"Eek," said Geoffrey.

He must be too drunk to move, Alex thought. Alex himself had consumed just enough to dash after Holmes. They stood in the entrance, peering into darkness.

"Gone," said the human.

"We'll track him down!" Holmes paused to light his bull's-eye lantern, button his long coat, and jam his deerstalker cap more firmly down over his ears. "Follow me."

No one else stirred as Holmes and Alex went out into the night. It was pitchy outside. The Hokas had better night vision than humans and Holmes' furry hand closed on Alex's to lead him. "Confound these cobblestones!" said the detective. "No tracks whatsoever. Well, come along." They trotted from the village.

"Where are we going?" asked Alex.

"Out by the path to Baskerville Hall," replied Holmes sharply. "You would hardly expect to find the Hound anyplace else, would you, Watson?"

Properly rebuked, Alex lapsed into silence, which he didn't have the courage to break until, after what seemed an endless time, they came to a halt. "Where are we now?" he inquired of the night.

"About midway between the village and the Hall," replied the voice of Holmes, from near the level of Alex's waist. "Compose yourself, Watson, and wait while I examine the area for clues." Alex felt his hand released and heard the sound of Holmes moving away and rustling about on the ground. "Aha!"

"Find something?" asked the human, looking nervously around him.

"Indeed I have, Watson," answered Holmes. "A seafaring man with red hair and a peg leg has recently passed by here on his way to drown a sackful of kittens."

Alex blinked. "What?"

"A seafaring man—" Holmes began again, patiently.

"But—" stammered Alex. "But how can you tell that?"

"Childishly simple, my dear Watson," said Holmes. The light pointed to the ground. "Do you see this small chip of wood?"

"Y-yes, I guess so."

"By its grain and seasoning, and the type of wear it has had, it is obviously a piece which has broken off a peg leg. A touch of tar upon it shows that it belongs to a seafaring man. But what would a seafaring man be doing on the moors at night?"

"That's what I'd like to know," said Alex.

"We may take it," Holmes went on, "that only some unusual reason could force him out with the Hound running loose. But when we realize that he is a red-headed man with a terrific temper and a sackful of kittens with which he is totally unable to put up with for another minute, it becomes obvious that he has sallied forth in a fit of exasperation to drown them."

Alex's brain, already spinning somewhat dizzily under the effect of the Hoka liquor, clutched frantically at this explanation, in an attempt to sort it out. But it seemed to slip through his fingers.

"What's all that got to do with the Hound, or the criminal we're after?" he asked weakly.

"Nothing, Watson," reproved Holmes sternly. "Why should it have?"

Baffled, Alex gave up.

Holmes poked around for a few more minutes, then spoke again. "If the Hound is truly dangerous, it should be sidling around to overwhelm us in the darkness. It should be along very shortly. Hah!" he rubbed his hands together. "Excellent!"

"I suppose it is," said Alex, feebly.

"You stay here, Watson," said Holmes, "and I will move on down the path a ways. If you see the creature, whistle." His lantern went out and the sound of his footsteps moved away.

Time seemed to stretch on interminably. Alex stood alone in the darkness, with the chill of the moor creeping into his bones as the liquor died within him, and wondered why he had ever let himself in for this in the first place. What would Tanni say? What earthly use would he be even if the Hound should appear? With his merely human night vision, he could let the beast stroll past within arm's reach and never know it. . . . Of course, he could probably hear it. . . .

Come to think of it, what kind of noise would a monster make when walking? Would it be a *pad-pad*, or a sort of *shuffle-shuffle-shuffle* like the sound on the path to his left?

The sound—*Yipe!*

The night was suddenly shattered. An enormous section of the blackness reared up and smashed into him with the solidity and impact of a brick wall. He went spinning down into the star-streaked oblivion of unconsciousness.

When he opened his eyes again, it was to sunlight streaming through the leaded windows of his room. His head was pounding, and he remembered some fantastic nightmare in which—hah!

Relief washing over him, he sank back into bed. Of course. He must have gotten roaring drunk last night and dreamed the whole weird business. His head was splitting. He put his hands up to it.

They touched a thick bandage.

Alex sat up as if pulled on a string. The two chairs which had been arranged to extend the bed for him went clattering to the floor. "Holmes!" he shouted. "Geoffrey!"

His door opened and the individuals in question entered, followed by Farmer Toowey. Holmes was fully dressed, fuming away on his pipe; Geoffrey looked red-eyed and haggard. "What happened?" asked Alex, wildly.

"You didn't whistle," said Holmes reproachfully.

"Aye, that yeou di'n't," put in the farmer. "When they boor yeou in, tha face were white nor a sheet, laike. Fair horrible it were, the look on tha face, lad."

"Then it wasn't a dream!" said Alex, shuddering.

"I—er—I saw you go out after the monster," said Geoffrey, looking guilty. "I tried to follow you, but I couldn't get moving for some reason." He felt gingerly of his own head.

"I saw a black shape attack you, Watson," added Holmes. "I think it was the Hound, even though that luminous face wasn't there. I shot at it but missed, and it fled over the moors. I couldn't pursue it with you lying there, so I carried you back. It's late afternoon now—you slept well, Watson!"

"It must have been the ppussjan," said Geoffrey with something of his old manner. "We're going to scour the moors for him today."

"No, Gregson," said Holmes. "I am convinced it was the Hound."

"Bah!" said Geoffrey. "That thing last night was only—was only—well, it was not a ppussjan. Some local animal, no doubt."

"Aye," nodded Farmer Toowey. "The Hound un were, that."

"Not the Hound!" yelled Geoffrey. "The ppussjan, do you hear? The Hound is pure superstition. There isn't any such animal."

Holmes wagged his finger. "Temper, temper, Gregson," he said.

"And stop calling me Gregson!" Geoffrey clutched his temples. "Oh, my head—!"

"My dear young friend," said Holmes patiently, "it will repay you to study my methods if you wish to advance in your profession. While you and Lestrade were out organizing a futile search party, I was studying the terrain and gathering clues. A clue is the detective's best friend, Gregson. I have five hundred measurements, six plaster casts of footprints, several threads torn from Sir Henry's coat by a splinter last night, and numerous other items. At a conservative estimate, I have gathered five pounds of clues."

"Listen." Geoffrey spoke with dreadful preciseness. "We're here to track down a dope smuggler, Holmes. A desperate criminal. We are not interested in country superstitions."

"I am, Gregson," smiled Holmes.

With an inarticulate snarl, Geoffrey turned and whirled out of the room. He was shaking. Holmes looked after him and tut-tutted. Then, turning: "Well, Watson, how do you feel now?"

Alex got carefully out of bed. "Not too bad," he admitted. "I've got a thumping headache, but an athetrine tablet will take care of it."

"Oh, that reminds me—" While Alex dressed, Holmes took a small flat case out of his pocket. When Alex looked that way again, Holmes was injecting himself with a hypodermic syringe.

"Hey!" cried the human. "What's that?"

"Morphine, Watson," said Holmes. "A seven percent solution. It stimulates the mind, I've found."

"Morphine!" Alex cried. Here was an IBI man currently present for the purpose of running down a dope smuggler and one of his Hokas had just produced—"OH, NO!"

Holmes leaned over and whispered in some embarrassment: "Well, actually, Watson, you're right. It's really just distilled water. I've written off for morphine several times, but they never send me any. So—well, one has one's position to keep up, you know."

"Oh," Alex feebly mopped his brow. "Of course."

While he stowed away a man-sized dinner, Holmes climbed up on the roof and lowered himself down the chimney in search of possible clues. He emerged black but cheerful. "Nothing, Watson," he reported. "But we must be thorough." Then, briskly: "Now come. We've work to do."

"Where?" asked Alex. "With the search party?"

"Oh, no. They will only alarm some harmless wild animals, I fear. We are going exploring elsewhere. Farmer Toowey here has kindly agreed to assist us."

"S'archin', laike," nodded the old Hoka.

As they emerged into the sunlight, Alex saw the search party, a hundred or so local yokels who had gathered under Lestrade's direction with clubs, pitchforks, and flails to beat the bush for the Hound—or for the ppussjan, if it came to that. One enthusiastic farmer drove a huge "horse"-drawn reaping machine. Geoffrey was scurrying up and down the line, screaming as he tried to bring some order into it. Alex felt sorry for him.

They struck out down the path across the moor. "First we're off to Baskerville Hall," said Holmes. "There's something deucedly odd about Sir Henry Baskerville. He disappears for weeks, and then reappears last night, terrified by his ancestral curse, only to dash out onto the very moor which it is prowling. Where has he been in the interim, Watson? Where is he now?"

"Hm—yes," agreed Alex. "This Hound business and the ppussjan—do you think that there could be some connection between the two?"

"Never reason before you have all the facts, Watson," said Holmes. "It is the cardinal sin of all young police officers such as our impetuous friend Gregson."

Alex couldn't help agreeing. Geoffrey was so intent on his main assignment that he just didn't take time to consider the environment; to him, this planet was only a backdrop for his search. Of course, he was probably a cool head ordinarily, but Sherlock Holmes could unseat anyone's sanity.

Alex remembered that he was unarmed. Geoffrey had a raythrower, but this party only had Holmes's revolver and Toowey's gnarled staff. He gulped and tried to dismiss thoughts of the thing that had slugged him last night. "A nice day," he remarked to Holmes.

"It is, is it not? However," said Holmes, brightening up, "some of the most bloodcurdling crimes have been committed on fine days. There was, for example, the Case of the Dismembered Bishop—I don't believe I have ever told you about it, Watson. Do you have your notebook to hand?"

"Why, no," said Alex, somewhat startled.

"A pity," said Holmes. "I could have told you not only about the Dismembered Bishop, but about the Leaping Caterpillar, the Strange Case of the Case of Scotch, and the Great Ghastly Case—all very interesting problems. How is your memory?" he asked suddenly.

"Why—good, I guess," said Alex.

"Then I will tell you about the Case of the Leaping Caterpillar, which is the shortest of the lot," commenced Holmes. "It was considerably before your time, Watson. I was just beginning to attract attention with my work; and one day there was a knock on the door and in came the strangest—"

"Here be Baskerville Hall, laike," said Farmer Toowey.

An imposing Tudoresque pile loomed behind its screen of trees. They went up to the door and knocked. It opened and a corpulent Hoka in butler's black regarded them with frosty eyes. "Tradesmen's entrance in the rear," he said.

"Hey!" cried Alex.

The butler took cognizance of his humanness and became respectful. "I beg your pardon, sir," he said. "I am somewhat near-sighted and— I am sorry, sir, but Sir Henry is not at home."

"Where is he, then?" asked Holmes, sharply.

"In his grave, sir," said the butler, sepulchrally.

"Huh?" said Alex.

"His grave?" barked Holmes. "Quick, man! Where is he buried?"

"In the belly of the Hound, sir. If you will pardon the expression."

"Aye, aye," nodded Farmer Toowey. "Yan Hound, ee be a hungry un, ee be."

A few questions elicited the information that Sir Henry, a bachelor, had disappeared one day several weeks ago while walking on the moors, and had not been heard from since. The butler was surprised to learn that he had been seen only last night, and brightened visibly. "I hope he comes back soon, sir," he said. "I wish to give notice. Much as I admire Sir Henry, I cannot continue to serve an employer who may at any moment be devoured by monsters."

"Well," said Holmes, pulling out a tape measure, "to work, Watson."

"Oh, no, you don't!" This time Alex asserted himself. He couldn't see waiting around all night while Holmes measured this monstrosity of a mansion. "We've got a ppussjan to catch, remember?"

"Just a little measurement," begged Holmes.

"No!"

"Not even one?"

"All right." Jones relented at the wistful tone. "Just one."

Holmes beamed and, with a few deft motions, measured the butler.

"I must say, Watson, that you can be quite tyrannical at times," he said. Then, returning to Hoka normal: "Still, without my Boswell, where would I be?" He set off at a brisk trot, his furry legs twinkling in the late sunlight. Alex and Toowey stretched themselves to catch up.

They were well out on the moor again when the detective stopped and, his nose twitching with eagerness, leaned over a small bush from which one broken limb trailed on the ground. "What's that?" asked Alex.

"A broken bush, Watson," said Holmes snappishly. "Surely even you can see that."

"I know. But what about it?"

"Come, Watson," said Holmes, sternly. "Does not this broken bush convey some message to you? You know my methods. Apply them."

Alex felt a sudden wave of sympathy for the original Dr. Watson. Up until now he had never realized the devilish cruelty inherent in that simple command to apply the Holmesian methods. Apply them—how? He stared fiercely at the bush, which continued to ignore him, without being able to deduce more than that it was (a) a bush and (b) broken.

"Uh—a high wind?" he asked hesitantly.

"Ridiculous, Watson," retorted Holmes. "The broken limb is green; doubtless it was snapped last night by something large passing by in haste. Yes, Watson, this confirms my suspicions. The Hound has passed this way on its way to its lair, and the branch points us the direction."

"They be tu Grimpen Mire, a be," said Farmer Toowey dubiously. "Yan mire be impassable, un be."

"Obviously it is not, if the Hound is there," said Holmes. "Where it can go, we can follow. Come, Watson!" And he trotted off, his small body bristling with excitement.

They went through the brush for some minutes until they came to a wide boggy stretch with a large signboard in front of it.

GRIMPEN MIRE
Four Miles Square
Danger!!!!!!

"Watch closely, Watson," said Holmes. "The creature has obviously leaped from tussock to tussock. We will follow his path, watching for trampled grass or broken twigs. Now, then!" And bounding past the boundary sign, Holmes landed on a little patch of turf, from which he immediately soared to another one.

Alex hesitated, gulped, and followed him. It was not easy to progress in jumps of a meter or more, and Holmes, bouncing from spot to spot, soon pulled away. Farmer Toowey cursed and grunted behind Alex. "Eigh, ma oold boons can't tyke the leaping na moor, they can't," he muttered when they paused to rest. "If we'd knowed the Mire were tu be zo much swink, we'd never a builted un, book or no book."

"You made it yourselves?" asked Alex. "It's artificial?"

"Aye, lad, that un be. 'Twas in the book, Grimpen Mire, an' un swall'd many a man doon, un did. Many brave hee-arts lie asleep in un deep." He added apologetically: "Ow-ers be no zo grimly, though un tried hard. Ow-ers, yeou oonly get tha feet muddy, a-crossing o' 't. Zo we stay well away fran it, yeou understand."

Alex sighed.

The sun was almost under the hills now, and long shadows swept down the moor. Alex looked back, but could not make out any sign of Hall, village, or search party. A lonesome spot—not exactly the best place to meet a demoniac Hound, or even a ppussjan. Glancing ahead, he could not discern Holmes either, and he put on more speed.

An island—more accurately, a large hill—rose above the quaking mud. Alex and Toowey reached it with a final leap. They broke through a wall of trees and brush screening its stony crest. Here grew a wide thick patch of purple flowers. Alex halted, looked at them, and muttered an oath. He'd seen those blossoms depicted often enough in news articles.

"Nixl weed," he said. "So this *is* the ppussjan hideout!"

Dusk came swiftly as the sun disappeared. Alex remembered again that he was unarmed and strained wildly through the gathering dimness. "Holmes!" he called. "Holmes! I say, where are you, old fellow?" He snapped his fingers and swore. *Damn! Now I'm doing it!*

A roar came from beyond the hilltop. Jones leaped back. A tree stabbed him with a sharp branch. Whirling around, he struck out at the assailant. "Ouch!" he yelled. "Heavens to Betsy!" he added, though not in precisely those words.

The roar lifted again, a bass bellow that rumbled down to a savage snarling. Alex clutched at Farmer Toowey's smock. "What's that?" he gasped. "What's happening to Holmes?"

"Might be Hound's got un," offered Toowey, stolidly. "We hears un eatin', laike."

Alex dismissed the bloodthirsty notion with a frantic gesture. "Don't be ridiculous," he said.

"Ridiculous I may be," said Toowey stubbornly, "but they girt Hound be hungry, for zartin sure."

Alex's fear-tautened ears caught a new sound—footsteps from over the hill. "It's—coming this way," he hissed.

Toowey muttered something that sounded like "dessert."

Setting his teeth, Alex plunged forward. He topped the hill and sprang, striking a small solid body and crashing to earth. "I say, Watson," came Holmes's dry, testy voice, "this really won't do at all. I have told you a hundred times that such impetuosity ruins more good police officers than any other fault in the catalogue."

"Holmes!" Alex picked himself up, breathing hard. "My God, Holmes, it's you! But that other noise—the bellowing—"

"That," said Holmes, "was Sir Henry Baskerville when I took the gag out of his mouth. Now come along, gentlemen, and see what I have found."

Alex and Toowey followed him through the nixl patch and down the rocky slope beyond it. Holmes drew aside a bush and revealed a yawning blackness. "I thought the Hound would shelter in a burrow," he said, "and assumed he would camouflage its entrance. So I merely checked the bushes. Do come in, Watson, and relax."

Alex crawled after Holmes. The tunnel widened into an artificial cave, about two meters high and three square, lined with a spray-plastic—not too bad a place. By the vague light of Holmes's bull's-eye, Alex saw a small cot, a cookstove, a radio transceiver, and a few luxuries. The latter, apparently, included a middle-aged Hoka in the tattered remnants of a once-fine tweed suit. He had been fat, from the way his skin hung about him, but was woefully thin and dirty now. It hadn't hurt his voice, though—he was still swearing in a loud bass unusual for the species, as he stripped the last of his bonds from him.

"Damned impertinence," he said. "Man isn't even safe on his own grounds anymore. And the rascal had the infernal nerve to take over the family legend—my ancestral curse, dammit!"

"Calm down, Sir Henry," said Holmes. "You're safe now."

"I'm going to write to my M.P.," mumbled the real Baskerville. "I'll tell him a thing or two, I will. There'll be questions asked in the House of Commons, egad!"

Alex sat down on the cot and peered through the gloom. "What happened to you, Sir Henry?" he asked.

"Damned monster accosted me right on my own moor," said the Hoka, indignantly. "Drew a gun on me, he did. Forced me into this noisome hole. Had the unmitigated gall to take a mask of my face. Since then he's kept me on bread and water. Not even fresh bread, by Godfrey! It—it isn't British! I've been tied up in this hole for weeks. The only exercise I got was harvesting his blinking weed for him. When he went away, he'd tie me up and gag me—" Sir Henry drew an outraged breath. "So help me, he gagged me *with my own school tie!*"

"Kept as slave and possibly hostage," commented Holmes. "Hm. Yes, we're dealing with a desperate fellow. But Watson, see here what I have to show you." He reached into a box and pulled out a limp black object with an air of triumph. "What do you think of this, Watson?"

Alex stretched it out: a plastimask of a fanged monstrous head, grinning like a toothpaste ad. When he held it in shadow, he saw the luminous spots on it. The Hound's head!

"Holmes!" he cried. "The Hound is the—the—"

"Ppussjan," supplied Holmes.

"How do you do?" said a new voice, politely.

Whirling around, Holmes, Alex, Toowey, and Sir Henry managed, in the narrow space, to tie themselves in knots. When they had gotten untangled, they looked down the barrel of a raythrower. Behind it was a figure muffled shapelessly in a great, trailing black coat, but with the head of Sir Henry above it.

"Number Ten!" gulped Alex.

"Exactly," said the ppussjan. His voice had a Hoka squeakiness, but the tone was cold. "Fortunately, I got back from scouting around before you could lay an ambush for me. It was pathetic, watching that search party. The last I saw of them, they were headed for Northumberland."

"They'll find you," said Alex, with a dry voice. "You don't dare hurt us."

"Don't I?" asked the ppussjan, brightly.

"I zuppoze yeou du, at that," said Toowey.

Alex realized sickly that if the ppussjan's hideout had been good up to now, it would probably be good until his gang arrived to rescue him. In any case, he, Alexander Braithwaite Jones, wouldn't be around to see.

But that was impossible. Such things didn't happen to him. He was League plenipotentiary to Toka, not a character in some improbable melodrama, waiting to be shot. He—

A sudden wild thought tossed out of his spinning brain: "Look

here, Ten, if you ray us you'll sear all your equipment here too."
He had to try again; no audible sounds had come out the first
time.

"Why, thanks," said the ppussjan. "I'll set the gun to narrow-
beam." Its muzzle never wavered as he adjusted the focusing
stud. "Now," he asked, "have you any prayers to say?"

"I—" Toowey licked his lips. "Wull yeou alloo me to zay one
poem all t' way through? It have given me gree-at coomfort, it
have."

"Go ahead, then."

"By the shores of Gitchee Gumee—"

Alex knelt too—and one long human leg reached out and his
foot crashed down on Holmes' lantern. His own body followed,
hugging the floor as total darkness whelmed the cave. The raybeam sizzled over him—but, being narrow, missed and splatted
the farther wall.

"Yoiks!" shouted Sir Henry, throwing himself at the invisible
ppussjan. He tripped over Alex and went rolling to the floor. Alex
got out from underneath, clutched at something, and slugged
hard. The other slugged back.

"Take that!" roared Alex. "And that!"

"Oh, no!" said Sherlock Holmes in the darkness. "Not again,
Watson!"

They whirled, colliding with each other, and groped toward the
sounds of fighting. Alex clutched at an arm. "Friend or
ppussjan?" he bellowed.

A raybeam scorched by him for answer. He fell to the floor,
grabbing for the ppussjan's skinny legs. Holmes climbed over
him to attack the enemy. The ppussjan fired once more, wildly,
then Holmes got his gun hand and clung. Farmer Toowey yelled a
Hoka battle cry, whirled his staff over his head, and clubbed Sir
Henry.

Holmes wrenched the ppussjan's raythrower loose. It clattered
to the floor. The ppussjan twisted in Alex's grasp, pulling his leg
free. Alex got hold of his coat. The ppussjan slipped out of it and
went skidding across the floor, fumbling for the gun. Alex fought
the heavy coat for some seconds before realizing that it was
empty.

Holmes was there at the same time as Number Ten, snatching

the raythrower from the ppussjan's grasp. Ten clawed out, caught a smooth solid object falling from Holmes' pocket, and snarled in triumph. Backing away, he collided with Alex. "Oops, sorry," said Alex, and went on groping around the floor.

The ppussjan found the light switch and snapped it. The radiance caught a tangle of three Hokas and one human. He pointed his weapon. "All right!" he screeched. "I've got you now!"

"Give that back!" said Holmes indignantly, drawing his revolver.

The ppussjan looked down at his own hand. It was clutching Sherlock Holmes' pipe.

Whitcomb Geoffrey staggered into the George and Dragon and grabbed the wall for support. He was gaunt and unshaven. His clothes were in rags. His hair was full of burrs. His shoes were full of mud. Every now and then he twitched, and his lips moved. A night and half a day trying to superintend a Hoka search party was too much for any man, even an IBI man.

Alexander Jones, Sherlock Holmes, Farmer Toowey, and Sir Henry Baskerville looked sympathetically up from the high tea which the landlord was serving them. The ppussjan looked up too, but with less amiability. His vulpine face sported a large black eye, and his four-legged body was lashed to a chair with Sir Henry's old school tie. His wrists were bound with Sir Henry's regimental colors.

"I say, Gregson, you've had rather a thin time of it, haven't you?" asked Holmes. "Do come have a spot of tea."

"Whee-ar's the s'arch party, lad?" asked Farmer Toowey.

"When I left them," said Geoffrey, dully, "they were resisting arrest at Potteringham Castle. The earl objected to their dragging his duckpond."

"Wull, wull, lad, the-all ull be back soon, laike," said Toowey, gently.

Geoffrey's bloodshot eyes fell on Number Ten. He was too tired to say more than: "So you got him after all."

"Oh, yes," said Alex. "Want to take him back to Head-quarters?"

With the first real spirit he had shown since he had come in,

Geoffrey sighed. "Take him back?" he breathed. "I can actually *leave* this planet?"

He collapsed into a chair. Sherlock Holmes refilled his pipe and leaned his short furry form back into his own seat.

"This has been an interesting little case," he said. "In some ways it reminds me of the Adventure of the Two Fried Eggs, and I think, my dear Watson, that it may be of some small value to your little chronicles. Have you your notebook ready? . . . Good. For your benefit, Gregson, I shall explain my deductions, for you are in many ways a promising man who could profit by instruction."

Geoffrey's lips started moving again.

"I have already explained the discrepancies of Sir Henry's appearance in the tavern," went on Holmes implacably. "I also thought that the recent renewed activity of the Hound, which time-wise fitted in so well with the ppussjan's arrival, might well be traceable to our criminal. Indeed, he probably picked this hideout because it did have such a legend. If the natives were frightened of the Hound, you see, they would be less likely to venture abroad and interfere with Number Ten's activities; and anything they did notice would be attributed to the Hound and dismissed by those outsiders who did not take the superstition seriously. Sir Henry's disappearance was, of course, part of this program of terrorization; but also, the ppussjan needed a Hoka face. He would have to appear in the local villages from time to time, you see, to purchase food and to find out whether or not he was being hunted by your bureau, Gregson. Watson has been good enough to explain to me the process by which your civilization can cast a mask in spray-plastic. The ppussjan's overcoat is an ingenious, adaptable garment; by a quick adjustment, it can be made to seem either like the body of a monster, or, if he walks on his hind legs, the covering of a somewhat stout Hoka. Thus, the ppussjan could be himself, or Sir Henry Baskerville, or the Hound of the Baskervilles, just as it suited him."

"Clever fella," murmured Sir Henry. "But dashed impudent, don't y'know. That sort of thing just isn't done. It isn't playing the game."

"The ppussjan must have picked up a rumor about our

descent," continued Holmes. "An aircraft makes quite a local sensation. He had to investigate and see if the flyers were after him and, if so, how hot they might be on his trail. He broke into the tavern in the Sir Henry disguise, learned enough for his purposes, and went out the window. Then he appeared again in the Hound form. This was an attempt to divert our attention from himself and send us scampering off after a non-existent Hound— as, indeed, Lestrade's search party was primarily doing when last heard from. When we pursued him that night, he tried to do away with the good Watson, but fortunately I drove him off in time. Thereafter he skulked about, spying on the search party, until finally he returned to his lair. But I was already there, waiting to trap him."

That, thought Alex, was glossing the facts a trifle. However—

Holmes elevated his black nose in the air and blew a huge cloud of nonchalant smoke. "And so," he said smugly, "ends the Adventure of the Misplaced Hound."

Alex looked at him. Dammit—the worst of the business was that Holmes was right. He'd been right all along. In his own Hoka fashion, he had done a truly magnificent job of detection. Honesty swept Alex off his feet and he spoke without thinking.

"Holmes—by the Lord Harry, Holmes," he said, "this—this is sheer genius."

No sooner were the words out of his lips than he realized what he had done. But it was too late now—too late to avoid the answer that Holmes must inevitably give. Alex clutched his hands together and braced his tired body, resolved to see the thing through like a man. Sherlock Holmes smiled, took his pipe from between his teeth, and opened his mouth. Through a great, thundering mist, Alexander Jones heard THE WORDS.

"Not at all. *Elementary, my dear Watson!*"

The Thing Waiting Outside
by
Barbara Williamson

In the introduction I said that Holmes was "undefined"; that, in referring to him, we did not have to identify him. The same is true of many of the Sherlockian characters and stories. The mere mention is enough. You'll see what I mean in this story.

The Thing Waiting Outside

by Barbara Williamson

A cold wind came down from the hills that night and in their room under the peaked roof the children turned their faces toward the sound.

"It's only the wind," the father said.

"Just the wind," said the mother.

There were two beds in the room, a dresser painted white, and under the windows, a table with small bright chairs.

The walls of the room were light yellow, like the first spring sunlight. In their glow the dolls and fire engines, the pasteboard castle with its miniature knights, even the sad-faced Harlequin puppet, shimmered with warmth. The plush animals became as soft as down, and the mane on the rocking horse was a crest of foam.

The children, a boy of eight and a girl of six, were already in their beds. The light glistened on their faces, their pale silken hair. They were beautiful children. Everyone said so, even strangers, and their parents always smiled and placed proud hands on their shining heads.

111

Now in the yellow light with the wind brushing the windows, the children listened to their father.

He sat on the side of the boy's bed and spoke quietly. The mother sat with the girl, her fingers now and then touching the sleeve of her daughter's nightgown. The faces of both parents were troubled.

The father said, "You do understand about the books? Why I had to take them away?"

The boy did not turn his eyes from his father's face, but he could feel the emptiness of the shelves across the room.

He said, "Will you ever put them back?"

His father laid a hand on the boy's shoulder. "Yes, of course," he said. "In time. I *want* you to read, to enjoy your books." He looked now at the girl and smiled. "I'm very proud of both of you. You read so well and learn so quickly."

The mother smiled too and gave the girl's hand a gentle squeeze.

The father said, "I think maybe this whole thing is my fault. I gave you too many books, encouraged you to read to the point of neglecting other things that are important. So for a while the only books I want you to read are your school books. You'll do other things—paint pictures, play games. I'll teach you chess, I think. You'll both like that."

"And we'll do things together," the mother said. "Take bike rides and walks up into the hills. And when it's spring, we'll have a croquet set on the lawn. And we'll go on picnics."

The children looked at their parents with wide dark eyes. And after a moment the boy said, "That will be nice."

"Yes," said the girl. "Nice."

The mother and father glanced at each other and then the father leaned over and cupped a hand under the boy's chin.

"You know now, don't you, that you did not really see and speak to the people in the books. They were only here in your imagination. You did not *see* the Lilliputians or *talk* to the Red Queen. You did not *see* the cave dwellers or *watch* the tiger eat one of them. They were not *here* in this room. You know that now, don't you?"

The boy looked steadily into his father's eyes.

"Yes," he said, "I know."

The girl nodded her head when the father turned to her. "We know," she said.

"Imagination is a wonderful thing," the father said to both of them. "But it has to be watched, or like a fire it can get out of control. You'll remember that, won't you?"

"Yes," the boy said, and again the girl nodded, her long hair gleaming in the light.

The father smiled and got to his feet. The mother rose too and smoothed the blankets on both beds. Then they each kissed the children good night with little murmurs of love and reassurance.

"Tomorrow," the father said, "we'll make some plans."

"Yes," the children said, and closed their eyes.

After the mother and father were gone and the room was dark, the children lay still for what seemed to them a long time. The wind rattled the windows and beyond the hills the moon began to rise.

At last the girl turned to her brother. "Is it time?" she asked.

The boy didn't answer. Instead, he threw back his blanket and crossed the room to the windows. Below, the fields were silvered by the moon, but the hills were a black hulk against the sky.

"Anything could come down from there," he said. "Anything."

The girl came to stand beside him, and together they looked out into the night and thought about the thing waiting outside.

Then the girl said, "Will you take them the book now?"

"Yes," the boy said.

He turned from the windows and went to the dresser. Kneeling on the floor, he pulled open a bottom drawer and felt carefully beneath the socks and undershirts. The girl came over and knelt beside him. Their white faces flowered in the darkness of the room.

They both smiled when the boy took the book out of its hiding place. They rose from the floor and the boy clasped the book in his arms. He said, "Don't start until I get back."

"Oh, I won't," the girl said. "I wouldn't."

Still holding the book close, the boy went to the door of the room, opened it softly, and stepped out into the hall.

It was a large house and very old, and deep inside it the wind was only a whisper of sound. The boy listened for a moment, then started down the stairs. The carpet was thick under his bare feet and the railing felt as cold as stone beneath his hand.

Downstairs, a faint spicy smell from the day's baking still lingered in the air. He walked to the back of the house, past dark rooms where mirrors winked from the light in the hall, and night lay thick across the floors.

The mother and father were in the room next to the kitchen. There was a fire in a small grate and empty coffee cups on a table. On the walls were photographs of the children. They looked out into the room with secret smiles.

The mother was seated on the sofa near a shaded lamp. Her lap was full of pink yarn and her knitting needles flashed in the firelight.

The father leaned back in a big leather chair, his eyes on the ceiling, his fingers curled around the bowl of his favorite pipe.

The fire sighed and sparks rose up the chimney. The boy's eyes flicked to the corners of the room where the shadows had retreated from the firelight.

From the doorway he said, "I couldn't sleep until I brought you this." And he went into the room toward his parents, holding the book out to them.

"I hid it, but that wasn't right, was it?"

They came to him then. His mother took him into her arms and kissed him, and his father said that he was a fine honest boy.

The mother held him in her lap for a few minutes and warmed his feet with her hands, and her eyes glistened in the light of the fire. They spoke softly to him for a time and he listened and answered "yes" and "no" at the right times, and then he yawned and said that he was sleepy and could he please go back to bed?

They took him to the stairs and kissed him and he went up alone without looking back.

In the room at the top of the house the girl was waiting for him. He nodded his head and then they climbed into their beds and joined hands across the narrow space between. Moonlight lay on the floor in cold slabs and the wind now washed against the windows with a shushing sound.

"Now," the boy said, gripping the girl's hand tightly. "And, remember, it's harder when the book is somewhere else."

They did not move for a long time. Their eyes stared at the

ceiling without blinking. Sweat began to glisten on their faces and their breathing grew short and labored. The room flowed around them. Shadow and light merged and parted like streams in the sea.

When the sounds from below began to reach them, they still did not move. Their joined hands, slick with sweat, held firm. Their muscles strained and corded. Their eyes burned and swam with the shifting light and darkness.

At last the sounds from the bottom of the house stopped. Silence fell around them, cooling their faces, soothing their feverish eyes.

The boy listened and then said, "It's done. You know what to do now, don't you?"

"Yes," the girl said. She slid her hand out of his, brushed her hair back from her face, and closed her eyes. She smiled and thought of a garden filled with flowers. There was a table in the center of the garden and on the table were china plates. Each plate held a rainbow of iced cakes. There were pink ones and yellow ones and some thick with chocolate. Her tongue flicked over her lips as she thought of how sweet they would taste.

The boy thought of ships—tall ships with white sails. He brought a warm wind out of the south and sent the ships tossing on a sea that was both blue and green. Waves foamed over the decks and the sailors slipped and laughed, while above their heads gulls wheeled in the sky, their wings flashing in the sun.

At the time agreed upon, just as the windows began to lighten, the children rose from their beds and went downstairs.

The house was very cold. The shadows were turning to gray and in the room next to the kitchen the fire was dead, it coals turned to feathery ash.

The mother lay in a corner of the room, near the outside wall. The father was a few feet away. He still held the fireplace poker in his hand.

The boy's eyes moved over the room quickly. "I'll find the book," he said. "You go open the door to the terrace."

"Why that one?"

The boy gave her a hard look. "Because that's the one with the catch that slips. It had to get in someway, didn't it?"

The girl turned, then she looked back and said. "Then can we have breakfast?"

The boy had begun moving around the room, looking under tables, poking under the sofa. "There's no time," he said.

"But I'm hungry!"

"I don't care," the boy said. "It's the cleaning lady's day and we have to be asleep when she gets here. We'll eat later."

"Maybe pancakes? With syrup?"

The boy didn't look at her. "Maybe," he said. "Now go open the door like I told you."

The girl stuck her tongue out at him. "I wish I was the oldest," she said.

"Well, you're not," the boy said, turning and glaring at her. "Now go and do like I said."

The girl tossed her hair back in a gesture of defiance, but she left the room, not hurrying, and in the hall she began to hum a little tune to annoy him.

The boy did not notice. He was becoming anxious now. Where could the book be? It wasn't on the table. And it couldn't be out of the room. He saw it then, on the floor, under the shattered lamp.

He hurried to it and his hands were shaking when he picked it up, brushing the bits of glass away. He examined it carefully, turning the pages, running his fingers over the smooth binding, the embossed letters of that title. Then he smiled. It was all right. There weren't even any spatters of blood.

He closed the covers and hugged the book to his chest. A great joy welled inside him. It was one of his favorite stories. Very soon, he promised himself, he would read *The Hound of the Baskervilles* again.

A Father's Tale

by

Sterling E. Lanier

Any good Baker Street Irregular knows that Sherlock Holmes claimed that his grandmother was the sister of a French painter named Vernet—not Verner. He also knows that Holmes refers, at one point in the tales, to the case of "the giant rat of Sumatra," for which he felt the world was not prepared.

Now read the following story.

A Father's Tale

by Sterling E. Lanier

"You certainly seem to like the tropics, sir," said a younger member. It was one of the dull summer evenings in the club. The outside fetor in New York City was unbelievable. Heat, accumulated off the sidewalks, hung in the air. Manhattan was hardly a Summer Holiday, despite the claims of its mayor. It was simply New York. The City, a place one had to work in or probably die in.

"I suppose you have a point there," Ffellowes answered. The library was air-conditioned, but all of us who recently had come in from the streets were sweating, with one exception. Our British member was utterly cool, though he had come in after most of us.

"Heat," said Ffellowes, as he took a sip of his Scotch, "is, after all, relative, especially in my case. Rela*tives*, I should say.

"But many of your tales, if you'll pardon me, in fact most of them, have been, well—set in the tropics," the young member kept on.

Ffellowes stared coldly at him. "I was not aware, young man, that I had told any *tales*."

119

At this point, Mason Williams, the resident irritant, who could not let the brigadier alone, exploded. "Hadn't told any tales! Haw-haw, haw-haw!"

To my amazement, and, I may add, to the credit of the new election committee, this piece of rudeness was quashed at once, and by the same younger fellow who had started the whole thing.

He turned on Williams, stared him in the eye, and said, "I don't believe you and I were speaking, sir. I was waiting for Brigadier Ffellowes to comment." Williams shut up like a clam. It was beautiful.

Ffellowes smiled quietly. His feelings about Williams were well-known, if equally unexpressed. A man who'd been in all of Her Majesty's Forces, seemingly including all the intelligence outfits, is hardly to be thrown off gear by a type like Williams. But the defense pleased him.

"Yes," he confessed, "I *do* like the tropics. Always go there when I can. But—and I stress this—it was a certain hereditary bias. I acquired it, one might say, in the genes. You see, my father, and for that matter his, had it as well."

Again the young member stuck his neck out. Those of us, the old crowd, who were praying that we would get a story, simply kept on praying. Ffellowes was not mean, or petty, but he hated questions. But the boy plugged on.

"My God, sir," he bored in, "you mean your father had some of the same kind of weird experiences you've had?"

I don't know to this day why the brigadier, ordinarily the touchiest of men, was so offbeat this evening. But he didn't either dummy up or leave. Maybe, just maybe, he was getting so fed up with Williams he didn't want to let the young fellow down. Anyway, those of us who knew him leaned forward. Of course, Mason Williams did too. He hated Ffellowes but never enough to miss a story, which is, I suppose, an indication that he isn't completely mindless.

"If you care to hear this particular account, gentlemen," began Ffellowes, "you will have to take it second-hand, as it were. I wasn't there myself, and all I know comes from my father. However—he *was* there, and I may say that I will strongly resent [here he did not quite look at Williams] any imputation that he

spoke to me anything but the absolute truth." There was silence.
Total. Williams had lost too many encounters.

Said Ffellowes, "The whole thing started off the west coast of
Sumatra. My father had been doing a spell of service with old
Brooke of Sarawak, the second of the so-called White Rajahs,
C.V. that would be. Anyway, Dad was on vacation, leave, or
what have you. The Brookes, to whom he'd been 'seconded,' as
the saying goes, from the Indian Army, were most generous to
those who served them. And my father wanted to see a few new
areas and get about a bit. This was in the fall of 1881, mind you,
when things were different.

"So there he was, coming down the Sumatran coast, in one of
Brooke's own private trading *prahus*, captained by old *Dato
Burung*, picked crew and all that, when the storm hit.

"It was a bad one, that storm, but he had a largish craft, as
those things went, a big *Prau Mayang*, a sort of merchant ship of
those waters. No engine, of course, but a sturdy craft, sixty feet
long, well capable of taking all the local weathers, save perhaps
for a real typhoon, which this was not. They all battened down to
ride out the storm. They had no trouble.

"Sure enough, the next morning was calm and clear. And off
the lee side, within sight of the green west Sumatran coast, was a
wreck. It wasn't much, but the remnants of another *prau*, a *prau
bedang*, the local light craft used for fishing, smuggling, and
what have you. Ordinarily, this much smaller vessel would have
carried two modified lateen sails, or local variants, but now both
masts were gone, snapped off at the deck, obviously by the
previous night's storm. The fragile hulk was wallowing in the
deep milky swells, which were the only trace of the earlier wind.

"My father's ship bore down on her. He had given no orders,
but a ship in trouble in these waters was fair game to anyone.
Occasionally, hapless folk were even rescued. Dad stood on the
quarter-deck in his whites, and that was quite enough to make
sure there would be no throat cutting. Forbidding anything else
would have been silly. Next to him stood his personal servant, old
Umpa. This latter was a renegade Moro from the Sulus, but a
wonderful man. He was at least sixty, but as lean and wiry as a
boy. Whatever my father did was all right with him, and anything
anyone else did was wrong, just so long as my father opposed it,
mind you.

"To his surprise, as the bigger craft wore, to come up under the wreck's lee, a hand was raised. Beaten down though the little craft had been, there was someone still left alive. Dad's vessel launched a rowing boat, and in no time the sole survivor of the wreck was helped up to the poop and placed before him. To his further amazement, it was not a Sundanese fisherman who confronted him, but a Caucasian.

"The man was dressed quite decently, in tropical whites, and even had the remnants of a celluloid collar. Aside from the obvious ravages of the sea, it was plain that some time must have passed since the other had known any amenities of civilization. His whites, now faded, were torn at the knees, badly stained with green slime and ripped at various places. His shoes were in an equally parlous condition, almost without soles. Yet, the man still had an air about him. He was tall, a youngish man, sallow and aquiline in feature, with a hawk nose. Despite his rags, he bore himself as a person of consequence. His beard was only a day or two grown.

" 'Captain Ffellowes, Second Rajput Rifles, very much at your service,' said my father, as this curious piece of human flotsam stared at him. 'Can I be of some service?'

"The answer was peculiar. 'Never yet, sir, have I failed in a commission. I should not like this occasion to be the first. With your permission, we will go below.' With that, this orphan of the gale fell flat on his face, so quickly that not even my father or the ship's captain could catch him as he slumped.

"They bent, both of them, quickly enough when the man fell. As my father reached down to take his head, the gray eyes opened.

" 'At all costs, watch for Matilda Briggs,' said the unknown, in low and quite even tones. The lids shut and the man passed into total and complete unconsciousness. It was obvious to my father that he had only been sustaining himself by an intense effort of will. What the last piece of nonsense meant was certainly obscure. Who on earth was Matilda Briggs, and why should she be sought? As they carried the man below to my father's cabin, he had decided the chap was simply delirious. On the other hand, he was obviously a man of education, and his precise speech betrayed the university graduate. One can be excused of snobbery at this point. There were not so many of this type about in the backwaters of the world in those days, you know, despite what Kipling may have written on the subject. Most educated Englishmen in Southeast Asia had jobs and rather strictured ones at that. The casual drifter or 'remittance man' was a later type than one found in the 1880's, and had to wait for Willie Maugham to portray him.

"Well, my father took his mystery man below; the crew looted the remnants of the little *prau* (and found nothing, I may say, including any evidence of anyone else; they told the skipper that the mad *Orang Blanda* must have taken her out alone); and the White Rajah's ship set sail and continued on her way down the Sumatran coast.

"Dad looked after the chap as best he could. Westerners, Europeans, if you like, though my father would have jibbed at the phrase since he thought that sort of thing began at Calais, did this sort of thing without much thinking then. There were so few of them, you see, surrounded by the great mysterious mass of Asia. Outside the British fief, as the Old Man said, one felt A.C.I., or Asia Closing In. No doubt the feeling of the average G.I. in Viet Nam a few years ago. I know what they meant, having spent enough time out in those regions.

"First, the chap was, as I have said, a lean, tough-looking creature. As he lay there on my father's bed in the stern cabin, even in utter exhaustion and repose, his sharp features were set in commanding lines. His clothes, or rather their remains, which the native servants stripped off at my father's orders, revealed nothing whatsoever of their owner's past. Yet, as the ragged coat was pulled off the tattered shirt, something fell to the cabin deck with a tinkle and a glitter. My father picked it up at once and found himself holding a man's heavy gold ring, set with an immense sapphire of the purest water. Was this the unknown's? Had he stolen it? No papers, and my father made it plain that he felt no compunction in looking for them, were on the castaway's person. Save for the ring, and his rags, he appeared to own nothing.

"For a day, as the *prau* ran slowly down the coast, my father nursed the stranger as tenderly as a woman could have done.

There was no fever, but the man's life had almost run out, nonetheless. It was simple exhaustion carried to the nth degree. Whatever the derelict had been doing, he had almost, as you chaps say, 'burned himself out' in the doing of it. Dad sponged and swabbed him, changed his personal linen, and directed the servants he had with him, as they all fought for the man's life. The ship's cook, an inspired Buginese, wrought mightily with the stores at his command, and nourishing soups were forced down the patient's lips, even though he lay in total unconsciousness.

"On the second day, my father was sitting by the man's bed, turning over in his hand the sapphire ring, when he was startled to hear a voice. Looking up, he saw that the patient was regarding both him and also what he held.

" 'I once refused an emerald of rather more value,' was the unknown's comment. 'I can assure you, for whatever my assurances are worth, that the object that you hold is indeed my personal property and not the loot of some native temple.' The man turned his head and looked out the nearest of the cabin ports within reach. Through it, one could discern the green shoreline in the near distance. He turned back to my father and smiled, though in a curiously icy way.

" 'The object you hold, sir, is a recompense for some small services, to the reigning family currently responsible for the archipelago which we appear to be skirting. I should be vastly obliged for its return since it has some small sentimental value.'

"Having no reason to do otherwise, Dad instantly surrendered the ring.

" 'My thanks,' was the languid comment. 'I assume that I also have you to thank for my treatment on board this somewhat piratical vessel?'

"The question was delivered in such an insolent tone that my father rose to his feet, ready to justify himself at length. He was waved back to his cushion by a commanding arm. After a pause, the unknown spoke.

" ' As an Englishman, and presumably a patriot, I have some small need of your assistance.' The face seemed to brood for a moment, before the man spoke again; then he stared in a glacial way directly at my father, running his gaze from top to toe before speaking again. His words appeared addressed to himself, a sort of soliloquy.

" 'Hmm, English, an officer, probably Sandhurst—Woolwich gives one rather less flexibility—on leave, or else extended service; speaks fluent Malay; seconded to some petty ruler as a guide into civilization, perhaps; at any rate, tolerably familiar with the local scene.'

"At this cold-blooded, and quite accurate appraisal (my family has indeed sent its males to Sandhurst for some time), my father continued to sit, waiting for the next comment from his bizarre guest.

" 'Sir,' said the other, sitting up as he spoke, and fixing my father with a steely glare, 'you are in a position to assist all of humanity. I flatter myself that never have I engaged in a problem of more importance, and, furthermore, one with no precedents whatsoever. Aside from one vaguely analogous occurrence in Recife, in '77, we are breaking fresh ground.'

"As he delivered this cryptic series of remarks, the man clapped, yes, actually clapped his hands, while his eyes, always piercing, lit up with glee, or some similar emotion. My father decided on the spot that the chap was deranged, if not under the influence of one of those subtle illnesses in which the East abounds. But he was brought back at once by the next question, delivered in the same piercing, almost strident, voice.

" 'What is our latitude, sir? How far south have we been taken since I was picked up?' Such was the immense authority conveyed by the strange voyager's personality, that my father had no thought of not answering. Since he himself took the sights with a sextant every dawn, he was able to give an accurate reply at once. The other lay back, obviously in thought.

"Rousing himself after a moment he seemed to relax, and his chiseled features broke into a pleasant smile as he stared at my father.

" 'I fear you think me mad,' he said simply, 'or else ill. But I assure you that I am neither. The Black Formosa Corruption has never touched me, nor yet Tapanuli Fever. I am immune, I fancy, to the miasmas of this coast, thought I take no credit for the status. In fact, I believe it to be hereditary. If the world would pay more attention to that forgotten Bohemian monk, Mendel, we should be in a position to learn much . . . but I digress.' Once more he stared keenly at my father, then seemed to come to some private decision.

" 'Would you, sir, be good enough to place yourself under my orders for the immediate future? I can promise you danger, great danger, little or no reward, but—and you have my word, which I may say has never yet been called into question—you would be serving your country and indeed all of humanity in aiding me. If what I have learned is any evidence, the entire world, and I am not given to idle speculation, is in the gravest of perils.' He paused again. 'Moreover, I can not at this point take you into my full confidence. It would mean, for the moment, that you would have to follow my instructions without question. Is this prospect of any attraction?'

"My father was somewhat taken aback by this sudden spate of words. Indeed, he was both irritated and impressed, at one and the same time, by the masterful way the stranger played upon him.

" 'I should be happy, sir, or rather happier, if I had your name,' he said stiffly. To his complete surprise, the other clapped his hands again and fell back on his couch, laughing softly.

" 'Oh, perfect!' The man was genuinely amused. 'Of course, my name would solve everything.' He ceased laughing and sat up in the bed with a quick motion, and once he did so, all humor left the scene.

" 'My name is—well, call me Verner. It is the name of a distant connection and bluntly speaking—not my own. But it will serve. As to any other *bona fides*, I fear you will have to forgive me. I simply cannot say more. Again, what do you say to my proposal?'

"My father was somewhat disconcerted by his guest's manners, but—and I stress this—one cannot realize what the circumstances were unless one had been there."

As Ffellowes spoke, and perhaps because he spoke, we *were* there, in the quiet waters off Sumatra, long, long ago. The silence of the library in the club became the silence of the East. Honking taxis, bawling doormen, straining buses, all the normal New York noises heard through our shuttered windows, were gone. Instead, with quickened breathing, we heard the tinkle of *gamilans* and the whine of tropic mosquitoes, the shift of the tide over the reefs, and smelled the pungent scent of frangipani blossoms. I stole one look at Mason Williams and then relaxed. He had his mouth open and was just as hung up as the rest of us. The brigadier continued.

" 'I am astounded, sir, at your presumption,' my father said. 'Here you are a—'

" '—veritable castaway and runagate, no doubt the sweepings of some Asian gutter,' finished the other in crisp tones, putting my father's unspoken words into life. 'Nevertheless, what I have said to you is so deadly in earnest that if you will not agree to aid me, I must ask that you put me afoot at once, on yonder inhospitable shore, from whence, as you must have discerned, I have recently fled.' He stared again at my father's face, his piercing eyes seeming to probe beyond the mere skin. 'Come, man, give me your decision. I cannot idle away the hours in your yacht's saloon, no matter how luxurious. Either aid me, on my terms, mind you, or let me go!'

" ' 'What do you need, then?' It was my father's tentative capitulation. I can only say in his defense, if he should need one, that as he told me the story, Verner's manner was such as somehow did not brook any opposition.

" 'Hah,' said Verner. 'You are with me. Trust the Bulldog.' My father professed to misunderstand the man, though the unedifying implications were plain.

" 'I wish all of your maps, at once, particularly of this coast,' was Verner's next remark. 'I have not been in these waters at all. I need the very best charts you possess.'

"My father bustled about, found all the maps he had, and as he had made something of a study of the area, he had all the best Dutch naval charts and whatnot. He brought them down into the big stern cabin. There, he found that in his absence, there had been a palace revolution of sorts. His captain, *Dato* Ali Burung, was on his knees before Mr. Verner, beating his head on the carpet, or rather, the straw matting.

"When the Asian arose, sensing my father's arrival, he had no shame on his flat features. 'We are going to help the *Tuan Vanah, Tuan*, are we not?' was what the chap said. Really, as my father put it, it wasn't enough that the strange traveler had seduced *him;* he had also somehow had the same effect on the toughest native skipper in the South China Sea! Whoever and whatever he was, Mr. Verner had, as you fellows put it, 'control.'

" 'I am tentatively prepared to assist you in your quest, Mr. Verner.' My Old Man had given his commitment, and beyond 'unbelievable, but utterly true to type,' he heard no further particulars from his uninvited guest, who relapsed into silence.

"The next morning, they stood in to the coast. Western Sumatra in those days was much as it is today, I expect. They were well north of the Mentawi isles at the time, and just a bit south of the Batus. In there were, and no doubt still are, a thousand little anchorages. My father, or rather, old *Dato Burung*, found one of them. It was a tiny river, flowing into the sea under nipa palms, which almost arched over the entrance. It was the sort of place a Westerner wouldn't expect to launch a log canoe, but from which they had been turning out big seagoing vessels since well before the Christian era.

"There was even a small village, a *kampong*, as they say in those parts. The people thought they were pirates, my father said, and turned out the town for the ship. But Mr. Verner wanted nothing from them. He had ascertained that my father had a number of Martini-Henry rifles aboard, perhaps from old Burung. Even in those days, this was hardly the latest thing, but in any of the backwaters of Asia, a breech-loading rifle, even the old Martini, was a thing of rare worth. At any rate, Verner had taken control of the arms locker and twelve of the skipper's prize thugs were armed and standing guard on the beach.

"I daresay you wonder what my father was doing, to let himself and his ship be commandeered in this casual way. All I can give you is the story he told me. Verner, whoever he was, had simply 'taken over.' Dad told me that he violently resented everything the man suggested, but could not raise any objection, at least beyond commonplaces. He simply was no longer in charge, and somehow he had come to accept it.

" 'Where are we going?' said Verner in answer to a question. 'Where I tell you, which is, as the crow is supposed to reckon matters, some twenty miles due north. There, hopefully, we will find a certain ship. This latter, we may or may not board. In any case, my orders are final. Is that quite understood?'

"The fellow's commands to the natives were delivered, I may say, in excellent Coast Malay. The timid folk of the local village came out and gave everyone garlands of flowers. No doubt, it was not the first time it had happened, but invaders who wanted nothing beyond food, and even paid for that, were something new. Yet, in retrospect, there may have been other reasons. . . .

"Verner, as if he had nothing to do with it at all, stood on the beach among the mangroves, waiting for my father to give all the orders. Finally, Dad asked him what he wanted next. He confessed to me in after years that the man was so much in charge, that if he had said 'jump in the river,' the crew would have done so despite the abundant knobs of salt-water crocodiles, imitating tree stumps on every shallow bank and bar.

"The guest of the sea was now wearing one of my father's linen suits although he refused a solar topee and went hatless. His ruined boots had been replaced by sandals, but the fact was, as Dad put it, Verner could have worn a loincloth, or some sort of sarong, and still have been as much in charge as if he had been the supreme Rajah of Bandung. One simply gave up arguing when around him. You tolerated his presence because the only alternative was killing him!

"'We must have food for two days and two nights,' said Verner to my father. 'We shall be going north along the coast for about that distance. Would you be good enough to order your remaining ship's people to remain in these parts for some four days. No, better five. Some mischance may delay us. After that, they may head north, until they either meet us—or do not.'

"Since the orders appeared already to have been given, and since the twelve toughest members of the crew of my father's *prau*, all armed to the teeth with not only their native cutlery but with rifles from my father's arms locker as well, were waiting, this latter would appear to have been only courtesy. But it was not. Verner himself made that plain.

"'Captain Ffellowes, I much regret the outward appearance of these matters,' he told my father. 'While I personally have no doubt of your trustworthiness, the simple folk you command feel rather more strongly concerning my mission. In fact, though you might attempt to divert them from their purpose, and, be it said, mine as well, you would do little more than present them with your carcass as a species of local signpost. Possibly, indeed, probably, impaled as well, on bamboo shoots. Should you desire this new impalement on your coat of arms (ghastly pun, really), you have only to urge my immediate arrest.'

"Frankly, as my father put it to me, the man was becoming an incubus, and he seemed to have no sense at all of what was due a fellow Englishman. Although my father was allowed his pistols, Colt's matched Bisleys at it happens, on his belt, two of the twelve hearties from the crew flanked him at all times. It was more than clear that he was along on sufferance. Twice, Verner came to a halt as they crawled through the vile coastal scrub behind the mangroves, but it was not my father whom he consulted, but rather old Burung, the skipper of the *prau*. The man himself seemed to feel somewhat abashed by this insolent favoritism of a native, and at one of the rest stops, he actually spoke to my father in some terms of apology. 'See here, Captain,' he said, 'it is a capital mistake not to accept the best local information one can get.' My father was by this time too affronted by Verner's behavior to pay him much heed. Yet—the man, by his very presence, somehow brooked no interference. Dad simply nodded. He felt, he told me later, it was as if he were in a dream, or suspended in space. The whole thing, from the arrival on board his vessel of Verner and all that had happened subsequently, seemed to be a walking nightmare. He wondered, how could all this be happening? The only rock in a failing world was his personal man, Umpa, who trudged sturdily along beside him. He, at least, seemed faithful to his master.

"Have I failed to mention the heat? It was bad enough at sea, off the coast, but here it was almost unbearable. The party was following a winding trail along the shore, though somewhat back from it, which wound through green coco palms, jackfruit plantations gone wild, rambutan and pure jungle. Sometimes they were under dank shade, with great tropical hardwoods towering overhead, shutting off the sun; the next moment they would break out into heavy yellowish rattan and lantana brush growth and the saber-edged grasses of the coast. This would be hacked through by the advance guard with their myriad steel weapons. The next instant they would be in slippery mud under the giant trees again. Leeches and ticks fell upon their necks at every instant; gnats and mosquitoes assaulted them continuously, but they kept moving through innumerable muddy bogs and across many small tidal creeks as well.

"As if this were not bad enough, Burung, as well as some of the other natives and Verner too, were constantly stooping over patches of mud, in order to see what appeared to be quite ordinary traces of game. Once, late in the afternoon, they called my father over and showed him, in high glee, some daub or other which seemed important to them.

"'Look here, Captain,' said Verner. 'This can hardly fail to interest an old *shikari*, such as yourself!'

"My father looked and saw some spoor or other of an animal, large enough to be sure, in the bank mud of one of the many small estuaries through which they had just stumbled. The trace had four clawed footprints and was otherwise without meaning. It was indeed wet, that is, recent, with the water oozing in around the rim of the track, but beyond being the trace of some no doubt harmless creature, probably distorted by expansion, it appeared to have no significance whatever.

"My father's attitude seemed to annoy Verner a great deal, and without any further argument the man signaled to the others that they must press on. As they did so, Dad heard Verner say, as if to himself, 'Microcephalus! A case of simian survival!' The meaning of these phrases escaped him.

"At length, even Verner, who seemed made of iron, had to call a halt. He spoke to *Dato* Burung in low tones, and a camp was set up. My father, now stumbling with fatigue and insect-bitten to the limit, was gently passed along the line of marchers, until placed in the circle formed around the tiny fire they had lit. At this point, he related, he would not have cared much if they had told him that he was the main course in the evening meal.

"He roused himself, though, when he saw Verner seated next to him on the same rotting log. The fellow was almost as cool-looking as he had been on the *prau* after his recovery and, to my father's amazement, was in the act of fitting a clean paper collar to his very tattered shirt. God knows where he got them.

"At my father's gaze, something must have penetrated this strange person's subconscious mind. He finished dealing with his collar and without any affectation laid his hand on my father's knee.

"'I fear that you are still in doubt, my dear chap,' he said in vibrant tones. 'We are now far enough from the hue and cry so that one may elaborate without any fear of indiscretion. Pray tell me how I can serve you. Is there any matter on your mind?' The tones were as soft and caressing as those of a woman, and the man's whole attitude so charged with sympathy that my father almost wept. Exhausted and bemused as he was by what had transpired around him in the last twenty-four hours, he nevertheless retained enough energy to ask why this extraordinary jaunt through a trackless wilderness was necessary.

" 'The matter is quite plain,' returned his singular congener. 'We are going to call upon a local ruler who is apparently dead, a native people who, though certainly native, are not people, and a ship due to be charged with more misery than any vessel that ever floated on this planet's seas. Finally we shall, I trust, destroy the scientific works of one Van Ouisthoven, who has been seemingly dead for fifteen years.'

"This flood of lunacy was too much for my father, who had been both physically and mentally taxed almost beyond endurance. He fell asleep, slumped over his own rotting log, even as he heard the final words of Verner's explanation. Yet the words stayed in his memory, so much so that even at his life's end, he could still recite them to me.

"It was not, however, to be a sleep-filled night. The noises of the great tropical rain forest were no doubt designed to make newcomers uncomfortable, but my father was an old stager at this sort of thing. Yet the cries of the civet cats, the hooting of the fish owls, the usual noises of insect and tree frog, none of these would have been sufficient to wake Dad. Suddenly, as he recollected, about 1 A.M., Verner and old Burung shook him awake. 'Listen,' hissed Verner, who actually grasped him by the collar.

"At first, my father heard nothing. There were the normal tropic sounds, the night wind in the great trees, the innumerable insects, locusts and such, the faraway cry of a sleepy gibbon, and that was all. But Verner's grip remained tight on his collar, and so—he listened. He could smell the reek of old Burung on the other side, full of garlic and menace, but the silence and the attention of the two finally got to him as well.

"Then he heard it. Over all the normal night noises, he heard the chatter of a squirrel. No one can mistake that nasty, scolding sound, and it came first from one side of the camp and then the other. The sound is the same in the Temperate Zone as it is in the tropics. But—and mind you, my father was an old tropic hand and a noted *shikari*—squirrels are not animals of the night. No scientist to this day has found anything but the flying squirrels active at night. And they are silent, or almost so. Also, this was deeper in pitch.

"Mixed with the chattering was a gruff, snarling bark, though that seemed to come only at intervals. Anything else he might have thought was shaken out of him by Verner. 'That is the enemy, Captain. They have already taken one sentry. Do you now feel my precautions to be unnecessary?'

"If this were not enough, the next thing was a sort of strangled choking noise from the other side of camp. Verner darted off like a flash, and came back almost as quickly. 'Another gone,' he said. 'We must move on in the morning, or they will pick us off like so many flies on a side of beef.' My father roused himself long enough to see that two more of the crew were detailed to stand sentry go, and then he relapsed once more into exhausted slumber. But, as he lay down, he was very conscious that something out in the great black forest was a hideous danger, clear and present. He fell asleep with dread on his soul.

"My father remembered nothing until he was roughly shaken in the first light of morning. He felt, and was, filthy, as well as being still tired, confused, and angry at the way Verner had somehow pirated the loyalty of his men. Then he remembered the incidents of the night. He looked over and saw the very man himself, bent over a log which he was using as a table, in deep converse with my father's, or Rajah Brooke's, own captain, Burung. Ignoring the native crewman who was trying to give him sustenance in the form of cold rice, my father lurched over to the duo, who were his captors as he then felt.

"Verner looked up coldly at first, then seeing who had caused the interruption, smiled. It was the same glacial smile, to be sure, a mere rictus, but the strange man actually rose from his seat, and, as if by osmosis, so did *Dato* Burung.

" 'Just the man we wanted,' said Verner. 'My dear chap, do come and look at this map. It purports to be the mouth of the river Lubuk Rajah. I fear you will be disappointed to learn that it was once considered by some to be the Biblical Ophir. The whole idea is, of course, beyond any reasoned belief. I, myself, when in the *Mekran*, found that . . . Still, a most interesting and primitive

area, geologically speaking. There is a young Dutch physician in
these islands, Dubois, I believe, who is laying the ground for
some splendid work on human origins. He is unknown to you?
Strange how the body controls the mind, in terms of limitation,
that is.'

"My father, who was, on his own admission to me given many
years later on, only half awake, ignored this rambling and stared
at the map which had been spread out on the rude table before
him. There was indeed a river mouth and a small harbor. As an
officer of the British Army, he was familiar with planes and
gradients of the landscape, but there were other things on this
map. There were lines, in various colors, extending around a
central area. This central part appeared to be a settlement of some
sort. In short, it looked like any typical village on any Southeast
Asian coast, as observed and recorded by a European cartog-
rapher. Except for the odd lines, that is.

"He next heard his mentor, for so Verner had come to seem, in
the same tone, but in excellent Malay, state the following: 'Those
are their lines. They have an inner and an outer defensive circuit.
We shall have to somehow go between them. Do you have any
suggestions?'

" 'Look here, Verner,' said my father. 'What the Hell are you
planning to do?' Nothing but fatigue, he told me, would have
made him use language of this degree of coarseness.

" 'I had thought it would have been apparent to any child with
even a board school education,' said Verner, turning back to stare
at him with those strange eyes. 'I propose to destroy this entire
village, root and branch, females, young, the whole—as our
American cousins put it—shebang. All at once. And I fear that I
am compelled to ask for your direct assistance in the matter.'

"My father stared at him. He was, after all, a British officer,
charged with spreading our native virtues, *Pax Britannica* and all
that it implied in those days. He was told now that he was to
assist in totally obliterating some native village in a foreign
colonial possession! It was fantastic! Do please remember this
was long before genocide became a word in the English
language.

"*Dato* Burung said something to Verner in Malay, but so fast
and low that my father totally failed to grasp it.

" 'Quite so,' said Verner, 'but we have none and should we

seek a prisoner, we stand the risk of further alerting all the others. No, I think the *Tuan*, Captain, will have to sleep. Then, perhaps he and I may make the trail together, and once and for all see what Van Ouisthoven's work has come to. Strange that this whole matter should have grown from a simple assessment of mining machinery.' This last sentence was in English.

"My father was at this point utterly out of his wits and strength, and did indeed fall silent. His next memories as he listened were those of hearing Verner say, in his clipped tones, and musingly in English, 'There are strange rhythms in world events, yet none stranger than that of unpaid businessmen!'

"They were now on the march in the usual blazing dawn. They had wound, in the previous day's journey, much closer to the coast than he had thought. Only a few mangroves and giant Java plums kept them from the glare of light, which now burst over the hills to the east. The day brought with it the inevitable cloud of insect horrors to replace the night's mosquitoes. His face puffed up and his eyes swollen, my father faced Verner—the man had the same catlike neatness, despite their march—at a trail fork and demanded to know who was in charge.

"He looked at my father coolly enough. His first words cut off anything my father was impelled to say, quite short.

"Do you know, Captain, anything about general assurance companies? No? I rather thought not. Then you will have heard nothing of Messrs. Morrison, Morrison and Dodd. You will be pleased to know that a highly respectable firm, of Mincing Lane, no less, is the cause of your present discomfort.' On receiving nothing but the blankest of looks from Dad, he continued in the same light, jocular vein, obviously amused to make some mystery of his remarks, as though, Dad said, they were not mysterious enough already.

"'All I know, sir,' interrupted my father, 'is that you have mishandled me in the most outrageous fashion, suborned and subverted my officers and men, the employees of His Highness, the Rajah of Sarawak, and finally taken us away on some dubious journey for an unnamed purpose. I insist, sir, that you tell me what—' At this point my father fell silent, for as his voice rose, a wave of Verner's hand had caused a cloth to be thrown over his mouth by one of the burliest of his own crewmen, and despite his struggles, he was flung back upon a nearby tree trunk in the most compelling way. During all this, Verner continued to regard him in the most placid manner. When he had waited, as my father was compelled to admit, for his struggles to cease, he again waved his hand and the swaddling was removed. Meanwhile, Dad had seen old Umpa, his faithful servant, sworn to guard him with his life, quietly picking his teeth across the way!

" 'Captain,' said Verner, leaning forward and staring into my father's eyes, 'behave yourself!'

"It was the rebuke one gives a child, and, my father was free to state, entirely successful. He sat quietly; the gag was withdrawn, and he stood in silence while listening to his interlocutor.

" 'In a short time, Captain,' said the cold voice, 'we are going to carry out a murderous assault, by stealth, upon what appears to be a peaceful village. I cannot, even at this date, take you entirely into my confidence. However, I give you a few morsels of thought to mull over. Your men, starting with the captain, are the picked officers of the *Rajah Muda* of Sarawak. Think, man! Would they be likely to go over to a complete stranger such as myself, a castaway of no known antecedents, without the most compelling of reasons? Your own servant, that Moro savage, is with us. Do you dare exclude yourself?' "

There was a silence in the club library at this, and Ffellowes, who had lit a cigar, pulled on it gently before resuming. We were all so caught up that he could have said almost anything, but, even so, this was a point most of us had missed. Why indeed had the faithful crew of his Rajah's vessel turned coat so fast over to this wandering stranger?

" 'The answer is simple, as are indeed most answers,' resumed Verner to my father. 'They believe most strongly in what I am doing. Why do you not ask them?'

" '*Dato* Burung,' said Dad to the old Bajau skipper. 'Why do you obey the strange *Tuan*? Why do you guard me as a prisoner?' He looked into the old man's jet eyes for the first time, seeing him not as a part of the ship, but as a *man*.

" '*Tuan*,' the old man spoke most respectfully. 'We have heard in the islands for many moons, and some few suns, that there will come a time when we will all rule ourselves. But, *Tuan*, not through those who are Not-men. We go now, under this strange

Tuan's orders, to kill the Not-men. Only men should rule men. The *Orang Blanda*, even the great ones, are silly, but—you are *men*, of whatever strange, mad country. But—never Not-men, this is against the Law of the Prophet. These are *Efreets*, something not to be borne. They must be killed.' The old pirate sighed and caressed his long drooping mustaches. 'It is quite simple, really.'

"This last piece of lunacy, as Dad told me, should have convinced any sane man that he had no chance. Instead, maddeningly, it swung him completely over to the other side. You see, he *knew* old Burung, and trusted him; had now for over a year served with him and his crew. Then there was Umpa, his Moro servant. He had been saved from execution by Dad's personal intervention. And he was a *hadji*, had made the Mecca pilgrimage. He now stared at my father and nodded his head. If these men believed . . .

"My father's response rather startled Verner in fact, if anything could startle a man as much in control of himself as that cold fish.

" 'I'm your man,' Dad said simply, stretching out his hand. 'What do we do next?'

"Verner stared at him for a moment, then a lean hand clasped his. 'Thank you, Captain,' he said, and nothing more. 'Now—I badly need your help. The innermost grounds of this place are unknown to me. I escaped, more by luck than anything else, from what seems to be the outer perimeter. As you must have guessed, we are not too far from the place off which I was so fortunate as to have you encounter me. There is a ship in the harbor there which must at any hazard be prevented from leaving. She must in fact be destroyed. She is the *Matilda Briggs*, of American registry, out of Tampa in the state of Florida, I think. Her charter is under grave suspicion. A bark of some seven hundred tons. No ship in the world has ever carried such a cargo of future misery in the history of the human race. I repeat, she must be destroyed, *at all costs.*'

" 'Of what does this cargo consist?' my father asked.

" 'Females and infants in arms, in all probability,' was the cool answer. The man's face was grave, however, and it was evident that he was not in jest. My father could say no more. He was now committed, on the sole basis of common trust.

" 'Now,' continued Verner, in his usual icy manner, but

speaking Malay, 'Let us plan our next move.' The six remaining crewmen moved in closer. They obviously knew something portended. The other two had been made guards, to watch both trails, north and south.

" 'See here,' cried Verner, pointing to the map. 'This is the weak point, here at this juncture of slopes. It is very plain that here is where we must strike.' Then he said a curious thing, almost an aside, a remark baffling to my father. 'May God defend the right. If it *is* the right.' The comment was so unlike Verner's usual detached attitude that it stuck in Dad's memory.

" 'We shall be well off enough if the *Dolfjin* does not play us false,' continued the master of the expedition. He seemed to be talking to himself as much as anyone else. 'She's only two hundred and fifty tons, but she carries two twelve pounders. And yet my last message may not have got through.'

"With no more remarks, Verner proceeded to dispose of the whole party. Two men, the crewmen with the best edged weapons, were sent on ahead to act as an advance guard. The two sentries were called in and made a rear party. The remaining four, including old Burung, plus my father and Verner, made up the central column. Dad loosened his revolvers in their holsters. He had been in some rough work more than once; yet he felt somehow that this business would take rank with the best of them. Verner seemed to carry no weapon at all, beyond a straight stick of some heavy wood he had cut.

"They were now on an obvious trail. It was early morning and the light was fair, despite the oppressive heat, even under the dark overhang of the giant trees. Moreover, the party was now heading inland, a bit away from the sea, in a northeasterly direction. Suddenly, as if by some species of legerdemain, they were confronted with an open area. The jungle simply stopped, and before them lay, in the morning light, a European village. Allowing for the tropics, there were fenced, brush-bordered fields, low peak-roof houses, chimneys curling with smoke, and in the middle distance a larger structure, hard to see through the morning mist, but also peak-roofed, which might have served as the headquarters of the squire, or what have you, with no trouble. Anything less likely on the Sumatran coast than this rustic view would be hard to imagine. It was as if a segment of Bavaria, or perhaps Switzerland, had been removed bodily to the tropics. To make the scene complete, off to the left was a tiny harbor, empty save for a three-masted bark at anchor. She was surrounded by boats.

"'They have learned well,' said Verner in cryptic tones. 'Come on, you men. We should have had some opposition by now. They must be leaving and we can afford no wait. There lies the *Matilda Briggs*.'

"Even as he spoke, they were surrounded. My father was a man of few words at the best of times, and in this description (I may say," said Ffellowes at this point, "I was a child of my father's old age) he always became somewhat incoherent.

"There were many of them, all larger than man-size. Their pointed faces were drawn back from the great yellow chisel teeth, which snapped and chattered as they came on. They barked, too, like giant dogs. They had been hiding in the growth at the edge of the fields, and now they rushed in upon the small party, their clawed hands, yes, *hands*, clutching great crooked knives and other edged tools. The early morning air was still, no wind or even a shadow of a breath; and as my father put it, their stink, an acrid bitter reek, came on before them. It was inconceivable, but it was happening. Even the stumpy, naked tails that flailed the air behind them as they scuttered forward on their hind legs seemed to add no more unbelievability to the whole scene. It was monstrous, incredible, impossible—and it was happening!

"Then, the nineteenth century, as my father put it, justified itself. All of the crew, as any of Brooke's men had to, knew how to shoot. The sharp crack of the Martinis rang out in the muggy air.

"The men could see the harbor, even as they fought. There was a stream of small boats putting out to the ship at anchor, shuttling back and forth. In between pauses in the fighting, each side drew breath, so to speak. Had they not had the advantage of firearms, my father told me, I venture to say that the small party of ten would have been overwhelmed in an instant. Even so, the courage of the creatures, or ferocity, rather, was astonishing. They removed their dead and wounded after each onslaught, and as fast as this was done, returned to the attack. Automatically, Verner took one flank and my father the other. *Dato* Burung, the old scoundrel, stayed with the center. Between them, somehow or other, they managed to hold the tiny line. More than once the monsters came to close quarters, but each time they were beaten back with cold steel. Verner, using only his heavy stick, disabled at least two of them personally, the stick revolving in a curious pinwheel manner, of point and side, that my father declared to be miraculous in its effect. But the attacks never ceased. There was, even though my father could not grasp the whole of the matter, an element of desperation about the way the creatures behaved, which was almost suicidal. Despite their immense strength, and the fact that their bulk much exceeded that of a man, they were clumsy with their weapons, and not only unskillful, but seemingly untrained in their usage. Save for a few barks and snarls at the outset, they were utterly silent.

"The whole affair could not have exceeded a quarter hour, but when it was over, my father felt that it had been going on for most of the morning. As suddenly as they had come, the monstrous enemy vanished, drawing off into the rice fields and the scrub which lined then. He was astonished to note the same placid harbor below and the small craft plying busily to and from the ship at anchor, so quick had been the onslaught.

" 'Now,' said Verner, breaking in on his thoughts abruptly. 'We have two objectives, Captain. Yonder largish building, which abuts on the hill slope, is surely the central situation of these inimical creatures and must have been Van Ouisthoven's head-quarters. As you can see, there are open-faced mine workings behind it, and a conduit as well. This it indeed must be, the *point d'appui*, of your section. I, on the other hand, will have to deal with the vessel in the harbor and attempt to ensure its total destruction. Am I clear?'

"If he was not clear, he had at least given orders; and a British officer, once he has accepted a superior, obeys orders, or did in those benighted days, before all this crapulous nonsense about morality came into the picture." (I have got to say here that this is the only time I ever heard Ffellowes do any "bitching" and he told me afterward that he simply was repeating what his father had said.)

"The idea of a 'section,' which in the British Army implied the use of a company or more, was laughable. My father," said

Ffellowes, "found his first amusement at Verner's misuse of military language somehow consoling. The man was not God, after all, and did not know everything. This was a military operation and had best be run on military lines. Of the eight 'lower ranks' who had begun the fight, three were incapacitated, one being, in point of fact, dead; the other two, badly wounded and in no condition to move at all. Of the remainder, all had cuts and bruises, including both Umpa and old Burung, who had bound a great flap of cut skin, blood and all, back under his turban. But they could go on.

"In the upshot, my father took three men, Verner two.

" 'Should we not meet again, my thanks for your support,' said Verner in his chilly manner. 'It may comfort you to know that you have been involved in a matter far beyond the normal purlieu of the average Indian Army officer.' A cheery farewell, indeed! In addition, ammunition was running low. Each man had no more than twenty-five rounds for his rifle, and my father no more than that for his two revolvers. He mentioned this latter to Verner and was dismissed with a wave of his hand.

" 'Pray rendezvous at the harbor, my dear Ffellowes,' was all he got in response. With that, the man was off, his grubby white suit soon vanishing around the lower end of the forest. To do the man justice, my father never thought him a coward. And he still carried only his heavy stick.

"There was nothing left to do but head for the central building, the transplanted seat of the local squirearchy, or whatever. It seemed, through the morning haze, to sit in the center of the fields, against the hill behind; and as Verner had said, there was the scar on the green slope beyond it, the red earth visible in the morning sun, which clearly showed that something or other was being worked. Indeed, there was even a glitter of twin rails. My father was in the infantry, not the engineers, but he could see a railway if it were thrust at him. Some dim meaning of the horror that Verner had hinted at now came upon him. Something monstrous and inchoate, in terms of the world at large, lay before him. The busy little boats, shuttling out to the ship, the placid harbor, the frenzied attack by the great, tool-wielding beasts, all began to fall into a dreadful pattern. The sight of those shining rails, leading from the central building to the mine on the hill, crystallized it, into a fear which must at some time haunt the dreams of every thinking person.

"When I tell you that my father was a convinced antievolutionist, who thought Darwin a moral degenerate, the matter may become clearer still. Or may not.

"A narrow path led downslope through the fields, or rather paddies, for rice seemed to be the crop grown. Dense brush of the usual rattan and other thorny plants lined it, and the party tensed themselves for an attack. But none came. In the morning heat, so hot that a mist obscured the hills in the distance, only faint chittering cries and barks came from far away. Each moment the little party of blood-stained, ragged men tensed as they rounded a curve between banks of thick scrub. The men could no longer see the harbor and sometimes could see no more than a few feet ahead. Yet the hideous things appeared to have withdrawn, at least for the time.

"Nevertheless, the trace they followed seemed to lead in the direction of the large building, and once or twice they caught a glimpse of the raw face of the hill which lay behind it, over the tops of the fringing shrubbery.

"At length, when my father estimated that they must have covered a mile or more, Umpa, his old servant, who was in the lead, held up a hand in warning. They froze, and then Umpa signaled to my father to join them. As Dad stole up and as he crouched beside the old savage, an amazing sight met his eyes.

"Before them rose a gentle slope, of clipped grass, rising for a hundred yards to the veranda of the large building they had seen in the distance. The path, which was almost a tunnel under the overhanging scrub, debouched onto this lawn, for it was nothing less, quite abruptly; and as my father looked about, he could see other openings of a similar nature all around the fringe of the brush.

"But the building itself was even more startling. Minus the broad veranda, it was nothing more than a Dutch farmhouse, of the sort one can still see in Zeeland, though much larger than most. There was the peaked roof, the stuccoed walls, with wooden beams set between the stucco as facing, and even wooden shutters on the high-arched windows. Small balconies held massive urns full of bright flowers, and near the door were set large geometric flower beds, also bright with scarlet blooms. The only thing missing was a blonde maid in starched cap and wooden shoes, chevying hens away from the stoop. A more unlikely edifice under the circumstances would be hard to envisage.

"No smoke curled from the high brick chimneys though, and there was no sign of life. My father could make nothing of this, but he had his orders, and he waved to the men to follow him. Half crouching, half running, they raced across the lawn, all of them trying to see in every direction at once, waiting for an attack from any or all sides to overwhelm them. They were a little more than halfway when the big front door opened suddenly. Every weapon went up as one, and they all halted in their tracks. Yet no one fired.

"Before them stood an old bearded gentleman, his ruddy face and snowy hair making him look like a tropical version of Saint Nick, a conceit not much accentuated by his costume, which consisted of a rather soiled duck jacket and equally dirty sarong. Old as he obviously was, there was no mistaking his urgency. His sharp blue eyes had nothing senile about them, and he waved them forward to him with a gesture of both command and urgency, peering about as he did so in a way that made his meaning plain, as plain indeed as his silence. My father also waved the others on, and in an instant they were in the hall of the house and the heavy door was shut and bolted behind them.

"The old chap addressed my father in sharp tones. When he saw that his Dutch gutturals were unintelligible, he switched to good, though accented, English. 'Are there no more of you? This is madness! We need at least a regiment to deal with my Folk. Did not my messages make this plain? And now they are *leaving!* You are too late!' His despair would have been comic had my father not seen what he had just seen.

" 'Who the deuce are you, old chap,' he asked, 'and what on earth are you doing here?' He wanted to know much more, such as how the old man was still alive and a few other obvious things like that.

"His question seemed to stun the old gentleman. 'Who am I? I am Van Ouisthoven. This is my place, *Kampong De Kan*, my house, my laboratory. Who else should I be?'

"My father had an excellent memory. This was the name Verner had twice mentioned, that of a man 'dead for fifteen years.' Verner then, did not posses the key to all knowledge, despite his air of omniscience. But the old man was clutching my father's sleeve.

" 'Did you not come in answer to my messages? Don't you know what has been happening? You have been fighting—you have met the Folk, that is obvious. Why are you here, then, if not to stop them? And, God help us, why so *few?*'

"In a few sentences, my father told the history of the past few days. The old chap was sharp as a needle, and he listened intently.

" 'So—I see. Maybe a message did get through, maybe not, But, anyway, this other Englishman comes and he knows or guesses something. There was a disturbance some four days ago, and Grixchox (or something like that) would tell me nothing. So he gets away from them then; a brave man to come here alone to face the Folk! And you find him, and he, how to put it, takes over you and your ship.' His eyes grew thoughtful, then focused.

" 'Listen. Everything rests on that ship out there. It must *not* get out, you understand me! I have been a prisoner here for a long while. But they do not kill me. They still remember that I taught *them!* But they do not know all my secrets. When they begin to learn, they scare me; I get just a few things in. But them—they are clever, they made me *not* nervous, they make me think I am their God, and all the time—among themselves—they plot. When the day comes, they kill all my Javanese boys quickly, yes, and their women and the little ones too. Only me they save. I can still teach them something, and—they do not forget that without me, they never *be!* Now, come fast. We have things to get. They are all down at the boat; that is why you got here alive, my friend. Come.'

"With no more words, he led them to the interior of the house, which went way back into the hill and was far larger than it appeared from the outside. The place was beautifully kept, by the way, old pictures on the walls, the floor spotless, rattan carpets here and there, and so on.

"Finally, Van Ouisthoven stopped at what was to outward appearances a blank section of wall between two large doors.

Murmuring to himself in soft tones, the old man ran his fingers over the wall, an inlaid one of varicolored native woods. Then he gave a gasp of satisfaction and pressed hard. Silently, a great panel slid aside, and there before them lay a snug closet, perhaps ten feet deep and as much high and wide. In it were various shapes, covered with heavy canvas. The old Hollander flung this aside, and from my father and the others came gasps in their turn.

"Oiled and gleaming on its tripod base, funnel hopper feed mechanism seated in place, sat the fat brass cylinder of a Gatling gun! It was the small model, invented for the use of your New York police, I believe; but there were enough of them in service in the British and Indian Army that my father was fully conversant with its operation. Behind lay a stack of boxes, wrapped in brown oilskin, which could be nothing but its ammunition. A stand of Martini rifles and more ammunition stood next to it.

"'Get it out, at once,' shouted Van Ouisthoven, 'we get it down to the harbor and those ungrateful *schlems* learn something they didn't learn yet. But hurry! That crook Yankee what skippers the *Matilda Briggs*, he'll take them all off yet if we don't hurry! They have been giving him my gold for years!'

"In a few words, my father told the others what he wanted. One man carried four boxes of ammunition for the gun. The other two took the weapon itself, one being Umpa, who carried the tripod and another box. My father slung two rifles and gave the old Dutchman another, at the same time taking a pouch of rifle cartridges. They were all laden, but not so much that they could not make good time. The urgency of what they were doing—though, to be sure, even my father only half understood it—somehow communicated itself to all of them.

"As they left the front door, my father was amazed to see the old man take a large box of wax vestas from his jacket pocket and calmly light a tall bamboo screen just inside the door. As it took fire, Van Ouisthoven turned to my father and said sadly, 'It must go. The whole thing. If some should survive, they must have nothing to come back to. All must go. And it is suitable. Here it started.' There was nothing in his eyes as he spoke but grim determination, and Dad could only begin to grasp what it must have cost the old chap. But he knew his history, and he remembered the men who cheerfully flooded their Dutch country-side in 1587 to turn back the Prince of Parma's Spanish Army.

"With no more words, the five of them set off down across the lawn and into another trail, this time headed for the harbor. Behind them a plume of black smoke came out the open door and began to rise in the heat of the steaming tropic mists.

"As they entered the new track, clear through the morning air came the distant sound of a rifle shot, followed by others. With no word spoken, they all began to run, their various loads seeming light as they did. Van Ouisthoven's age was a mystery to my father, but he kept up gamely, his white beard jutting forward and his rifle at the ready.

"The trail they were on was a goodish bit broader than the narrow trace on which they had first approached the house, beaten smooth with much use, and presenting no obstruction to movement. They kept alert, the two Europeans guarding the flanks and moving first. The rifle fire continued in the distance, and grew louder as they advanced. How long they ran would be impossible to estimate, but suddenly they came into the open and saw a panorama which stayed riveted in their memories. My father could describe it, after a fifth glass of port, as if it had been only the day before.

"The tiny bay lay before them, a broad stretch of yellow sand skirting a calm blue lagoon. Some hundreds of yards offshore lay the bark at anchor, a shabby enough craft, her brown hull paint peeling, patched sails half up but idle in the almost windless air. Between her and the shore, boats, three of them, none large, plied steadily with paddles, all heading for the ship.

"Directly in front of my father and his group, Verner and his three seamen fronted the monsters. It was a curious situation. The three seamen, including Burung, were prone, firing at intervals, in unison, and only when there was a rush. Their ammunition must have been almost exhausted. Behind them, Verner leaned on his crude cane, somehow conveying an air of casual urbanity, as if bored by the whole proceedings, his shabby garments even now appearing neat, despite their rips and tatters. My father, who disliked the man intensely, was always careful to aver, never-theless, that he carried himself in a very gentlemanly manner at all times.

"There were bodies on the sand between Verner's people and the Folk. Huge bodies covered with yellow-brown fur, great ivory chisel teeth fixed in death grimaces, strange hairy hands still clutching their crude knives. Behind them, in turn, were the rest of the Folk, the great males, in a circle, their horrid faces turned toward their enemies, their gruff barking notes and shriller chatter filling the air. Even as my father saw them, they were massing for another rush. In back of the ring of raging creatures were a mass of smaller brutes, many of them no larger than children. The Folk, or at least some of them, had been brought to bay, and their females and young were the cause."

As we heard this story, those of us who knew Ffellowes saw something we had seldom seen. I mean, the man was *feeling!* As he told the final moments of this tale, the man was really moved. He illustrated his story with jerky hand motions, and there was actual sweat on his forehead! Whatever the truth of his yarns, and I have long since suspended judgment on them, there is no doubt about one thing, in this one anyway. The guy felt it! And it was supposed to have happened to his *father* back long before any of us were born!

He went on. "My father wasted no time. Several crisp orders and the Gatling was set up, with Dad holding the yoke bars. Old Umpa was the ammunition loader and emptied the first box of shells into the hopper feed.

" 'Get down, Verner, get down flat!' Dad bellowed. Verner, whose back was to them, fell as if struck dead. The others being prone already, a clear field of fire was possible. Dad began to turn the crank.

"The bellow of the Gatling drowned out all other noises, and my father transversed it back and forth as coldly as if he had been on a target range. Old Umpa, his dark, scarred visage expressionless, broke open the boxes and emptied cartridges into the hopper as calmly as if he were shelling nuts. The result was appalling. The great furry brutes went down like nine-pins, and as fast as those in front fell, the others behind followed. It was over in five minutes.

"My father stopped firing and the bluish smoke drifted in the faint breeze. The water at the beach edge was red, and so too were the sands. It looked like a slaughterhouse. The bulky carasses lay in their gory death like so many shot muskrats, which indeed they resembled, save in size.

"Verner rose from the sand and dusted himself off in a precise, almost mincing way. His three trusties also got up, old Burung in the lead, and walked over to us.

" 'You have justified my belief in you, Captain,' he said in his usual icy tones. 'These dangerous vermin were tolerably close to terminating a career which had not been without some small distinction. And who is this, pray tell?'

"It was a considerable pleasure for my father to introduce Van Ouisthoven to Mr. Verner, though the latter was, to be sure, as imperturbable as usual.

" 'I see that the reports of your death, *mijnheer*, have been considerably exaggerated.' Verner's voice was even chiller than its normal wont. 'You have much to answer for, sir. You have imperiled the entire human race by your meddling in matters better left to Providence.'

"His rebuke, however, went unnoticed. For even Verner had forgotten the ship. Now, with a cry, the old Hollander pointed, and we all remembered her. Under easy sail, square sails set on the two foremasts, and gaff on the mizzen, the *Matilda Briggs* was standing out to sea. The three small boats which had been plying to and from shore drifted on the tide.

"It was a beautiful scene, really. There was the brown ship, as lovely as only a sailing vessel can be, the azure waters, the fringe of *nipa* and coco palms on the shore, and then the open sea beyond the harbor's mouth. But it was horror! One thing had been made plain to my father; that the ship must not escape. And here she was, stealing out to sea, and they were helpless. The Gatling, though unparalleled at close range, was useless beyond two hundred yards, and the ship was thrice that already. Everyone stood in numb silence, and simply watched her go. And saw her end.

"Around the corner of the northern point of the bay came the bow of a small black steamer with white upper works. And as she appeared, she began to fire, first the bow gun and then the stern, as soon as they could bear upon the target. She was not large, but on her staff she wore the blue, red, and white of the navy of Holland. In silence the little crowd on the beach watched the annihilation of the *Matilda Briggs*. The two guns the gunboat used were not of great caliber, but the bark was a fragile thing, wood-built, old and hard-used. Her masts fell in seconds, and the fires kindled by the exploding shells were all over her in another instant. Ceaselessly, remorselessly, the warship fired. When she stopped and the echoes of her guns no longer resounded in one's ears, there was nothing on the surface of the lagoon, nothing but a smear of oily muck, some oily smoke, a litter of wood scraps, and the dark fins of countless sharks.

" 'The *Dolfjin* has justified the Dutch naval estimates, indeed those of the entire mass of all the world's navies,' came the didactic comment of Verner over my father's shoulder. 'A curious reflection on the rise of modern fleets, that one minute gunboat should prove the probable savior of the human race. She came only just in time,' he added.

"But my father was not really listening to Verner. He was watching Van Ouisthoven instead. The old man was walking slowly down the beach to the pile of bodies where the Folk lay, the males in front of their females and young. For some reason, my father followed him as he skirted the fringe of the mass of dead creatures and advanced slowly and with head bent on the last heap at the water's edge.

"While my father stood silent behind him, the old fellow began to pull the bodies apart in the last heap, the one nearest the water, ignoring the warm blood that stained his arms and clothing. Persistently, he tugged and hauled, shoving the great carcasses aside, until at last he was rewarded.

"Something moved under his hands, and his motions grew more excited. My father drew one of his revolvers and stood waiting, poised for any eventuality.

"A blunt-nosed head appeared from under one of the larger shapes, and into the bright sun of noon wiggled a small furry creature, no more than three feet high. In one arm it clutched something flat, but the other hand it held out to Van Ouisthoven, squeaking plaintively as it did so. The man whom it addressed stood silent, his shoulders seeming to stoop even more, if possible. Then in the absence of sound, Van Ouisthoven held out one hand—to my father. In the same bleak silence, as if no other noise could be allowed, my father handed over the revolver he held. He saw tears pouring down Van Ouisthoven's face. There was a shot. My father confessed he had his eyes closed at this juncture. Then a second shot.

"When Dad could bear to look again, two figures were clasped together. The old Hollander lay hugging the small shape of the last of the Folk, a bullet in his own brain. Beside them on the sand lay the object which the little thing had been holding so tightly. My father stirred it with his foot. It was a Dutch primer, brightly illustrated in color, with pictures of children in Holland at play.

"The next scene of the drama, or what have you, took place in the captain's cabin of His Netherlandish Majesty's ship, the *Dolfjin*. They were headed down the coast to pick up my father's *prau*. The Dutch naval officer had ceased his questions, and the interminable voice of Verner had taken up the tale. Through a fog of fatigue blended with irritation, my father tried to follow what the man was saying. His comprehensive dislike of the fellow's personality was palliated only by a genuine admiration of the man's attainments and perserverance.

" 'It becomes quite clear, I think, to all present, that no report of this affair must reach any but the few constituted authorities, those who are cognizant to some extent, that is, of the problem. Were the facts to be made plain, I fear, some scientific rascals would be able to reproduce the late Van Ouisthoven's work. While he had a good degree from Leyden, he was hardly, save in sheer persistence, a genius, and it is highly possible . . .'

"Here, my father, who could not forget the old man's death, made some ejaculation or even swore, though this was most unlike him.

" 'My dear Ffellowes,' said Verner, his voice losing some of its habitual *sang-froid*. 'No one is more cognizant than myself of that unfortunate man's dilemma. He must, perforce, destroy the very thing he had created. His last moments, which I also observed, were charged with remorse and grief. Yet, what choice had he? Or, indeed, any of us? His final actions, awful though they may appear to an observer, gave him rank with the leaders of the human race. He raised Caliban from the depths and to the depths he dispatched him.'

"My father said nothing. He was too sunk in weariness and

sadness to venture further. Yet—for one moment, Verner's wiry hand had pressed his shoulder, and he felt the unspoken sympathy which the other could not express in any other way, both to the dead, and to himself. There was a silence.

" 'To resume,' Verner continued, his high querulous voice cutting off any debate, 'the facts are indeed singular. They stem, in fact, from the unpaid bills of the Manchester firm of machinery manufacturers. These people, whose name is in the highest degree inconsequential to this story, retained in turn, my employers, Messrs. Morrison, Morrison and Dodd, who act not only as appraisers of various mechanical artifices and manufacturers, but also, in a subsidiary vein, as assurers of the same. Thus are great affairs put in train! The bills of the original company were not being paid! A steady and reliable account had ceased payment, without prior notice! An outrage, in the ordered community of business! What transpired? Morrison, Morrison and Dodd were called in and found themselves at sea, literally and figuratively. The account was in the great Dutch island of Sumatra. Some ten thousands of pounds sterling were owed. The Dutch, when appealed to, could give no assistance.

" 'The area in question was remote and feverish, on the so-called Tapanuli coast. Few ships called there. In any case, the Hollands Government could hardly prosecute a bankrupt on behalf of an English firm. They declined action. So the matter stood. But do not undervalue the persistence of the English man of business. He will follow a bad debt to the end. Hence my appearance in this matter, brought about by devious means and my own desires, let it be said.

" 'When the matter was first put to me, I was at first totally uninterested. It seemed to have little of consequence, and less of any noteworthy quality about it. I was resistant to the idea of my services being engaged. Yet, I made a few preliminary moves. One of these was to frequent the numerous haunts in the areas of the London docks, where information on this part of the world might be ascertained, if patience were applied.

" 'My patience was rewarded. Some mouthings of a dying lascar seaman in a den of the vilest description caused me to accept the commission. What the fellow said was vague and in the highest degree inconclusive. Nevertheless, it brought me out here to the East. For, in speaking of the very area of coast in which we now find ourselves, he said something of great interest. "Do not go there," he choked out. "That is the land of the Not-men. Men like you and me, we are killed on sight!"

" 'So, by strange methods, including enlisting persons so lofty in stature they may not be mentioned on this vessel, through a previous indebtedness to my humble person, I secured the right to go anywhere in these islands. And also to ask for the aid of such Dutch naval craft as might be available. In fact, I could tell my colleague here to sink anything he saw moving on this coast.

" 'And so by circuitous means,' continued Verner, 'I came to one Cornelius Van Ouisthoven, the original bad debtor of my employers. The man was presumed dead. Not one relative in his family had heard from him for many years. But—and a large BUT it was—he had ordered mining machinery, railway machinery, all sorts of machinery, and had not paid for it, that is, after a certain point in time.

" 'I found myself with a curious and unsolvable equation, involving this hitherto unknown Dutch gentleman, whose background I was at some pains to look into. Added to him there was some unpaid-for machinery, and finally, as I drew closer to the area in question, more and more rumors about a land where *men* were not welcome!

" 'So curious were all these circumstances that I felt I must investigate in person. I did so, and the results were as you know. I found myself the prisoner of these creatures the old gentleman chose to call "the Folk."

" 'I managed to escape and even flee the harbor in one of the native craft whose previous owners, no doubt innocent fishermen, the Folk had slain. These vessels, which were beyond their management, were left drawn up on the beach.

" 'I have not been so fortunate as to secure Van Ouisthoven's notes, but I rather fancy I can piece together the main *membra*.

" 'Briefly, the old man was a biologist, and one of extraordinary patience. He bred some native rodent, almost certainly *Rhizomys sumatrensis*, the local, so-called "bamboo rat," to extraordinary size. In my dissecting days at Barts, various genera of the *Rodentia* were exposed to me, and I well remember noting that this particular species had very well-developed paws, quite resembling hands, in fact.

" 'Hands come before brains, you know. This is the most recent opinion. Without grasping organs, our peculiar human brains would be worthless. So, the old recluse went on with his work. And, from what you tell me, Ffellowes, he succeeded.

" 'Brain is an inevitable increment of size at this rate. These vermin are quite clever enough as it is. Someone at the British Museum has deduced that there are four thousand species of rodents on the planet already. But if we are to be supplanted, let it be in due course. Even the old man agreed with that at the end.'

"And there," said Ffellowes, extinguishing his cigar, "my story, or 'tale' if you like, Williams, ends. My father was returned to his own vessel, he continued his cruise through the islands, and no report of any of this exists anywhere, unless it be in some hidden archives of the Kingdom of the Netherlands. That is all."

There was a longer silence this time. It was broken by the younger member who had brought on the whole business in the first place.

"But, Brigadier, with all respect, sir, there is something vaguely familiar about all this. Who was this man, Verner, or whatever he called himself? He sounds like some creature of fiction himself."

Ffellowes' answer was—well—typical. He stared at the young man coldly, but not in anger.

"Possible, no doubt. Since I never read sensational literature, I fear that I am in no position to give an answer. I have nothing to go on, you understand, but my father's unsupported word. I have always felt that sufficient!"

After a much longer silence, the brigadier was found to have gone, as silently as always. And, as usual, no one else seemed to have anything to say.

The Adventure of the Extraterrestrial

by

Mack Reynolds

Since all good Sherlockians are firm in the belief that Holmes is immortal, but not necessarily ever-youthful, it follows that some cases must be dealt with by Holmes as a very old man. Consequently, though a senile Holmes would seem a contradiction in terms, the possibility must be faced.

The Adventure of
The Extraterrestrial

by Mack Reynolds

From the chess problem, over which he had been nodding, my companion slowly raised his head. His age-crooked fingers relinquished their hold on the knight—I suspected he had forgotten the square from which he had originally lifted it—and he leaned back.

His once lean, hawklike face worked before he cackled, "We are about to have company, Doctor."

London was lost in fog, a heavy autumnal curtain shutting the city away from our lodgings in Baker Street, and at first there was only the distant hum of diminished traffic that was the pulse of the city and the several small noises of water dripping; then I heard the low purr of a heavy vehicle, traveling a short distance, stopping, then coming forward again.

"Must be looking for this number," the aged detective prattled. "Who else at this hour of the night, eh?"

"Whom else," I said. Sometimes I suspect he thinks himself

157

living in the days of nearly half a century ago, when clients were continually presenting themselves at odd hours. I have wondered if it wasn't a mistake to allow his relatives to coax me into returning to the rooms at 221B Baker Street to act as his companion in his final years. They had explained, at the time convincingly, that the octogenarian sleuth had never been happy on the bee farm in Sussex to which he had retired at the age of sixty in 1914.

"Eh," he was saying, listening intently. "He has left his car just a few doors away. He has gone to the door, eh? He has flashed his torch on the number. Heh, that is not the number, but it cannot be far away. Now, eh? He returns to his car but does not get in. He is too close to the address for that. He locks it, eh? And here he is, here he is."

Frankly, I had thought the old gaffer in one of his daydreams but his once keen eyes, now slightly rheumy, were fixed on the night bell. When it jangled, he chortled satisfaction, pushed himself to his feet, grasped his stick, and made his way to the speaking tube where he invited our visitor to come up.

In a few moments there was a tap on the door of our lodgings and I crossed the room and opened it.

Across the threshold stepped a youngish, black-haired man whose smooth shaven face was partly concealed by horn-rimmed glasses with dark panes. He was clothed in fashion and his well-tailored suit went far toward hiding his excessive weight. I had an impression of over-indulgence at the table—and possibly at the cabaret.

My companion, in a burst of lucidity which admittedly set me back, said happily, "Ah! A pleasure to see you again, Mr. Norwood. And how is Sir Alexander, your father?"

The newcomer stared at him. "For heaven's sake, man! It has been thirty years since you set eyes on me in 1903. I was a child of five or six. I had expected to have to introduce myself, even to remind you of my father."

Chuckling to himself, my companion motioned him to a seat. "Not at all, not at all. The details of the case upon which I worked for your admirable father are still quite clear in my mind. Quite clear. Always thought of it as . . . just a minute . . .

the Riddle of Closton Manor. Eh? Riddle of Closton Manor. As for recognizing your features, I assure you, young man, you resemble your father. Spittin' image, as the Americans say, eh? Isn't that what the Americans say, Doctor? Damn bounders."

"I wouldn't know," I said coolly. Actually, it was time for his bed and I disliked to see him aroused by company.

The retired detective lowered himself cautiously into his chair and reached for his pipe and tobacco, observing me slyly from the side of his eyes. He knew he wasn't supposed to smoke this late at night. He chortled with satisfaction, I suspected at thwarting me, and said, "I assume, young man, you are here on matters of personal interest rather than on an errand for Sir Alexander, eh?"

The newcomer lifted his eyes to me.

My friend chuckled in what I can only name a puerile fashion and said, "The doctor is my valued assistant." He introduced us, then lit his pipe, dropping the match on the floor, as said through the smoke, with a certain deprecation which irritated me, "His discretion is as great as my own. Eh? Great as my own."

We nodded politely to each other and the young man began his story. "Sir, my father has a great deal of respect for you."

"The feeling is reciprocated. Your father impressed me as a man of integrity and one with an unusual sense of duty and humanity, eh?" He chuckled again, and I suspected he was getting a childish pleasure at doing so well before me.

I felt, however, that Peter Norwood wasn't overly pleased with these words from my friend. He hesitated before saying, "Then you will be sorry to hear that there is evidence that his mind is beginning to slip."

A shadow crossed the face of the former detective. "I am indeed. Your words distress me. But then, let me see. Sir Alexander must be in his late seventies." To hear him, one would never have suspected his full decade of seniority, the old hypocrite.

Norwood nodded. "Seventy-eight." He hesitated again. "You asked me whether my visit was personal or on behalf of my father. Actually, I am on his errand, but in fact I think it should be me you consider your client."

"Ah?" my aged companion muttered. He made a steeple of his bent fingers as in days of old and I must admit there was a sparkle of intelligence behind watery eyes. Old his clay might be, but there was still in him the ancient bloodhound catching a distant whiff of a chase to come—were he about to rise to it.

Peter Norwood pushed out his plump lips in what was almost a pout. "I shall put it bluntly, sir. My father has only a few years to live and he is about to dispose frivolously of the greater part of his fortune."

"You are his heir?" I asked.

Norwood nodded. "His sole heir. If in these last years of his life my father wastes away the family fortune, it is I who will suffer."

My friend's mouth worked several times, unhappily. "Frivolous waste? Doesn't sound like your father, young man."

"My father is contemplating leaving the greater part of his estate to a group of charlatans and, if I may resort to idiom, crackpots. The World Defense Society, they call themselves." Peter Norwood could not control a sneer. He looked from one of us to the other. "You have heard of it, perhaps?"

We both shook our heads.

"Please elucidate," I said.

"This group and my father, who is a charter member, are of the opinion that there are aliens in London."

"Aliens?" I blurted. "But what could be more obvious? Of course there are aliens in London."

Peter Norwood turned his eyes to me. "Aliens from space," he said. "Extraterrestrials." He threw up his hands in disgust. "Men from Mars. Spaceships, I suppose. All that sort of rot."

Even my friend was surprised at this turn. "Eh? You say Sir Alexander supports this belief? Why?"

The young man's rounded face reflected his disgust. "He has a fantastic collection of *proof*. He has devoted the past two years to the accumulation of it. Flying saucers, unidentified objects in the sky. The case of Kasper Hauser. That sort of thing. Stuff and nonsense, of course."

The elderly detective leaned back and closed his eyes, and for a moment I thought he had gone to sleep, as can be his wont when he gets tired, or bored with the conversation. But he said, quite lucidly, "You say you are on an errand for your father?"

"Actually, it was I who planted the idea in his head," Peter Norwood admitted. "As I have said, Father has a considerable respect for your methods, sir. I will not deny that he and I have had several heated discussions on his phobia. In the midst of the last one, I suggested that since he thinks so highly of you, that he hire your services to investigate the presence of these aliens. As a result of that argument, I am here, ostensibly to employ you in his behalf to seek out these . . . these little green men from Mars."

My companion opened his rheumy eyes. "But you said I should consider you to be my actual client."

Peter Norwood spread his hands. "I realize, sir, that you no longer practice, that you have long since retired. However, I implore you to take this assignment. To pretend you actually seek these so-called extraterrestrials, supposedly running wild about London, and then to report to my father that after a thorough search you can find no such aliens from space. Needless to say, I shall reward you amply."

I thought I understood his point. "You wish to have drawn up a supposed report of an investigation and present it to your father in hopes his neurosis will be cured?"

The young man shook his head emphatically. "That would not be sufficient, Doctor. My father is not an easily deceived man. The investigation would have to be made, and seriously so, and reported possibly in a step-by-step manner. Otherwise, the old fool will realize he is being duped."

The term *old fool* had slipped out, but in a manner I could sympathize with Peter Norwood.

My companion was in deep thought—or drowsing. I could not remember the adventure that he chose to think of as the Riddle of Closton Manor, but it was manifest that his regard for Sir Alexander must have been high indeed and that he was torn by this regard and by the young man's—what seemed to me—understandable position.

He wasn't asleep. He said slowly, "Aside from the fact that I

have retired, this is not the sort of thing upon which I worked."
He seemed petulant.

"Of course not," the other agreed, placatingly. "But then the
fee—"

"It isn't a matter of fee."

Norwood blinked behind his lenses, but held his tongue.

The octogenarian puffed his pipe in irritation and squirmed in
his chair. He muttered finally, "I assume your father wishes me to
come to Closton Manor to discuss my employment of this
project, eh?"

I snorted. The idea was ridiculous. The former sleuth seldom
left our rooms except for a short stroll up and down the street for
exercise.

"That was the purpose of my visit, supposedly. To bring you to
him so that he might go over the matter with you. However, I can
see that such a journey would—"

To my amazement, the aged detective slapped the arm of his
chair and said, "Young man, expect me at your home tomorrow
afternoon."

Before I could protest, Peter Norwood came to his feet. He
was manifestly pleased. "You shall not regret this, sir. I'll see
that your time—ah, financially, that is—is not wasted."

The aged face of the other worked, but he said nothing in reply
to that. It was obvious that the young man assumed his interest
was venial and that the former sleuth had lost caste by his
decision.

I saw Norwood to the door in silence.

When I returned I stood over my aged friend and began, "Now
look here—"

But he glowered up at me stubbornly and said in what I must
describe as a blathering tone, "No reason I can't take a trip into
the country for a breath of air, Doctor. I don't see why you think
you're more fit than I, eh? Practically the same age."

I said, in an attempt to be biting, "Perhaps my fitness as
compared to your own is based on the fact that as a young man
stationed in the Near East I learned to make yogurt a daily item of
diet, whilst at the same time you were wielding a hypodermic
needle loaded with a certain crystalline alkaloid which shall
remain nameless."

"Yogurt, heh, heh," he chortled in a manner which could but emphasize to me his caducity. He reached absently for his violin, probably having forgotten that two of the strings were broken.

In spite of my protests, at ten in the morning we embarked on the train for Durwood, the nearest village to the ancestral home, Closton Manor, of the Norwood family. I had looked up the title in Burke's Peerage and found the baronetcy an ancient and distinguished one originally granted on the field of battle by Richard the First in the Holy Land. More recently, bearers of the title had distinguished themselves in India and the Sudan.

We arrived in Durwood shortly after twelve and proceeded to Closton Manor by dog cart. A middle-aged, work bent servant had been awaiting the train. After introducing himself as Mullins and stating that Master Peter had sent him, he lapsed into silence which he maintained until we reached the manor.

We entered the extensive and rambling house by a side entrance where we were met by young Norwood himself and conducted by way of a narrow staircase to the rooms of Sir Alexander. I must admit that my retired detective friend was in uncommonly good condition, having slept the whole way from London. His most lucid moments, I believe, were invariably immediately after he had awakened.

Sir Alexander was seated in a small study which was well stocked with books, pamphlets, and aged manuscripts. In fact, the only description would be to say it was overstocked. Great piles of tomes leaned against walls or balanced precariously without support. But in spite of the fact that manifestly considerable study was done in the room, the light was dim, as a result of rather heavily curtained windows.

Sir Alexander sat deep in an upholstered chair, wrapped in a steamer rug as though for warmth. His chin rested upon his chest and his sunken eyes looked at us from over his pince-nez. A thin mustache and beard, both gray, and a fringe of gray hair seen from under the skull cap he wore, ornamented his thin ascetic face, white within the darkness of his immediate environment.

"Ah, my friend," he said in a cultured, well-modulated voice. "We meet again." His eyes sparkled with a youth his body belied. He held out a hand to be shaken.

The retired sleuth, using his cane as though it was no more than an affectation, rose to the occasion. "A great pleasure to renew our acquaintanceship, Sir Alexander. May I present my friend?" He introduced us with a flare I hadn't witnessed in him for years.

It was my turn to shake the proffered hand and I found it warm and firm. First impressions deceive. Sir Alexander was considerably further from his grave than his son had led us to believe.

Peter Norwood said, "Would you prefer I leave, Father, while you discuss your business with our visitors?"

The baronet gestured with a slight motion. "If you don't mind, my boy. I shall see you at tea, if not before."

Young Norwood bowed to us, winking whilst his back was to his father, and excused himself.

When we were alone, Sir Alexander chuckled wryly. "Peter, I am afraid, is of the opinion that I am somewhat around the bend."

The former sleuth had lowered himself gingerly into a chair and was now fumbling in his jacket pocket for pipe and tobacco. "Suppose you tell us this from the beginning, eh?"

The other cocked his head to one side and eyed him, frowning, and probably noticing for the first time how considerably my companion had aged since last they had met. However, he said, finally, "I am afraid I am working under a handicap. I have no doubt that your minds have already been somewhat prejudiced."

I cleared my throat, if the truth be known, surprised at his approach. I had expected mental infirmity, but found no outward signs of it. Was it possible the man was pulling his son's leg?

My companion, who was bringing his match in contact with the shag he had fumbled into his pipe, rose to the occasion again, his voice being quite firm as he said, "I consider myself without prejudice, Sir Alexander, as you have had cause to know in the past."

A flush touched the other's face. "Forgive me, my dear friend. Hadn't it been for your toleration three decades ago, I would be dead today." He looked away from us for the moment, as though seeking a starting point to his narrative.

"I suppose there is no beginning," he said finally. "This matter has been coming to my attention, piece by piece, fragment by fragment, throughout my adult life. Only recently have I given it the attention it deserves." He hesitated for a moment, then said to me, "Doctor, if you please, would you hand me that book on the top of the pile there to your left?"

I was able to reach the book and hand it to him without leaving my chair.

Sir Alexander said, "You gentlemen are both familiar with H. Spencer Jones, I assume?"

I said, "The Astronomer Royal, of course."

The other lifted the book. "You are acquainted with his work, 'Life on Other Worlds'?"

"Afraid not, eh," the retired detective said. I shook my head.

"Let me read you a passage or two." Our host thumbed quickly through the volume. "Here, for instance."

He began reading *"With the universe constructed on so vast a scale, it would seem inherently improbable that our small earth can be the only home of life."* He skipped over some pages. "And here: . . . *It seems reasonable to suppose that whenever in the universe the proper conditions arise, life must inevitably come into existence. This is the view that is generally accepted by biologists."*

He began to look for more passages.

"Never mind," my friend wheezed. "I accept what you offer, eh. That is, I accept the possibility. Possibility, not probability. Other life forms might be present somewhere in the universe." He chortled. "Let me say, Sir Alexander, that it is an extensive universe."

The old gaffer was outdoing himself, I had to admit. I had expected him to be drowsing by this time.

Our host nodded agreeably. "It is indeed. However, please pass me that magazine to your right there, Doctor."

He took up the magazine and thumbed through it. "Ah, here. This is an article by a young German chap, Willy Ley. A chap more than ordinarily interested in the prospects of man's conquest of space. Here we are: ". . . *We are justified in believing in life on Mars—hardy plant life. The color changes which we can see are explained most logically and most simply by assuming vegetation."* He skipped some lines, then went on. *"Of terrestrial plants, lichen might survive transplanting to Mars and one may imagine that some of the desert flora of Tibet could be adapted. At any event, conditions are such that life as we know it would find the going tough, but not impossible."*

Sir Alexander broke off and looked at us questioningly.

I said, "I submit, Sir Alexander, that the presence on Mars of lichens, and the possible presence on some far distant star of even intelligent life, does not mean that alien life forms are scampering about the streets of London!"

The other was visibly becoming animated by the discussion. He leaned forward. "Ah, my dear Doctor, do you not see the point? When you grant the existence of life elsewhere than on Earth, you must admit the possible corollary."

I scowled at him and said, "Perhaps I have missed something."

Sir Alexander said quickly, "Don't you see? If there is life elsewhere in the universe, we must suppose one of three things. It is either less advanced than we, equally advanced, or it is more advanced than we."

My former detective friend chortled again. "That about covers everything, eh, Sir Alexander?"

"Of course. However, now please understand that already here on Earth man is beginning to reach for the stars. The Willy Ley I quoted from is an example of the thousands of young men who see tomorrow's exploration of the moon, and, in the comparatively near future, of the solar system. And they dream of eventual travel to the stars." He leaned forward again to stress his earnestness. "If we grant the possibility of intelligent life elsewhere, then we must grant the possibility that it is further along the path toward conquest of space. Our race, gentlemen, is a young one. Our fellow intelligent life forms might have several millions of years of growth behind them."

Neither of us had an answer to this. In my own case, there was just too much to assimilate. And I suspected my friend had lost the thread of thought.

Sir Alexander pointed a thin finger at us for emphasis. "If man is already laying plans for exploration beyond his own planet, why should not our neighbors in space have already taken such steps?"

I said, barely keeping irritation suppressed, "You have made a theoretical case for the possibility of alien life forms, and their desire to reach beyond their own worlds. But you have said nothing definite, thus far. Thus far, it is all in the realm of hypothesis. You have some concrete proof, Sir Alexander?"

Our host tossed the magazine to a cluttered desk and pursed his lips. He said, "I have never shaken the hand of an extraterrestrial, my friend."

My companion chortled, "Heh, jolly good, eh?" Evidently, he had been following the conversation after all.

But Sir Alexander raised his gray eyebrows at me. "Perhaps one day I shall, Doctor. Who knows?" He turned back to my companion. "For literally centuries men have been sighting strange flying objects. Long before the Wright brothers, unidentified flying objects, saucer shaped, cigar shaped, ball shaped, have been seen by reputable witnesses. Literally hundreds of such sightings have been recorded by Charles Fort, the American."

"American?" my friend muttered. "Blighter."

"But, Sir Alexander," I protested, "the man is commonly regarded as a fool, a fanatic, if not a charlatan."

The thin gray eyebrows went up again. "By whom, Doctor? I suggest that his critics so regard him. And those who have raised our still immature science to the pedestal and cry wrath against all who do not worship. But there are many tens of thousands of persons who regard Fort as a keen brain capable of revealing the shortcomings of many of our so-called scientific beliefs."

"I have never bothered to read him," I said, possibly a bit snappish in tone.

My retired detective friend's mouth worked unhappily. He said, "You have other, eh, evidence?"

The baronet motioned to his room, cluttered as it was with a thousand manuscripts, newspaper clippings, books, and pamphlets. "For years I have been gathering data which in many respects duplicates that of Charles Fort. Accounts of strange sightings, both on land and sea. Accounts of strange people seen, strange animals, impossible phenomena."

I was becoming impatient. "And you believe them from some foreign planet?"

He frowned at me. "Don't misunderstand, Doctor. I assume no definite position as yet. But I do wish to know. Frankly, I am willing to place the greater part of my fortune at the disposal of the World Defense Society if it can be proven to me that there is danger of invasion of our planet by aliens. Thus far, the evidence presented has been insufficient to convince me." He turned to my friend. "That is why I wish your services. I have great confidence in you. If there are aliens in London, as my associates would have it, I wish to know. If they are dangerous to our way of life, I wish to be foremost in the defense."

He looked down at his aged body. "Unfortunately, my years prevent my services in other than a financial manner."

I was capable of nothing beyond staring at him. Was he asking the blind to lead the blind? My friend, who I suspected of tottering along the edge of dotardism, and I, myself, for that matter, were a good decade older than he. But here he was, suggesting he hire our services because his years prevented him from activity.

However, my companion, with a thump of his cane, came suddenly to life and pushed himself to his feet with an aggressiveness that would have done him credit twenty years earlier. "I shall take the assignment, Sir Alexander." To me, his attitude indicated that his intention was to dash out upon the moors and begin immediate search for little green men.

It was too late now. I tried to rescue something from the debris, for the sake of young Norwood. "Under one condition, Sir Alexander."

The baronet's eyes pierced me. "And it is?"

"We shall guarantee to investigate to the best of our abilities. However, if it is found to our satisfaction there is no evidence of such aliens, you must pledge to drop the World Defense Society and your interests in alien life forms."

Sir Alexander sank back into his chair and remained silent for a long moment. Finally he said, his voice low, "Very well, Doctor. I trust you both."

There had been practically no conversation from my companion either from or to Closton Manor. He had drowsed both ways. Indeed, on the return, exhausted from his efforts, I suppose, he had snored most atrociously so that we had the compartment to ourselves. It was not until that evening when we were seated before the fire that he discussed the case—if the farce may be called a case—with me.

Over the steeple of his fingertips, which he affected when pretending still to retain his faculties, he peered at me quizzically. "What are your opinions on this matter, my good Doctor?" he asked. "I assume you have formed opinions, eh?"

If the truth must be known, I was somewhat surprised that he remembered the events of the morning. Anything out of the ordinary routine had a tendency to magnify his growing signs of senile dementia, in my professional observation.

I shrugged deprecation. "Sir Alexander seems an admirable enough man, but I am afraid he has—" I hesitated.

"Slipped around the bend? Very good, eh? His own term. Very good, eh? We used to say balmy. The blue Johnnies, the pink spiders. Slipped around the bend. Very good, heh, heh."

"Unfortunately," I said coolly, at his senile levity, "I feel sorry for young Norwood, his son. Frankly, I think his only recourse is to the courts, unless you are able to convince his father to forgo this fantastic hobby."

He eyed me slyly, with what I can only call that cunning you sometimes find in those failing with age. "Doctor, I am afraid young Norwood has anticipated you." He chuckled to himself, as though over some secret knowledge. "Thinks I'm pulling chestnuts out of the fire for him."

"What?" I said, cutting off his prattle. My face must have mirrored my lack of understanding—if, indeed, there was understanding to be found in his maunderings.

He shook a finger at me in puerile superiority. "If that whelp attempted to have his father committed merely on the grounds that he collected books and magazine articles on a rather fanciful subject, he would be rejected by the courts, eh? However, if he could prove that his father, ah, squandered money by hiring an overaged detective, then I submit that few courts of law would do other than turn the estate over to our young friend." He chortled sourly. "Imagine, hiring an old-timer such as myself to stalk Bug Eyed Monsters."

"Bug Eyed Monsters?" I said.

No chuckles, and I began to suspect his moment of lucidity had passed. But then he said, cryptogrammatically, "Your reading has been neglected, Doctor."

I got back to the point. "Then you believe that Peter Norwood is deliberately provoking his father along these lines in order to hasten the date of his inheritance?"

He worked his mouth, unhappily. "Manifestly, Sir Alexander is in excellent health, considering his age. He might live another five years . . . ."

"At least," I muttered.

". . . Which makes it understandable that young Peter might be impatient for the title and the estate."

I became agitated at the old codger, in spite of myself. "Then, confound it, why did you accept this ridiculous case?"

My companion shrugged his bony shoulders in a petulant movement that to me accented his caducity. "Can't you see, eh? If I had refused, the ungrateful hound would have gone elsewhere. There are private investigators in London who would gladly cooperate with him. At least I have Sir Alexander's interests at heart."

I suspected he was having delusions again about his abilities to perform in the manner of yesteryear. However, I merely grunted and said, "I am not too sure but that the boy is right. Perhaps his father has slipped mentally to the point where he is incapable of handling his affairs. After all—aliens from space. I ask you!"

But my aged friend had closed his eyes in either sleep or thought and so I retreated to my book.

Approximately ten minutes later and without lifting his lids he wheezed, "Doctor, if there are aliens from space in this city, why should they have picked London, eh? Why London? Why not Moscow, Paris, Rome, New York, Tokyo, eh? Why not Tokyo?"

It had been years since I had thought him able to concentrate on one subject for so lengthy a time. I sighed, and marked my place with a finger. Usually he had drowsed off by this time of the evening, sometimes muttering in his sleep about Moriarty, or some other foe of half a century before. I said, trying to keep impatience from my voice, "Perhaps they are in those cities, too."

He opened one eye, looked at me with a moist accusation. "No. Let us grant there are such aliens present, eh? And let us grant that they are in London."

"Very well," I humored him.

His wavering voice turned thoughtful. "Manifestly, they are keeping their presence here on Earth a secret for motives of their own. If this is their policy it then follows that they must limit their number, eh?"

"Why so?" I sighed, wishing to return to my tome.

"Because it would be considerably more difficult to keep the presence of a hundred aliens from the attention of we Earthlings than it would be one or two. If they're here, *if* they're here, Doctor, there are but a few."

I nodded, finding tolerant amusement in my aged friend's mental exercises. In fact, I was quite proud of him, especially at this time of the day. "That is plausible," I encouraged him.

"Why then," he muttered petulantly, "are they in London rather than elsewhere?"

I followed along with him, tolerantly. "But that is obvious. London is the largest city in the world. You might say, the capital of the world. If these extraterrestrials are investigating Earth and mankind, here would be the place to start."

He opened his eyes fully and snorted at me. "Your patriotism overshadows your ability to appreciate statistics, Doctor. In the first instance, London is no longer the largest city. Tokyo is, and even metropolitan New York exceeds our capital."

I began to sputter, I must admit, but he chortled what I can only describe as senile contempt of my opinions and went on. "And New York is the commercial center of the world and its largest port. Beyond that, it is Washington which has become the political center of the world. Damn Yankees."

I was miffed at his childish know-it-all attitude. "Very well, then, you answer the question. Why should they choose London, given the ridiculously fanciful idea that such creatures exist at all?"

"Only one reason, Doctor," he chortled, obviously inanely pleased with himself. "The British Museum."

"I admit I don't follow you," I said coldly.

His rheumy eyes were once more superior. "London may not

be the population leader, eh? Nor the political head. But if I were one of Sir Alexander's BEMs . . ."

"BEMs?" I said.

He chortled again, but went on. ". . . making a study of this planet, I would spend a good deal of time in the British Museum. It holds more data than any other museum or library. I submit that if there are aliens in London, investigating our customs and institutions, they are manifestly devoting considerable time to the British Museum."

He pushed himself to his feet, yawning sleepily. "And it is there, my dear Doctor, I shall begin my investigation tomorrow."

I suspected that by the morrow he would have forgotten the whole matter, but I humored him. "Then you plan to go through with this, to make the motions of investigating the presence of space aliens?"

"Eh? Indeed I do, Doctor." His tone was petulant. "Pray recall, I gave my pledge to Sir Alexander." He began toddling off toward his room, depending on his cane.

I said after him in exasperation, "Just what is a BEM?"

He cackled an inner, secret amusement. "A Bug Eyed Monster."

To my astonishment, I saw little of the once great detective in the next few days. In fact, such was his energy that I was prone to wonder, as I have had occasion to before, whether he had made a contact, as the Americanism has it, and found some pusher who was supplying him with a need that I had thought long since cured. Manifestly, however, he was taking his task seriously. Indeed, on two different occasions I found him leaving our rooms in disguise, once as an elderly woman, once as a professorial looking scholar. On both occasions he winked at me, but vouchsafed no explanation and no description of his supposed progress. I could but worry that my old friend, in the burden of his years, was in a fantasy of belief that this ridiculous affair was as serious as the adventures of a quarter of a century ago, and more, when his faculties were at their height.

On the fifth day, shortly after a breakfast at which he had encouraged no conversation pertinent to the case of Sir Alexander Norwood, but had sat trying to impress me by pretending to be in deep thought, he asked to borrow my exposure meter. This was a device I had acquired but recently, after having received a rather complicated German camera as a birthday gift from a near relative. I was a bit nervous about his absent-mindedly leaving the gadget somewhere, but couldn't find it in me to refuse the old duffer.

To my relief, he returned it that night and then, before maundering off to bed, requested that if in the morning I was able that I locate Alfred, the captain of his group of street gamins which he was amused to name his Baker Street Irregulars, and have him at our rooms by noon.

At that, I could but stare blankly at the door to his bedroom through which he had just passed.

Alfred, rest his soul, had fallen in His Majesty's service at Mons in 1915, and the balance of my friend's Irregulars had gone their way, largely to prison, if the truth be told.

My conscience now struck me. I had allowed my companion— my ward might be the better term—to become so overwrought in his belief that he was again working on a major case, that his mind had slipped over the edge of dotardism to the point where he was now living in a complete world of fantasy. Alfred indeed.

By morning I had resolved to make an ending of the whole affair, to bring matters to a head and to wind up insisting that my companion return to the sedentary existence that we had become resigned to before the appearance of Peter Norwood.

To accomplish this, I took me to the streets, in the late morning, and accosted the first ten- or eleven-year old I spied. He was a ragged, wise looking chap, his voice considerably more raucous even than that of his ragamuffin companions. If the truth be known, and if my memory served me correctly, he somewhat resembled the Alfred of long ago, who had, in his time, played on these very same streets.

I said, "See here, young fellow, would you like to make half a crown?"

He looked at me for a long, calculating minute. "Doing *wot?*" he said, his tone implying, *I've 'eard about your type gent, I 'ave.*

I refrained from giving him the back of my hand and explained what I had in mind, and after jacking up the price to three shillings he agreed.

So it was that when the retired detective appeared at noon, swinging his cane, rather than hobbling upon it, he bid me a cheery afternoon and clapped the boy on the back. He looked every bit as though he had shed twenty years in the excitement of his endeavors, and came immediately to the point.

"Alfred," he said, "do you think you might find three or four other boys for an assignment this afternoon?"

The lad had been standing, his arms akimbo, his bright eyes flashing, before the other. Now he touched his cap and said, "I thinks so, sir. Right away, sir?"

"Right away, Alfred. Scamper now."

Manifestly, I was taken aback. "Just a minute!" I rapped, thinking to spring my trap. I turned accusingly to the companion of my declining years. "See here, just who do you think this young chap is?"

The former detective blinked his rheumy eyes, as though it were I who had slipped over the precipice of puerility. "Why, it's Alfred. Surely, my good Doctor, you must remember his grandfather who was so often of service to us in the old days. We have managed to become friends during my morning strolls along the street."

I closed my eyes and counted slowly. When I reopened them, the boy was gone in a rattle of shoes upon the stairs.

"And how," I asked, perhaps testily, "goes the investigation of the men from Mars?"

He had sunk wearily into his chair. Some of his elan of but a moment ago dropped away and I could see him working his slack mouth. However, his thin eyebrows raised and he asked, "Why do you think them from Mars, Doctor, eh?"

His matter-of-fact inquiry unsettled me. "Really," I said. "I was but jesting, you know."

"Oh." He mumbled something, in his old manner, and closed his eyes and I assumed his morning exertions had exhausted him to the point of putting him a-napping.

So, though burning with curiosity, I sat down in my own chair and took up a medical digest I had been perusing.

However, he was not asleep. Without opening his eyes he said in what I can only call the blathering tone I had become used to in the past few years, "Doctor, do you realize how blasted difficult an alien, far in advance of our own science, could make it to detect him, eh? How blasted difficult?"

"I rather fancy he could," I agreed, encouraging him in a way simply to find out what in the world he had been up to, but at the same time still a bit peeved over the Alfred misunderstanding.

"One chink in the armor," he prattled. "One chink in the armor, eh?"

"A chink?" I said.

He opened his eyes, as though accusingly. "Gadgetry, Doctor. Couldn't keep him using his gadgetry." He closed his eyes and chuckled.

I was exasperated, I must admit. "I am not sure I follow you," I said coldly.

This time he didn't bother to raise his lids. "Simple deduction, Doctor. Suppose he is making records of some of the books and manuscripts, eh? In the library section of the British Museum. And to use a camera of our culture, he must carry heavy volumes a distance in order to get sufficient light. He would be tempted, sorely tempted, to use a camera or some device, of his own culture. One that would photograph in an impossibly poor light."

"Good heavens," I ejaculated. "You borrowed my light meter this morning!"

He chortled his senile pose of superiority for a moment, then nodded with an irritating air of accomplishment. "Doctor, there is a . . . ah . . . person daily appearing at the library. According to your light meter, and according to the most advanced works I could find on photography, there is no lens or film of such speed now manufactured that could take such photos in the light he was using."

Before I could assimilate his words, there was a rush and a clatter on the stairs coupled with our good landlady's indignantly raised voice; the door was thrown open without ceremony and young Alfred burst into the room followed pell-mell by a trio of grinning urchins.

"Here we are, sir," cried Alfred, closing the door and marching up to my friend, followed by his companions.

"So I see," the aged detective wheezed. "Mystery to me how you can manage to act so quickly." He fumbled forth four florins from his pocket. "These shall be yours for what should be a simple task for such active young men." He cackled as though he had made a humorous sally. "I want you to follow a rather elusive chap from the British Museum to his lodgings."

The old gaffer's rheumy eyes almost gleamed. He chortled, "I am sure you will. And where the most cautious persons might suspect an adult who is going to keep a suspicious eye on a shouting, playing lad?" He chuckled to himself again so that I suspected he had lost his train of thought, but then he said, "And now, lads, let us be off to assume a strategic point near the museum entrance."

"I don't suppose," I said, possibly a trifle wistfully, "that you need further assistance?" Could it be that, caught up in the excitement, I was reacting like an old fire horse?

However, he said, "Not today, Doctor, not today. Afraid your arthritic joints are not quite up to the pace today." His voice trailed off into utterly indistinct drivel, even as he left the door, and the last I made out was something pertaining to yogurt.

I stared after him in some indignation, but they were gone, the boys' feet clattering down the stairs.

I heard no more of the case for three days, and then, suddenly, it came to a head, though not exactly to a conclusion. If there can be said to be a conclusion at all.

We were seated early in the evening in our usual places, I with book in hand, my ex-detective friend tinkering with his .455 Webley, a weapon with which he was once remarkably accurate but which of recent years has caused me to wince each time he handles it. One of these days, I am going to throw away his supply of shells.

"Ah," he muttered finally, "our friend Peter Norwood is here for his report." I must admit that his newfangled hearing device is effective; with it his ears are considerably better than my own.

Even as he spoke, I could hear a knock at the door and faintly our landlady's voice. In moments there was another knock, this time at our own door.

I opened and welcomed the young man in, for indeed it was he. Peter Norwood's face was slightly flushed, undoubtedly from a surfeit of good food and rare vintages, for it was shortly after the regular supper hour.

He looked at us, the wine preventing him from disguising a somewhat belligerent attitude. "How long is this to take?" he demanded. "How long does it take to cook up a reasonable story for the old boy?"

The former detective did not arise from his chair. He said, mildly I thought, "I sent my report to your father this morning, Mr. Norwood." Which was lucid enough, but then he chuckled under his breath in what I can only describe as inane fashion.

"Ah?" Norwood blinked at him, momentarily taken aback. "Well," he said, reaching for a pocket, "I suppose then there is nothing more than to pay you off." There was a contemptuous undertone in his words.

"Unnecessary. No fee. I am retired, young fellow. No longer dependent upon my profession." He waggled a bent finger at the other. "But if there had been, I should have submitted my bill to Sir Alexander. It was his commission, eh?"

Peter Norwood scowled his incomprehension. Evidently, he began to smell a rat for his eyes narrowed and he growled, "What did you report, sir? Though I warn you, it will make no difference."

My aged friend fumbled through his pockets petulantly, finally coming up with a badly wrinkled carbon copy of a letter which he had obviously laboriously pounded out upon my typewriter. He handed it to me, obviously to be read aloud.

This was the first I knew of it; however, I read.

My dear Sir Alexander: This will convey to you my belief that your interest is well founded, and that your hobby, that of investigating the possibility of the existence of life forms on other planets and/or in other star systems, is an intelligent one. I have uncovered sufficient data to indicate further investigation by yourself and the group with which you are affiliated would not be amiss.

He had signed it very normally. Frankly, I had no idea he was capable of composing so coherent a letter, no matter how puerile the content.

Peter Norwood was glaring at him. He stuttered, "I . . . I

suppose you think you have thwarted me by this . . . this piece of lying nonsense?"

My friend chuckled his affirmation, obviously as pleased as punch with himself.

"You realize, you old fool," the young man snapped, "that no court in the land would fail to commit my . . ."

But the other was wagging an age-bent finger at him, his watery eyes still capable of a dim spark of fire. "It will never come to court, young fellow. Eh? This case has taken a full week of my time. I didn't spend it all in chasing elusive extraterrestrials. I warn you, young man. I warn you that if Sir Alexander is brought before the courts in an attempt on your part to secure management of his affairs, I shall reveal your own secret."

And with that he leered in a most senile fashion.

He could not have been more effective had he struck the other across the face. Peter Norwood staggered back, obviously deeply distressed. His flushed features went pale.

The former detective chortled. "Yes, yes. My time was not wasted. I have no intention of making a report on the subject to your father, eh. Nor to, shall we say, others who might be concerned. I bid you to take heed"—he leered again, the obscene leer of an old man beyond vice himself—"and now, to take your leave." His voice dribbled off into a chuckle again, as though in thinking of young Norwood's secret.

Without another word the young man staggered from our rooms.

"Confound it," I blurted. "This whole thing escapes me. I am in the dark. What sort of secret of that bounder's were you able to ferret out?"

He wheezed his inane laugh, until I began to suspect all over again complete dotardism, but finally he chortled, "Come now, my dear Doctor. We have here a young whelp obviously the victim of his sensual vices, eh? In spite of what must be a considerable allowance in view of his big cars and his fine clothing." And then with a return to the terminology of yesteryear, "You know my methods. Utilize them." He began his idiotic chuckling again.

"You mean . . ."

"I mean I haven't the slightest idea what the young hound's

secret might be. Gambling, a young woman, or whatever. But I would wager that there *is* such a secret, or more than one."

I chuckled myself, seeing the humor of the situation. "But my dear fellow, that report you submitted to Sir Alexander. Do you think it well to encourage him in his delusions?"

He had found his pipe and now loaded it, probably, in his childish cunning, thinking that in the discussion I would fail to notice his smoking at this late hour. "I submit, Doctor," he prattled, "in the first instance it is a harmless hobby that will fill the hours for an old man whose mind is still keen."

"And in the second instance?" I prompted.

"Ah. In the second instance, the report was in good faith." He chuckled again, vaguely, and for a moment I thought he had lost the thread, but it came back to him.

"I assume you have deduced from my activities that I located an individual at the museum who was making an extensive collection of photographs, eh? Photos of periodicals, books, pamphlets."

I nodded encouragingly.

"Well," he babbled, "with the assistance of my Baker Street Irregulars I was able to trace him to his rooms." He watched me slyly from the side of his eyes. "Eventually, I was even able to search them. Eh?"

I leaned forward, my interest manifest. "And what did you find?"

"Nothing."

"Nothing? *You*, the outstanding sleuth of our era, found nothing?"

He had lit his pipe and now waggled the extinguished match at me. "Negative assistance, Doctor. Negative evidence, but not without value. The man's—I use the term with reservations, eh?—the *man's* apartment was devoid of any records, personal effects, or anything whatsoever which might give a clue to his identity."

"A spy!" I blurted.

He wheezed his disgust at my opinion. "A spy for whom, eh? Anyway it was too late. Our bird had flown."

"A spy for some foreign power . . ."

He chuckled. "Very foreign indeed."

". . . Some power such as Russia, or Germany. Possibly France or the United States. Each nation has its quota of agents."

His rheumy eyes held an expression of contempt. "I submit, Doctor, that none of the nations you name need sneak into the British Museum for such information as is there. It is open to the public, which includes the members of the diplomatic corps of these countries."

Had the matter ended here and without further development, I must be truthful with my readers, it is unlikely that I should have recorded this last of the famed sleuth's adventures. For I had come increasingly of the opinion that he had slipped irrevocably over the edge of the precipice of senility, and it was painful enough to report these activities of a once great mind. However, the postscript of the whole matter is such that I am left admittedly unsatisfied and pass on to other followers of the career of the world's most immortal detective the bare facts, without final conclusion.

For it was but the night following the above mentioned conversation that a knock came upon the door. There had been no preliminary ringing of the bell, no sounds of our landlady answering the door below. Nothing save the knock.

My friend scowled, fiddled with his hearing device petulantly, his once hawklike face in puzzlement such as he seldom admitted to. He muttered something under his breath, even as I answered the summons.

The man at our threshold was possibly thirty-five years of age, impeccably dressed, and bore himself with an air of confidence all but condescending. Perhaps still miffed at my unsatisfactory conversation with the aged sleuth the night before, I said snappishly, "Yes, my good man?"

The other said, "My business, sir, is with . . ."

"Heh!" the aged detective cackled. "Señor Mercado-Mendez. Or should I say, Herr Doktor Bechstein? Or, still again, Mr. James Phillimore? So, we meet again, eh? How long has it been since our confrontation on the cutter *Alicia?*"

To say I was startled would be understatement. I have recorded, long since, the mysterious episode of the *Alicia* which sailed one spring morning into a small patch of mist from where she never again emerged, nor was anything further heard of herself and the crew. One of the few adventures of my detective friend, while still in his prime, which he had failed to solve. Nor could I have failed to place the name Phillimore, who, long years since, had stepped back into his own house to get his umbrella and was never more seen in this world. Another adventure never solved.

But, as I have said, our newcomer was at most in his mid-thirties and the two cases I mention took place during the Boer War, when the other could have been but a child.

However, he bowed and, ignoring me, addressed my companion, though never stepping within the limits of our rooms.

"Congratulations, sir. I did not expect recognition or would have taken precautions."

The aged detective grunted. "Precious good they would have done you, eh? I never close a case, señor. Even that of Isadore Persano still rankles me."

And once again it came back to me. The third adventure never solved by the greatest brain ever to concentrate upon the science of criminal detection. Isadore Persano, the well-known journalist and duelist, who was found stark raving mad with a matchbox in front of him which contained a remarkable worm said to be unknown to science.

And now I could but note that Señor Mercado-Mendez, if that was his name, stood in the shadows for good cause. His visage was such as to be that of a poorly embalmed corpse, waxlike in complexion so that I wondered if it could be a mask. Only the unnatural sharpness of his eyes indicated his face lived.

He bowed again. "In the past, sir, it has not been necessary to contact you directly, though on the several occasions you mention you came dangerously near stumbling upon information not meant for you—nor anyone else."

There came a tension in the air, and the mouth of my old friend worked. "I deduce, Señor Mercado-Mendez, that you are not of this world."

I would have expected that bit of drivel to have been enough to send anyone off, without further discussion, but our newcomer merely stared for long moments, as though considering the old duffer's words.

Finally, still ignoring me, he said, "I have come to warn you, sir, that the Galactic Council cannot permit you to continue interfering with legitimate student research conducted with all care not to upset the internal affairs of your, shall we say, somewhat unique culture."

Obviously, the man was as mentally incompetent as was my friend, who could at least claim the infirmity of age. I began to take issue. However, he turned but briefly and his eyes gleamed warning as a cobra's eyes gleam warning, and I grew still again.

The once great detective shifted in his chair, petulantly. "So far as I am concerned, the case was closed. However, I cannot speak for Sir Alexander and the World Defense Society."

There was a glint of amusement in the other's startling eyes. "We will not worry about Sir Alexander's group, sir. We have had our Sir Alexanders before." There returned the element of condescension to the stranger's voice. "Nor need you worry about preserving the integrity of your planet. Your desire in that direction is as nothing compared to that of the Galactic Council's Bureau of Archaeology and Ethnology, Department of Research in Living Primitive Cultures."

There was a long moment of silence and when my friend spoke again there was a slow care in his voice which brought me to memories of long years before, when the famed sleuth was feeling his way to the solution of a problem beyond the ken of ordinary minds.

"I deduce further," he said, "that your own position is similar to that of a police official . . . perhaps guardian were the better term."

The other made a very human shrug, twisted his mouth wryly, and bowed. His eyes came again to me and I had the impression of being quickly weighed and rejected as an element to be considered in this nonsensical verbal duel. He said agreeably, "The Council is desirous of protecting such planets as your own; admittedly there are elements who would exploit your culture, in its infancy. I am the Council's servant."

Perhaps it was that the aged detective was growing weary of the condescension in the other's tone. He took on a snappish quality. "I begin to suspect, Señor Mercado-Mendez, the solution to many of the great unsolved crimes of the world. The disappearance, for example, of the Great Mogul diamond, eh? The spiriting away of the Aztec treasure following the *noche triste* of Hernando Cortés. The theft of the sarcophagus of Alexander the Macedonian, eh? The unbelievable tomb robberies of the Pharaohs. The . . ."

Had the stranger's face been capable of a flush, it was manifest that one would have appeared at this point. He held up a hand to quell the cataloguing. "Admittedly, the best of guardians can sometimes fail."

The great detective's face sharpened in such wise that I knew, from long past experience, that he had arrived at a conclusion satisfactory to him. I snorted inwardly. He was having his delusions again.

He said, his voice resisting wavering, "I submit the following. In this world today, the nations are deep in international intrigue, war threatens, and all prepare. Major nations send agents to every continent. Is it not manifest, señor, that a British undercover operative masquerading as an Arab would have immense difficulty detecting a first-rate German undercover agent masquerading as an Arab in the same town? But an Arab native would be much better equipped to detect the slight flaws in the German's disguise, eh?"

All of which was obviously beside what little point there had seemed to be in the conversation before, so far as I could see, and I had about decided to suggest to the newcomer that he was trying the strength of my companion with all this claptrap, and that it might be well for him to be on his way.

However, Señor Mercado-Mendez, if that was truly his name, seemed to find meaning where I had not. His tone had now lost the amused tolerance of his earlier words. He said, "You suggest . . ."

The aged detective nodded as he relit his pipe. "Manifestly."

The other was quietly thoughtful. "In what capacity would you expect to act?"

"Heh," my companion snorted. "As you should well know, my following has been that of a consulting detective, señor. And my fees, I might add, not minimal."

From whence the old codger was drawing his resources I shall never know, though I will admit that by this time my own were giving out to the point that my bed's attractions were wooing me. I said, "Hasn't there been quite enough of this drivel? Neither of you makes sense to me. If I gather anything at all, it is that my octogenarian, ah, patient is offering himself as an employee. I submit . . ." But they were ignoring me.

There was condescension again in the younger one's tone. "Fifty years ago, sir, perhaps your offer would have had its elements."

The once great sleuth lifted an age-bent hand and waggled it negatively. "Señor, I need hardly point out the manifest answer to that." He cackled his inane amusement. "Your own appearance after all these years is ample indication that your people have, shall we say, discovered what Friar Roger Bacon once named the *Elixir Vitae.*"

There was a lengthy silence. Finally, "I see. And you are correct; your fees, sir, are far from minimal. However, it is not the practice of the Galactic Council to interfere with the natural progress of primitive planets by introduction of medical techniques beyond . . ."

The bent hand was waggling negatively again.

I suppressed a yawn. Was this to go on forever? What in the world were they getting at?

My friend said, "Obviously, Señor Mercado-Mendez, all rules must have their exceptions. If your council's work is to be successful, you need a"—his chuckle had the inane quality to which I object—"shall we say, aborigine, agent on your staff. Come, señor, you know my abilities, my methods."

The strange visitor seemed to have reached some decision. "It is not for me to decide. Can you come to consult my immediate superiors?"

To my admitted amazement, the retired sleuth banged the arm of his chair and wavered to his feet. "Immediately, señor," he cackled.

"Now see here," I protested. "This has gone much too far. I cannot permit my . . . my *charge* to be taken out at this hour, after a full week overladen with activity. I say . . ."

"Hush up, Doctor," the old codger muttered, on his way for muffler and coat. "Charge indeed."

Weary as I was, I resolved on firmness. "I warn you, I shall no longer put up with all this balderdash. If you insist upon wandering out into the night, at your age, I submit that I have no intention of assisting you. I shall remain right here."

He grunted puerile amusement, managed to get into his things without assistance, and turned to our strange visitor. "Let us be on our way, señor."

Admittedly, I stared after them in my amazement for long moments after they were gone. Perhaps it was my own weariness, but I must confess being unable to detect the sound of their passage down the stairs and out the front door. But then, as I have reported, my hearing is not what it once was.

In the morning he had not returned, nor the next.

I could not but recall long decades before when he had vanished from my ken for some years. But the difference is manifest. An octogenarian does not roam about the streets of London with no companion other than a driveling madman who prates about being the representative of a galactic council, or whatever he called it.

Debating whether to call the police, and hesitating in view of my old friend's reputation—long years ago he was dubbed the immortal detective—there came back to me some of his words that I had not understood at the time. Perhaps there was a slight clue there.

I went to the encyclopedia and looked up Friar Roger Bacon and the term *Elixir Vitae*.

Friar Roger Bacon, 13th century alchemist and metaphysician. One of the most prominent of those who sought the elixir of life which would grant immortality, and the philosopher's stone to transmute base metals into gold.

I grunted and returned the volume to its place. Nothing there but more nonsense of the type they had prattled back and forth to each other two nights earlier.

But still I refrain from phoning the authorities.

Back to me, down through the years, come the words I have heard a score of times over. *When you have eliminated the impossible, whatever remains, however improbable, must be the truth.*

And back to me also continue to come the very last words my friend chortled at me as he left our rooms with the mysterious Señor Mercado-Mendez.

"Yogurt, heh, heh."

A Scarletin Study

by

Philip José Farmer

(writing as Jonathan Swift Sommers III)

There's no reason why the Sherlock Holmes spirit ought to be restricted to Homo sapiens. Anyone who has seen pictures in which Rin Tin Tin or Lassie were featured knows very well that dogs are more intelligent than humans beings. Well, then—

A Scarletin Study

by Jonathan Swift Somers III
(Philip José Farmer)

BEING A REPRINT FROM THE REMINISCENCES OF
JOHANN H. WEISSTEIN, DR. MED., LATE OF THE AUTO-
BAHN PATROL MEDICAL DEPARTMENT.

Foreword

Ralph von Wau Wau's first case as a private investigator is not his
most complicated or curious. It does, however, illustrate remarkably well my colleague's peculiar talents. And it is, after all, his
first case, and one should proceed chronologically in these
chronicles. It is also the only case I know of in which not the
painting but the painter was stolen. And it is, to me, most
memorable because through it I met the woman who will always
be for me *the woman.*

Consider this scene. Von Wau Wau; his enemy, Detective-
Lieutenant Strasse; myself; and the lovely Lisa Scarletin, all
standing before a large painting in a room in a Hamburg police
station. Von Wau Wau studies the painting while we wonder if

189

he's right in his contention that it is not only a work of art but a map. Its canvas bears, among other things, the images of Sherlock Holmes in lederhosen, Sir Francis Bacon, a green horse, a mirror, Christ coming from the tomb, Tarzan, a waistcoat, the Wizard of Oz in a balloon, an ancient king of Babylon with a dietary problem, and a banana tree.

But let me begin at the beginning.

Chapter I
HERR RALPH VON WAU WAU

In the year 1978 I took my degree of Doctor of Medicine of the University of Cologne and proceeded to Hamburg to go through the course prescribed for surgeons in the Autobahn Patrol. Having completed my studies there, I was duly attached to the Fifth North-Rhine Westphalia Anti-Oiljackers as assistant surgeon. The campaign against the notorious Rottenfranzer Gang brought honors and promotions to many, but for me it was nothing but misfortune and disaster. At the fatal battle of the Emmerich Off-Ramp, I was struck on the shoulder by a missile which shattered the bone. I should have fallen into the hands of the murderous Rottenfranzer himself but for the devotion and courage shown by Morgen, my paramedic aide, who threw me across a Volkswagen and succeeded in driving safely across the Patrol lines.

At the base hospital at Hamburg (and it really is base), I seemed on the road to recovery when I was struck down with an extremely rare malady. At least, I have read of only one case similar to mine. This was, peculiarly, the affliction of another doctor, though he was an Englishman and suffered his wounds a hundred years before on another continent. My case was written up in medical journals and then in general periodicals all over the world. The affliction itself became known popularly as "the peregrinating pain," though the scientific name, which I prefer for understandable reasons, was "Weisstein's Syndrome." The popular name arose from the fact that the occasional suffering it caused me did not remain at the site of the original wound. At times, the pain traveled downward and lodged in my leg. This was a cause célèbre, scientifically speaking, nor was the mystery solved until some years later. (In *The Wonder of the Wandering Wound,* not yet published.)

However, I rallied and had improved enough to be able to walk or limp about the wards, and even to bask a little on the veranda when smog or fog permitted, when I was struck down by *Weltschmerz,* that curse of Central Europe. For months my mind was despaired of, and when at last I came to myself, six months had passed. With my health perhaps not irretrievably ruined, but all ability to wield the knife as a surgeon vanished, I was discharged by a paternal government with permission to spend the rest of my life improving it. (The health, not the life, I mean.) I had neither kith nor kin nor kinder and was therefore as free as the air, which, given my small social security and disability pension, seemed to be what I was expected to eat. Within a few months the state of my finances had become so alarming that I was forced to completely alter my life style. I decided to look around for some considerably less pretentious and expensive domicile than the Hamburg Hilton.

On the very day I'd come to this conclusion, I was standing at the Kennzeichen Bar when someone tapped me on the shoulder. Wincing (it was the wounded shoulder), I turned around. I recognized young blonde Stampfert, who had been an anesthetist under me at the Neustadt Hospital. (I've had a broad experience of women in many nations and on three continents, so much so in fact that I'd considered entering gynecology.) Stampfert had a beautiful body but a drab personality. I was lonely, however, and I hailed her enthusiastically. She, in turn, seemed glad to see me, I suppose because she wanted to flaunt her newly acquired engagement ring. The first thing I knew, I had invited her to lunch. We took the bus to the Neu Bornholt, and on the way I outlined my adventures of the past year.

"Poor devil!" she said. "So what's happening now?"

"Looking for a cheap apartment," I said. "But I doubt that it's possible to get a decent place at a reasonable rate. The housing shortage and its partner, inflation, will be with us for a long time."

"That's a funny thing," Stampfert said. "You're the second . . . person . . . today who has said almost those exact words."

"And who was the first?"

"Someone who's just started a new professional career," Stampfert said. "He's having a hard go of it just now. He's looking for a roommate to share not only expenses but a partnership. Someone who's experienced in police work. You seem to fit the bill. The only thing is . . ."

She hesitated, and I said, "If he's easy to get along with, I'd be delighted to share the expenses with him. And work is something I need badly."

"Well, there's more to it than that, though he is easy to get along with. Lovable, in fact."

She hesitated, then said, "Are you allergic to animals?"

I stared at her and said, "Not at all. Why, does this man have pets?"

"Not exactly," Stampfert said, looking rather strange.

"Well, then, what is it?"

"There is a dog," she said. "A highly intelligent . . . police dog."

"Don't tell me this fellow is blind?" I said. "Not that it will matter, of course."

"Just color blind," she said. "His name is Ralph."

"Yes, go on," I said. "What about Herr Ralph?"

"That's his first name," Stampfert said. "His full name is Ralph von Wau Wau."

"What?" I said, and then I guffawed. "A man whose last name is a dog's bark?" (In Germany "wau wau"—pronounced vau vau—corresponds to the English "bow wow.")

Suddenly, I said, "Ach!" I had just remembered where I had heard, or rather read, of von Wau Wau.

"What you're saying," I said slowly, "is that the dog is also the fellow who wants to share the apartment and is looking for a partner?"

Stampfert nodded.

Chapter II
THE SCIENCE OF ODOROLOGY

And so, fifteen minutes later, we entered the apartment building at 12 Bellener Street and took the elevator to the second story.

Stampfert rang the bell at 2K, and a moment later the door swung in. This operation had been effected by an electrical motor controlled by an on-off button on a control panel set on the floor in a corner. This, it was obvious, had been pressed by the paw of the dog now trotting toward us. He was the largest police dog I've ever seen, weighing approximately one hundred and sixty pounds. He had keen eyes which were the deep lucid brown of a bottle of maple syrup at times and at other times the opaque rich brown of a frankfurter. His face was black, and his back bore a black saddlemark.

"Herr Doktor Weisstein, Herr Ralph von Wau Wau," said Stampfert.

He grinned, or at least opened his jaws, to reveal some very long and sharp teeth.

"Come in, please, and make yourself at home," he said.

Though I'd been warned, I was startled. His mouth did not move while the words came from his throat. The words were excellent standard High German. But the voice was that of a long-dead American movie actor.

Humphrey Bogart's, to be exact.

I would have picked Basil Rathbone's, but *de gustibus non est disputandum*. Especially someone with teeth like Ralph's. There was no mystery or magic about the voice, though the effect, even to the prepared, was weird. The voice, like his high intelligence, was a triumph of German science. A dog (or any animal) lacks the mouth structure and vocal cords to reproduce human sounds intelligibly. This deficiency had been overcome by implanting a small nuclear-powered voder in Ralph's throat. This was connected by an artificial-protein neural complex to the speech center of the dog's brain. Before he could activate the voder, Ralph had to think of three code words. This was necessary, since otherwise he would be speaking whenever he thought in verbal terms. Inflection of the spoken words was automatic, responding to the emotional tone of Ralph's thoughts.

"What about pouring us a drink, sweetheart?" he said to Stampfert. "Park it there, buddy," he said to me, indicating with a paw a large and comfortable easy chair. I did so, unsure whether or not I should resent his familiarity. I decided not to do so. After all, what could, or should, one expect from a dog who has by his own admission seen *The Maltese Falcon* forty-nine times? Of course, I found this out later, just as I discovered later that his manner of address varied bewilderingly, often in the middle of a sentence.

Stampfert prepared the drinks at a well-stocked bar in the corner of the rather large living room. She made herself a tequila with lemon and salt, gave me the requested double Duggan's Dew o' Kirkintilloch on the rocks, and poured out three shots of King's Ransom Scotch in a rock-crystal saucer on the floor. The dog began lapping it; then seeing me raise my eyebrows, he said, "I'm a private eye, Doc. It's in the best tradition that P.I.'s drink. I always try to follow human traditions—when it pleases me. And if my drinking from a saucer offends you, I *can* hold a glass between my paws. But why the hell should I?"

"No reason at all," I said hastily.

He ceased drinking and jumped up onto a sofa, where he sat down facing us. "You two have been drinking at the Kennzeichen," he said. "You are old customers there. And then, later, you had lunch at the Neu Bornholt. Doctor Stampfert said you were coming in the taxi, but you changed your mind and took the bus."

There was a silence which lasted until I understood that I was supposed to comment on this. I could only say, "Well?"

"The babe didn't tell me any of this," Ralph said somewhat testily. "I was just demonstrating something that a mere human being could not have known."

"Mere?" I said just as testily.

Ralph shrugged, which was quite an accomplishment when one considers that dogs don't really have shoulders.

"Sorry, Doc. Don't get your bowels in an uproar. No offense."

"Very well," I said. "How did you know all this?"

And now that I came to think about it, I did wonder how he knew.

"The Kennzeichen is the only restaurant in town which gives a stein of Lowenbrau to each habitue as he enters the bar," von Wau Wau said. "You two obviously prefer other drinks, but you could not turn down the free drink. If you had not been at the Kennzeichen, I would not have smelled Lowenbrau on your breath. You then went to the Neu Bornholt for lunch. It serves a salad with its house dressing, the peculiar ingredients of which I detected with my sense of smell. This, as you know, is a million times keener than a human's. If you had come in a taxi, as the dame said you meant to do, you would be stinking much more strongly of kerosene. Your clothes and hair have absorbed a certain amount of that from being on the streets, of course, along with the high-sulfur coal now burned in many automobiles. But I deduce—olfactorily—that you took instead one of the electrically operated, fuel-celled, relatively odorless buses. Am I correct?"

"I would have said that it was amazing, but of course your nose makes it easy for you," I said.

"An extremely distinguished colleague of mine," Ralph said, "undoubtedly the most distinguished, once said that it is the first quality of a criminal investigator to see through a disguise. I would modify that to the *second* quality. The first is that he should smell through a disguise."

Though he seemed somewhat nettled, he became more genial after a few more laps from the saucer. So did I after a few more sips from my glass. He even gave me permission to smoke, provided that I did it under a special vent placed over my easy chair.

"Cuban make," he said, sniffing after I had lit up. *"La Roja Paloma de la Revolucion."*

"Now that is astounding!" I said. I was also astounded to find Stampfert on my lap.

"It's nothing," he said. "I started to write a trifling little monograph on the subtle distinctions among cigar odors, but I realized that it would make a massive textbook before I was finished. And who could use it?"

"What are you doing here?" I said to Stampfert. "This is business. I don't want to give Herr von Wau Wau the wrong impression."

"You didn't used to mind," she said, giggling. "But I'm here because I want to smoke, too, and this is the only vent he has, and he told me not to smoke unless I sat under it."

Under the circumstances, it was not easy to carry on a coherent conversation with the dog, but we managed. I told him that I had read something of his life. I knew that his parents had been the property of the Hamburg Police Department. He was one of a litter of eight, all mutated to some degree since they and their parents had been subjected to scientific experiments. These had been conducted by the biologists of *das Institut und die Tankstelle fur Gehirntaschenspielerei*. But his high intelligence was the result of biosurgery. Although his brain was no larger than it should have been for a dog his size, its complexity was comparable to that of a human's. The scientists had used artificial protein to make billions of new nerve circuits in his cerebrum. This had been done, however, at the expense of his cerebellum or hindbrain. As a result, he had very little subconscious and hence could not dream.

As everybody now knows, failure to dream results in a progressive psychosis and eventual mental breakdown. To rectify this, Ralph created dreams during the day, recorded them audiovisually, and fed them into his brain at night. I don't have space to go into this in detail in this narrative, but a full description will be found in *The Case of the Stolen Dreams*. (Not yet published.)

When Ralph was still a young pup, an explosion had wrecked the Institute and killed his siblings and the scientists responsible for his sapiency. Ralph was taken over again by the Police Department and sent to school. He attended obedience school and the other courses requisite for a trained *Schutzhund* canine. But he was the only pup who also attended classes in reading, writing, and arithmetic.

Ralph was now twenty-eight years old but looked five. Some attributed this anomaly to the mutation experiments. Others claimed that the scientists had perfected an age-delaying elixir which had been administered to Ralph and his siblings. If the explosion had not destroyed the records, the world might now have the elixir at its disposal. (More of this in *A Short Case of Longevity,* n.y.p.)

Ralph's existence had been hidden for many years from all except a few policemen and officials sworn to silence. It was believed that publicity would reduce his effectiveness in his detective work. But recently the case had come to the attention of the public because of Ralph's own doing. Fed up with being a mere police dog, proud and ambitious, he had resigned to become a private investigator. His application for a license had, of course, resulted in an uproar. Mass mediapersons had descended on Hamburg in droves, herds, coveys, and gaggles. There was in fact litigation against him in the courts, but pending the result of this, Ralph von Wau Wau was proceeding as if he were a free agent. (For the conclusion of this famous case, see *The Caper of Kupper, the Copper's Keeper,* n.y.p.)

But whether or not he was the property of the police department, he was still very dependent upon human beings. Hence, his search for a roommate and a partner.

I told him something about myself. He listened quietly and then said, "I like your odor, buddy. It's an honest one and uncondescending. I'd like you to come in with me."

"I'd be delighted," I said. "But there is only one bedroom . . ."

"All yours," he said. "My tastes are Spartan. Or perhaps I should say canine. The other bedroom has been converted to a laboratory, as you have observed. But I sleep in it on a pile of blankets under a table. You may have all the privacy you need, bring all the women you want, as long as you're not noisy about it. I think we should get one thing straight though. I'm the senior partner here. If that offends your human chauvinism, then we'll call it quits before we start, amigo."

"I forsee no cause for friction," I replied, and I stood up to walk over to Ralph to shake hands. Unfortunately, I had forgotten that Stampfert was still on my lap. She thumped into the floor on her buttocks and yelled with pain and indignation. It was, I admit, stupid—well, at least an unwise, action. Stampfert, cursing, headed toward the door. Ralph looked at my outstretched hand and said, "Get this straight, mac. I never shake hands or sit up and beg."

I dropped my hand and said, "Of course."

The door opened. I turned to see Stampfert, still rubbing her fanny, going out the door.

"Auf Wiedersehen," I said.

"Not if I can help it, you jerk," she said.

"She always did take offense too easily," I said to Ralph.

I left a few minutes later to pick up my belongings from the hotel. When I re-entered his door with my suitcases in hand, I suddenly stopped. Ralph was sitting on the sofa, his eyes bright, his huge red tongue hanging out, and his breath coming in deep happy pants. Across from him sat one of the loveliest women I have ever seen. Evidently she had done something to change his mood because his manner of address was now quite different.

"Come in, my dear Weisstein," he said. "Your first case as my colleague is about to begin."

Chapter III
THE STATEMENT
OF THE CASE

An optimist is one who ignores, or forgets, experience. I am an optimist. Which is another way of saying that I fell in love with Lisa Scarletin at once. As I stared at this striking yet petite woman with the curly chestnut hair and great lustrous brown eyes, I completely forgot that I was still holding the two heavy suitcases. Not until after we had been introduced, and she looked down amusedly, did I realize what a foolish figure I made. Red-faced, I eased them down and took her dainty hand in mine. As I kissed it, I smelled the subtle fragrance of a particularly delightful—and, I must confess, aphrodisiacal—perfume.

"No doubt you have read, or seen on TV, reports of Mrs. Scarletin's missing husband?" my partner said. "Even if you do not know of his disappearance, you surely have heard of such a famous artist?"

"My knowledge of art is not nil," I said coldly. The tone of my voice reflected my inward coldness, the dying glow of delight on first seeing her. So, she was married! I should have known on seeing her ring. But I had been too overcome for it to make an immediate impression.

Alfred Scarletin, as my reader must surely know, was a wealthy painter who had become very famous in the past decade. Personally, I consider the works of the so-called Fauve Mauve school to be outrageous nonsense, a thumbing of the nose at commonsense. I would sooner have the originals of the *Katzenjammer Kids* comic strip hung up in the museum than any of the maniac creations of Scarletin and his kind. But, whatever his failure of artistic taste, he certainly possessed a true eye for women. He had married the beautiful Lisa Maria Mohrstein only three years ago. And now there was speculation that she might be a widow.

At which thought, the warm glow returned.

A. Scarletin, as I remembered, had gone for a walk on a May evening two months ago and had failed to return home. At first, it was feared that he had been kidnapped. But, when no ransom was demanded, that theory was discarded.

When I had told Ralph what I knew of the case, he nodded.

"As of last night there has been a new development in the case," he said. "And Mrs. Scarletin has come to me because she is extremely dissatisfied with the progress—lack of it, rather— that the police have made. Mrs. Scarletin, please tell Doctor Weisstein what you have told me."

She fixed her bright but deep brown eyes upon me and in a voice as lovely as her eyes—not to mention her figure—sketched in the events of yesterday. Ralph, I noticed, sat with his head cocked and his ears pricked up. I did not know it then, but he had asked her to repeat the story because he wanted to listen to her inflections again. He could detect subtle tones that would escape the less sensitive ears of humans. As he was often to say, "I cannot only *smell* hidden emotions, my dear Weisstein, I can also *hear* them."

"At about seven last evening, as I was getting ready to go out . . ." she said.

With whom? I thought, feeling jealousy burn through my chest but knowing that I had no right to feel such.

". . . Lieutenant Strasse of the Hamburg Metropolitan Police phoned me. He said that he had something important to show me and asked if I would come down to headquarters. I agreed, of course, and took a taxi down. There the sergeant took me into a room and showed me a painting. I was astounded. I had never seen it before, but I knew at once that it was my husband's work. I did not need his signature—in its usual place in the upper right-hand corner—to know that. I told the sergeant that and then I said, 'This must mean that Alfred is still alive! But where in the world did you get it?'

"He replied that it had come to the attention of the police only that morning. A wealthy merchant, Herr Lausitz, had died a week before. The lawyer supervising the inventory of his estate found this painting in a locked room in Lausitz's mansion. It was only one of many valuable objets d'art which had been stolen. Lausitz was not suspected of being a thief except in the sense that he had undoubtedly purchased stolen goods or commissioned the thefts. The collection was valued at many millions of marks. The lawyer had notified the police, who identified the painting as my husband's because of the signature."

"You may be sure that Strasse would never have been able to identify a Scarletin by its style alone," Ralph said sarcastically.

Her delicate eyebrows arched. "Ach! So that's the way it is! The lieutenant did not take it kindly when I told him that I was thinking of consulting you. But that was later.

"Anyway, I told Strasse that this was evidence that Alfred was still alive. Or at least had been until very recently. I know that it would take my husband at least a month and a half to have painted it—if he were under pressure. Strasse said that it could be: one, a forgery; or, two, Alfred might have painted it before he disappeared. I told him that it was no forgery; I could tell at a glance. And what did he mean, it was painted some time ago? I knew exactly—from day to day—what my husband worked on."

She stopped, looked at me, and reddened slightly.

"That isn't true. My husband visited his mistress at least three times a week. I did not know about her until after he disappeared, when the police reported to me that he had been seeing her . . . Hilda Speck . . . for about two years. However, according to the police, Alfred had not been doing any painting in her apartment. Of course, she could have removed all evidence, though Strasse tells me that she would have been unable to get rid of all traces of pigments and hairs from brushes."

What a beast that Scarletin was! I thought, how could anybody married to this glorious woman pay any attention to another woman?

"I have made some inquiries about Hilda Speck," Ralph said. "First, she has an excellent alibi, what the English call ironclad. She was visiting friends in Bremen two days before Scarletin disappeared. She did not return to Hamburg until two days afterward. As for her background, she worked as a typist-clerk for an export firm until two years ago when Scarletin began supporting her. She has no criminal record, but her brother has been arrested several times for extortion and assault. He escaped conviction each time. He is a huge obese man, as ugly as his sister is beautiful. He is nicknamed, appropriately enough, *Flusspferd*. (Hippopotamus. Literally, river-horse.) His whereabouts have been unknown for about four months."

He sat silent for a moment, then he went to the telephone. This lay on the floor; beside it was a curious instrument. I saw its function the moment Ralph put one paw on its long, thin but blunt end and slipped the other paw snugly into a funnel-shaped cup at the opposite end. With the thin end he punched the buttons on the telephone.

A police officer answered over the loudspeaker. Ralph asked for Lt. Strasse. The officer said that he was not in the station. Ralph left a message, but when he turned off the phone, he said, "Strasse won't answer for a while, but eventually his curiosity will get the better of him."

It is difficult to tell when a dog is smiling, but I will swear that Ralph was doing more than just exposing his teeth. And his eyes seemed to twinkle.

Suddenly, he raised a paw and said, quietly, "No sound, please."

We stared at him. None of us heard anything, but it was evident he did. He jumped to the control panel on the floor and pushed the on button. Then he dashed toward the door, which swung inward. A man wearing a stethoscope stood looking stupidly at us. Seeing Ralph bounding at him, he yelled and turned to run. Ralph struck him on the back and sent him crashing against the opposite wall of the hallway. I ran to aid him, but to my surprise Ralph trotted back into the room. It was then that I saw the little device attached to the door. The man rose glaring and unsteadily to his feet. He was just above minimum height for a policeman and looked as if he were thirty-five years old. He had a narrow face with a long nose and small close-set black eyes.

"Doctor Weisstein," Ralph said. "Lieutenant Strasse."

Strasse did not acknowledge me. Instead, he tore off the device and put it with the stethoscope in his jacket pocket. Some of his paleness disappeared.

"That eavesdropper device is illegal in America and should be here," Ralph said.

"So should talking dogs," Strasse said. He bowed to Mrs. Scarletin and clicked his heels.

Ralph gave several short barks, which I found out later was his equivalent of laughter. He said, "No need to ask you why you were spying on us. You're stuck in this case, and you hoped to overhear me say something that would give you a clue. Really, my dear Lieutenant!"

Strasse turned red, but he spoke up bravely enough.

"Mrs. Scarletin, you can hire this . . . this . . . hairy four-footed Holmes . . ."

"I take that as a compliment," Ralph murmured.

". . . if you wish, but you cannot discharge the police. Moreover, there is grave doubt about the legality of his private investigator's license, and you might get into trouble if you persist in hiring him."

"Mrs. Scarletin is well aware of the legal ramifications, my dear Strasse," Ralph said coolly. "She is also confident that I will win my case. Meantime, the authorities have permitted me to practice. If you dispute this, you may phone the mayor himself."

"You . . . you!" Strasse sputtered. "Just because you once saved His Honor's child!"

"Let's drop all this time-wasting nonsense," Ralph said. "I would like to examine the painting myself. I believe that it may contain the key to Scarletin's whereabouts."

"That is police property," Strasse said. "As long as I have anything to say about it, you won't put your long nose into a police building. Not unless you do so as a prisoner."

I was astonished at the hatred that leaped and crackled between these two like discharges in a Van de Graaff generator. I did not learn until later that Strasse was the man to whom Ralph had been assigned when he started police work. At first they got along well, but as it became evident that Ralph was much the more intelligent, Strasse became jealous. He did not, however, ask for another dog. He was taking most of the credit for the cases cracked by Ralph, and he was rising rapidly in rank because of Ralph. By the time the dog resigned from the force, Strasse had become a lieutenant. Since then he had bungled two cases, and the person responsible for Strasse's rapid rise was now obvious to all.

"Pardon me," Ralph said. "The police may be holding the painting as evidence, but it is clearly Mrs. Scarletin's property. However, I think I'll cut through the red tape. I'll just make a complaint to His Honor."

"Very well," Strasse said, turning pale again. "But I'll go with you to make sure that you don't tamper with the evidence."

"And to learn all you can," Ralph said, barking laughter. "Weisstein, would you bring along that little kit there? It contains the tools of my trade."

Chapter IV
LIGHT IN THE DARKNESS,
COURTESY OF VON WAU WAU

On the way to the station in the taxi (Strasse having refused us use of a police vehicle), Ralph told me a little more of Alfred Scarletin.

"He is the son of an American teacher who became a German citizen and of a Hamburg woman. Naturally, he speaks English like a native of California. He became interested in painting at a very early age and since his early adolescence has tramped through Germany painting both urban and rural scenes. He is extremely handsome, hence, attracts women, has a photographic memory, and is an excellent draftsman. His paintings were quite conventional until the past ten years when he founded the Fauve Mauve school. He is learned in both German and English literature and has a fondness for the works of Frank Baum and Lewis Carroll. He often uses characters from them in his paintings. Both writers, by the way, were fond of puns."

"I am well aware of that," I said stiffly. After all, one does not like to be considered ignorant by a dog. "And all this means?"

"It may mean all or nothing."

About ten minutes later, we were in a large room in which many articles, the jetsam and flotsam of crime, were displayed. Mrs. Scarletin led us to the painting (though we needed no leading), and we stood before it. Strasse, off to one side, regarded us suspiciously. I could make no sense out of the painting and said so even though I did not want to offend Mrs. Scarletin. She, however, laughed and said my reaction was that of many people.

Ralph studied it for a long time and then said, "It may be that my suspicions are correct. We shall see."

"About what?" Strasse said, coming closer and leaning forward to peer at the many figures on the canvas.

"We can presume that Mrs. Scarletin knows all her husband's works—until the time he disappeared. This appeared afterward, and so we can presume that he painted it within the last two months. It's evident that he was kidnapped not for ransom but for the money to be made from the sale of new paintings by Scarletin. They must have threatened him with death if he did not paint new works for them. He has done at least one for them and probably has done, or is doing, more for them.

"They can't sell Scarletins on the open market. But there are enough fanatical and unscrupulous collectors to pay very large sums for their private collections. Lausitz was one such. Scarletin is held prisoner and, we suppose, would like to escape. He can't do so, but he is an intelligent man, and he thinks of a way to get a message out. He knows his paintings are being sold, even if he isn't told so. Ergo, why not put a message in his painting?"

"How wonderful!" Mrs. Scarletin said and she patted Ralph's head. Ralph wagged his tail, and I felt a thrust of jealousy.

"Nonsense!" Strasse growled. "He must have known that the painting would go to a private collector who could not reveal that Scarletin was a prisoner. One, he'd be put in jail himself for having taken part in an illegal transaction. Two, why should he suspect that the painting contained a message? Three, I don't believe there is any message there!"

"Scarletin would be desperate and so willing to take a long chance," Ralph said. "At least, it'd be better than doing nothing. He could hope that the collector might get an attack of conscience and tell the police. This is not very likely, I'll admit. He could hope that the collector would be unable to keep from showing the work off to a few close friends. Perhaps one of these might tell the police, and so the painting would come into the hands of the police. Among them might be an intelligent and well-educated person who would perceive the meaning of the painting. I'll admit, however, that neither of these theories is likely."

Strasse snorted.

"And then there was the very slight chance—which never-theless occurred—that the collector would die. And so the legal inventory of his estate would turn up a Scarletin. And some person just might be able to read the meaning in this—if there is any."

"Just what I was going to say," Strasse said.

"Even if what you say happened did happen," he continued, "his kidnappers wouldn't pass on the painting without examining it. The first thing they'd suspect would be a hidden message. It's so obvious."

"You didn't think so a moment ago," Ralph said. "But you are right . . . in agreeing with me. Now, let us hypothesize. Scarletin, a work of art, but he wishes to embody in it a message. Probably a map of sorts which will lead the police—or someone else looking for him—directly to the place where he is kept prisoner.

"How is he to do this without detection by the kidnappers? He has to be subtle enough to escape their inspection. *How* subtle depends, I would imagine, on their education and perceptivity. But too subtle a message will go over everybody's head. And he is limited in his choice of symbols by the situation, by the names or professions of his kidnappers—if he knows them—and by the particular location of his prison—if he knows that."

"If, if, if!" Strasse said, throwing his hands up in the air.

"If me no ifs," Ralph said. "But first let us consider that Scarletin is equally at home in German or English. He loves the pun-loving Carroll and Baum. So, perhaps, due to the contingencies of the situation, he is forced to pun in both languages."

"It would be like him," Mrs. Scarletin said. "But is it likely that he would use this method when he would know that very few people would be capable of understanding him?"

"As I said, it was a long shot, madame. But better than nothing.

"Now, Weisstein, whatever else I am, I am a dog. Hence, I am color blind. (But not throughout his career. See *The Adventure of the Tired Color Man,* to be published.) Please describe the colors of each object on this canvas."

Strasse sniggered, but we ignored him. When I had finished, Ralph said, "Thank you, my dear Weisstein. Now, let us separate the significant from the insignificant. Though, as a matter of fact, in this case even the insignificant is significant. Notice the two painted walls which divide the painting into three parts—like Gaul. One starts from the middle of the left-hand side and curves up to the middle of the upper edge. The other starts in the middle of the right-hand side and curves down to the middle of the lower side. All three parts are filled with strange and seemingly unrelated—and often seemingly unintelligible—objects. The Fauve Mauve apologists, however, maintain that their creations come from the collective unconscious, not the individual or personal, and so are intelligible to everybody."

"Damned nonsense!" I said, forgetting Lisa in my indignation.

"Not in this case, I suspect," Ralph said. "Now, notice that the two walls, which look much like the Great Wall of China, bear many zeros on their tops. And that within the area these walls enclose, other zeros are scattered. Does this mean nothing to you?"

"Zero equals nothing," I said.

"A rudimentary observation, Doctor, but valid," Ralph said. "I would say that Scarletin is telling us that the objects within the walls mean nothing. It is the central portion that bears the message. There are no zeros there."

"Prove it," Strasse said.

"The first step first—if one can find it. Observe in the upper right-hand corner the strange figure of a man. The upper half is, obviously, Sherlock Holmes, with his deerstalker hat, cloak, pipe—though whether his meditative brierroot or disputatious clay can't be determined—and his magnifying glass in hand. The lower half, with the lederhosen and so on, obviously indicates a Bavarian in particular and a German in general. The demi-figure of Holmes means two things to the earnest seeker after the truth. One, that we are to use detective methods on this painting. Two, that half of the puzzle is in English. The lower half means that half of the puzzle is in German. Which I anticipated."

"Preposterous!" Strasse said. "And just what does that next figure, the one in sixteenth-century costume, mean?"

"Ah, yes, the torso of a bald and bearded gentleman with an Elizabethan ruff around his neck. He is writing with a pen on a sheet of paper. There is a title on the upper part of the paper. Doctor, please look at it through the magnifying glass which you'll find in my kit."

Chapter V
MORE DAWNING LIGHT

I did so, and I said, "I can barely make it out. Scarletin must have used a glass to do it. It says *New Atlantis.*"

"Does that suggest anything to anybody?" Ralph said.

Obviously it did to him, but he was enjoying the sensation of being more intelligent than the humans around him. I resented his attitude somewhat, and yet I could understand it. He had been patronized by too many humans for too long a time.

"The great scholar and statesman Francis Bacon wrote the *New Atlantis,*" I said suddenly. Ralph winked at me, and I cried, "Bacon! Scarletin's mistress is Hilda Speck!"

(*Speck* in German means *bacon.*)

"You have put one foot forward, my dear Weisstein," Ralph said. "Now let us see you bring up the other."

"The Bacon, with the next two figures, comprise a group separate from the others," I said. "Obviously, they are to be considered as closely related. But I confess that I cannot make much sense out of Bacon, a green horse, and a house with an attic window from which a woman with an owl on her shoulder leans. Nor do I know the significance of the tendril which connects all of them."

"Stuck in the mud, eh, kid?" Ralph said, startling me. But I was to get used to his swift transitions from the persona of Holmes to Spade and others and back again.

"Tell me, Doc, is the green of the oats-burner of any particular shade?"

"Hmm," I said.

"It's Nile green," Lisa said.

"You're certainly a model client, sweetheart," Ralph said. "Very well, my dear sawbones, does this mean nothing to you? Yes? What about you, Strasse?"

Strasse muttered something.

Lisa said, *"Nilpferd!"*

"Yes," Ralph said. *"Nilpferd.* (Nile-horse.) Another word for hippopotamus. And Hilda Speck's brother is nicknamed *Hippopotamus.* Now for the next figure, the house with the woman looking out the attic and bearing an owl on her shoulder. Tell me, Strasse, does the Hippo have any special pals? One who is perhaps, Greek? From the city of Athens?"

Strasse sputtered and said, "Somebody in the department has been feeding you information. I'll . . ."

"Not at all," Ralph said. "Obviously, the attic and the woman with the owl are the significant parts of the image. *Dachstube* (attic) conveys no meaning in German, but if we use the English translation, we are on the way to light. The word has two meanings in English. If capitalized, Attic, it refers to the ancient Athenian language or culture and, in a broader sense, to Greece as a whole. Note that the German adjective *attisch* is similar to the English *Attic.* To clinch this, Scarletin painted a woman with an owl on her shoulder. Who else could this be but the goddess of wisdom, patron deity of Athens? Scarletin was taking a chance on using her, since his kidnappers, even if they did not get beyond high school, might have encountered Athena. But they might not remember her, and, anyway, Scarletin had to use some redundancy to make sure his message got across. I would not be surprised if we do not run across considerable redundancy here."

"And the tendrils?" I said.

"A pun in German, my dear Doctor. *Ranke* (tendril) is similar to *Ranke* (intrigues). The three figures are bound together by the tendril of intrigue."

Strasse coughed and said, "And the mirror beneath the house with the attic?"

"Observe that the yellow brick road starts from the mirror and curves to the left or westward. I suggest that Scarletin means here that the road actually goes to the right or eastward. Mirror images are in reverse, of course."

"What road?" Strasse said.

Ralph rolled his eyes and shook his head.

"Surely the kidnappers made my husband explain the symbolism?" Lisa said. "They would be very suspicious that he might do exactly what he did do."

"There would be nothing to keep him from a false explanation," Ralph said. "So far, it is obvious that Scarletin has named the criminals. How he was able to identify them or to locate his place of imprisonment, I don't know. Time and deduction—with a little luck—will reveal all. Could we have a road map of Germany, please?"

"I'm no dog to fetch and carry," Strasse grumbled, but he obtained a map nevertheless. This was the large Mair's, scale of 1:750,000, used primarily to indicate the autobahn system. Strasse unfolded it and pinned it to the wall with the upper part of Germany showing.

"If Scarletin had put, say, an American hamburger at the beginning of the brick road, its meaning would have been obvious even to the *dummkopf* kidnappers," Ralph said. "He credited his searchers—if any—with intelligence. They would realize the road has to start where the crime started—in Hamburg."

He was silent while comparing the map and the painting. After a while the fidgeting Strasse said, "Come, man! I mean, dog! You . . ."

"You mean Herr von Wau Wau, yes?" Ralph said.

Strasse became red-faced again, but after a struggle he said, "Of course. Herr von Wau Wau. How do you interpret this, this mess of a mystery?"

"You'll note that there are many figures along the yellow brick road until one gets to the large moon rising behind the castle. All these figures have halos over their heads. This puzzled me until I understood that the halos are also zeros. We are to pay no attention to the figures beneath them.

"But the moon behind the castle? Look at the map. Two of the roads running southeast out of Hamburg meet just above the city of Luneburg. A *burg* is a castle, but the *Lune* doesn't mean anything in German in this context. It is, however, similar to the English *lunar,* hence the moon. And the yellow brick road goes south from there.

"I must confess that I am now at a loss. So, we get in a car and travel to Luneburg and south of it while I study the map and the painting."

"We can't take the painting with us; it's too big!" Strasse said.

"I have it all in here," Ralph said, tapping his head with his paw. "But I suggest we take a color Polaroid shot of the painting for you who have weak memories," and he grinned at Strasse.

Chapter VI
FOLLOW THE YELLOW
BRICK ROAD

Strasse did not like it, but he could not proceed without Ralph, and Ralph insisted that Mrs. Scarletin and I be brought along. First, he sent two men to watch Hilda Speck and to make sure she did not try to leave town—as the Americans say. He had no evidence to arrest her as yet, nor did he really think—I believe—that he was going to have any.

The dog, Lisa, and I got into the rear of a large police limousine, steam-driven, of course. Strasse sat in the front with the driver. Another car, which kept in radio contact with us, was to follow us at a distance of a kilometer.

An hour later, we were just north of Luneburg. A half hour later, still going south, we were just north of the town of Uelzen. It was still daylight, and so I could easily see the photo of the painting which I held. The yellow road on it ran south of the moon rising behind the castle (Luneburg) and extended a little south of a group of three strange figures. These were a hornless sheep (probably a female), a section of an overhead railway, and an archer with a medieval Japanese coiffure and medieval clothes.

Below this group the road split. Two roads wound toward the walls in the upper and lower parts of the picture and eventually went through them. The other curved almost due south to the left and then went through or by some more puzzling figures.

The first was a representation of a man (he looked like the risen Jesus) coming from a tomb set in the middle of some trees. To its right and a little lower was a waistcoat. Next was what looked like William Penn, the Quaker. Following it was a man in a leopard loincloth with two large apes at his heels.

Next was a man dressed in clothes such as the ancient Mesopotamian people wore. He was down on all fours, his head bent close to the grass. Beside him was a banana tree.

Across the road was a large hot-air balloon with a bald-headed man in the wicker basket. On the side of the bag in large letters were: O.Z.

Across the road from it were what looked like two large Vikings wading through a sea. Behind them was the outline of a fleet of dragon-prowed longships and the silhouette of a horde of horn-helmeted bearded men. The two leaders were approaching a body of naked warriors, colored blue, standing in horse-drawn chariots.

South of these was a woman dressed in mid-Victorian clothes, hoopskirts and all, and behind her a mansion typical of the pre–Civil War American south. By it was a tavern, if the drunks lying outside it and the board hanging over the doorway meant anything. The sign was too small to contain even letters written under a magnifying glass.

A little to the left, the road terminated in a pair of hands tearing a package from another pair of hands.

Just before we got to Uelzen, Strasse said, "How do you know that we're on the right road?"

"Consider the sheep, the raised section of railway, and the Japanese archer," Ralph said. "In English, *U* is pronounced exactly like the word for the female sheep—*ewe*. An elevated railway is colloquially an *el*. The Japanese archer could be a Samurai, but I do not think so. He is a *Zen* archer. Thus, *U, el,* and *zen* or the German city of Uelzen."

"All of this seems so easy, so apparent, now that you've pointed it out," I said.

"Hindsight has twenty/twenty vision," he said somewhat bitterly.

"And the rest?" I said.

"The town of Esterholz is not so difficult. Would you care to try?"

"Another English-German hybrid pun," I said, with more confidence than I felt. "*Ester* sounds much like *Easter,* hence the risen Christ. And the wood is the *holz*, of course. *Holt,* archaic English for a small wood or copse, by the way, comes from the same Germanic root as *holz.*"

"And the Weste (waistcoat)?" Ralph said.

"I would guess that that means to take the road west of Esterholz," I said somewhat more confidently.

"Excellent, Doctor," he said. "And the Quaker?"

"I really don't know," I said, chagrined because Lisa had been looking admiringly at me.

He gave his short barking laughter and said, "And neither do I, my dear fellow! I am sure that some of these symbols, perhaps most, have a meaning which will not be apparent until we have studied the neighborhood."

Seven kilometers southeast of Uelzen, we turned into the village of Esterholz and then west onto the road to Wrestede. Looking at the hands tearing loose the package from the other pair, I suddenly cried out, "Of course! Wrestede! Suggesting the English, *wrested!* The hands are *wresting* the package away! Then that means that Scarletin is a prisoner somewhere between Esterholz and Wrestede!"

"Give that man the big stuffed teddy bear," Ralph said. "OK, toots, so where is Scarletin?"

I fell silent. The others said nothing, but the increasing tension was making us sweat. We all looked waxy and pale in the light of the sinking sun. In half an hour, night would be on us.

"Slow down so I can read the names on the gateways of the farms," Ralph said. The driver obeyed, and presently Ralph said, "Ach!"

I could see nothing which reminded me of a Quaker.

"The owner of that farm is named Fuchs (fox)," I said.

"Yes, and the founder of the Society of Friends, or The Quakers, was George Fox," he said.

He added a moment later, "As I remember it, it was in this area that some particularly bestial—or should I say human?—murders occurred in 1845. A man named Wilhelm Graustock was finally caught and convicted."

I had never heard of this case, but, as I was to find out, Ralph had an immense knowledge of sensational literature. He seemed to know the details of every horror committed in the last two centuries.

"What is the connection between Herr Graustock and this figure which is obviously Tarzan?" I said.

"Graustock is remarkably similar in sound to Greystoke," he said. "As you may or may not know, the lord of the jungle was also Lord Greystoke of the British peerage. As a fact, Graustock and Greystoke both mean exactly the same thing, a gray stick or pole. They have common Germanic roots. Ach, there it is! The descendants of the infamous butcher still hold his property, but are, I believe, singularly peaceful farmers."

"And the man on all fours by a banana tree?" Strasse growled. It hurt him to ask, but he could not push back his curiosity.

Ralph burst out laughing again. "Another example of redundancy, I believe. And the most difficult to figure out. A tough one, sweetheart. Want to put in your two pfennigs' worth?"

"Aw, go find a fireplug," Strasse said, at which Ralph laughed even more loudly.

"Unless I'm mistaken," Ralph said, "the next two images stand for a word, not a thing. They symbolize *nebanan* (next door). The question is, next door to what? The Graustock farm or the places indicated by the balloon and the battle tableau and the antebellum scene? I see nothing as yet which indicates that we are on or about to hit the bull's-eye. Continue at the same speed, driver."

There was silence for a minute. I refused to speak because of my pride. Finally, Lisa said, "For heaven's sake, Herr von Wau Wau, I'm dying of curiosity! How did you ever get *nebanan*?"

"The man on all fours with his head close to the ground looks to me like ancient Nebuchadnezzar, the Babylonian king who went mad and ate grass. By him is the banana (Banane) tree. Collapse those two words into one, à la Lewis Carroll and his portmanteau words, and you have *nebanan* (next to)."

"This Scarletin is crazy," Strasse said.

"If he is, he has a utilitarian madness," Ralph said.

"You're out of your mind, too!" Strasse said triumphantly. "Look!" And he pointed at a name painted on the wall. Neb Bannons.

Ralph was silent for a few seconds while Strasse laughed, and then he said, quietly, "Well, I was wrong in the particular but right in the principle. Ach! Here we are! Maintain the same speed driver! The rest of you, look straight ahead, don't gawk! Someone may be watching from the house, but they won't think it suspicious if they see a dog looking out of the window!"

I did as he said, but I strained out of the corners of my eyes to see both sides of the road. On my right were some fields of barley. On my left I caught a glimpse of a gateway with a name over it in large white-painted letters: Schindeler. We went past that and by a field on my left in which two stallions stood by the fence looking at us. On my right was a sign against a stone wall which said: Bergmann.

Ralph said delightedly, "That's it!"

I felt even more stupid.

"Don't stop until we get around the curve ahead and out of sight of the Schindeler house," Ralph said.

A moment later, we were parked beyond the curve and pointed west. The car which had been trailing us by several kilometers reported by radio that it had stopped near the Graustock farm.

"All right!" Strasse said fiercely. "Things seem to have worked out! But before I move in, I want to make sure I'm not arresting the wrong people. Just how did you figure this one out?"

"Button your lip and flap your ears, sweetheart," Ralph said. "Take the balloon with O.Z. on it. That continues the yellow brick road motif. You noticed the name Bergmann (miner)? A Bergmann is a man who digs, right? Well, for those of you who may have forgotten, the natal or Nebraskan name of the Wizard of Oz was Diggs."

Strasse looked as if he were going to have an apoplectic fit. "And what about those ancient Teutonic warriors and those naked blue men in chariots across the road from the balloon?" he shouted.

"Those Teutonic warriors were Anglo-Saxons, and they were invading ancient Britain. The Britons were tattooed blue and often went into battle naked. As all educated persons know," he added, grinning. "As for the two leaders of the Anglo-Saxons, traditionally they were named Hengist and Horsa. Both names meant *horse*. In fact, as you know, *Hengst* is a German word for stallion, and *Ross* also means horse. Ross is cognate with the Old English *hrossa*, meaning horse."

"God preserve me from any case like this one in the future!" Strasse said. "Very well, we won't pause in this madness! What does this pre–Civil War house with the Southern belle before it and the tavern by it mean? How do you know that it means that Scarletin is prisoner there?"

"The tableau suggests, among other things, the book and the movie *Gone With the Wind*," Ralph said. "You probably haven't read the book, Strasse, but you surely must have seen the movie. The heroine's name is Scarlett O'Hara, right, pal? And a *tavern*, in English, is also an *inn*. Scarlett-inn, get it?"

A few minutes later, Ralph said, "If you don't control yourself, my dear Strasse, your men will have to put you in a strait jacket."

The policeman ceased his bellowing but not his trembling, took a few deep breaths, followed by a deep draught from a bottle in the glove compartment, breathed schnapps all over us, and said, "So! Life is not easy! And duty calls! Let us proceed to make the raid upon the farmhouse as agreed upon!"

Chapter VII
NO EMERALD CITY FOR ME

An hour after dark, policemen burst into the front and rear doors of the Schindeler house. By then it had been ascertained that the house had been rented by a man giving the name of Albert Habicht. This was Hilda Speck's brother, Albert Speck, the Hippopotamus. His companion was a Wilhelm Erlesohn, a tall skinny man nicknamed *die Giraffe*. A fine zoological pair, both now behind bars.

Hilda Speck was also convicted but managed to escape a year later. But we were to cross her path again. (*The Case of the Seeing Eye Man.*) Alfred Scarletin was painting another canvas with the same message but different symbols when we collared his kidnappers. He threw down his brush and took his lovely wife into his arms, and my heart went into a decaying orbit around my hopes. Apparently, despite his infidelity, she still loved him.

Most of this case was explained, but there was still an important question to be answered. How had Scarletin known where he was?

"The kidnaping took place in daylight in the midst of a large crowd," Scarletin said. "Erlesohn jammed a gun which he had in his coat pocket against my back. I did as he said and got into the back of a delivery van double-parked nearby. Erlesohn then rendered me unconscious with a drug injected by a hypodermic syringe. When I woke up, I was in this house. I have been confined to this room ever since, which, as you see, is large and has a southern exposure and a heavily barred skylight and large heavily barred windows. I was told that I would be held until I had painted twelve paintings. These would be sufficient for the two men to become quite wealthy through sales to rich but unscrupulous collectors. Then I would be released.

"I did not believe them of course. After the twelve paintings were done, they would kill me and bury me somewhere in the woods. I listened often at the door late at night and overheard the two men, who drank much, talking loudly. That is how I found out their names. I also discovered that Hilda was in on the plot, though I'd suspected that all along. You see, I had quit her only a few days before I was kidnapped, and she was desperate because she no longer had an income.

"As for how I knew where I was, that is not so remarkable. I have a photographic memory, and I have tramped up and down Germany painting in my youth and early middle age. I have been along this road a number of times on foot when I was a teen-ager. In fact, I once painted the Graustock farmhouse. It is true that I had forgotten this, but after a while the memory came back. After all, I looked out the window every day and saw the Graustock farm.

"And now, tell me, who is the man responsible for reading my message? He must be an extraordinary man."

"No man," I said, feeling like Ulysses in Polyphemus' cave.

"Ach, then, it was you, Lisa?" he cried.

"It's yours truly, sweetheart," the voice of Humphrey Bogart said.

Scarletin is a very composed man, but he has fainted at least once in his life.

Chapter VIII
THE CONCLUSION

It was deep in winter with the fuel shortage most critical. We were sitting in our apartment trying to keep warm by the radiations from the TV set. The Scotch helped, and I was trying to forget our discomfort by glancing over my notes and listening to the records of our cases since the Scarletin case. Had Ralph and I, in that relatively short span of time, really experienced the affair of the aluminum creche, the adventures of the human camel and the Old-School Thai, and the distressing business with the terrible Venetian, Granelli? The latter, by the way, is being written up under the title: *The Doge Whose Barque Was Worse Than His Bight*.

At last, I put the notes and records to one side and picked up a book. Too many memories were making me uncomfortable. A long silence followed, broken when Ralph said, "You may not have lost her after all, my dear Weisstein."

I started, and I said, "How did you know I was thinking of her?"

Ralph grinned (at least, I think he was grinning). He said, "Even the lead-brained Strasse would know that you cannot forget her big brown eyes, her smiles, her deep rich tones, her figure, and her etcetera. What else these many months would evoke those sighs, those moping stares, those frequent attacks of insomnia and absent-mindedness? It is evident at this moment that you are not at all as deep in one of C. S. Forester's fine sea stories as you pretend.

"But cheer up! The fair Lisa may yet have good cause to divorce her artistic but philandering spouse. Or she may become a widow."

"What makes you say that?" I cried.

"I've been thinking that it might not be just a coincidence that old Lausitz died after he purchased Scarletin's painting. I've been sniffing around the painting—literally and figuratively—and I think there's one Hamburger that's gone rotten."

"You suspect Scarletin of murder!" I said. "But how could he have killed Lausitz?"

"I don't know yet, pal," he said. "But I will. You can bet your booties I will. Old murders are like old bones—I dig them up."

And he was right, but that adventure was not to happen for another six months.

Voiceover
by
Edward Wellen

Another dog—this time as a lower-class cockney; the type that appeared in the canon as the original Baker Street Irregulars, after which the society is named. Watch for the rhyming slang. By the end of the story, you'll be able to understand it without help.

Voiceover

by Edward Wellen

"Arf a mo, Watson," said the cockney spaniel.

I stopped in midstride and my closing fist froze short of the doorknob. I turned my head stiffly and glared at the dog. Blooming cheek. Its all-too-intelligent gaze did not slink away from mine.

"Gabriel" was Holmes's original appellation for the canine simulacrum, but because it tracked by scent and because "I suppose" is cockney rhyming slang for "nose" we generally called it "I Suppose."

My glare widened to take in Holmes lounging moodily in his Morris chair. Why couldn't Holmes have utilized barkless Basenji biochips?

"Really, Holmes. How can you allow this, this mechanism, to address me so familiarly?"

The carefully stained and moth-eaten dressing gown stirred as Holmes came out of his pipe dream. His gaze shot to I Suppose and I had a spectral impression that the two exchanged subliminal winks. It could have been my imagination. It shames me to admit that I had grown jealous of their rapport. At the same time, there seemed something so supernatural about it that I stood in awe of their mutual empathy, their ready responsiveness to one another. I felt quite prepared to believe the explanation was telepathy.

"I'm sure I Suppose meant no offense, Watson," Holmes drawled. "Would calling you 'guv'nor' be more to your liking?"

"Much more," I said forcefully.

"Done," he said.

Eyeing me steadily, I Suppose touched a paw to his brow with a bob of mock humility. "Righto, guv'nor. Nah then, me old china, would you tell us 'ow you discovered I'm not really a dog?"

China, china plate: mate. Still cheeky. Incorrigible. But the question hooked me. My mind took me back through mist. "It was an evening not long after Mr. Holmes brought you home. He had told me merely that you were a good sniffer-out of clues and of course I accepted that. But on the evening I speak of I happened to be playing solitaire; you looked over my shoulder and advised me to play the red queen on the black king. When I got over my choler at your kibitzing, I recalled that real dogs see no color at all and I knew you had to be a thing of biochips."

"Bravo, Watson," Holmes said, after a moment of almost shocked silence. I had the eerie feeling that he and I Suppose subliminally exchanged uneasy glances. Then he went on. "I see that living with me has rubbed off on you. You've learned to apply my methods."

I swelled with pleasure. "Coming from you, Holmes . . ."

"Not at all, my dear fellow." He smiled a twitch of a smile. "Now that we've cleared up several side issues, Watson, you should find yourself free to wonder why I Suppose called out to you just as you made to slip away."

I blinked "How did you know that I was about to sally forth, Holmes? You seemed to be off in a world of your own and I thought you so unaware of my presence that you would not notice my absence."

Holmes waved that away. "Don't sidetrack yourself again, Watson. I handed you a line of inquiry. Pursue it."

I narrowed my glare once more to I Suppose, whose tail lazily thumped the Turkey carpet. "Very well," I said. "Why?"

I Suppose's nose remained on his paws and one imperturbable eye cocked at me. "It's a real scratch an itch today, guv'nor. I detect acid fallout from the Mount Saint 'Elens eruption of Fursday last. If you've a mind to venture outdoors you'd be wise to don decon suit and breathing mask."

I felt a twinge (not in shoulder or leg, for it was not physical but mental), one of guilt. Here I had been overready to take offense—and I Suppose had spoken up to do me a good turn. I gave a cough of apology.

Apparently that was not good enough. I Suppose shot a near-subliminal wink at Holmes before addressing me once more. " 'Aving it orf wiv a bird, guv'nor?"

I spluttered.

While I was still trying to shape words to my outrage, I Suppose went on.

"Where's he orf to, 'Olmes?"

I stared blankly and a chill traversed my spine. Where indeed had I been off to? I could not for the life of me come up with the answer. I tossed my head in an affectation of indifference, while casting an anxious ear for Holmes's reply.

"That should be obvious, I Suppose," said Holmes without a preliminary draw on his pipe. "Dr. Watson's left hand is carrying his black bag."

So it was.

I Suppose made no bones about his scorn. " 'E's orf 'is tuppenny."

Tupenny. Cockney rhyming slang. The trail leads backward through twopenny loaf, loaf, loaf of bread: head. The mangy cur had just now said I was off my head.

Holmes leaped in as I made to rival Mount St. Helens. He spoke in as kindly a tone as I had ever heard him use. "Dear old fellow, do come back and sit down. About to make your rounds, were you?" He shook his head sadly. "Have you forgotten that you've retired, Watson? You've given up your practice. There are no patients you must visit."

"Senile, that's wot." Muffled, but I heard it.

Holmes turned reprovingly toward I Suppose. But it was true. I had lost track of time and events. How else explain the mental fog I found myself in almost constantly?

Numbly I moved away from the door and sought a chair to sink into. Both Holmes and I Suppose watched unblinking, though I sensed pity from even I Suppose. All the more unnerved, I clutched visually at the hands of the clock on the mantelpiece. The hands stood at a minute to ten. P.M. or A.M.? P.M. I knew that much. And the date? The thirtieth of October. There! I had not lost all track. Something tickled my mind.

"Why are 'is mince pies on the dickory dock, 'Olmes?"

I Suppose's voice derailed my train of thought and I remained staring foggily at the clock, in a puzzlement as to what I had just now had in mind.

Holmes glanced at the face of the clock, consulted his wristcom, and took one puff before answering I Suppose. "This is the evening of October thirtieth. It has struck the good doctor that we have failed as yet to deal with the anachronism of daylight savings. He is about to perform the ceremony of moving the hands in salute to drowned Greenwich."

Thanks to Holmes, I now knew what I had been intending. Still, I would not have put it so fancifully. It was just something that had to be done and I was the one to do it.

Taking a surreptitious look at my own wristcom and confirming that it had automatically reset itself, I made for the ancient clock, reckoning to turn the hour hand eleven hours ahead to put it one hour back, when the street doorbell sounded, simultaneously with the clock's chiming ten.

Holmes put up his hand as though to hush the clock. The ears of I Suppose pricked up, the nose wrinkled.

Over the intercom system we heard the Mrs. Hudson voice of the door. "Do you have an appointment, sir?"

The visitor's voice was gruff. "No, but—"

"Kindly identify yourself."

An impatient snort. "If Sherlock 'Olmes is all 'e's cracked up to be, 'e'll know 'oo I am by the time I've climbed to 'is rooms."

"I'm sorry, sir, but—"

This, however, was a challenge Holmes could not pass up.

His face brightened in the most lively manner and he sprang to his feet. He projected his voice toward the intercom hidden in the tantalus. "It's quite all right, Mrs. Hudson. Kindly admit the gentleman."

"Very well, Mr. Holmes."

I heard the hiss as the caller passed through the front door's air lock. I whirled to watch I Suppose, who would already be analyzing whiffs of air piped in from the air lock, air laced with discreet vacuumings from the caller's person.

Then I whirled back to watch Holmes, who with a touch of a hidden button transformed the picture of General Gordon on the wall into a monitor screen. The image on the screen remained a mystery to me. I saw only a stocky figure in decon suit and breathing mask.

After the sprinklers rinsed and the hot air jets dried, the caller took off the decon suit and the breathing mask and hung them on pegs. But that got me no forrarder. Not that I tried. I may have had the urge to seek telling detail but out of habit I deferred to Holmes. The face was just a face—the map of Britain before the Drowning. Then even that blurred and vanished as the inner door opened and the caller stepped out of the air lock and made for the stairs. But Holmes, restoring General Gordon, nodded in satisfaction. "The Lord Harry."

I stared at my friend. "Holmes, you surprise me. I've never known you to swear."

Holmes stared back, then chuckled. I flushed as he exchanged a near-subliminal wink with I Suppose and the latter snickered. "You misheard me, Watson. I did not say 'By the Lord Harry,' which would have meant I was taking the name of the Devil in vain. I said 'Lord Harry,' by which I mean Lord Harry Nash. Surely you have heard that name."

"That goes without saying, Holmes," I said, and racked my brain. The mist cleared. "A famous, not to say notorious, personage. A latterday Dick Whittington—though with none of the latter's philanthropic instincts. Head of the multinational conglomerate United Unlimited, many of whose companies have been implicated in environmental disasters. Unless I'm sorely mistaken, he's been called responsible for the great carbon spill that hastened the melting of the polar ice caps." I felt the heat of an angry flush on my face. "By the Lord Harry, indeed!"

"Language, Watson." However, Holmes was smiling. "But an excellent brief on our prospective client. Now to discover what has brought this peerless entrepreneur to our door. Kindly open it and admit him." Then he raised his voice and sent it toward the door. "Do come in, Lord Nash."

I opened the door and caught Lord Nash striding forward on the landing, his hands in his pockets as though he never doubted he would not have to knock: the mark of a man whose position and power gained him entry anywhere.

He entered with the merest nod to me, sharp eyes heavy lids summing the room's occupants and furnishings up at a glance. The lids lowered further, hiding what he thought of us. The hands remained in the pockets, and it struck me that this was the aggressively defensive posture of one unsure he would be offered a handshake.

And indeed Holmes passed the occasion by, though I doubted not he could have learned much by it, tactilely and visually. Holmes has standards and it was clear he did not think Lord Nash measured up to them. Holmes gestured toward a chair. A case is a case and a client is a client. With another curt nod, Lord Nash took it.

A knowing smile formed on his shrewd face as his eyes lit on the Persian slipper, the pipe collection, the beeswax dummy made for Colonel Moran to shoot at, Von Herder's airgun, the Amati violin, the deerstalker hat, the magnifying glass, the gold snuffbox with a great amethyst in the center of the lid, the gasogene, the hypodermic needle, the *Encyclopedia Britannica,* Bunyan's *The Holy War,* Boccaccio's *Decameron,* Flaubert's *Letters,* Murger's *Scenes de la vie de Boheme, The Origin of Tree Worship, Practical Handbook of Bee Culture,* the picture of General Gordon, and the unanswered correspondence pinned to the mantelpiece with a jackknife.

His smile broadened. "Capital. Very like the real thing."

Holmes spoke coldly. "I beg your pardon."

Lord Nash unpocketed his right hand and waved it mollifyingly. "No offense intended." He glanced at his wristcom and spoke more rapidly. "Let's skip the amenities and get down to brass tacks. I 'ave to 'ook it before the hour. First, though, I'd like to know 'ow you knew my name. I've taken pains to stay unphotographed. Wot's the fiddle?"

Involuntarily I swung my gaze to the Amati, then realized that Lord Nash had employed cockney rhyming slang. Fiddle, fiddlestick: trick.

Holmes had not made the same mistake. "Simplicity itself," Holmes said offhandedly but less coldly. "It is after all my job to take notice of details. Very well, then. Your decon suit bears decals warning potential kidnappers that the wearer has alarm and tracer implants. To make you a target you had to be high in either politics or business. You've never lost the unmistakable accent of one born within the sound of Bow Bells, which is to say a four-point-five-mile radius of Saint Mary-le-Bow in East Old London, now sadly clanging with the tides, unheard."

Lord Nash's sunlamp color heightened. "I never tried to lose it."

"More credit to you. But it ruled out political eminence; a public speaker would have greatly softened his cockney accent over the years. Once you removed your protective outerwear and stood in your business suit, the first item to catch my eye was your old school tie."

Lord Nash gave a harsh laugh. "My old—"

With a lift of a hand Holmes halted him. "I know; your school was the school of hard knocks. And your tie bespeaks your pride in your humble origins. The tie bears a pattern of stylized oil and chemical drums. You made your original pile in salvage and waste disposal. Next, when you shot your right cuff—and not-so-incidentally the cufflink has the initials HN—I saw you were wearing a Wristocrat™ com system timepiece. Left-handed persons usually wear wristcoms on the right hand, the dominant hand having an easier time of it when it comes to manipulating the miniature buttons. Harry Nash's childhood nickname was Lefty."

Lord Nash's turn to lift his hand. "Good enough. I guess I've come to the right place after all. Let's not waste any more—" He interrupted himself with a sharp question. "This bloke 'ere one of yer Baker Street Irregulars?"

I looked around to see who Lord Nash meant. It dawned on me that he meant me.

Holmes said somewhat shortly, "This is Dr. Watson."

Lord Nash frowned. "But 'e—"

"Shall we get on to your problem, to the reason you sought me out?"

Lord Nash was a man of quick decisions. He gave a slight shrug, then leaned forward. "By all means. Time's short. I don't want my voice to 'ear me."

I blinked, so failed to see whether or not Holmes blinked likewise.

The cockney accent went on. "I'm not a madman. I came to consult you rather than the authorities. I thought you at least would not prejudge me."

Holmes nodded coolly. "Pray proceed."

"My voice is telling me to go to the hequatorial regions."

Holmes lifted an eyebrow. "To Hades?"

Lord Nash was not a man used to having his statements questioned. "When I say hequatorial regions I mean hequatorial regions."

Before Holmes could draw him out further the clock struck the quarter hour. Lord Nash automatically glanced at the clock. It read ten-fifteen. He paled and shot a look at his Wristocrat™. From where I stood I could see its digits. Nine-fifteen.

To my astonishment, I Suppose snarled at Lord Nash.

Paying I Suppose no mind, Lord Nash pointed a trembling hand at the clock. He had to try twice before the words came. "Is that the old time?"

Holmes nodded. "'Spring forward, fall back.'"

"Wot?"

"Have you forgotten the mnemonic?"

"No. I forgot it was time for the switch from daylight savings to standard." His voice quivered. "It's an hour later than I fought. My voice 'eard me. I'm done for."

I Suppose eyed him scornfully. "Garn."

"Straight," whimpered Lord Nash. "Done for."

I stared at a spreading stain. Lord Nash had wet his pants. I Suppose had smelled the fear.

Lord Nash had been so cocky till now I could only wonder at his sudden attack of panic.

He stared in fearful fascination at his watch. "We'll know for sure in nine minutes."

Holmes eyed him keenly. "Just what do you expect to happen nine minutes hence?"

Lord Nash's gaze remained locked on the seconds count of his

Wristocrat™. He answered in a whisper. "The voice will punish me for 'aving broken our pact by even speaking of it."

Acidly Holmes said, "Thus far you've done nothing more than waste my time as well as yours in dropping veiled hints of a so-called voice. Would it not be advisable, and more profitable, to tell us about this voice that so frightens you? I gather you hear it at certain times, and that it in turn hears you. Pray be more forthcoming in the eight minutes remaining. If I but knew the voice's nature I might be better armed to deal with it."

Lord Nash nodded quickly. "I 'ave it all down." He raised a finger, then reached his hand into an inside pocket. His face registered dismay, which would have been ludicrous had it not been so evocative of terror, as he felt around and came out empty-handed. "I 'ad it all down on paper. The paper's gone. 'Ow'd the voice manage that fiddle?"

Holmes countered with a question of his own. "What was on the paper?"

Lord Nash opened his mouth, but no words came. It seemed clear that his fear of the voice froze his speech center.

I Suppose growled, "Use your tuppenny, mate. Nuffink can do it like rhyming cant. It's the fiddle if you want to rabbit."

Rabbit, rabbit and pork: talk.

Lord Nash looked shakily hopeful and nodded. He struggled, and got out, "Tea leaf Jeremiah."

I Suppose murmured, "Tea leaf: thief. Jeremiah. fire."

Excitedly I said, "Steal fire? Like Prometheus?"

Lord Nash looked blank. "'Oo's 'e when 'e's at 'ome?"

Holmes eyed me reprovingly. "Please, Watson. Allow me to conduct the interrogation." He turned to Lord Nash. "Your . . . voice is commanding you to steal fire?" Finding a relieved expression on Lord Nash's face, Holmes went on. "Does this have to do with the equatorial regions?" And after getting quick bobbing nods, "With volcanoes in the equatorial belt?" Then, following even quicker nods, "So your voice is telling you to trigger eruptions of volcanoes in the equatorial belt?" A deep sigh and a bowing nod from Lord Nash sent Holmes musing aloud. "Your whole career bears the mark of Cain. Early on you struck a Faustian bargain with some entity. Your 'voice.' This entity is either from the outside or the inside, equally real in either case. For years you have been gaining power and wealth while destroying the environment. Why the sudden concern? Why are you struggling to warn us of more catastrophes to come, and implicating yourself as you do so?"

Lord Nash's face worked. He gazed past us all, beyond the walls. "Me poor little twist. 'Er Gawd forbid born wiv no ham and eggs. Can you ever forgive me, duck?"

I Suppose translated. "Twist, twist and twirl: girl. Gawd forbid: kid. Ham and eggs: legs."

"The sins of the fathers," Holmes said sadly. His face and voice hardened. "I take it a grandchild of yours has a birth defect attributable to hazardous chemicals? And I presume one of your companies disposed of these toxic wastes improperly?"

Lord Nash bowed his head miserably.

Holmes went on at him remorselessly. "So now you're on a guilt trip. You wish to break with the demonic force whose voice has directed your antisocial behavior."

The bowed head nodded. Then the head jerked upward as though pulled by a string and the eyeballs rolled toward the ceiling. "The voice! I 'ear it!"

Holmes leapt to Lord Nash's side and his hands gripped Lord Nash's arm. "Quick, man! Where does the voice come from?" His own voice was loud, as though to override the one audible to Lord Nash alone. "You must know. Speak."

Lord Nash listened in a trance, a trance he seemed fighting to break out of. "Is it—? No. Nearer the hot-cross bun." He croaked out the words before stiffening again.

"Hot-cross bun: sun," I Suppose said, in a whisper as though to keep from distracting.

"Get a fix on the voice, man," Holmes said in a near-shout. "You can do it." He tightened the vise to lend the man his strength.

All at once Lord Nash stared with the stare of blinding insight, his mind's eye piercing the last veil. "Now I know 'oo they are, where they are."

"For God's sake, man, who? Where? Try to tell us."

"Just one dicky bird," I Suppose put in.

Dicky bird: word.

Sweat beaded Lord Nash's brow. He got out more than one word. "Rise and fall over stick of joss . . ."

Then his head twisted and his body jerked, as though undergoing the violence of a gallows drop, and everything went slack and he sank to the floor.

Even as I knelt in what I knew to be the empty gesture of feeling for a pulse in the carotid, I was thinking *Aha! I have it!* But out of deference I waited for I Suppose to come out with the translation. By this time it was obvious to me that Holmes had programmed I Suppose to bone up on cockney rhyming slang because the underworld made use of it as cant. Far be it for me to keep I Suppose from doing its thing. But I Suppose for once stood mute as a Basenji.

If I Suppose did not recognize "rise and fall" and "stick of joss" as cockney rhyming slang, then those phrases were not in the lexicon. Obviously I had jumped to the wrong conclusion. I felt glad I had held my tongue.

"Well?" said Holmes.

I Suppose had no compunctions about beating me to the diagnosis. " 'E's done for."

Somewhat miffed, I rendered a second—and fuller—opinion. "I wager an autopsy would show a massive stroke. The man's beyond help."

Holmes looked positively grim. "This is murder. Murder done not only in my presence but my premises. The voice has struck me in the face with the gauntlet. I have no choice but to accept the challenge."

I Suppose cocked his head and asked in tone of practicality, "Wot's the protocol? Do we get on the dog and bone to the bottles?"

Dog and bone: phone. Bottles, bottles and stoppers: coppers.

Holmes spoke firmly. "No. Time is of the essence, and that would be a waste of it. New New Scotland Yard would dismiss the murder as death by natural causes—Watson's stroke. I can hear the commissioner, if we ever got that high, laugh at our talk of a voice. No matter that the three of us could bear witness to Lord Nash's dread of it." He shook his head and strode to the window overlooking the street and raised the shade to peer out. He fixed an eye of resolve on the world. "We must locate this voice and deal with it before it finds another susceptible human to carry out its damnable work."

I shivered as he spoke. At that very moment it seemed to me that the voice of a tempter felt its way through the maze of my mind and whispered of power and glory if I but did its will.

It may be that I ought to have let it think it was having its way, but the deadly strength I sensed behind the sensuous whisper filled me with dread—and Lord Nash's body lay before me as a warning sign.

I said nothing of this inward struggle to Holmes, of how nearly I had come under the sway of some evil force, but his eyes were keen on my face.

He exchanged a wink with I Suppose before jollying me. "For an old campaigner who's seen death in all bloody phases, you look shaken, Watson, positively pale. Do you good to get a breath of even stale air."

I Suppose got up on all fours. "If you're stepping outside I'm going along o' you."

"No fear," Holmes said. "If I'm not mistaken, we'll have need of your expertise."

"How's that?" I asked.

"There's no limousine below in the street. Lord Nash evidently came here either by autocar that he did not ask to wait or by shank's mare. Unless we find Lord Nash's address on his person, I Suppose will have to sniff that out."

I Suppose fairly swelled.

Holmes knelt to look at Lord Nash's boots.

"Why the butcher's 'ook at 'is daisy roots?" I Suppose queried querulously.

"To see if they have beeper soles. As I feared, they do not. Apparently he took into account that his boots might fall into the hands of those with good or bad cause to retrace his secretive movements, to locate his safe houses, his caches, his drops, his rendezvous points."

He went deftly as a pickpocket through the corpse's clothing. A fruitless search. He rose with a sigh. "All as I feared. No wallet, no keys, no ID. A person such as Lord Nash needs only palmprint or voiceprint to see him through any day's activities." He traded his dressing gown for a navvy's pea jacket.

As he changed he addressed I Suppose, who had quite perked

up again. "What can you tell us of Lord Nash's most recent movements?"

"Pony and trap?" I Suppose said coarsely. (I will not translate.) "Only 'aving a bit o' fun, gentlemen. I know the sort o' fing you mean." The cynosure for the moment, he sat up on his haunches. " 'E made 'is way 'ere on 'is own plates o' meat. On the way 'e stopped in at a rub-a-dub and 'ad a tiddly or two, like 'e was getting up 'is nerve to come and see us. Wot 'e 'ad was a pig's ear and mother's ru-in; a hot pertater spilled someone else's laugh and titter on 'is whistle and flute, because it's on that and not on 'is bref. While 'e was there, 'e 'ad a rabbit wiv a brass nail, then went to the men's for a 'it and miss. Suiting up again, 'e set out once more. Doubtless feeling 'e'd 'ad too much tiddly on an empty stomach, 'e paused at a lollipop to feed 'is boat race a bit o' Andy McNish. After which 'e came straight 'ere."

Which is to say our late client had come on foot, halting at a pub for a few drinks. Beer and gin; someone, a waiter most likely, spilled a mild and bitter on Lord Nash's suit—that particular drink was not on Lord Nash's breath. While there, he chatted with a streetwalker and relieved himself. Then he came directly to our lodgings, stopping once for fish and chips.

"Brilliant, I Suppose," said Holmes. "Do you think you can retrace those movements to the very pub?"

"A piece o' shiver and shake," I Suppose said immodestly. Holmes rubbed his hands together. "Then we're off." He smiled at me, then his face lengthened. "One moment, Watson."

For a heartbeat or two I though he meant to leave me behind; I could not guess why. But he swiftly broke out his makeup kit and sat me down for the application of a mustache. A disguise! I thought in delight, not stopping to wonder why I, with my forgettable puddingy face and not Holmes with his distinctive features, should be the one who needed disguise. While I admired myself in the mirror, he himself put on a pair of dark glasses. The better to observe while unseen to observe, I thought. Ah, how foresighted the man was.

We went downstairs, into the airlock, and took our outerwear off the pegs. Holmes helped I Suppose suit up, then suited up himself. Meanwhile I put on my decon suit and made sure my breathing mask fitted without disturbing the truly magnificent mustache.

As we left the airlock and stepped outside I felt the familiar frisson. The snugness of our lodgings became a nostalgic memory. The real world was shadowy, grim as doom, the air an inversion of nature.

In the roadway autocabs streaked to and fro like dirty turbulences, guided by buried wires. On the sidewalks a few darkling figures moved, their beeper soles recording their traversal of the geodetic mosaic.

If Old London had been The Smoke, New London, arisen in the Highlands after the melting ice caps drowned the sceptered isle's—and the world's—coasts, was, thanks to the prevailing acid rain, The Poison.

I Suppose and Holmes held a colloquy.

"Wot's it to be, 'Olmes, flounder and dab or ball o' chalk?"

"Shank's mare's faster," Holmes said.

And at the pace Holmes set, we should indeed make better time walking than cabbing.

"This way, then, gents," I Suppose said, and we followed—I, at least, blindly trusting. Every now and then I Suppose paused cursorily to cock a leg, blazing a trail with a minim of personal scent. I made a face, yet found it oddly reassuring as indicating that I Suppose could backtrack himself and lead us safely home should for some reason our own beeper soles, or the grid itself, fail us.

Once, a burly form loomed menacingly in the mist, but it proved to be a bobby, who touched his stick to his helmet in passing. "Nasty night, persons. Watch your step at all times."

"A real scratch an itch," I Suppose said.

Though the gutter language embarrassed me, I smiled to myself at the chauvinistic machismo. For a sham dog, I Suppose had "bitch" a good deal on the mind.

"Thank you, officer," I said, to make up for I Suppose's lack of good taste and good manners.

The bobby vanished, but left behind a wisp of thought. Scotland Yard that was, was now fittingly in Scotland, though renamed New New Scotland Yard.

The mist made it easy to believe that the natural world and the supernatural world intersected. Musing that all interfaces are ultimately fuzzy—for at the subatomic level will you not find particles of A on B's side of the interface and particles of B on A's side? —I tripped on a curb.

"Curb yer toe, guv'nor," said I Suppose with a malicious laugh. "Mind wot the peeler said. Watch yer step."

I would have said something I might have regretted had not I Suppose just then imitated a setter pointing.

Holmes's keen eyes picked out the sign sooner than mine. "The very fish and chips shop, eh?"

"Too right, 'Olmes. 'Ere's the Andy McNish lollipop 'is lordship patronized."

As we drew nearer I saw it was more in the nature of a stand. Under its ionizing canopy a lone customer was placing a palm to the credit panel and pressing selection keys. We strode by, onward into the mist.

I had lost track and could not make out the street sign when we reached the next corner. "Do you know where we are?"

"In the loop-the-loop." In the soup.

A bit of give-and-take on the order of: Q. Where was Moses when the light went out? A. In the dark.

"Really, Holmes," I said. "You must take a firmer hand with I Suppose."

"Gabriel," Holmes said forbiddingly.

"Sorry, guv'nor," I Suppose thus prompted said to me unrepentantly. "Sorry you take it amiss when I'm only 'aving a bit o' sport. We're at the norfeast Jack 'Orner of New Camden Square."

"'Thank you," I said stittly.

"Shouldn't be much farver. Just up the frog and toad."

Good as his word, I Suppose soon came to a halt alongside a building front. The neon legend bled into the mist. The Cormorant.

"This 'ere's the rub-a-dub 'is lordship stopped in at."

We entered, unsuited in the airlock, Holmes snapped a leash on I Suppose, and breathing air weary of recycling we emerged to face the blast of spirited sound and spiritous atmosphere.

Pseudowindows looked out on cloudless climes. The regulars at the bar and in the booths turned to stare at us with territorial imperative in their eyes. Then a loud voice from behind the bar stopped us in our tracks.

" 'Old on there, you lot. No animals allowed in 'ere." The

barman had a red face, at least for the moment, and his build was an advert for his stout.

Holmes turned the dark glasses full on the barman. "That stricture, my good man, if you know anything about the law, does not apply to seeing-eye dogs."

"Oh. Ah. Er. Sorry, sir. Carry on. But do try and keep 'im from getting underfoot or making a mess."

"I beg your pardon," said I Suppose, growing stiff-legged. The barman dropped the glass he had been polishing.

Holmes spotted an empty booth, took me by the arm to turn me toward it, and whispered for me to stake our claim and hold a place while he and I Suppose repaired to the loo.

I had barely seated myself when a woman with a young shape and old eyes locked those eyes on me and sashayed that shape toward the booth.

"All alone, dearie?" She displayed an alarming amount of tooth and gum. She wore a shrinkwrap dress and I wondered how she breathed, but she definitely breathed. Before I could remonstrate, she slid in and sat down beside me. "You don't mind a bit o' company, do you, love?" Before I could say I was here with friends, she added, "I knew at first sight you were a good sort." She leaned back to take me in. "Slumming, are you?"

She knew a gentleman when she saw one.

"Why, no," I got out.

She leaned forward. I felt something jump inside me. Her hand resting on my thigh wakened strange stirrings. I glanced uneasily around to see who watched. What kept Holmes and I Suppose?

An ancient waiter appeared and stood listlessly facing me.

"I'll 'ave a laugh and titter," the woman said.

"And your gentleman friend?"

The tips of my ears felt aflame. "The same," I said.

While we awaited the waiter's return sweat loosened my mustache. I felt it come unstuck. I caught it as it fell.

The woman raised a minimal eyebrow. "Wot 'ave we 'ere? You looking to cost Alf 'is license? Never you mind, I won't grass." She helped stick the mustache back on. "Big for yer age, ain't you, love? Does yer muvver know yer aht?" She rubbed up against me.

The waiter returned. My mug slopped over as he set it down. He made to set the woman's down, missed badly, and spilled her mild and bitter over my suit. The woman was quick to help wipe it. Despite my irritation I felt sorry for the gaffer, who kept mumbling apologetically.

I Suppose growled at the man. I Suppose and Holmes had come back from the loo. Holmes was too busy focusing his dark lenses on the woman to tell I Suppose to mind his manners. I reproved I Suppose. "Don't you feel sorry for the poor old fellow?" I imagine I felt a certain kinship for the waiter, my mind going back to I Suppose's slur of senility earlier aimed at me.

"Brown Bess and Brown Joe." Yes and no. I Suppose spoke absently, his attention following Holmes's toward the woman I Suppose muzzled her dress.

"Forward thing," she said.

"Same perfume as on 'is lordship," I Suppose stated. He sniffed my clothing. "And it's just now rubbed off on the guv'nor."

Plainly not liking this turn of events, and squirming under Holmes's unnerving dark glasses, the woman slid away from me as though making ready to leave the booth.

Holmes and I Suppose blocked her way.

"This is the place, beyond any shadow of doubt," I Suppose went on conversationally. " 'Is lordship was at the urinal. Didn't quite belly up to it. I recognized 'is 'it and miss "

The woman tried to squeeze past Holmes, but he clamped a hand on her arm.

"Not so fast, my dear." The one hand immobilized her while the other dipped into her cleavage and come up with my gold tie pin, which he handed to me warm with her body heat.

"Amazing, Holmes," I said, all agape. "What made you suspect?"

"You had your tie pin on when Gabriel and I split for the john: quite without it when we came back."

" 'Ow it works, guv'nor," I Suppose said condescendingly, "the 'ot pertater spills the tiddly over the sucker's whistle and flute, the brass nail 'elps wipe 'im orf—and 'elps 'erself to wot's in 'is skyrocket while she's at it."

The woman's free hand flew protectively to her bosom. The waiter, I saw, had made himself scarce.

"The Cormorant," Holmes said with a snort. He seemed high; the game was afoot. "Cormorant, indeed. Rather, The Den of Thieves."

The babble had suddenly stilled and his words hung as in a balloon in the room's breathy silence. I felt the regulars' baleful looks. This could turn uglier than it already was. Without relaxing his grip on the woman, Holmes swung his dark glasses toward the crowd, then slowly flashed the badge pinned to the underside of his pea jacket's lapel. It was that of honorary sheriff of Salt Lake County, Utah, but it served well enough.

"Blimey," the barman said. "It's a fair cop." He shrugged and went back to polishing glasses.

That defused the moment. The babble rebuilt.

Holmes turned back to the woman. "What else have you lifted this evening, young woman?"

"Nuffink," she said sulkily.

"Under the Cain and Abel," I Suppose said.

And under the table, where she had apparently just now while we were distracted ditched it, lay a folded sheet of paper. I Suppose retrieved it. Carefully Holmes took it from I Suppose's jaws, and one-handedly unfolded and smoothed the creases so it lay flat on the table.

It was a sheet of printout on a letterhead. The logo consisted of the monogram HN on a field of chemical drums.

"By the Lord Harry!" I permitted to escape.

"Just so, Watson," Holmes said as through glasses darkly he scanned the printout. He picked it up and handed it to me. "What do you make of it?"

Columns of dates and times filled the upper half of the sheet, graphics the bottom. I made out the latter to be curves plotted from the former. "It appears to be a record of durations ranging over a period of years, increasing from slightly less than five minutes to slightly less than twenty-nine minutes, then decreasing, and so on, cyclically."

"Excellent, Watson." Holmes turned again to the woman. "Had the man you took this from said anything about it to you?"

She shook her head sullenly.

"So you do not know what it is, except that it belonged to one HN. Do you know who this HN was?"

She frowned and, as though piezoelectrically, flashes of fear shone in her eyes. "Was?"

"You're quick on the uptake," Holmes said admiringly. "Yes, was. He died not an hour ago."

She took a quick swallow of my mild and bitter, then said stoutly, "I 'ad nuffink to do wiv that."

Holmes held the dark lenses on her. "But from the logo on the paper you knew or guessed his identity. Having whizzed the only thing of seeming value on his person, you figured that it might bring a reward for its return or that it might be worth something to a business rival of Lord N's. Do I read you right?"

"Right and left," she said with a flash of spirit.

Holmes smiled, released his grip, and moved aside. "That's all. You're free to go." And he even bowed as she slipped past.

We stood watching her maneuver her curves across the floor to the airlock. At the last, she tossed a sweet smile over her shoulder and such foul words came from those fair lips as I do not care to repeat.

The noise level in the Cormorant was hardly conducive to sensible discussion, and the atmosphere to unconstrained deduction, so we left not long after. I breathed easier to find that the woman had not slashed our decon suits.

Back in our digs, we took time now, as in Holmes's urgent desire to retrace Lord Nash's last movements we had not done before, to stash the corpse in the deep freeze against the moment Holmes was ready to hand it and the solution over to New New Scotland Yard, then made ourselves comfortable. Holmes screened the mysterious printout in General Gordon's space and we sat studying it.

Between puffs on his pipe, Holmes put the case. "Lord Nash meant to show us this as having to do with the source of the voice. It was missing, we have found it. What does it tell us? Clearly, it is a time log, recording Lord Nash's sessions with the voice. Can the voice have been a voice from the future? Does intercourse between past and future entail a time lag, a variable one at that?"

He did not wait for answer but went on, with the distancing effect of one thinking as he spoke, probing for his own questions and answers. "On the other hand, Lord Nash used the phrase 'nearer the hot-cross bun,' which Gabriel renders as 'nearer the sun.' That would indicate the source to be a planet of the solar system. Aha! Mars!"

Holmes's curriculum had deliberately omitted study of the makeup and workings of the solar system as unneccesary to a consulting detective; such mundane details only cluttered the mind.

I could hold myself in no longer. "Not Mars, Holmes. Venus. It has to be Venus."

His mouth opened. He filled it with "Oh?" Then, "How on earth do you know that?"

"Mars is farther from the sun. Venus is nearer. Mars's mean distance from the sun is roughly one-and-a-half astronomical units. Venus's is roughly three-fourths an a.u. That means—"

Holmes lifted his hand. "You've made your point, Watson. Spare me."

Sufficient unto the day. I had broadened his horizons more than enough.

Heedless, I persisted. "Besides, the sign of Mars is ♂"—I drew it in the air—"whereas the sign for Venus is ♀."

He looked puzzled. "I fail to see—"

"Allow me," I said, with unaccustomed confidence. "'Rise and fall over stick of joss.'"

He looked blank, then eyed I Suppose accusingly.

"Don't blame I Suppose," I said quickly. "The phrases aren't in his cockney rhyming slang vocabulary."

"Ta, guv'nor," I Suppose said. "'E's right, 'Olmes. I've never come across the bleeding fings."

"Lord Nash," I said, "a human under pressure, needing rhyming phrases for words never yet paired with them, invented the rhyming phrases on the spot. No machine, confronting the unexpected, could have programmed itself to do that."

" 'Old 'ard, guv'nor."

"Rise and fall: ball. Stick of joss: cross. Ball over cross equals the sign for Venus."

I considered during the silence that fell, then ventured my comment. "I find 'rise and fall' elegant, as evoking bounce. But while stick of joss suggests the religious burning of incense, I'm not so happy with it. For my part, I should have preferred 'nowhere to doss' as better evoking 'no room at the inn' and 'Foxes have holes, and birds of the air have nests; but the Son of man hath not where to lay his head.'" I shrugged. "However. Yes, all in all, Lord Nash did extremely well for one in extremis." I grew brisk. "If you'll permit me, Holmes, I'll call up on the screen recorded terrestrial observations of Venus."

Holmes remained frozen-faced, but with a jerk of his hand he gave me the go-ahead.

I accessed the astronomical data base and loaded the pertinent ephemeris. I studied the figures on the screen and compared them with Lord Nash's printout. "It all fits! The voice comes only when New London's in line of sight of Venus. Lord Nash's regular plotting of these contacts gives us curves corresponding to the swing of Venus from west of the sun, when it's a morning star, to east of the sun, when it's the evening star. Venus's minimum distance from Earth, taking place at inferior conjunction, is twenty-six million miles. Venus's maximum distance from Earth, at superior conjunction, is one hundred sixty million miles. Apparently the 'voice'—some sort of thought-wave—travels at light-speed, one hundred eighty-six thousand, two hundred eighty miles per second." I worked my wristcom. "That gives us roughly two point three-two-six minutes for near and roughly fourteen point three-one-five minutes for far. Multiply each by two—the round trip—and you get a low of five minutes and a high of twenty-nine minutes, just as Lord Nash's graph shows."

Deduction swept me along. An exhilarating feeling, attributable I am sure to something more than or beyond oxygen or adrenaline. "This brings us to the matter of motive. I'm afraid I can't visualize a life form that thrives on sulfuric acid. But the Venereans"—I shed my Victorian prudery and came right out with that monicker in place of the namby-pamby "Venusians"—"do, and their aim in communicating with Lord Nash and bending him to their will must surely be to venusform Terra in anticipation of a takeover."

The fire had gone out of Holmes's pipe and he now knocked out the ashes. "I think you've hit on it, Watson. Congratulations."

"Thank you, Holmes." I waited, but I Suppose did not complement the compliment. However, I was too keyed up to mind. "Holmes," I said excitedly, with the creepy-crawly sensation of enlightenment prickling my flesh, "I do believe the Venereans have been at this for a long time. Think, did not the industrial revolution's satanic mills, burning fossil fuels, give rise to the greenhouse effect? From James Watt of the steam engine to James Watt of oil leases, and latterly Lord Nash, Venerean agents have been among us!"

"You may have a point there, Watson," Holmes said quietly, working fiercely on the dottle.

"Right on 'is loaf," I Suppose muttered.

"The Venereans," I said, "are growing bolder or getting impatient. Lord Nash may have fought the switch from high-sulfur coal to low-sulfur coal, have resisted the costly installation of scrubbers to remove sulfur dioxide from plant emissions, have contested laws mandating double-walled storage tanks, but environmentalists have been making inroads, slowing the deadly process. Why else would the Venerean voice have been pressing him to nuke, or otherwise trigger, eruptions in the equatorial regions? Volcanoes there, you know, put out more sulfur than those at the higher latitudes."

Holmes nodded. "Sulfur dioxide couples with water vapor to bring forth sulfuric acid droplets—acid rain."

He was once more in his element; chemistry was one of his strong points. So I now deferred to him.

"What now, Holmes?"

Holmes sat more erect, though I thought he looked somewhat wan. "Even without further deliberate sabotaging by Venusian tools such as Lord Nash, the greenhousing will continue if we Terrans do little more than we have done to reverse it. That is up to the world as a whole to deal with. As for present company, our immediate problem is to find some way of forcing the Venusians to stop their sinister but dexterous venusforming of Terra."

I stepped to the window and raised the blind. By the grandfather clock and our other timepieces it was morning. By eyeball it was a timeless limbo. I craved to grab handfuls of the foul air to fling back at the Venereans. But that—and the analogy here was with Antaeus and Mother Earth—would merely strengthen the Venereans.

Turning from the window, I found Holmes once more—to my glad surprise—smilingly alert.

"Holmes, you appear almost cocky. Do you have some scheme?"

"Yes. And believe me, Watson, it is some scheme."

"What—"

"Curb your impatience, Watson. This waits on the voice. With Lord Nash out of it, Venus must find another human receiver, some sensitive not all that insensible to blandishment and the promise of power. That is what we have to be on the lookout for: the signs that someone is carrying on Lord Nash's job. Then we will strike."

My mind flashed to the corpse in the deep freeze. "What of the meanwhile? Lord Nash's people will be looking for him."

Holmes pursed his lips, then shook his head. "No fear of a hue and cry. He's legendary as Howard Hughes for his mysterious comings and goings."

"Then what about New New Scotland Yard? Won't the authorities hold us to account for not reporting his demise?"

"His number's up when we say it is. We have but to let him thaw when we're ready."

"I hope you know what you're doing, Holmes," I said dubiously.

Holmes relit his pipe. "Leave it to me, Watson. Leave it to me."

I left it to him.

After two weeks I was still leaving it to him, not nagging him about his seeming indifference to the lack of progress. He lounged about the lodgings, doing nothing but play the violin or pipedream. Or try out a new toy, some state-of-the art device that he hoped would aid him in his private-eye work.

This particular morning it was a laser pistol. I heard the snap of the beam and smelled burned air as he sat in his armchair and picked out VR on the wall.

From the lavatory, where I happened to be engaged in shaving my face, I heard Holmes languidly ask I Suppose, "What's . . . Watson up to?"

" 'E's giving 'imself a dig in the grave," I Suppose said, and rapped out a laugh I didn't at all care for.

I had been frowning to see the growth so sparse, and I was, as you might say, in a lather when I strode to the doorway and hurled my hand mirror at I Suppose.

Holmes, on the point of punctuating the revered initials, fired the laser pistol just as the mirror sliced past him I-Supposewards. The beam, rebounding from the reflecting surface, struck Holmes full in the chest, pierced Holmes's clothing, and Holmes, and the chairback, and seared the wall behind him.

I heard the yip from I Suppose as the mirror found its mark, then a shattering as the mirror rebounded to the floor. I did not look to see: it was Holmes my gaze fixed on. The poor fellow lay back slackly in the chair, his eyes empty. A roaring stillness filled the room. I stood frozen.

The tunnel walls of the hole in him showed the golden gleam of circuitry.

"A robot," I whispered.

"Walking computer." I Suppose corrected me with a snarl. "See wot you done? I 'ope yer satisfied."

"How can that be?" I said in the same whisper.

" 'Ow can it not be," I Suppose came back in the same snarl. "Time you used yer loaf for something besides a titfer rack. Ain't it sunk in that 'Olmes bloody well 'as to be an artifact? Wot was 'e in the first place but only a literary construct? Then fervent fans raised funds and set up the Sherlock 'Olmes Foundation to fashion a computerized simulacrum, and 'e came into being a quarter century ago."

This was too much for me. My head swam, and I doubt not I should have collapsed in a parade-ground faint had not a noise resounded in my head, a noise so loud I closed my eyes. Once the pain passed, I felt in control of myself again. It was as though one of the more powerful brands of sonic cleanser had rattled my brain clear. Somehow I knew it to be I Suppose's doing.

"Thanks," I said. "I needed that."

Without more ado, I grabbed Holmes's magnifying glass and sprang to his side to assess the damage. By the looks of it, the shot had gutted Holmes's message center. I smashed open the tantalus and cannibalized the intercom for wiring and chips.

Gently I freed the laser pistol from Holmes's grasp to forestall further damage to anyone or anything should Holmes twitch. As I worked to bridge the gaps in Holmes, my mind, with a mind of its own, ruminated about the sound that had snapped me out of my funk. I Suppose—and Holmes—had unexpected capacities.

Despite my self-recriminations and urgent ministrations, I smiled. Their "supernatural" rapport, forsooth! They communicated at dog-whistle frequency, in tones pitched too high for my ears.

I finished the last bit of soldering. Holmes stirred under my hand before I could draw his dressing gown more tightly about him to cover the hole till I found a patch. Life came back to his eyes. He glanced at me almost mischievously, then his gaze shot to the window.

"In the nick of time, Watson," he said in quite nearly his old voice, though with overtones of Mrs. Hudson. "The game's afoot."

"Thank the Lord," I breathed. Then, trying to match Holmes's self-possession, "What do you mean, Holmes, the game's afoot? The Venerean voice has finally found its new pawn? But how can you know that?"

"Just look out the window, Watson."

"A real scratch an itch of a fog," said I Suppose. "A Brighton pier 'un."

Brighton pier: queer.

"What's queer about it?" I asked.

"Look sharp, Watson," said Holmes, "and answer yourself."

I peered out. "By the Lord Harry! It's raining split peas!"

"Not only that," I Suppose said, nose to the window sash and snuffing strongly. "I smell smoked brisket of beef, celery, onion, butter, sugar, salt, white pepper, and flour."

"Most unnatural!" I exclaimed.

"Not at all, Watson. Entirely natural if you examine the list of ingredients and ask yourself what they form the recipe for."

"Pea soup!" I ejaculated.

"Quite so, Watson. Pea soup. Literal pea soup. And what does that suggest?"

"A human agency?"

"Precisely. This is the sign I have been waiting for. It tells me that the voice has been in contact with someone in the vicinity, someone who has cast his or her lot with the Venusians, selling humanity out in exchange for the promise of personal power. This someone has evidently taken all too literally the order to produce a pea-soup fog."

I Suppose snickered. "Guess we ort to give fanks 'e received pea as p-e-a."

Holmes turned on I Suppose chidingly. "You'd be better occupied, Gabriel, tracking the pea soup to its source."

I Suppose hung his head. "Too right, 'Olmes." Then he lifted his head and wagged his tail. "Just suit me up and I'm orf."

"Good Gabriel. Good fellow."

And with that Holmes led the way down to the airlock. Holmes saw I Suppose off with a word in his ear, then Holmes and I climbed back to our rooms to wait I Suppose's return.

Holmes sat in his armchair with his eyes closed but with an attentiveness that told me he kept in constant touch with I Suppose over the dog-whistle frequency. I did not stir for fear of breaking their contact, their rapport.

After only a half hour by the clock by an eon by my own reckoning, Holmes gave a beatific sigh and opened his eyes. "We've done it, Watson."

"Wonderful! What have we done?"

"Our Gabriel hound had no trouble locating the source: a canning factory—a subsidiary of United Unlimited, by the by—that was spewing the soup from its stacks instead of sealing it in cans. Gabriel slipped inside the plant without difficulty. The plant is highly automated and there are few people about. The smell of fear, mixed with sweaty elation, led him directly to one of the few, a computer operator by the name of Winthrop Morrill. On my instructions, Gabriel blasted the dupe's brain with a message for relay to the Venusians, telling them that their dastardly plot has been uncovered and warning them that Terra will terraform Venus unless Venus desists from venusforming Terra. As for Morrill, the blast will leave his mind foggy, no longer of use to the Venusians, and he most likely will remember little if anything of the entire episode. There you have it, Watson. I believe I can say we have saved Earth from a terrible fate."

"Bravo, Holmes!" I said without stint.

He waved his hand. "Kudos are due I Suppose as well. Oh, and of course, yourself. Your contribution was, shall I say, astronomical."

"Not at all, Holmes," I said, though naturally gratified. Hunting for something to do to hide my blushes, I bent to pick up the shards of the mirror that had been the cause of damage to my friend. "Blast the blasted thing!" I had cut myself on a splinter of glass. Blood flowed. And with it, thought; thought like a streak of dark turbulence in the fog. "Holmes, I'm human!"

Holmes looked round quickly at me as I knelt thus, then he puffed on his pipe and followed the smoke ceilingward with his gaze.

"Did you hear me, Holmes? I said I'm human."

He sighed from his depths. "I know, Watson. I've been aware for some time that this moment would have to come. I know too that I shall be glad when it is out, but that makes it no easier to get out." He took a deep breath and sat straighter. "Very well. Listen to the story of your life. Thirteen years ago I felt overwhelmingly the need that had been instilled in me for a Watson. I suppose I could have materialized my Watson in the same manner as I later built Gabriel, but I had the notion of repaying Sir Arthur Conan Doyle for bringing me back to life after Reichenbach Falls." He erased air with his hand. "I know, that was a paper resurrection. But memory and mimicry interface in me, and I am my canonical history as much as I am my functioning computerized self. And so, with the thought of repaying my debt to my creator, I secretly made my way to that part of Hampshire where Minstead is, was, located. I had to work fast, as the world's oceans were still rising rapidly and the area was on the point of drowning. On the sopping grounds of a home in Minstead I played resurrection man in the dead of night, dark lantern and all. What I dug for lay beneath a carved British oak headstone, inscribed SIR ARTHUR CONAN DOYLE, 22 MAY 1859, STEEL TRUE, BLADE STRAIGHT. In short, Watson, you are a clone, grown and still growing from a splinter of bone, a trace of gristle, robbed from his grave."

Memory and mimicry interfaced, just as Holmes had said, making the past the present. I knew I was in our New Baker Street lodgings, yet at the same time I knew I was in shock on the Afghanistani front, having just taken a Jezail bullet. I had memories of childhood and adulthood, of medical education and practice of medicine, yet I had the physique of an adolescent, though an overgrown burly one. My body bore the requisite scars of my military campaigning—plastic surgery?—but my voice had only just changed and I had yet to grow some sort of mustache.

I Suppose's voice brought me back to the present present. "Tell me somefink, guv'nor, do clones 'ave belly buttons?" He had unvelcroed himself out of his decon suit and turned the doorknob with his jaws. He grinned at me. " 'Ow's that for a larf, guv'nor?" He threw back his head to howl in laughter.

I reached for the poker and raised it.

Too late I Suppose saw it coming.

"Arf—"

His last bow-wow.

It was a good feeling, and purged me, though I knew deep down that sooner or later either Holmes or myself would have to resurrect I Suppose.

Holmes said, "Really, Watson." But there was a wealth of understanding in his voice.

And that night, with a grin, I laid me loaf on me weeping willow to plow the deep.

The Adventure of the Metal Murderer
by
Fred Saberhagen

What small hints are enough to fasten our mind on the incomparable, the unique. Mention "Baker Street" and that is enough. Have someone say "Elementary" and that is enough. It is even almost enough to refer to someone as a "tall man."

The Adventure of the Metal Murderer

by Fred Saberhagen

It had the shape of a man, the brain of an electronic devil.

It and the machines like it were the best imitations of men and women that the berserkers, murderous machines themselves, were able to devise and build. Still they could be seen as obvious frauds when closely inspected by any humans.

"Only twenty-nine accounted for?" the supervisor of Defense demanded sharply. Strapped into his combat chair, he was gazing intently through the semitransparent information screen before him, into space. The nearby bulk of Earth was armored in the dun-brown of defensive force fields, the normal colors of land and water and air invisible.

"Only twenty-nine." The answer arrived on the flagship's bridge amid a sharp sputtering of electrical noise. The tortured voice continued. "And it's quite certain now that there were thirty to begin with."

"Then where's the other one?"

251

There was no reply.

All of Earth's defensive forces were still on full alert, though the attack had been tiny, no more than an attempt at infiltration, and seemed to have been thoroughly repelled. Berserkers, remnants of an ancient interstellar war, were mortal enemies of everything that lived and the greatest danger to humanity that the universe had yet revealed.

A small blur leaped over Earth's dun-brown limb, hurtling along on a course that would bring it within a few hundred kilometers of the supervisor's craft. This was Power Station One, a tamed black hole. In time of peace the power-hungry billions on the planet drew from it half their needed energy. Station One was visible to the eye only as a slight, flowing distortion of the stars beyond.

Another report was coming in. "We are searching space for the missing berserker android, Supervisor."

"You had damned well better be."

"The infiltrating enemy craft had padded containers for thirty androids, as shown by computer analysis of its debris. We must assume that all containers were filled."

Life and death were in the supervisor's tones. "Is there any possibility that the missing unit got past you to the surface?"

"Negative, Supervisor." There was a slight pause. "At least we know it did not reach the surface in our time."

"Our time? What does that mean, babbler? How could . . . ah."

The black hole flashed by. Not really tamed, though that was a reassuring word, and humans applied it frequently. Just harnessed, more or less.

Suppose—and, given the location of the skirmish, the supposition was not unlikely—that berserker android number thirty had been propelled, by some accident of combat, directly at Station One. It could easily have entered the black hole. According to the latest theories, it might conceivably have survived to reemerge intact into the universe, projected out of the hole as its own tangible image in a burst of virtual-particle radiation.

Theory dictated that in such a case the reemergence must take place before the falling in. The supervisor crisply issued orders.

At once his computers on the world below, the Earth Defense Conglomerate, took up the problem, giving it highest priority. What could one berserker android do to Earth? Probably not much. But to the supervisor, and to those who worked for him, defense was a sacred task. The temple of Earth's safety had been horribly profaned.

To produce the first answers took the machines eleven minutes.

"Number thirty did go into the black hole, sir. Neither we nor the enemy could very well have foreseen such a result, but—"

"What is the probability that the android emerged intact?"

"Because of the peculiar angle at which it entered, approximately sixty-nine percent."

"That high!"

"And there is a forty-nine-percent chance that it will reach the surface of the earth in functional condition, at some point in our past. However, the computers offer reassurance. As the enemy device must have been programmed for some subtle attack upon our present society, it is not likely to be able to do much damage at the time and place where it—"

"Your skull contains a vacuum of a truly intergalactic order. *I* will tell *you* and the computers when it has become possible for us to feel even the slightest degree of reassurance. Meanwhile, get me more figures."

The next word from the ground came twenty minutes later.

"There is a ninety-two-percent chance that the landing of the android on the surface, if that occurred, was within one hundred kilometers of fifty-one degrees, eleven minutes north latitude; zero degrees, seven minutes west longitude."

"And the time?"

"Ninety-eight-percent probability of January 1, 1880, Christian Era, plus or minus ten standard years."

A landmass, a great clouded island, was presented to the supervisor on his screen.

"Recommended course of action?"

It took the ED Conglomerate an hour and a half to answer that.

The first two volunteers perished in attempted launchings before the method could be improved enough to offer a reasonable chance of survival. When the third man was ready, he was called in, just before launching, for a last private meeting with the supervisor.

The supervisor looked him up and down, taking in his outlandish dress, strange hairstyle, and all the rest. He did not ask whether the volunteer was ready but began bluntly: "It has now been confirmed that whether you win or lose back there, you will never be able to return to your own time."

"Yes, sir. I had assumed that would be the case."

"Very well." The supervisor consulted data spread before him. "We are still uncertain as to just how the enemy is armed. Something subtle, doubtless, suitable for a saboteur on the Earth of our own time—in addition, of course, to the superhuman physical strength and speed you must expect to face. There are the scrambling or the switching mindbeams to be considered; either could damage any human society. There are the pattern bombs, designed to disable our defense computers by seeding them with random information. There are always possibilities of biological warfare. You have your disguised medical kit? Yes, I see. And of course there is always the chance of something new."

"Yes, sir." The volunteer looked as ready as anyone could. The supervisor went to him, opening his arms for a ritual farewell embrace.

He blinked away some London rain, pulled out his heavy ticking timepiece as if he were checking the hour, and stood on the pavement before the theater as if he were waiting for a friend. The instrument in his hand throbbed with a silent, extra vibration in addition to its ticking, and this special signal had now taken on a character that meant the enemy machine was very near to him. It was probably within a radius of fifty meters.

A poster on the front of the theater read:

THE IMPROVED AUTOMATON CHESS PLAYER
MARVEL OF THE AGE
UNDER NEW MANAGEMENT

"The real problem, sir," proclaimed one top-hatted man nearby, in conversation with another, "is not whether a machine can be made to win at chess, but whether it may possibly be made to play at all."

No, that is not the real problem, sir, the agent from the future thought. *But count yourself fortunate that you can still believe it is.*

He bought a ticket and went in, taking a seat. When a sizable audience had gathered, there was a short lecture by a short man in evening dress, who had something predatory about him and also something frightened, despite the glibness and the rehearsed humor of his talk.

At length the chess player itself appeared. It was a desklike box with a figure seated behind it, the whole assemby wheeled out on stage by assistants. The figure was that of a huge man in Turkish garb. Quite obviously a mannequin or a dummy of some kind, it bobbed slightly with the motion of the rolling desk, to which its chair was fixed. Now the agent could feel the excited vibration of his watch without even putting a hand into his pocket.

The predatory man cracked another joke, displayed a hideous smile, then, from among several chess players in the audience who raised their hands—the agent was not among them—he selected one to challenge the automaton. The challenger ascended to the stage, where the pieces were being set out on a board fastened to the rolling desk, and the doors in the front of the desk were being opened to show that there was nothing but machinery inside.

The agent noted that there were no candles on this desk, as there had been on that of Maelzel's chess player a few decades earlier. Maelzel's automaton had been a earlier fraud, of course. Candles had been placed on its box to mask the odor of burning wax from the candle needed by the man who was so cunningly hidden inside amid the dummy gears. The year in which the agent had arrived was still too early, he knew, for electric lights, at least the kind that would be handy for such a hidden human to use. Add the fact that this chess player's opponent was allowed to sit much closer than Maelzel's had ever been, and it became a pretty safe deduction that no human being was concealed inside the box and figure on this stage.

Therefore . . .

The agent might, if he stood up in the audience, get a clear shot at it right now. But should he aim at the figure or the box? And he could not be sure how it was armed. And who would stop it if he tried and failed? Already it had learned enough to survive in nineteenth-century London. Probably it had already killed, to further its designs—"under new management" indeed.

No, now that he had located his enemy, he must plan thoroughly and work patiently. Deep in thought, he left the theater amid the crowd at the conclusion of the performance and started on foot back to the rooms that he had just begun to share on Baker Street. A minor difficulty at his launching into the black hole had cost him some equipment, including most of his counterfeit money. There had not been time as yet for his adopted profession to bring him much income; so he was for the time being in straitened financial circumstances.

He must plan. Suppose, now, that he were to approach the frightened little man in evening dress. By now that one ought to have begun to understand what kind of a tiger he was riding. The agent might approach him in the guise of—

A sudden tap-tapping began in the agent's watch pocket. It was a signal quite distinct from any previously generated by his fake watch. It meant that the enemy had managed to detect his detector; it was in fact locked onto it and tracking.

Sweat mingled with the drizzle on the agent's face as he began to run. It must have discovered him in the theater, though probably it could not then single him out in the crowd. Avoiding horse-drawn cabs, four-wheelers, and an omnibus, he turned out of Oxford Street to Baker Street and slowed to a fast walk for the short distance remaining. He could not throw away the telltale watch, for he would be unable to track the enemy without it. But neither did he dare retain it on his person.

As the agent burst into the sitting room, his roommate looked up, with his usual, somewhat shallow, smile, from a leisurely job of taking books out of a crate and putting them on shelves.

"I say," the agent began, in mingled relief and urgency, "something rather important has come up, and I find there are two errands I must undertake at once. Might I impose one of them on you?''

The agent's own brisk errand took him no farther than just across the street. There, in the doorway of Camden House, he shrank back, trying to breathe silently. He had not moved when, three minutes later, there approached from the direction of Oxford Street a tall figure that the agent suspected was not human; its hat was pulled down, and the lower portion of its face was muffled in bandages. Across the street it paused, seemed to consult a pocket watch of its own, then turned to ring the bell. Had the agent been absolutely sure it was his quarry, he would have shot it in the back. But without his watch, he would have to get closer to be absolutely sure.

After a moment's questioning from the landlady, the figure was admitted. The agent waited for two minutes. Then he drew a deep breath, gathered up his courage, and went after it.

The thing standing alone at a window turned to face him as he entered the sitting room, and now he was sure of what it was. The eyes above the bandaged lower face were not the Turk's eyes, but they were not human, either.

The white swathing muffled its gruff voice. "You are the doctor?''

"Ah, it is my fellow lodger that you want.'' The agent threw a careless glance toward the desk where he had looked up the watch, the desk on which some papers bearing his roommate's name were scattered. "He is out at the moment, as you see, but we can expect him presently. I take it you are a patient.''

The thing said, in its wrong voice, "I have been referred to him. It seems the doctor and I share a certain common background. Therefore the good landlady has let me wait in here. I trust my presence is no inconvenience.''

"Not in the least. Pray take a seat, Mr.—?''

What name the berserker might have given, the agent never learned. The bell sounded below, suspending conversation. He heard the servant girl answering the door, and a moment later his roommate's brisk feet on the stairs. The death machine took a small object from its pocket and sidestepped a little to get a clear view past the agent toward the door.

Turning his back upon the enemy, as if with the casual purpose of greeting the man about to enter, the agent casually drew from his own pocket a quite functional briar pipe, which was designed to serve another function, too. Then he turned his head and fired the pipe at the berserker from under his own left armpit.

For a human being he was uncannily fast, and for a berserker the android was meanly slow and clumsy, being designed primarily for imitation, not dueling. Their weapons triggered at the same instant.

Explosions racked and destroyed the enemy, blasts shatteringly powerful but compactly limited in space, self-damping and almost silent.

The agent was hit, too. Staggering, he knew with his last clear thought just what weapon the enemy had carried—the switching mindbeam. Then for a moment he could no longer think at all. He was dimly aware of being down on one knee and of his fellow lodger, who had just entered, standing stunned a step inside the door.

At last the agent could move again, and he shakily pocketed his pipe. The ruined body of the enemy was almost vaporized already. It must have been built to self-destruct when damaged badly, so that humanity might never learn its secrets. Already it was no more than a puddle of heavy mist, warping in slow tendrils out the slightly open window to mingle with the fog.

The man still standing near the door had put out a hand to steady himself against the wall. "The jeweler . . . did not have your watch," he muttered dazedly.

I have won, thought the agent dully. It was a *joy*less thought because with it came slow realization of the price of his success. Three quarters of his intellect, at least, was gone, the superior pattern of his brain-cell connections scattered. No. Not scattered. The switching mindbeam would have reimposed the pattern of his neurons somewhere farther down its pathway . . . *there,* behind those gray eyes with their newly penetrating gaze.

"Obviously, sending me out for your watch was a ruse." His roommate's voice was suddenly crisper, more assured than it had been. "Also, I perceive that your desk has just been broken into, by someone who thought it mine." The tone softened somewhat.

"Come, man, I bear you no ill will. Your secret, if honorable, shall be safe. But it is plain that you are not what you have represented yourself to be."

The agent got to his feet, pulling at his sandy hair, trying desperately to think. "How—how do you know?"

"Elementary!" the tall man snapped.

Slaves of Silver
by
Gene Wolfe

Next to space travel, the most consummately science fictional plotline involves robots. It would be astonishing therefore if there failed to be a robot story included in this collection. There's no need to be astonished. Here it is.

Slaves of Silver

by Gene Wolfe

The day I formed my connection with March B. Street has
remained extraordinarily well fixed in my memory. This shows,
of course, that my unconscious—my monitor, I should say; you
must pardon me if I sometimes slip into these anthropomorphic
terms; it's the influence of my profession— What was I saying?
Oh, yes. My monitor, which of course sorts through my stored
data during maintenance periods and wipes the obsolete material
out of core, regards the connection as quite important. A tenuous
connection, you will say. Yes, but it has endured.

The hour was late. I had finished the last of my house calls and
it was raining. I may be more careful of my physical well-being
than I should be, but my profession makes me so and, after all,
quite a number of people depend on me. At any rate, instead of
walking to my quarters as was my custom I bought a paper and
seated myself in a kiosk to read and await the eventual arrival of
the monorail.

In twenty minutes I had read everything of interest and laid the
paper on the bench beside my bag. After some five minutes spent

watching the gray rain and thinking about some of my more troublesome patients I picked it up again and began (my room being, in several respects, less than satisfactory) to leaf through the real estate ads. I believe I can still remember the exact wording:

Single Professional wishes to share apt. (exp. clst.) Quiet hbts, no entrtnng. Cr8/mo.

The cost was below what I was paying for my room and the idea of an apartment—even if it were only an expanded closet and would have to be shared—was appealing. It was closer to the center of the city than was my room, and on the same mono line. I thought about it as I boarded, and when we reached the stop nearest it (Cathedral) I got off.

The building was old and small, faced with unlightened concrete time had turned nearly black. The address I sought was on the twenty-seventh floor; what had once been a single apartment had been opened out into a complex by means of space expanders, whose all-prevading hum greeted me as I opened the door. One had, for a moment, the sensation of tumbling head first into gulfs of emptiness. Then a little woman, the landlady, came fluttering up to ask what it was I wanted. She was, as I saw at once, a declassed human.

I showed her the ad. "Ah," she said. "That's Mr. Street, but I don't think he'll be wanting any of your sort. Of course, that's up to him."

I could have mentioned the Civil Liberties Act, but I only said, "He's a human, then? The ad said, 'Single Professional.' Naturally I thought—"

"Well, you would, wouldn't you," the little woman said, looking at the ad again over my shoulder. "He's not like me. I mean even if he is declassed, he's still young. Mr. Street's a strange one."

"You don't mind if I inquire, then?"

"Oh, no. I just don't want to see you disappointed." She was looking at my bag. "You're a doctor?"

"A bio-mechanic."

"That's what we used to call them—doctors. It's over there."

It had been a hat and coat closet, I suppose, in the original apartment. There was a small brass plate on the door:

MARCH B. STREET
CONSULTING
ENGINEER
&
DETECTIVE

I was reading it for the second time when the door opened and I asked, quite without thinking how it might sound, "What in the world does a consulting engineer do?"

"He consults," Mr. March Street answered. "Are you a client, sir?"

And that was how I met him. I should have been impressed—I mean, had I known—but as it was I was only flustered. I told him I had come about the apartment and he asked me in very politely It was an immense place, filled to bursting with machines in various stages of disassembly and furniture. "Not pretty," Mr. Street remarked, "but it's home."

"I had no idea it would be so big. You must have—"

"Three expanders, each six hundred horsepower. There's plenty of space out there between the galaxies, so why not pull it down here where we need it?"

"The cost, I should say, for one thing. I suppose that's why you want to—"

"Share the apartment? Yes, that's one reason. How do you like the place?"

"You mean you'd consider me? I should think   "

"Do you know you talk very slowly? It makes it damned difficult not to interrupt you. No, I wouldn't prefer a human. Sit down, won't you? What's your name?"

"Westing," I said. "It's a silly name, really—like naming a human Tommy or Jimmy. But the old 'Westinghouse' was out of style when I was assembled."

"Which makes you about fifty-six, confirmed by the degree of wear I see at your knee seals, which are originals. You're a bio-mechanic, by your bag—which should be handy. You haven't much money; you're honest—and obviously not much of a talker. You came here by mono, and I'd almost be willing to swear you presently live high up in a fairly new building."

"How in the world—"

"Quite simple, really, Westing. You haven't money or you wouldn't be interested in an apartment. You're honest or you'd have money—no one has more and better chances to steal than a bio-mechanic. When a passenger with a transfer boards the mono the conductor rips up the ticket and, half the time, drops it on the floor—and one is stuck to your foot with gum. And lightened concrete and plastic facades have given us buildings so tall and spindly-framed that the upper floors sway under the wind load like ships. People who live or work in them take to bracing themselves the way sailors used to—as I notice you're doing on that settee."

"You are an extraordinary person," I managed to say, "and it makes me all the more surprised—" And here I am afraid I stopped speaking and leaned forward to stare at him.

"Extraordinary in more ways than one, I'm afraid," Street said. "But although I assure you I will engage you as my physician if I am ever ill, I haven't done so yet."

"Quite so," I admitted. I relaxed, but I was still puzzled.

"Are you still interested in sharing my little apartment, then? Shall I show you about?"

"No," I said.

"I understand," Street said, "and I apologize for having wasted your time, Doctor."

"I don't want to be shown the door, either." Though I was upset, I must admit I felt a thrill of somewhat guilty pleasure at being able to contradict my host. "I want to sit here and think for a minute."

"Of course," Street said, and was silent.

Living with a declassed human (and there was no use in my deceiving myself—that was what was being proposed) was a raffish sort of thing. It was bound to hurt my practice, but then my practice was largely among declassed humans already and could not get much worse. The vast spaces of the apartment, even littered as they were, were attractive after years in a single cramped room.

But most of all, or so I like to think, it was the personality of Street himself which decided me—and the fact that I detected in him, perhaps only by some professional instinct not wholly rational, a physical abnormality I could not quite classify. And there was, in addition, the pleasing thought of surprising my few friends, all of whom, I knew, thought me much too stuffy to do any such outlandish thing. I was giving Street my money—half a month's rent on the apartment—when he froze, head cocked, to listen to some sound from the foyer.

After a moment he said, "We have a visitor, Westing. Hear him?"

"I heard someone out there."

"The light and tottering step is that of our good landlady, Mrs. Nash. But there is another tread—dignified, yet nervous. Almost certainly a client."

"Or someone else to ask about the apartment," I suggested.

"No."

Before I could object to this flat contradiction the door opened to show the birdlike woman who had admitted us. She ushered in a distinguished-looking person well over two meters tall, whose polished and lavish solid chrome trim gave unmistakable evidence, if not of wealth, then at least of a sufficiency I—and millions of others—would only envy all our lives.

"You are Street?" he asked, looking at me with a somewhat puzzled expression.

"This is my associate, Dr. Westing," Street said. "I am the man you came to see, Commissioner Electric. Won't you sit down?"

"I'm flattered that you know my name," Electric said.

"Over there, past the nickelodeon," Street told him, "you'll see a cleared spot for tri-D displays. There are several cameras around it. Whenever a man I don't know appears I photograph the image for later reference. You were interviewed three months ago in connection with your request for additional expanders for the hiring hall, made necessary by the depressed state of the economy."

"Yes." Electric nodded and it was plain that Street's recital of these simple facts, accurate as it was, had depressed still further spirits already hovering at the brink of despair. "You have no conception, Mr. Street, of how ironic it seems that I should hear now—here—of that routine request for funds, and so be reminded of those days when our hall was filled to bursting with the deactivated."

"From which," Street said slowly, "I take it that the place is now empty—or nearly so. I must say I am surprised; I had believed the economy to be in worse condition—if that is possible—than it was three months past."

"It is," Electric admitted. "And your first supposition is also correct—the hall, though not empty, is far from crowded."

"Ah," said Street.

"This thing has been driving me to the brink of reprogramming for six weeks now. The deactivated are being stolen. The police pretend to be accomplishing something; but it's obvious they are helpless—they're only going through the motions now. Last night a relative of mine—I won't name him, but he is a highly placed military officer—suggested that I come to you. He didn't mention you were a declassed human, and I suppose he knew that if he had I wouldn't have come, but now that I've seen you I'm willing to take a chance."

"That's kind of you," Street said dryly. "In the event I succeed in preventing further thefts by bringing the criminals to justice my fee will be—" He named an astronomical sum.

"And in the event further thefts are not prevented?"

"My expenses only."

"Done. You realize that these thefts strike at the very fabric of our society, Mr. Street. The old rallying cry, *Free markets and free robots,* may be a joke now to some, but it has built our civilization. Robots are assembled when the demand for labor exceeds the supply. When supply exceeds demand—that is, in practical terms, when the excess cybercitizens can't make a living—they turn themselves in at the hiring hall, where they're deactivated until they're needed again. If news of these shortages should leak out—"

"Who would turn himself in to be stolen, eh?" said Street. "I see what you mean."

"Precisely. The unemployed would resort to begging and theft, just as in the old days. We already have—I hope you'll excuse me—enough of a problem with declassed humans. You yourself are obviously an exception, but you must know what most of them are like."

"Most of us," Street replied mildly, "are like my landlady: people who lost class because they refused death at the end of their natural lifespans. It's not very easy to learn to earn your living when for a hundred years of life society has handed you an income big enough to make you rich."

It wasn't really my affair, but I couldn't help saying, "But if you can help Commissioner Electric, Street, you'll be helping your own people in exactly this area."

Street turned his eyes—which were of an intense blue, as though his photosensors were arcing—to me. "Is that so, Doctor? I'm afraid I don't quite follow you."

Electric said, "I should think it's obvious. Surely the motive for stealing our deactivated workers must be the desire to use them as forced labor, presumably in a secret factory of some sort. If this is being done, the criminals are competing illegally with everyone trying to earn an honest living—including the declassed."

I nodded my emphatic agreement. The thought of an illicit factory, perhaps in a cavern or abandoned mine, filled with dim figures laboring without cease under the threat of destruction, had already come to haunt my imagination.

"Slaves of silver," I muttered half aloud, "toiling in the dark."

"Possibly," Street said. "But I can think of other possibilities—possibilities you might find more shocking still."

"In any event," Commissioner Electric put in, "you will want to visit the hiring hall."

"Yes, but not in company with you. I consider it quite possible that the entrance may be watched. Human beings do visit the hall from time to time, I assume?"

"Yes, usually to engage domestics."

"Excellent. Under what circumstances would you deal with such visitors personally?"

"I would not ordinarily do so at all, unless all my subordinates were engaged."

Street looked at me. "You seem to want to be a party to this, Westing. Are you game to visit the hiring hall with me? You must consider that you may disappear—for that matter we both may."

"Oh, no," Electric protested, "the disappearances occur only after dark, when the hall is closed."

"Certainly I'll come."

Street smiled. "I thought you would. Commissioner, we will follow you in one half hour. See to it that when we arrive your subordinates are engaged."

When the commissioner had gone I was able to ask Street the question that had been nagging at my mind during the entire interview.

"Street, for God's own sake, how was it you know Commissioner Electric hadn't come about the apartment before Mrs. Nash had opened the door?"

"Be a good fellow and look in the drawer of the inlaid rosewood table you'll find on the other side of that camera obscura to the left of the tri-D stage, and I'll tell you. You ought to find a recording ammeter in there. We'll need it."

I didn't know what a camera obscura was, but fortunately the rosewood table was a rather striking piece and only one instrument was in its drawer, lying amid a litter of tarot cards and bridge score pads. I held it up for Street to see and he nodded. "That's it. You see, Westing, when someone arrives in answer to a newspaper ad he almost invariably—ninety-two point-six percent of the time, according to my calculation—carries the paper with him and shows it to the person who answers the door. When I failed to hear the telltale rattle of the popular press as our visitor addressed Mrs. Nash I knew there was little chance that he had come about the apartment."

"Astounding!"

"Oh, it's not so much," Street said modestly. "But get a move on, won't you? It wouldn't do to ride down in the same elevator with Electric—but on the other hand it's seldom a waste of askance to view a public official with it. We're going to shadow him."

Despite Street's suspicions, Commissioner Electric did nothing untoward that I could see while we followed him. To give him time to prepare for us, as Street said, we idled for a quarter of an hour or more at the window of a tri-D store near the hall. The show being carried on the display set inside was utterly banal and I could swear that Street did not give it even a fraction of his attention. He stood, absorbed in his own thoughts, while I fidgeted.

The hiring hall, when Electric guided us around it, we found to be a huge place; impressive from outside but immensely larger within and filled with the hum of expanders. The corridors were lined with persons of every age and state of repair—they stretched for slightly curved miles like the vistas seen in opposed mirrors. Gaping spaces showed where the disappearances had taken place, but, sinister as they were, in time they seemed a relief from the staring regard of those thousands of unseeing eyes. Street asked for data on each theft and recorded the date and the number of persons missing in a notebook; but there seemed to be no pattern to the crimes, save that all the disappearances took place at night.

At last we came to the end of that vast building. Commissioner Electric did not ask Street for his opinion of the case (though I could see he wanted to), nor did Street give it. But once we were fairly away from him, Street pacing impatiently alongside the sidewalk while I trotted to keep up, he broke forth in an irascible tirade of self-abuse: "Westing, this thing is as simple as a two-foot piece of aluminum conduit and I'm confident I know everything about it—except what I need to know. And I have no idea of how I'm going to find the answer. I know the robots are taken—I think. And I believe I know why. The question is: Who is responsible? If I could get the patrol to cooperate—"

He lapsed into a sour silence, unbroken until we were once more back in the huge, littered apartment I had not yet learned to call "ours." Indeed, my arrangement with Street was so recent that I had not yet had an opportunity to shift my possessions from my old room or to terminate my tenancy there. I excused myself—though Street seemed hardly to notice—and attended to these things.

When I returned nothing had changed. Street sat, as before, wrapped in gloom. And I, reduced to despondency by his example and with nothing better to do in any case, sat watching him. After an hour had passed he rose from his chair and for a few moments wandered disconsolately about the apartment, only to return to the same seat and throw himself down, his face blacker—if that were possible—than before.

"Street—" I ventured.

"Eh?" He looked up. "Westing? That's your name, isn't it? You still here?"

"Yes. I've been watching you for some time. While I realize you have, no doubt, a regular medical advisor, you were once kind enough to say that you might call me. On the strength of that—"

"Well, out with it, man. What is it?"

"There will be no fee, of course. I was going to say that though I don't know what means of chemical reality enhancement you employ, it would appear to me that it has been a considerable time—"

"Since my last fix? Believe me, it has." He laughed, a reaction I thought encouraging.

"Then I would suggest—"

"I don't use drugs, Westing. None at all."

"I didn't mean to suggest anything strong—just a few pinks, say, or—"

"I mean it, Westing. I don't use pinks. Or blues. Or even whites. I don't use anything except food, and little enough of that, water and air."

"You're serious?"

"Absolutely."

"Street, I find this incredible. We were taught at medical school that human beings—being, after all, a species evolved for a savanna landscape rather than our climax civilization—were unable to maintain their sanity without pharmaceutical relief."

"That may well be true, Westing. Nevertheless, I do not use any."

This was too much for me to absorb at once and while I tried to encode it Street fell back into his former gloom.

"Street," I said again.

"What is it this time?"

"Do you remember? When we first met I said that I detected in you, perhaps only by some professional instinct not wholly rational, a physical abnormality I could not quite classify?"

"You didn't say anything of the sort. You may have thought it."

"I did. And I was right. Man, you don't know how good this makes me feel."

"I have some comprehension of the intellectual rewards attendant on successful deduction."

"I'm sure you do. But now, if I may say so, a too-avid pursuit of those rewards has led you to a severe state of depression. A stimulant of some sort—"

"Not at all, Westing. Thought is my drug—and believe me it is both stimulating and frustrating. My need is for a soporific, and your conversation fills the bill better than anything you could prescribe."

This was said in so cheerful and bantering a way, albeit with a barely perceptible touch of bitterness, that I could not resent it— and, indeed, the marked improvement this little spate of talk had brought to Street's mien emboldened me to continue at whatever risk to my vanity.

So I answered, "Your powers of concentration, admirable as they are, may yet be your undoing. Do you remember the quarter-hour we spent in front of a store window? Where the tri-D had such poor reception? I addressed you several times, but I would swear you heard none of my questions."

"I heard every one of your questions," Street said, "and since none admitted to intelligent responses I ignored them all. And that tri-D, if not of the most exquisite quality, was at least better than passable. I apologize if I sound peevish, but really, Westing, you must learn to observe."

"I am not an engineer," I replied, perhaps rather too stiffly, "and so I cannot say if the reception in fact was at fault—but acute observation is a necessity in my profession and I can assure you that the color stability of the set on display was abominable."

"Nonsense. I was looking directly at it for the entire time and I could, if necessary, describe each stupidity of programming in sequence."

"Maybe you could," I said. "And I don't doubt your assertion that you were watching with commendable attention while we waited outside the hiring hall. But you quite obviously failed to observe it when we *left*. You were talking excitedly, as I recall— and as you spoke we passed the window again. The actors were blushing—if I may use that expression here—a sort of reddish-orange. Then they turned greenish blue, than really blue, and finally a shade of bright, cool green. In fact, they went through that whole cycle several times just during the time it took us to walk past the window."

The effect of this perhaps overly detailed and argumentative statement on Street was extraordinary. Instead of countering with argument or denial, as I confess I expected, for a few moments he simply stared silently at me. Then he jumped to his feet and for half a minute or more paced the room in silent agitation, twice tripping over the same ball-clawed foot of the same late Victorian commode.

At last he turned almost fiercely back to me and announced: "Westing, I believe I can recall the precise words I addressed to you as we passed that display. I will repeat them to you now and I want you to tell me the exact point at which you noticed the color instability you mentioned. I said: 'Westing, this thing is as simple as a two-foot piece of aluminum conduit and I'm confident I know everything about it—except what I need to know. And I have no idea of how I'm going to find the answer. I know how the robots are taken—I think. And I believe I know why. The question is: Who is responsible? If I could get the patrol to cooperate—' at which point I broke off, I believe. Now, precisely where did you notice the reddish orange color you mentioned—I believe that was the hue you noticed originally?"

"To the best of my recollection, Street, it coincided with the word *believe*."

"I said, 'I know how the robots are taken—I think. And I *believe*—' and at that point you noticed that the figures in the tri-D illusion blushed a color you have described as a reddish orange. Is that correct?"

Dumfounded, I nodded.

"Excellent. Among my other antiques, Westing, I have asembled a collection of paintings. Would it interest you to see them? You would be conferring a favor of no mean magnitude upon me."

"I don't see how—but certainly, if you wish."

"Excellent again; particularly if, while drinking in their loveliness, you would take the trouble to point out to me the shades which most closely match the four colors you saw when the tri-D malfunctioned. But please be most exact—if the match is not perfect, you need not inform me."

For an hour or more we pored over Street's pictures, which were astoundingly varied and, for the most part, in a poor state of preservation. In size they ranged from Indian miniatures smaller than coins to a Biblical cyclorama five meters high and (so Street told me) more than three kilometers in length. The greenish-blue long escaped us, but at last I located it in an execrable depiction of *Susanna and The Elders* and the art display was abruptly terminated. Street told me bluntly—his manner would have been offensive if it had not been so obvious that his mind was totally engaged on a problem of formidable proportions—to amuse myself and buried himself in an assortment of ratty books and dusty charts, one of which, as I particularly remember, was like a rainbow bent into a full circle, with the blazing colors melting into one another like the infinitesimal quantities in a differential equation.

While he pondered over these the hours of evening rolled past on silent rubber wheels. Others, their day's work done, might rest now; I waited. Humans, rich and fortunate or declassed, might sleep or busy themselves in those pointless naked tumblings which mean so little to us; Street worked. And at last I wondered if it might not be that we two were the only wakeful minds in the entire city.

Suddenly Street was shaking me by the shoulder. "Westing," he exclaimed. "I have it—let me show you." I explained that I had taken advantage of his concentration to edit my memory banks.

Street shrugged my mumblings aside. "Here," he said. "Look at this and let me explain. You told me, if you remember, that you saw a cycle of four colors and that this cycle was repeated several times."

"That's correct."

"Very well. Now observe. Has it ever occurred to you to wonder how *robots*—yourself included—speak?"

"I assume," I said with as much dignity as I could muster, "that somewhere in my monitor the various words of the English language are stored as vibration patterns and—"

"The Chinese system. No, I am convinced it must be something far more efficient. English is spoken with only a trifle more than sixty sounds; even the longest words are created by combining and recombining these—for examples we might use the *a* as it appears in *arm*, the *r* as in *rat* and the *ch* from *chair* to describe our inestimable landlady, Mrs. Nash. Combined in one fashion they give us *char*—her profession—but rearranged in another they contribute *arch*—her manner."

"You mean that all of spoken English can be stored in my central processing unit as a mere sixty-place linear array?"

"That is precisely what I've been saying."

"Street, that's marvelous! I'm not a religious man, but when I contemplate the ingenuity of those early programmers and systems analysts—"

"Exactly. Now, I do not know the order in which the various English sounds were listed, but there is an order which is very commonly used in the texts to which I have referred. It is to list the sounds alphabetically and, within the alphabetical sections, to order them from longest to shortest. Thus these lists begin with the long *a* of *ale*; followed by the half-long *a* of *chaotic*; and this is followed in turn by the circumflex *a* of *care*, so that the whole reads like a temperance lecture. What I have done here is to take these sounds and space them evenly along the visible spectrum." He held up a hand-drawn chart on which there were, however, no colors, but only a multitude of names.

"But," I objected, "only a few true colors exist and you said there were more than sixty—"

"A few *primary* colors," he returned, "but believe me, Westing, if the artists were to make up a pallet containing every oil and watercolor known to them there would be a great many more than sixty. As you may remember, you described the four colors you saw as reddish-orange, greenish-blue, true blue—which is just like you, Westing—and bright, cool green."

"Yes."

"Afterward, when you pointed out these colors on canvas, I was able to identify them as scarlet lake, cyan blue, blue, and viridian. Please observe that on my chart these correspond to the consonant sound *p*, the consonant *h*, the short *e* heard in *end* and the *l* sound of *late*."

I considered this remarkable statement for a moment, then replied, "You seem to believe that someone is trying to communicate, using the colors of the tri-D; but I do not see that the sounds to which you say these colors correspond possess any significance."

Street leaned back in his chair, smiling. "Let us suppose, Westing, that you came in late as it were, to the message. Catching the last sound of a repeated word, you supposed it to be the first. In short—"

"I see!" I exclaimed, leaping up. "'HELP!'"

"Precisely."

"But—"

"There's no more time to waste, Westing. I have only given this much explanation because I want you to be an intelligent witness to what I am about to do. You will observe that I have set up a tri-D camera before our viewing area, enabling me to record for my own use any image appearing there."

"Yes, you said something about that to Commissioner Electric."

"So I did. What I intend to do now is to code that store near the hiring hall and ask for a demonstration. At this late hour it seems improbable that anyone will be there but a robot clerk—and it's unlikely he will be implicated."

Street was pushing the coding buttons as he spoke and a clerk—a robot—appeared almost before he had finished the last word.

"I should prefer to deal with a human being," Street told him, displaying an excellent imitation of prejudice.

The clerk groveled. "Oh, I am sorry, sir. But my employers— and no person ever had better—have gone to snatch a few hours of deserved rest. If you would—"

"That's all right." Street cut him off. "You'll do. I'm interested in another tri-D and I want a demonstration."

"Very wise, sir. We have—"

"As it happens, I was passing your shop today and the set in your window looked attractive. I presume there would be a discount, since it's a demonstrator?"

"I would have to consult my masters," the clerk answered smoothly, "but I assume something might be arranged."

"Good."

"Is there any particular program—"

"I don't know what's on right now." For an instant Street feigned indecision. "Isn't *The Answer Man* always available?"

"Indeed he is, sir. Personal, Sexual, Scholarly, or Civil Affairs?"

"Civil Affairs, I think."

In an instant The Answer Man, a computer-generated illusion designed to give maximum reassurance in the field of civil affairs, appeared in the tri-D area.

He nodded politely to us and asked, "Would you like a general report—or have you specific fears?"

"I have heard rumors," Street said, "to the effect—well, the fact is that an old family servitor of mine is—uh—resting in the hiring hall. Is it quite safe?"

The Answer Man reassured him, but as he did so he (and indeed the entire illusion) blushed a series of colors as astonishing as it was—at least by me—unexpected.

"Names," Street prompted softly. "I must have names."

"I beg your pardon?" The Answer Man said, but as he spoke he coruscated anew with dazzling chromatic aberrations.

"I meant," Street returned easily, "that you would have to have my servant's name before you could properly reassure me. But it's really not necessary. I've heard—"

Abruptly The Answer Man vanished, replaced by the clerk robot.

"I'm terribly sorry," he said. "Something seems to be wrong with the color control. Could I show you another set?"

"Oh, no," Street told him. "The trouble is in the network signal. Didn't you get the announcement? Sunspots."

"Really?" The clerk looked relieved. "It's extraordinary that I should have missed it."

"I would say," Street sounded severe, "that in your position it was your duty to have heard it."

"I can't imagine— About an hour ago, could it have been? I had to leave—only momentarily—to dispose of the surplus water created by my fuel cells, but except for that—"

"No doubt that was it," Street said. "I wish you a good

evening, sir." He switched off the tri-D. "Westing, I've done it! I've got everything we need here."

"You mean that by going over the tapes you made and comparing them with your chart—"

"No, no, of course not," Street interrupted me testily. "I memorized the chart while you were asleep. The tapes are only for evidence."

"You mean that you understood—"

"Certainly. As well as I understand you now—though I must confess that before I heard that poor machine speak it had never occurred to me that the word *dread*, especially when given the slightly pre-Raphaelite pronunciation of our unfortunate friend, oould reoult in ouoh otartling beuuty."

"Strcct," I said, "you'rc toying with mc. With whom arc you communicating when you talk to those colors? And how were the deactivated robots stolen—and why?"

Street smiled, fingering a small cast iron "greedy-pig" coin bank he had picked up from the table beside his chair. "I am communicating, as I should think must be obvious, with one of the stolen robots. And the method of theft was by no means difficult—indeed, I'm surprised that it is not employed more often. A confederate of the thieves' concealed himself in the immensities of the hiring hall during the day. When all were gone he momentarily interrupted the flow of current to one of the expanders, with the result that the expander space returned to a position between the galaxies, carrying its contents with it. As you know, the exact portion of space taken by an expander is dependent on the fourth derivative of the sinusoidal voltage at the instant of startup, so it is most improbable that, upon being restarted a split second later, the expander should return the robots to their proper places. They are picked up instead by a deep-space freighter and eventually returned to Earth. The recording ammeter I contrived to fasten to the hall's main power supply while Electric was showing us around will tell us if anyone tries the little trick again, as well as convincing a court that might not otherwise believe my explanation."

"But the colors, Street? Are you trying to tell me that the National Broadcasting Authority itself is employing slave labor?"

"Not at all." Street looked grave, then smiled. I might almost say grinned at me. "The robots in the hiring hall are there because society can find no present use for them—but has it never occurred to you that the electronics they contain might themselves be useful?"

"You mean—"

Street nodded. "I do. A tri-D set requires considerable computing power: a quite complicated signal must be unscrambled almost instantly to produce the three-dimensional illusion. The central processing unit of a robot, however, would be more than equal to the task—and very economical, if it were free. Unfortunately—for them—the criminals made one mistake. A criminal always makes one mistake, Westing."

"They wired the speech centers to handle the color coding?"

"Precisely. I am proud of you."

I was so elated that I leaped to my feet and for a few moments paced the room feverishly. The triumph of justice—the chagrin of the criminal manufacturers! The glory that would be Street's and, to some degree as his friend, mine! At length a new thought struck me, coming with the clarity of the tolling of a great bell.

"Street—" I said.

"You look dashed, Westing."

"You have done society a great service."

"I know it—and the fee will be most useful. There is an early twentieth-century iron-claw machine in a junk shop over on four hundred and forty-fourth I've been lusting after. It needs a little work—the claw won't pick up anything now—but I think I can fix it."

"Street, it might be possible—Commissioner Electric possesses great influence—"

"What are you blathering about, Westing?"

"It might be possible for you to be reclassed. Have your birthright income restored."

"Are you insinuating, Westing, that you believe me to have been declassed for criminal activity?"

"But all human beings are born classed—and you're not old enough to have refused death."

"Believe me, Westing, my income is still in existence and—in a way—I am receiving it. You, as a bio-mechanic, should understand."

"You mean—"

"Yes. I have had a child by asexual reproduction. A child who duplicates precisely my own genetic makeup—a second self. The law, as you no doubt know, requires in such cases that the parent's income go to the child. He must be reared and educated."

"You could have married."

"I prefer to have a home. And no man has a home unless he is master of a place where he must please no one—a place where he can go and lock the door behind him."

This was what I had feared. I said, "In that case perhaps you won't want—I mean, with the money you'll be getting from Electric you won't need to share this apartment. I would quite understand, Street, really I would."

"You, Westing?" Street laughed. "You're no more in the way than a refrigerator."

God of the Naked Unicorn
by
Richard Lupoff
(writing as Ova Hamlet)

Here Sherlock Holmes is associated with other fictional heroes,
in the organization "Personages United in League as Protectors,"
which has a curious acronym. Oddly enough, it is Watson—the
neglected and often derided Watson—who is the hero.

God of the Naked Unicorn

by

Ova Hamlet
(Richard Lupoff)

I.

It was a chilly winter's evening and the sound of jingling coach bells attached to the harness of carriage horses penetrated both the swirling yellow fog of Limehouse where the Thames swerves and eddies and dark Lascar shapes flit through shaded passages, and the ancient rippled glass of the windows of my humble flat to remind even a sad old man that there were yet revelers at large in the city anticipating the joyous holiday of Nativity.

My mind fled back to earlier, and jollier, holiday seasons, seasons spent in my youth amidst the savage tribesmen of barbaric Afghanistan before a jezail bullet cut short my career in Her Majesty's service, causing me to be seconded home and returned, ultimately, to civil existence. At home in London I had attempted to support my modest needs by setting up practice in Harley Street, but had been forced to accept accommodations

285

with another person of my own class and station in order to make ends meet.

That had been the beginning of my long and happy association with the foremost consulting detective of our time—perhaps of any time. A confirmed bachelor, my associate had treated persons of the female persuasion with unstinting chivalry and kindness through all the time I had known him, yet on only one occasion had he permitted himself to entertain romantic notions concerning a member of the more gentle sex, and had, in all the years that followed the incident, refrained from ever speaking the name of the person involved.

On occasion of each of my own marriages he had congratulated myself and my bride effusively, assisted in supervising the packers and drayers in the removal of my personal belongings from our bachelor digs, and maintained a friendly if somewhat aloof interest in my well-being until such time as the exigencies of fate dictated the termination of my marital state and my return to our lodgings in Baker Street.

That was all ended now. The great detective had retired from practice and was devoting himself to the cultivation of bees on the Sussex Downs. My own latest assay upon the sea of matrimony having been brought up upon the sharp rocks of disaster I had returned to 221B to find my old home occupied by a stranger. Upon application to the ever faithful Mrs. Hudson I had been told, amidst the most pitiable wringing of hands and shedding of tears, that my associate—I should say, my former associate—had vacated, lock, stock, and Persian slipper. Gone, the good woman told me tremblingly, were the famous dagger, the files of news-cuttings, the phonograph and bust, the gasogene and the ill-famed needle.

Even the patriotic intitials V. R. marked in bullet holes knocked in Mrs. Hudson's treasured mahogany wainscotting had been patched and varnished over so that every trace of the former occupancy was excised, and only a false and sterile pseudo-hominess marked the chambers I had so long occupied.

So distraught was I upon learning of this turn of affairs that I was barely able to accept Mrs. Hudson's offer of kippers and scones washed down with a tumbler of Chateau Frontenac '09 before stumbling back into the chill night.

I was disconsolate!

In a state of financial as well as emotional impoverishment, I wandered the streets of the greatest of cities, rebounding from the well-padded bodies of late shoppers and early revelers, making my way under the guidance of some ill-understood instinct through quarters imperceptibly but steadily more shabby, disreputable, and dangerous. At last I found myself standing before the facade of the building which was shortly to become my abode.

A gas-lamp flickered fitfully behind me, casting weird and eerie shadows. The clop-clopping of horses' iron shoes upon cobblestones mingled with the creak of harness and the occasional distant scream which in Limehouse is best left uninvestigated, lest the self-designated Samaritan find himself sharing the misfortune of the one whom he had sought to assuage.

A yellowed pasteboard notice in a ground-floor window announced that a flat was available in the building—the condition of the pasteboard indicating that the flat had been unoccupied for some time—and by virtue of this ingenious deduction I was able shortly to bargain the ill-kempt and uncivil landlord to a price in keeping with my dangerously slim pocketbook.

Well had I learned the lessons of observation and deduction taught by my longtime associate—and now those lessons would pay me back for innumerable humiliations by the saving of considerable sterling to my endangered exchequer!

Hardly had I settled myself into my new domain when I heard the tread of a lightly-placed foot upon the landing outside my chambers, and then the knock of a small but determined hand upon the heavy and long-unattended door.

For an instant I permitted my fancy to imagine that the door would open to reveal a smartly-uniformed buttons—a street-arab of the sort sometimes employed by my associate—the homey, bustling form of Mrs. Hudson—perhaps even the tall, saturnine figure of my associate himself! But I had no more than begun to rise from the cushions of a shabby but comfortable armchair when reality smote down upon my consciousness and I realized that none of these knew the location of my new quarters. Far more likely would my caller prove to be some dark denizen of Limehouse here to test the mettle of a new tenant!

I pulled a small but powerful revolver from its place among my belongings and slipped it into the pocket of the dressing gown which I wore, then advanced cautiously toward the portal of the room and drew back the locking bar. Protesting loudly this imposition upon its seldom-exercised hinges, the door swung back and still farther back until there stood revealed in the opening to the landing the one person upon the face of the earth whom I would least have supposed to trace down my new whereabouts or to have reason of any nature ever to call upon me here.

Hardly could I so much as credit the evidence of my own eyes! We must have stood for fully fifteen seconds in silent tableau—I with my eyes widened and my very jaw, I am certain, hanging open in astonishment. I was suddenly and uncomfortably aware of the reduced surroundings in which my caller had found me, and of the shabbiness which I fear I had permitted to come upon my personal demesne. My hair, once a rich brown in hue, had grown gray and unkempt with the passing years. My mustache was yellowed with nicotine and stained with wines and porters. My dressing gown was threadbare and marked with the souvenirs of many a solitary meal.

While my visitor was as breathtaking a figure as ever I had beheld: handsome rather than beautiful, she had borne the years since our last encounter with that grace and imperturbability which had marked her at one phase of her career as the most famous beauty of the dramatic stage, and at another as the woman for whom a throne had been risked—and saved!

"May I enter?" asked The Woman.

Coloring to the very roots of my hair I stepped back and indicated that she might not merely enter, but would be the most welcome and most honored of guests. "I must apologize," I said, "for my boorish performance. Can you forgive me, Miss—I should say Madame—Your Highness—" I halted, uncertain of how even to address my distinguished visitor.

Yet even as I stammered and reddened, I could not keep myself from observing the appearance of The Woman.

She was as tall as I remembered her to be, a hand more so than myself and nearly of a height with my longtime associate. Her hair, piled high upon her magnificent head in the European vogue of the period, was of a raven glossiness that seemed to throw back the light of my flickering kerosene lamp with every movement of the flame. Her facial features were perfect, as perfect as I had remembered them to be on the occasion of our first meeting many years earlier, and her figure, as revealed by the closely fitted fashions of the era, which she carried with the aplomb of one long accustomed to the attentions of the finest fitters and couturiers of the continent, was as graceful and appealing as that of a school girl.

She had entered my humble chambers by now, and as I checked the landing behind her to ascertain that no footpad stood lurking in the musty darkness, The Woman ensconsed herself unassisted upon the plain-backed wooden chair which I was wont to utilize while wielding my pen in the pursuit of those modest exercises of literary embellishment about which my associate had so often chided me.

I turned and gazed down at my visitor, seating myself as near to her magnetic form as decorum might permit. At this closer range it was visible to me that her air of confident poise was not unstrained by some element of nervousness or even distress. I attempted to smile encouragingly at The Woman, and she responded as I hoped she would, her voice so cultured as largely to conceal the difficulty with which she maintained her equilibrium.

"May I come directly to the point, Doctor?" she inquired.

"Of course, of course, Miss—ah—"

"In private circumstances you may address me simply as Irene," she graciously responded.

I bowed my head in humble gratitude.

"You may feel some surprise at my tracking you down," The Woman said. "But I have come upon a matter of the greatest urgency. Once before I called upon you and your associate in an hour of grave crisis, and now that a problem of like proportion has arisen, I call upon you again."

"My associate is retired," I explained sadly. "If you wish, I will attempt to contact him by telegraph but he has indicated his complete dedication to apiarian enterprises and I hold grave doubts that he could be prevailed upon to leave Sussex."

"Then you must assist me. Please, Doctor, I would not have

come here or disturbed your solitude in any way were it not for the extreme nature of the present situation."

So saying she leaned forward and placed her cool and ungloved fingertips softly upon the back of my wrist. As if a galvanic current had passed from her organism to my own at the very touch of her fingers, I felt myself energized and inspired. The Woman was in trouble! And The Woman had come to me in her hour of need! I could never be so mean a bounder as to turn her away—surely not now when the very mantle of my mentor seemed about to fall upon my own uncertain shoulders.

"But of course, Your High—Irene." I felt myself reddening to the very roots of my hair at the pronunciation of her given name. "If you will be so kind as to wait a moment while I fetch notepad and writing instrument so as to record the salient details of your narrative—"

I rose and fetched foolscap and nib, then quickly returned to my place opposite this charming visitor. For a moment I thought to offer her tea and biscuits with marmalade, but refrained at the thought of the present condition of my larder and my pocketbook. "Pray proceed," I said.

"Thank you. I trust that I need not make mention of the location or manner of my current domicile, Doctor," The Woman began. Upon seeing my nodded response she said simply, "The God of the Naked Unicorn has been stolen."

"The God of the Naked Unicorn!" I exclaimed.

"The God of the Naked Unicorn!"

"No!" I blurted incredulously.

"Yes!" she replied coolly. "The God of the Naked Unicorn!"

"But—but how can that be? The greatest national art treasure of the nation of—"

"Shh!" She silenced me with a sound and a look and a renewed pressure of fingertips to wrist. "Please! Even in more familiar and secure quarters than these it would be unwise to mention the name of my adoptive motherland."

"Of course, of course," I murmured, recovering myself rapidly. "But I do not see how the God of the Naked Unicorn *could* be stolen! Is it not—but I have here a book of artistic reproductions, let us examine a print of the statue and see."

"It is burned into my memory, Doctor. I see it before my eyes day and night! For me, there is no need to examine an artist's poor rendering, but you may search your volume to find a representation of the great sculptor Mendez-Rubirosa's masterpiece!"

I crossed the room and returned with a heavy volume bound in olive linen-covered boards and opened it carefully, turning its cream-vellum leaves until I came to a steel engraving of the sculptor Mendez-Rubirosa's supreme achievement, the God of the Naked Unicorn. As I had recalled, the work had been cast in platinum and decorated with precious gems. The eyes of the god were rubies and those of the unicorns clustered worshipfully about the deity's feet were of sapphires and emeralds. The horns of the unicorns were of finest ivory inlaid with filigreed gold. The very base of the sculpture was a solid block of polished onyx inlaid with Pekin jade.

"But the God of the Naked Unicorn is the national treasure of Boh—" I caught myself barely in time. "If its theft is made public the very crown itself would be once more endangered."

"Quite so," the woman known as The Woman agreed. "And a message has been received threatening that the sculpture will be placed on public display in St. Wrycyxlwv's Square if a ransom of eighty trillion grudniks is not paid for its return. And a deadline is given of forty-eight hours hence! You can see, Doctor, how desperate my husband and I are. That is why I came to you! You alone—if your colleague insists upon remaining with his apian charges can help me!"

A million thoughts swirled through my poor brain at this juncture.

"St. Wrycyxlwv's Square!" I exclaimed.

"St. Wrycyxlwv's Square!" she affirmed.

"But that is the national gathering place of your nation's fiercest and most implacable enemy!"

"Precisely, Doctor."

I stroked my chin thoughtfully, painfully aware of the unsightly stubble of unshaved whiskers that marred my appearance.

"And eighty trillion grudniks!" I repeated.

"Yes, eighty trillion grudniks," she said.

"That would be—roughly—forty crowns, nine quid and thruppence," I computed.

"That—or as close as to make no practical difference," my charming visitor agreed.

"Forty-eight hours," I said.

"Approximately two days," The Woman equated.

"I see," I temporized, stroking my chin once again. "And tell me, Your High—I mean, Irene—have you and your husband made response to the demand?"

"My husband has instructed his chief minister to play for time while I traveled, in the utmost secrecy you understand of course, to seek your assistance. Yours and—" She paused briefly and cast her gaze through the mist-shrouded panes into the fog-swirled gaslight beyond "—but you say he is unavailable."

"And his distinguished brother—you of course recall his distinguished brother," I averred.

"Of course."

"Rusticated," I whispered.

"Rusticated?" she echoed, clearly aghast.

"Rusticated," I repeated.

The Woman reached into her lace-trimmed sleeve with the thin, aristocratic digits of one hand and pulled from it a tiny, dainty handkerchief. She dabbed briefly at her eyes. This was the moment, some inner demon prompted me to recall, at which an unscrupulous person of the male persuasion might initiate an advance in the guise of simple sympathy. But even as I sat berating my secret weakness The Woman regained control of herself. She replaced her handkerchief and regained her full composure.

"There is only one thing for it then, Doctor," she said firmly. "None other can help. You must come with me. You must give us your assistance!"

I rose and without a word slipped into mackintosh, mackinaw, and cape, cap and galoshes, and extended my arm to the grateful and trembling Irene.

The game, I mumbled grimly to myself at a level of vocalization well below the audible, is afoot!

II.

Leaving even my humble chambers I paused to set up the deadfall, intruder trap, burglar interdictory, automatic dageurro-type machine, and the bucket of water on top of the door. Then I drew in the latch-string and, turning to my charming companion, said "I am at your service, madame."

We made our way down the stairs, checking at each landing for the presence of footpads or traitors, and emerged safely into the Limehouse night. A fine mist had begun to fall, wetting the soot-blackened remnants of a previous snowfall into a gray and slippery slush. My companion and I made our way through shadowy, echo-filled by-lanes until we emerged upon the West India Dock Road, site of so many infamous deeds and unex-plained atrocities.

A shudder ran unrepressed through my form as we crossed a cobblestone-floored square. For a moment I imagined it St. Wrycyxlwv's Square, and before my mind's eye there arose the silvery-gray and jewel-sparked shape of the God of the Naked Unicorn—the national art treasure of The Woman's adoptive homeland and the potential cause of revolution and anarchy in that ancient landlocked principality!

Somewhere a scream rent the Limehouse night—whether that of a tramp beating her cautious way up the fog-shrouded Thames or of some poor unfortunate victim of the crime rampant in the streets of the ill-starred district, it was not for me to know.

A cab wheeled by, its curtains drawn, driver in muffled obscurity on the box, dark horses' accoutrements jingling and creaking with the movement of the steaming beasts.

My companion and I walked nervously through the impene-trable murk until, drawn by the lights of a lower-class establish-ment where the very scum of Limehouse roistered out their pitiful nights, we had the good fortune to see a cab roll up and discharge is passengers, a couple of debauched-looking mariners obviously somewhat the worse for wear and seeking a place in which to squander what poor remnants of their seamen's wage they retained after being gouged and cheated by parsimonious owners and dishonest pursers on their ship.

I was about to call the cabby when my companion stopped me with an urgent hiss and a pressure upon the arm.

A second cab pulled up before the tavern and as its load of unsavory occupants made their way from the conveyance we climbed into the cab and Irene delivered softly her instructions to the cabby who peered inquisitively through the trap into the passenger compartment.

The first cab had departed and my companion leaned toward me, saying, "I should have thought by now, Doctor, that you would know better than to engage the first cab you encountered."

"But it had only just arrived," I protested. "There could have been no way for a malefactor to know we would be seeking transportation just at this place in time to send a cab for us."

At this point our conversation was interrupted by a flash of light and a loud report from a point directly ahead of our cab. The other vehicle had exploded in a gout of flame, and tongues of orange licked upward among clouds of black, oily smoke.

"Incredible!" I gasped in amazement. "How did you—?"

The Woman smiled inscrutably as our driver carefully picked his way around the first cab, now violently ablaze and all but blocking the intersection where the West India Dock Road was met by a winding thoroughfare that made its way upward from the Thames and into a safer and more reputable quarter than Limehouse.

We passed through numerous thoroughfares, some of them bustling and lighted as if it were noonday, others eerie and shrouded, until I felt that there was no way I could ever retrace our passage, nor less deduce the location of the moment, when at last the cab drew up at a kiosk whence individuals dressed in every manner and description entered and emerged into the street.

I chivalrously went halfies with Irene as to the cost of the cab, despite the embarrassing deficit of my financial situation, and we climbed from the cab onto the wet cobblestones of yet another London square surrounded by shops and restaurants all closed at this hour of the night. Without a word my companion led me carefully toward the kiosk, and drew me with her down a flight of darkened and ill-kept stair-steps until we reached a platform illuminated by a form of lighting totally unfamiliar to me. The flames seemed to be wholly enclosed in miniature glass globes, and to burn with a peculiar regularity and stability that permitted neither flickering nor movement. How they obtained the air to sustain combustion was a puzzle beyond my comprehension, but my companion refused to remain still long enough for me to make inquiry.

She led me past a large painted notice board marking the area of Ladbroke Grove, and depositing tickets in a turnstile device we made our way across the platform to wait for—I knew not what! There were railroad tracks before us, and my induction that this was a station of some sort was borne out in a few minutes when a train of a type and model unfamiliar to me approached. The train halted and we climbed aboard a coach, took seats, and rode in a strange and uncomfortable silence until my companion indicated that it was time for us to exit the odd train.

We made our way back to the surface of the earth and I discovered that we were standing on the edge of a broad, level area as large as a cricket field and then some, but whose surface, rather than being of grass, was composed of a hard, gritty stuff that exhibited none of the usual give and responsiveness of a natural substance.

My companion led me by the hand across the hardened surface until we stood beside the strangest contraption it has ever been to my wonderment to behold.

The thing was as long as a coach and rested on wheels, two rather largish ones at one end and a small one at the other. Its main substance seemed to be devoted to a ridged cylinder some rod or so in length and covered with a stressed fabric now glistening wetly in the night's drizzle.

Two open cockpits were located on the upperside of the thing, with curved shields of celluloid or isenglass before each and a set of bewildering dials and knobs in one of them. Stubby projections extended from the sides and rear of the machine, and a large wooden device not dissimilar to a marine screw was attached to one end, mounted to a black and powerful looking machine that I could only guess to be a self-contained engine of the sort sometimes used in small experimental marine craft.

Oddest of all, four free-swinging vanes projected from a pole mounted on the top of the machine, their ends drooping of their own unsupported weight and their entirety creaking and swaying slightly with each variation in the icy, drenching wind.

My companion reached into the closer cockpit and pulled from it a headgear for herself and one for me, demonstrating wordlessly the manner in which it was to be worn. It was made of soft leather and wholly enclosed the wearer's cranial projection. A strap caught beneath the wearer's chin thereby insuring a snug and secure fit of the headgear, and a pair of goggles fitted with transparent lenses could be slipped in place to protect the eyes from wind or moisture or raised onto the forehead to facilitate an unencumbered view in time of eased conditions.

My companion placed one shapely foot upon the stubby projection that stood away from the side of the machine and climbed gracefully into the cockpit. By means of silent gestures she communicated her desire that I emulate her actions, and not wishing to distress this brave and competent person I acceded, climbing upon the projection and thence into the second cockpit where I found myself seated upon a not uncomfortable leather cushion.

My companion turned in her place and indicated by gestures that I was to secure my seating by clamping a webbed belt across my lap. Again I acceded, watched over my companion's shoulder as she belted herself into position, and gasped in amazement to see a grease-covered and canvas-coveralled mechanician suddenly appear from a nearby outbuilding, race across the open area to our machine, grasp the wooden member which I could not help dubbing (in my mind) an aerial screw in his hands, and whirl it.

My companion, having acknowledged the arrival of the mechanician with a single-handed thumbs-up gesture, adjusted some of the controls before her and the self-contained engine at the front of the strange little craft coughed and sputtered its way into life! After warming the engire for some minutes my companion again gestured to the mechanician who pulled a set of inconspicuous chocks from before the wheels of the vehicle, and we rolled forward at an astonishing rate of speed, the wind whipping past us making me grateful for the helmet and goggles provided by my companion.

Before I had time even to wonder at the destination of this unusual mechanically-propelled journey I was distracted by the sound of a strange *whoop-whoop-whoop* coming from directly overhead and obviously keeping perfect pace with our own progress. I cast my gaze above in hopes of detecting the source of the strange sounds and discovered that they were coming from the four vanes mounted on the low tower above the cockpit where I sat.

The vanes were revolving so rapidly that I could barely follow them with my eye, and startlement was piled upon startlement when I felt the odd craft into which I was helplessly strapped actually *rise* from the field it had been crossing and move unsupported through the thin air!

I must have shouted my astonishment, for my companion turned her countenance toward me with a grin of such total confidence and surety of self that I laughed aloud at my momentary panic and vowed inwardly that I should permit nothing to interfere with my enjoyment of this unprecedented experience. The God of the Naked Unicorn might be missing, the great detective might be inseparably devoted to his bees on the Sussex Downs—at this very moment, if not abed, he might be engaged in the delicate and perilous activity of segregating the queen—but all was well with myself, and I would take the pleasure that was offered to me and worry later about my problems.

We flew—yes, I use the word advisedly and with full awareness of the gravity of its employment—in a great circle over the edges of London, watching the sun rise over the distant Channel to the east, passing perhaps over the very cottage where my former associate now made his home and tended his bees, and then swung in a northerly direction, passing over dark green woodlands and lighter meadows, leaving behind us England, Wales, Scotland, and the Orkney Islands.

No word was spoken—none could have been heard over the steady droning of the engine that turned the aerial screw that gave us our forward headway through the sky and that dragged the windmilling vanes of our overhead rotors through their vital revolutions—but I was amazed, from time to time, to see my companion half-climb from her cockpit and reach down upon the stubby projections from the sides of the craft and retrieve small teardrop shaped containers of fuel which she emptied into a nozzle mounted on the body of the craft in front of her own celluloid shield.

The sun had risen fully now, the sky was a sparkling northern blue with only spotty clouds of pure white dotting its cerulean regularity, and neither land nor handiwork of man was visible on the sparkling aquatic surface beneath us. I know not how long we flew nor how far north we had proceeded, save to make note that the air around us was growing increasingly frigid and I increasingly grateful for the foresight that caused me to dress warmly before leaving my Limehouse chambers, when there appeared below us and in the far distance a glimmer of blinding white.

My companion reached for the last remaining fuel container mounted on the vehicle and emptied its contents into the nozzle she had used before her shield. Glancing over her shoulder toward me she pointed ahead of us and shouted a series of words which were lost to me in the drone of the engine and the rush of the air past my leather-covered ears.

But I soon came to understand the significance if not the actual content of her speech as, under her careful guidance, our little craft nosed downward and began a long, steady approach toward what I came now to recognize as nothing less than the great ice pack of the north polar regions of the planet! Lower and lower our little craft made its way, as the dark waters beneath our extended wheels gave way to jagged white icebergs, pack ice, and finally great glaciers.

The mountainous formation of the ice slipped beneath our droning craft as we sped through the lower reaches of the atmosphere, then gave way to a flat and level area of glistening white. We crossed this new expanse and at length my companion swung the craft into a pattern of tight circles, spiraling slowly downward before a formation I had initially taken to be an icy projection of unusual beauty and regularity, and only after many moments recognized for a building.

Here—in the northernmost wastes of the polar ice fields—was the handiwork of man! I nearly wept at the audacity and beauty of the construction, and was distracted from this train of thought only by the landing of the craft in which I rode. The vehicle rolled across the hard-packed snow and came to a halt near the entrance of the gorgeous building.

A gale sped across the gleaming ice cap and flung a playful spray of snow against the exposed lower half of my face. I ran my tongue around my lips, tasting the clear purity of the melting crystals. No sign of life or activity emerged from the glittering spires that confronted us. Neither greeter nor guard emerged from the arched entry of the edifice.

My companion climbed from her seat and vaulted gracefully to the icy surface upon which our craft rested. I followed her, feeling in my bones and sinews the difference in our age. Then, side by side, we made our way to the building.

Before we even reached its portals I said "Irene—what place is this? I thought that we were going to your capital. Instead we have reached the northern polar cap of the planet, a region always believed uninhabited save for polar bears, seals, and gulls. Yet we find this magnificent structure!

"I beseech you to elucidate!"

She turned upon me the dazzling smile that had melted the hearts and won the applause of audiences the world around and that had brought her to the side of one of the crowned heads of Europe in as dazzling a marriage as the century has seen. "Pray exercise patience for a few more minutes, Doctor. All will be made clear to you once we are inside the Fortress."

"The Fortress?" I echoed helplessly.

"The Fortress of Solitude. The structure, which appears to be part of the ice flow upon which it stands, is actually constructed of marble, pure white marble quarried from a secret deposit and transported here in utmost concealment. Within it are—those who have summoned you. Those whose willing agent it is my honor to be."

We strode beneath towering portals and through echoing corridors until at last we entered a chamber occupied by a single bronzed giant seated in a posture of intense meditation. As we entered the room he seemed momentarily to be stationary, but in a few seconds I realized that he was engaged in a series of the most amazing solitary exercises.

Before my very eyes he made his muscles work against each other, straining until a fine film of perspiration covered his mighty frame. He vocalized softly and I realized that he was juggling a number of a dozen figures in his head, multiplying, dividing,

extracting square and cube roots. He turned to an apparatus that
made sound waves of frequencies that disappeared beyond the
limits of audibility for me, but which he could, from the
expression on his face, detect.

At the end of the series he looked up at my companion and
myself. In a voice that commanded confidence and obedience he
spoke. "Hello, Patricia," he said informally. "I see he came with
you. I knew of course that he would."

He rose from his seat and crossed the room toward us,
embracing the woman known as The Woman in two mightily
muscled arms of bronze. Yet, for all the affection that was visible
in that embrace, it was clearly one of brotherly—or perhaps
cousinly—fondness, nothing more.

"And you, sir," the bronze giant said, turning toward myself
and extending a mighty hand in manly greeting, "you are none
other than John H. Watson, M.D., are you not?"

I gave him my hand in as strong a grip as I could muster, and
will confess that I felt pleased to receive it back in one piece, the
bones not crushed farther than they were, in the viselike grip of
the man of bronze. "I am indeed. And may I have the honor of
your own credentials, sir?"

He smiled most disarmingly and said, "Of course, of course.
My name is Clark Savage, Jr. I hold a few degrees myself, picked
up here and there over the years. Most of my friends just call me
Doc. I'd be honored if you would do the same!"

For some reason I felt more flattered than offended by the
offhandedness and informality of the man, and agreed to call him
by the name he preferred, Doc. "I suppose," I said in reply,
"that we might avoid some certain degree of confusion were you
to call me what my dearest friend does, simply Watson."

"I'll be happy to do just that," the bronze giant said.

"But did I not hear you address our female companion as
Patricia?"

Doc Savage nodded his bushy, copper-colored poll in agreement. "My cousin, you see."

Perturbed, I said "But is she not—" I turned to The Woman
and addressed her directly. "But are you not the former Irene
Adler, now Her Royal Highness—"

"Please!" the charming young woman interrupted. "To Doc I

am known as his cousin, Patricia Savage. To you and your associate, I am known in another persona. Let us leave it at that, I pray you."

Her words puzzled me no end, but I felt that I had no choice under the circumstances in which I found myself than to accede.

"You must forgive me, Watson," the bronze giant said. "My cousin has helped me in a minor deception that was necessary to get you here to my polar Fortress of Solitude. If word had become current in the capitals of the world of the meeting to which you have been secretly summoned, an outbreak of crime unprecedented in the entire history of our planet would be bound to take place."

"You mean   " I stuttered dumfoundedly, "—you mean that the God of the Naked Unicorn has not been stolen? It is not being ransomed for a sum of eighty trillion grudniks? It is not going to be displayed in St. Wrycyxlwv's Square if the ransom is not paid? This entire proceeding has been a hoax of some sort?"

"Oh, the robbery is real enough, Dr. Watson," The Woman stated. "The God of the Naked Unicorn is missing and everything that I described to you will happen if it is not recovered. But this is only one tiny part of a world-wide threat!"

"Exactly," Doc Savage said. "I have only myself returned from a trek across the earth, escaping the clutches of a fiend unparalleled in the annals of crime. What is taking place here today is nothing less than a council of war, a council of war against one who menaces the orderly structure and just proceedings of the entire world order. Someone whose very identity, no less his base of operations, is a mystery wrapped in a puzzle locked inside an enigma!"

"Well said," I applauded. "But is it just we three who stand between the forces of order and civilization and this fiend?"

"Not we three, Doctor," said The Woman. "I must leave you now. My role has been played, my exit speech spoken. It is time for me to leave the stage of this drama and return to the side of my husband, there to watch and pray for those into whose hands the very fate of the world may have been given!"

Once more she exchanged a chaste contact with the man of bronze, then shook my own hand heartily and disappeared from the room. In a moment I heard the sound of her machine as it coughed into life again, then began its steady droning and the *whoop-whoop-whoop* that meant its rotors were spinning, lifting its fabric-covered body into the chilly air above the arctic reaches, and then it faded slowly from audibility.

I stood, alone in the room, with the bronze giant Doc Savage.

"Please come with me, Watson," he said at last. I felt that I had no choice but to obey. Savage strode powerfully to a doorway, adjusted some device which I took to be an automatic guard of a type infinitely more advanced than those I had set in my Limehouse flat, and stood aside as I walked into the next room.

Here I found myself in a chamber that would have done proud the finest men's club of London, Chicago, or the European bund of exotic Shanghai.

Wood-paneled walls rose to a magnificently carved high ceiling from which hung old wrought-iron chandeliers. Candles guttered atmospherically while skillfully concealed lights of an artificial nature provided supplementary illumination. The walls were lined with row upon row of books in matched sets of the finest buckram and morocco binding; hand-stamped titles in finest gilt gave back the light of the room.

Across a deep-piled oriental carpet of infinite richness and exquisite workmanship, a small portion of the luxuriantly flagstoned flooring was exposed before the great ornate fireplace where there roared a jolly bonfire of the greatest beauty and the most subtle yet pleasing fragrance.

Overstuffed chairs of rich leather and masterfully carven dark woods stood about the room, and each, save for two conspicuously left vacant, was occupied by a man of imposing mien if slightly eccentric dress.

In one chair sat a muscular figure all in gray. Gray hair, gray complexion, gray tunic and trousers. As I stood, aghast, in the entranceway of the room, he turned dead, cold eyes toward me, taking me in from sturdy British boots to my own faded crop of hair. He nodded curtly, but did not speak.

In the chair beside him sat a man all in black, black clothing swathing him from head to foot save here and there where the scarlet flashing of his clothes was exposed. His collar was turned up about his face and the brim of a black slouch hat was pulled down. Only his brilliant flashing eyes and hawklike nose protruded between brim and collar. With one hand he played with a strange girasol ring that he wore upon a finger of the other.

Next to him was a man with a contrastingly open, boyish expression about his face, blond wavy hair, and sparkling blue eyes. He wore a tight-fitting jersey, tight trousers with a broad stripe running down their sides, and high, polished boots. He somehow impressed me as an American—as, strangely, did most of these men. But this one carried a further, distinctive feeling of being a great college athlete—a Harvard man, I guessed.

Beyond him another young, open-faced individual, this one wearing a red zip-suit that matched his curly red hair. And beyond him two more persons of muscular and athletic build—one nearly naked, clad only on jingling harness and jouncing weapons, the other wearing ordinary clothing that looked by far the worse for wear, while he himself seemed strong and competent.

There remained only two others. One was another figure in dark cloak and slouch hat, a figure strangely resembling the hawk-nosed man, save that in this latter case there was no red flashing to relieve the gloomy hues of the clothing he wore, but instead a network of silvery threads that covered his clothing, giving one the uncanny feeling of a gigantic spider's web.

The other was a young man of pleasant mien albeit with a touch of the indolent attitude of the very wealthy. He looked at me with open, friendly expression and I was therefore all the more startled to make note of his reversed collar and the monotonous coloration of his rather ordinary looking suit—of mild, jade green!

III.

"Gentlemen," I heard Doc Savage say from behind me, "may I present our final member—Dr. John H. Watson, late of 221B Baker Street, London, England.

"Dr. Watson," the bronze giant continued, "won't you walk in and make yourself at home. This is our library. The thousands of volumes that you see lining the walls of this room represent the biographies, published and secret, of the men gathered in this room. Even a few of your own works concerning your former associate have found their way into this room—as has your associate himself on more occasions than one!"

"Holmes—here?" I gasped. "Why, he never told me—he never so much as hinted—"

"No, Watson?" the bronze giant responded. "Did he never tell you of the years he spent in Tibet? Nor of those in the United States under the name of Altamont?"

"Of course!" I smote myself on the forehead with the heel of my hand. "Of course! And I never—"

"Don't be harsh on yourself, Watson. Now that the time has come for you to be of service, here you are at the Fortress of Solitude, and this is your chance to do a favor for the world—and for certain individuals within this world. But first, let me introduce our other members."

He took me by the elbow and I made my way around the circle of easy chairs, shaking hands in turn with each of the men I had previously observed. As I approached each he introduced himself to me:

"Richard Benson—the Avenger," said the man in gray.

"Kent Allard—the Shadow," the hawk-nosed man chuckled grimly.

"Gordon, Yale '34—my friends call me Flash."

"Curtis Newton, sir, sometimes known as Captain Future."

"John Carter, former captain, confederate cavalry."

"David Innes of Connecticut and the Empire of Pellucidar."

"Richard Wentworth," said the second of the black-clad men, "known to some as the Spider." Even as he shook my hand I detected a look of suspicion and jealousy pass between himself and the man who had identified himself as the Shadow.

And finally, the man in the green clergy suit. "*Om,*" he intoned, making an Oriental sign with his hands before extending one to me in western fashion. "Jethro Dumont of Park Avenue, New York. Also known as Dr. Charles Pali and—the Green Lama."

"I am honored," I managed to stammer, "I had never dreamed that any of you were real persons. I always thought you the figments of fevered imaginations."

"As indeed that same charge has been hurled against your good friend and associate of Baker Street, wouldn't you say, Watson?" It was the bronze giant Doc Savage.

I acknowledged that such was indeed the case. "I am assailed from both sides," I said. "On the one side there are those who maintain that my good friend and associate, whose cases I have chronicled to the best of my mean ability for these many years, is himself a creature of my own fevered imaginings and has no being in the real world at all.

"While on the other hand the gentleman who serves as my own literary agent, Dr. Arthur Conan Doyle, has himself been accused of writing the very narratives which I furnish to him and which he in turn peddles to the magazines in my behalf."

A chuckle of sympathetic agreement made its way around the circle of men in the room. I thought again of the volumes that covered the walls of this library—not one of my companions but whose exploits had merited the efforts of some chronicler like mine own self, however humble his talents.

"And this band, this assemblage of adventurers—do I see before me the entirety of their sort?" I asked the personages at large as I assumed the rich and comfortable chair offered me by Doc Savage.

Again there was a buzz of low-pitched discussion as the colorfully garbed figures exchanged comments upon my question. Then one of them—I believe it was the Yale man, Gordon—replied in the role of tacitly designated spokesman for them all.

"We hardy few are just the present representatives of a movement whose number is legion. From the days of our founder whose portrait hangs above the fireplace, to this moment, there have been hundreds of us. Their names are inscribed upon the scroll of honor which stands beside the window over there."

He gestured, first toward the painting to which he had referred, then to a tall, narrow window through the thermally opaqued panes of which the long arctic night was beginning to descend. I strode first to stand before the roaring fire and gazed upward at the gracefully executed and richly framed depiction above it. The painter had done his work in rich colors of deep brown, rust, and maroon. The face which gazed back at mine showed strength, intelligence, and a fine tincture of insouciant wit. The costume was that of a French chevalier of a former century. The small engraved plaque beneath the canvas bore but a single word in simple script: *D'Artagnan.*

Paying momentary silent homage to the subject of the portrait I strode across the rich carpet to the scroll previously indicated by the American Gordon. Its heading was a simple phrase the initial characters of which cleverly formed a word of but a single syllable, the relevance of which, I fear I must admit, quite escaped me. The heading of the scroll read Personages United in League as Protectors. The names subtended therefrom were indeed numerous, including not only all of those in the room (myself excepted, of course!) but also many others, of which a random selection included such familiar and unfamiliar appellations as Jules de Grandon, Anthony Rogers, Sir Dennis Nayland Smith, Jimmy Dale, Arsène Lupin, Kimball Kinnison, Nicholas Carter, Stephen Costigan, and entire columns more.

"A splendid company!" I could not help exclaiming when I had completed my perusal of the gilded scroll. "But if I may make so bold as to ask, how is this establishment maintained? By whose efforts are these facilities operated? Who builds the fire, prepares comestibles, serves libations?"

"Oh, we have flunkies aplenty, Dr. Watson," the young man in the red zip-suit supplied. I identified him at once as Curtis Newton. "Each of us contributes his own staff of assistants to the general service of the League. My own aides include Otho the android, Grag the robot, and Simon Wright the living brain."

"And mine," the Shadow stated with a sinister chuckle, "are the playboy Lamont Cranston, the chauffeur Moe Shrevnitz, the communications wizard Burbank, and the near-suicide Harry Vincent!"

In turn each of them named a group of bizarre assistants, each as peculiar and eccentric as his employer.

"Each of these," Doc Savage concluded, "serves his time in the kitchen, the armory, or elsewhere in the Fortress and other farflung outposts of the League between assignments in personal service to his respective employer."

"I comprehend," I stated, sipping idly at the beverage which had appeared, all unnoticed, beside my easy chair. I stopped and sniffed, surprised, at the contents of my glass. Sarsaparilla.

"And yet I am puzzled by one matter," I said, addressing myself once more to my hosts at large. In response they looked at me, to a man, with expressions of inquisitive anticipation. "Why," I brought myself at last to ask, "have you summoned me to this redoubt? You are clearly a band of the most capable and dashing of men. I know not what puzzle confronts you, other than the matter of the purloined God of the Naked Unicorn. Surely you do not require my own humble talents in the solution of this, which must pale before your eyes to the pettiest of puzzles."

Once more the chairmanship of the assemblage was assumed by Clark Savage, Jr. He strode to and fro, stationing himself at last before the crackling fire so that the flames, as they writhed and danced behind his heroic figure, cast monstrous shadows across the ornate library of the League. With his feet spread widely, his hands clasped behind his back, his magnificent chest thrown out and his proud head held high, his entire form back-lighted and semi-silhouetted against the dancing flames, he made as glorious a picture of masculine power and grace as ever I had beheld.

"John Watson," he intoned impressively, "what I'm about to tell you is a piece of information of the most sensitive and yet earth-shaking nature. I place you upon your honor as a junior associate of the Personages United in League as Protectors to reveal it to no one until such time as the case has been brought to a triumphant conclusion. Have I your solemn word, John Watson?"

"You have it, sir," I whispered. There was a lump in my throat and my eyes were oddly watery at that moment.

"Very well!" Doc Savage continued. "I must inform you that there is at large an arch-villain whose malific machinations utterly overshadow those of the most infamous evil-doers in the entire annals of the League!"

"Blacker than Cardinal Richelieu!" a voice cried out.

"More sinister than the insidious Dr. Fu Manchu!" added another.

"More brilliant than the revolutionist Ay-Artz of the planet Lemnis!"

"More treacherous than Hooja the Sly One!"

"More dangerous than Blacky Duquesne!"

"More ruthless than the master mind Ras Thavas!"

"More threatening than the very Napoleon of Crime himself!" added Doc Savage, bringing the list to a crashing conclusion. "The Napoleon of Crime?" I repeated incredulously. "You mean—you mean the warped genius Professor James Moriarty? But I thought he was dead—killed in the plunge into Reichenbach Falls!"

"Perhaps he was—and then again, perhaps he escaped, as did his rival and opponent in the epic struggle that had its culmination there in Switzerland. Many a man has seen fit to disappear, and what better hiding place than the grave, eh, Watson?"

Savage was now striding back and forth before the great fireplace, his titanic shadow swaying across the wooden beams and metal chandeliers above our heads. The other men in the room sat silently, expectantly, observing the exchange between their leader and myself. I vowed silently not to fail my absent associate in the upholding of his honor.

"In raising the name of the Napoleon of Crime," I said with some heat, "in making that reference, Doc Savage, you bring by implication the charge that my own associate has somehow failed to rid the earth of this menace!"

"Quite so," Doc Savage stated. "Your associate—Sherlock Holmes—is in the hands of a fiend before whom Professor Moriarty and these other petty peculators pale to a paltry puniness!"

He strode forward and stood over me, towering fully six feet and more into the air. "I am here only because a timely bit of aid by my cousin Patricia caused me to escape the clutches of this arch-fiend! I slipped through his net, but two companions with whom I was pursuing the missing God of the Naked Unicorn were less fortunate than I, and are at this time held in durance vile by the mad genius whose efforts may yet bring the entire fragile structure of civilization crashing to destruction!"

"*Two* companions?" I echoed dumbly. "*Two*? But who can they be?"

He crouched low, bringing his metallic-flecked eyes glimmeringly close to my own and pointed his finger at me significantly. "At this very moment there rest in the clutches of this brilliant maniac both Sherlock Holmes and Sir John Clayton, Lord Greystoke, the man known to the world at large as—Tarzan of the Apes!"

"Holmes *and* Greystoke? At one time? And very nearly yourself as well, Doc Savage?" I exclaimed. "Who can this devil be, and how can I assist in retrieving your associates from his clutches?"

"Wentworth, you are our supreme intellectual!" snapped Doc Savage to the personage in the spider-webbed cloak. "Enlighten Dr. Watson as to our strategy, will you please, while I retire briefly to extract a few square and cube roots?"

Doc Savage retreated to his own seat and the Spider began to speak in a low, insinuating voice that seemed almost to hypnotize the listener.

"This arch-fiend is unquestionably the most brilliant and most resourceful opponent any of us has ever faced," he averred. "Yet, Watson, as all who fight crime and anarchy know in the innermost recesses of their being, there has never lived an evildoer whose warped brain has not caused him to commit one fatal mistake that led to his being brought before the bar of justice and punished sooner or later. Sooner or later, Watson."

"The abduction of Tarzan, Holmes, and Doc Savage was to have taken place at the brilliant Exposition of European Progress where the God of the Naked Unicorn was on display." This was Richard Henry Benson, the Avenger, speaking. He fingered an odd dagger and an even odder-looking pistol as he spoke. "A brilliant replica of the God of the Naked Unicorn was substituted, a substitution that would escape the practiced eye of the most discerning lapidarist, and yet was discovered by a mere woman!"

"Yes, a mere woman!" Captain John Carter took up the narration. "A woman of protean nature whose admirers have identified her variously as the Princess Dejah Thoris of Helium—as Joan Randall, daughter of the commissioner of the interplanetary police authority—as Margo Lane, faithful friend and companion of the Shadow—as Jane Porter Clayton, Lady Greystoke—and as Miss Evangl Stewart of New York City's bohemian quarter Greenwich Village, among others!"

"This woman," Jethro Dumont intervened suavely, "*The* Woman, if you will, detected the clever substitution and sought to notify Sherlock Holmes, Lord Greystoke, and Doc Savage. She had alerted both Greystoke and Holmes and was speaking with Doc Savage when the first two members of the League, unaware of the presence of Doc, moved to uncover the fraud and fell into the trap of the arch-fiend!"

"I moved to their rescue," Savage concluded the tale, "but the evil-doer was prepared! He used the God of the Naked Unicorn to trap Holmes and Tarzan, and using them as bait nearly netted me as well! I escaped with my life and nothing more, and Holmes and Tarzan were spirited away, along with the God of the Naked Unicorn!"

"Then the threat of which Miss—The Woman spoke," I stammered, "the threat to display the God of the Naked Unicorn in St. Wrycyxlwv's Square—was merely a device? A hoax?"

"No, Dr. Watson," the Shadow interposed, "that threat is real, is all too real. But a far greater threat to the order and security of the world is posed by the madman who holds Sherlock Holmes and Tarzan of the Apes in his clutches at this moment!"

"I see, I see," I mumbled in stunned semi-coherency. "But then—then what role have you chosen for me to play in this drama? What can an humble physician and sometime biographer of the great do in this exigency?"

"You," said Doc Savage commandingly, "must solve the crime, rescue the victims, and save the order of world civilization, Dr. Watson!"

IV.

I fumbled in my lounging robe for my pipe, shoved aside the futile revolver with which I had foolishly menaced The Woman as she entered my Limehouse flat so seemingly long ago, and began to pace to and fro myself. My mind raced. My thoughts whirled about like bits of flotsam caught in a maelstrom. What would Holmes do, was all I could think at that moment, What would Holmes do, what would Holmes do?

At last I halted before Doc Savage and asked, "Did the villain leave behind any clue—any scrap of evidence, however trivial or meaningless it might seem to you?"

Furrows of puzzlement and concentration seemed to cut deep grooves into the brow of the man of bronze. At last he said, "There may be one thing, Watson, but it seemed so inconsequential at the time that I hardly took note of it, and hesitate to mention it to you now."

"Permit me to be the judge of that, please," I snapped in as Holmes-like a manner as I could muster. To my gratification the man of bronze responded as ever had witnesses under the questioning of Sherlock Holmes.

"The fiend had apparently developed a superscientific device of some sort which reduced the stature of his victims to that of pygmies, and he strode away with poor Holmes under one arm and Greystoke under the other."

"Yes," I said encouragingly, "pray continue."

"Well, Dr. Watson," Savage resumed, "as the fiend left the Exposition of European Progress he seemed to be mumbling something to himself. I could barely make out what it was he was saying. But it seemed to be something like *Angkor Wat, Angkor Wat.* But what could that possibly mean, Watson?"

I smiled condescendingly and turned to the assemblage who sat in awed silence at the confrontation between Savage and myself. By a tacit gesture I indicated that I would accept information from any of them.

"Is it an exotic drug?" one asked.

"The name of the fiend himself?" another attempted.

"A secret formula of some sort?" queried a third.

"Some religious talisman?" "A Princeton lineman?" "The greatest scientist of ancient Neptune?" "An obsolete nautical term?" "The seat of an obsolete monarchy?"

"That's it!" I cried encouragingly. "I knew that the knowledge lay somewhere among you! Angkor Wat is a city lost in the jungles of heathen Asia! We must seek this fiend and his victims in Angkor Wat!

"Quickly," I exclaimed, turning toward Doc Savage, "have transportation made ready at once! We depart for Angkor Wat this night!"

"Can I come along?" the Shadow asked, twisting the girasol ring on his finger.

"No, no, take me!" the Avenger put in.

"Me!" cried Gordon of Yale.

"Me!" shouted David Innes. "I know Tarzan personally!"

Soon they were all jumping from their seats, jostling one

another to approach closest to me and squabbling as to which among them should have the honor of accompanying me on my mission to rescue Sherlock Holmes and John Clayton, Lord Greystoke.

"This is a task for Doc Savage and myself alone," I told them as kindly but definitely as I could. "The remainder of you are to remain here and hold yourselves in readiness should there be a call for your services. Now, Savage," I addressed myself to the man of bronze, "have some of those well-known flunkies of your establishment make ready a vehicle suitable for transporting us to the lost city of Angkor Wat in the jungles of the faraway Orient!"

"Yes, sir!" he acceded.

Firmness, I vowed, would be the salient feature of my modus operandi from henceforward onward.

Within minutes a crew of grotesque creatures had prepared one of the strange flying machines, which Doc Savage informed me were known as autogyroes, with a plentiful supply of reserve fuel, a wicked-looking advanced-design gattling gun, and belts of ammunition. Almost before there was time to shake hands heartily with each member of the League we were leaving behind, Savage and I were airborne over the arctic wastes.

Before many hours had passed, our remarkable autogyro was *whoop-whoop-whooping* its way across the great Eurasian world-island, passing, at one moment, over the very St. Wrycyxlwv's Square where the God of the Naked Unicorn was to be displayed, to the distress of The Woman and the disordering of the stability of European civilization, in what was now little more than twenty-four hours, should Doc Savage and I fail in our mission.

We passed over the Germanic and Austro-Hungarian Empires, the semi-barbarous Slavic states to their east, fluttered dangerously through rigid snow-capped passes in the sinister Ural Mountains and into Asia. Nothing stopped us, nothing slowed us. Savage's flunkies had equipped the autogyro with numerous auxiliary tanks of fuel, and had thoughtfully provided for Savage and myself a huge wicker basket filled with delicate viands.

We passed over teeming Bombay, curved northward tossing clean-picked bones of squab onto the nomad-haunted sands of the Gobi Desert, hovered high above teeming hordes of heathen Chinese as we completed a repast of cold lobster in mayonnaise (dropping the empty carapaces of the aquatic arachnidae into the hands of awed Orientals) and moved at last across the bay of Tonkin, waving greetings to tramp steamers as they plied their routes, until we came once more over land and I saw far beneath the wheels of the autogyro the green lushness of the ancient jungle.

Shortly my companion and pilot pointed downward toward an opening in the jungle. Through the here widely-spaced palms I could see the pyramids and temples, collonades and pagodas of an antique metropolis, one lost for thousands of years and only of late rediscovered, to the awe and wonderment of even European scholars.

Doc Savage worked the controls of the autogyro and we dropped, dropped, dropped through the steaming tropical air, until the rubber-clad wheels of the aerial vehicle rolled to a rest atop the tallest pyramid in Angkor Wat.

We climbed from the autogyro and stood overlooking the ancient city. It was dawn in this quarter of the globe, and somewhere a wild creature screamed its greeting to the sun while great cats padded silently homeward from their nocturnal prowls and birds with feathers like brilliant jewels soared into the air in search of tropical fruits upon which to gorge themselves.

"There's only one place in a city like this where a maniac like our foe would make his headquarters!" Doc Savage growled. "That's in the high temple of the sun, and that's why I landed us where I did!"

Through the eerie stillness of the jungle metropolis we made our way down the giant granite steps of the pyramidal edifice, pausing now to gasp in awed admiration of the handicraft of some long-forgotten Asiatic artisan, now to kill a poisonous serpent, now to pot a brilliant-plumaged denizen of the airy reaches for the sheer fun and sport of it.

At last we reached the earth, and making our way to the grand collonade that gave onto the great chamber of the temple, we found the prison-chamber of the arch-fiend—but our prey had flown the coop! Savage and I stood aghast at the torture device of the maniac, chilled not so much by its massiveness—for it was

smaller than an ordinary kit bag—as by the malignant poten-
tialities revealed in its complex controls.

Clearly the fiend and his victims had been here shortly before
us and the villain had fled in haste, abandoning his infernal
device as he made good his escape. And yet, the very
carelessness exhibited by the malefactor suggested that he owned
as bad or worse and was keeping them somewhere other, to which
place he had repaired, victims in tow!

Savage and I sprinted back to the autogyro pausing only to
ferret out such clues as were required to determine the destination
of the fleeing fiend and his captives.

Thus pursued we them from Angkor Wat to bustling, modern
Tokio, thence to mystery-shrouded Easter Island where we
wandered among the strange monolithic sculptures in bafflement
until Doc Savage summoned the talents of the Green Lama by
remote communication. That luminary induced one of the weird
statues to reveal to Savage and myself that it had observed the
fiend and his two captives only minutes earlier than our arrival,
departing on a course dead-set for the American settlement of
Peoria in the province of Illinois.

We pounded our way across the Pacific, the autogyro's rotors
whoop-whoop-whooping as we fled from day back into night.

We passed above the gleaming lights of San Francisco harbor,
rose to frigid heights as we passed over the Rocky Mountains,
dropped low again to wave to a cowpoke here, a sourdough there,
as we saw the sun rise once again before we reached Peoria.

Less than a day left to us! My horrified mind's eye pictured the
scene in St. Wrycyxlwv's Square and the inevitable disintegration
of world order that must follow—especially in the absence of
those two saviors of the sane and the normal, Holmes and
Greystoke!

Each outpost of the fiend, as we uncovered it, revealed him to
have abandoned a similar but more fiendishly advanced model of
his infernal torture device, its case glistening, its control panel
studded with keys and levers, each marked with some arcane
abbreviation of alphabetical or cabbalistic significance known
only to the torturer—and, I inferred with a shudder—to Sherlock
Holmes and John Clayton!

From Illinois the trail led to an abandoned warehouse located on New York City's lower Seventh Avenue. Here Savage and I found more and different devices of the fiend's trade, and heard a distant door slam at the far end of the building even as our boots pounded angrily after the fleeing maniac.

We pursued him down a long tunnel that seemed to dip and curve away beneath the very bedrock of the Island of Manhattan, then there was a rumble—a flash—an uncanny sensation of twisting and wrenching, and Savage and I found ourselves standing side-by-side outside the very London kiosk where The Woman had brought me at the outset of my weird odyssey!

"Where now?" Savage gasped frantically, consulting a chronometer which he wore conveniently strapped to the wrist of one mighty bronze limb.

I thought for a moment, wondering where in the great metropolis the maniac would go. Suddenly I was seized by a stroke of inspiration. I grasped the bronzed giant by one elbow and with him raced to the nearest hack stand where we engaged the second carriage in line. I stammered my instructions to the cabby and he set off at a rapid clip, the hooves of the horses clop-clopping over the London cobblestones to my great comfort and relief until we drew up before a familiar old building where I had spent many happy years in the past.

I tossed a coin to the cabby and Savage and I raced up the stairs, hammered frantically at the doorway of the ground story flat, and urged its occupant, the owner and resident manager of the establishment, to join us in our mission above, and to bring her pass key with her as she did so!

As that good woman turned her key in the lock to the upper flat Savage burst open the door with a single thrust of his mighty bronze shoulder and I stepped past him, revolver in hand, and surveyed the scene within.

There I beheld the fiend seated at his infernal machine, operating its keys and levers with maniacal rapidity while upon the table beside him I saw the pitifully shrunken figures of Sherlock Holmes and John Clayton, dancing and twirling with each strike of the keys of the maniac's machine. To one side of the machine stood a huge stack of pages covered with typed writings. To the other stood an even taller stack of blank pages waiting to be covered with words.

A single sheet was in the fiend's machine, and each time he struck a key a new letter appeared upon the page, and with each word I could see the pain upon the faces of the two heroes growing greater as their stature grew less.

"Halt, fiend!" I shouted.

The maniac turned in his seat and leered maniacally up at Savage and myself. His hair was white, his face satanically handsome, yet marked with the signs of long debauchery and limitless self-indulgence.

"So, Savage—" he lipped grimly "—and Watson! You have found me, have you. Well, small good that will do you. No man can stand in the way of Albert Payson Agricola! You have played into my hands! You see—there are your two compatriots. All of the rest in your moronic League will follow! And I alone shall possess the God of the Naked Unicorn," and with that he gestured grandly toward a table on the opposite side of the room.

There, on the very mahogony where my gasogene had stood for so many years between Holmes's violin case and his hypodermic apparatus, there now reposed the silver and gem majesty of Mendez-Rubirosa's masterpiece, the God of the Naked Unicorn!

"And now," Agricola hissed triumphantly, "I shall add two more trophies to my collection of puppets and husks!"

He bent to the keyboard of his infernal device and struck this lever, then that. With each strike I either felt a jolt of galvanic dynamism scream through my own organism or saw poor Savage writhe in bronzed agony.

"Stop it!" I managed to howl at the fiend. "Stop it or—"

He struck still another key. SUDDENLY I FELT HUGELY MAGNIFIED AND EMPOWERED! I JERKED THE TRIGGER OF MY REVOLVER AND ALBERT PAYSON AGRICOLA FLUNG HIS ARMS OUTWARD! HIS ELBOW STRUck a lever on the machine and I returned to normal. I saw Doc Savage at my side massaging his painfully twisted limbs. I saw Sherlock Holmes and Tarzan of the Apes beginning with infinite slowness and yet by perceptible degrees to regain their proper form and stature.

Albert Payson Agricola fell to the carpet, a hole neatly drilled between his eyes.

From the wound there seemed to flow neither blood nor spattered brains but shred after shred of dry, yellow, smearily imprinted wood pulp paper.

Death in the Christmas Hour
by
James Powell

If we can involve ourselves with Sherlockian extraterrestrials, animals, and robots, why not toys? And if we're going to involve ourselves with toys, why not make it a Christmas story as well? Of course, the toys antedate our modern electrified, computerized ones, but then Holmes is Victorian in origin, remember.

Death in the Christmas Hour

by James Powell

In the first hour of Christmas morning animals can talk and toys come to life provided no humans are lurking about.

Several minutes after the last stroke of midnight had tolled over the snowy Christmas city, a Welsh corgi named Owen Glendower could be seen leading a young man on a leash past the houseware windows of McTammany's Department Store.

Austin W. Metcalfe, as this young person called himself, possessed a round face cluttered with glasses and a short-stemmed, fat-bowled pipe whose operation he had not yet mastered. A burgundy muffler was tucked up neatly under his chin. His hands and feet were warm in fleece-lined leather. Every button of his dark-blue overcoat was buttoned. He moved with a sedate and serious air, having by dint of application and high purpose risen to be second assistant curator of the Metropolitan Museum of Toys.

In other words—as Owen Glendower would be the first to admit—Metcalfe was a very, very pompous young ass. The dog

321

looked back over its shoulder as if about to unload a considerable burden of complaint. Poor square Metcalfe really needed his corners knocked off. The dog hoped some girl would come along crazy enough to take a liking to him and do the job before it was too late. Recently Metcalfe had met one who seemed to fit the bill. Owen Glendower had used his considerable powers of thought transference to inspire a phone call. (Half the good ideas humans get come from their pets. Owen Glendower didn't know where the other half came from.) But the young stick-in-the-mud wouldn't budge. The dog turned to mutter at a hydrant.

Though the wind was picking up, Metcalfe waited patiently in the falling snow, conscious of being a kindly and, he was sure, a beloved master. He'd have enjoyed dwelling on that but his pipe went out again and he had to struggle to relight it.

Meanwhile, around the corner and just ten feet from where he stood, the occupants of the largest of McTammany's toy windows were enjoying a fashion show. The Dick and Jane dolls were displaying their extensive wardrobes to an appreciative audience of frogs in frill collars, sows in dresses, and a variety of robots, those metal facsimiles of humanity who beeped, hummed, and flashed their approval in the most amazing manner considering that batteries were not included.

When Owen Glendower was ready, he coughed to warn the toys to freeze in their tracks and then led the young man around the corner so the whole window could see what an honest corgi had to put up with all year long. As for Metcalfe, he'd seen the window many times before. The museum had loaned its popular toy display and the young man's personal creation, "A Victorian Christmas," to McTammany's for the holidays. Metcalfe came daily to admire his handiwork on exhibit in the next window. But he always stopped here first. The antique toys never suffered from the comparison.

Unwilling to interrupt the toys' Christmas Hour any longer, Owen Glendower coughed again and led the way to Metcalfe's window. The young man's design represented a Victorian living room centering on a small alabaster fireplace. To its left stood a Christmas tree hung with brightly painted wooden ornaments and topped by a caroling angel.

Before the tree was a music-box ballerina on tiptoe and a blue-

and-yellow jack-in-the-box. On the hearth rug stood a Punch and Judy show with two fine hand puppets. The right of the fireplace was occupied by a grass-green wing chair and a matching hassock topped with a most elegant Victorian dollhouse whose procelain mistress stood at the door in a plum-colored hoop shirt. At the base of the hassock a nutcracker captain of hussars with fierce grin and drawn saber led a formation of toy soldiers in scarlet coats and bearskin hats.

Rather, that was how Metcalfe had laid out the exhibit. But tonight someone else's hand had been at work. The soldiers were nowhere to be seen. The hussar and the rest of the toys stood in a circle in front of the jack-in-the-box looking down at Judy, lying on the red Turkey carpet, a limp and strangely lifeless figure looking somehow less than a hand puppet without a hand in it.

And there was more uncanniness. The jack-in-the-box was out and nodding on its spring. But traffic vibrations sometimes triggered the box latch. And the hussar seemed atremble as though it had just snapped to attention. Still, that might have been Metcalfe's imagination. But where did that Sherlock Holmes doll come from? And why did Metcalfe have the distinct impression the little detective was on the verge of pointing an accusing finger?

Then he saw the teddy bear at Holmes's side and the light dawned. Miss Tinker, a department-store window dresser who'd helped him set up the museum display, said she always put her Teddy in one of the toy windows and please couldn't she sit him there on the wing chair? Well, Metcalfe'd had to laugh at that and explain how every toy, ornament, and piece of furniture in the display was an authentic Victorian artifact. Teddy bears were Edwardian. With bad grace she had accepted his compromise that she wrap up the bear and put it under the tree where more presents were needed. Why, he wondered, were the pretty ones all so feather-headed?

On the other hand, he hadn't been completely honest with her. The museum didn't have a Victorian Christmas-tree angel. Mr. Jacoby, their toy repair and reproduction wizard, had fashioned this one from parts of an Amelia Earhart doll damaged when the wire that held its monoplane to the ceiling above the Toys Conquer the Clouds display had broken. Metcalfe'd been tempted to call her up and confess. Now he was rather glad he hadn't. A Sherlock Holmes doll, indeed! Metcalfe relit his pipe and rocked back and forth on his heels, puffing with his hands clasped behind his back. Yes, he would definitely have to speak to the young lady about this. And about how the teddy bear got there, too.

Metcalfe might have stayed for some time, fuming, imagining his righteousness at this confrontation, but Owen Glendower gave a sigh of tedium and led him away, knowing that Mr. Metropolitan, the generous Armenian who was the museum's director and principal endower, had asked his second assistant curator to make an early-morning visit to the toy reliquary at the museum. Last Christmas morning the night watchman had reported discovering three dead alligators in a pool of blood in the Victorian Wing.

Asked to produce the carcasses, the man insisted he'd burned them in the furnace after cleaning up the mess. Asked to explain the disappearance of one of the finest of the Victorian dolls, the night watchman had professed ignorance. Metcalfe had been commissioned to drop in and smell the night watchman's breath to determine, as Mr. Metropolitan put it, "if the man's on the Christmas sauce."

As for where Teddy came from, the answer was the Midwest. Miss Ivy Tinker had brought him with her as a mascot when she moved East to take the job with McTammany's. For Teddy, mascoting was a kind of lonely, fallow time, waiting for Miss Ivy Tinker to get married and have children so he could get back to toying again. Teddy had spent his first Christmas Hour here in the East alone, pacing up and down with his paws in his pockets and nothing to do but kick at a corner of the rug.

To insure that wouldn't happen again, he had furrowed his brow and directed his powers of thought transference at Miss Ivy Tinker's sleeping head behind the bedroom door. The next morning over toast she announced that she'd dreamed she'd included him in one of her Christmas toy windows. And why not? The perfect cachet for a Tinker-dressed window. The stuffed bear wasn't surprised a bit. Half the good ideas humans get come from their toys. Teddy didn't know where the other half came from.

Teddy hadn't spent a boring Christmas Hour since. Last year he'd been right in the middle of McTammany's stuffed-animal window. On the stroke of midnight, in clopped the team of stuffed Clydesdales, the kangaroo pulled the spigot out of his pouch and told the old one about Australian beer being made out of kangaroo hops, and a great time'd been had by all. Teddy'd worn a hangover and a lopsided grin for the rest of the year.

And now it was the Christmas Hour again. Stretching at the first rush of vital power, Teddy felt the noisy paper and some constricting bond. His paw found the seam in the wrapping, located the end of the velvet bow, and pulled. With the toll of midnight sounding dimly in the distance, he emerged and found himself standing among a pile of presents under a Christmas tree. Farther out in the room he could see other toys coming to life. He was just about to join them when the sound of a muffled violin made him stop.

He lay his ear to the gay boxes one by one until he found the source. He stripped back the paper. The lid illustration on the box depicted night and fog and a doorway from another era. The number on the door was 221B. The name on the lamppost was Baker Street. Large bright letters declared: THE ORIGINAL SHERLOCK HOLMES DOLL. ANOTHER WONDERFUL CREATION FROM DOYLE TOYS.

Teddy opened the box. The doll inside wore a deerstalker cap and a coat with a cape. In addition to its violin and bow, which the doll lay aside with a smile, the other accessories included a magnifying glass, a calabash pipe, and a Persian slipper stuffed with shag.

"Thank you, my dear sir," said Sherlock Holmes, taking Teddy's proffered paw to help himself out of the box. "I've spent I don't know how many Christmases wedged down behind a radiator in the toy-department stockroom. I'm the sole survivor of an unpopular and long-forgotten line of dolls. I don't know whom to thank for being here."

"Miss Ivy Tinker needed more boxes for under the tree," said Teddy, introducing himself.

"Ursus arctus Rooseveltii? I hardly think so," said the detective. "And I did publish an anonymous monograph on stuffed animals." Reaching for his glass, he examined Teddy's eyes and the seam on his shoulder. "Your eyes are French glass manufactured by Homard et Fils. Your seams are a double stitch called English nightingale because, like that bird, it is only found in England east of the Severn and south of the Trent.

"Homard et Fils supplied only one company in that area, Tiddicomb and Weams. That firm produced stuffed bears only once. On the birth of Queen Victoria's son, Prince Leopold, in 1854, Tiddicomb and Weams presented the child with a papier-mâché replica of the House of Lords, complete with twelve stuffed bears dressed in stars and garters and full pontificals to represent the lords spiritual and temporal. This wonderful toy the teenaged prince later donated to an auction in aid of the victims of the great Chicago fire and it disappeared from sight in America. You, Teddy, are a Bear of the Realm."

Teddy's chest swelled with pride and his voice grew husky. "I believed it when Miss Ivy Tinker said I was a teddy bear. We stuffed animals are notoriously absent-minded."

"Well, come along, old fellow," said Holmes, taking his arm. "It's the Christmas Hour. The game's afoot. Time to wrap ourselves around a good stiff drink."

Teddy needed no urging. They strolled from under the tree together, walking to the beat of the carol being sung by the silver-voiced angel atop the tree—who, in the nature of Christmas-tree angels, preferred to spend the hour singing hymns of joy and praise.

Suddenly a captain of hussars blocked their way, a dozen redcoats at his back. The officer raised a suspicious eyebrow at Teddy and lay the point of his saber against his hairy breast. "Well, you ain't no alligator but you could be a rat in disguise," said the hussar, gnashing his teeth in a most threatening manner.

Teddy knocked the saber aside and growled as a Bear of the Realm might. "What I am is a bear."

Impressed by this lack of meekness, the officer said, "You mean one of those stuffed-animal chappies? Then welcome aboard. Captain Rataplan here. We can use anyone with spunk enough to stand beside us in this damned business."

"And just what business is that, Captain?" asked Holmes.

"Let's save that for over a drink once we've got the perimeter secure," said the hussar. "I see old Punch has opened for business."

Holmes followed the officer's finger over to the hearth rug where the two hand puppets were converting their stage into a bar, Punch polishing the counter with a rag while Judy set up the bottles and glasses.

But Teddy's gaze couldn't get past the music-box ballerina only a few feet away. She had the dancer's classic features, small head, large eyes, and long legs. Teddy tried to catch her attention by wiggling his ears. "A fine figure of a woman," agreed Captain Rataplan. "That's Allegretta. Gretta, we call her. Likes to play hard to get, don't you know. Well, I don't mind that in a woman. Faint heart ne'er won fair lady, eh?" He snorted fiercely and marched his men away.

Holmes and Teddy headed off across the carpet in the direction of the bar. As they passed the closed jack-in-the-box, Holmes remarked, "Jack seems to be a slug-a-bed."

Then they stopped and introduced themselves to the ballerina, who sat nursing a foot in her lap. "Come and join us for a drink," urged Teddy, wiggling his ears outrageously. "Tempus fugit."

"I'll be right along, okay?" she said through chewing gum. "Boy, are my dogs barking."

"After a year on tiptoe, dogs that didn't bark would be quite a clue indeed," observed Holmes with a smile which she answered with a blank stare.

At the bar Punch greeted them with a "What'll it be, gents?" in a squeaking batlike voice.

"Something with a splash of the old gasogene, Landlord, if you please," said Holmes. "A scotch whisky, I think."

"Make mine a gibson," said Teddy. The cocktail vice had spread quickly among creatures who only came to life one hour a year.

"So be it, gents," said Punch. But as the hunchback reached for the scotch he shouted over his shoulder, "Judy, where are you off to?"

"The olives," squeaked his female partner.

"Onions for gibsons, old hoss," scolded Punch. He mixed their drinks and when Judy came back from the icebox carrying a pickled onion on the point of an ice pick he served them. "Your health, gents," he declared, raising his own mug of beer. As they clinked their drinks, Punch turned once again to Judy and demanded, "Where now, old hoss?"

"An olive," she said, waving the ice pick. "Here comes Captain Rataplan for his martooni."

But the hussar heard her and shook his head. "My men come first. Twelve mugs of the nut-brown ale." Judy put the ice pick in the pocket of her smock and obediently set to filling the mugs.

Turning to Holmes and his bear companion, Captain Rataplan said, "Getting back to the alligator situation, the damned things feed on sewer rats all year round. So come Christmas Hour we're a delicious change of pace and they swarm up and make a try for us. No problem. We can give as good as we get. And alligators are a stupid, muscle-bound crew.

"But then there are the rats. Cowards, but smart as whips. Gentlemen, one of these years the rats are going to talk the alligators into an alliance. What I see coming against us is an army of alligators each with a rat riding on its neck whispering orders in its ear. Mark my words, when that day dawns toydom will vanish from human memory and dogs and cats won't be far behind."

"A grim prospect, Captain," said Holmes gravely. "Let's hope the rats never get the idea."

But as Rataplan left with his mugs of ale on a tray, some of the gloom went with him. After a few pulls at his drink, Holmes leaned back with his elbows on the bar and said, "Rat masterminds astride alligators or not, Teddy, it's great to be alive again. I miss only one thing: a mystery to be solved. No, I'm a liar, Teddy. Two things."

"And what's the other, Holmes?" asked Teddy, chewing the onion from his gibson.

Sherlock Holmes did not answer. He straightened up. "Speak of the devil!" he exclaimed. "Excuse me, old man, won't you?" And taking off his cap, the detective strode across to the hassock where a woman stood smiling at him. Not a woman but *The* Woman. "Can it be you, Miss Adler? I mean, Mrs. Godfrey Norton." For that indeed was the married name of the heroine of "A Scandal in Bohemia."

"Good morning, Mr. Holmes," smiled the woman. "And it is

Irene Adler. I assumed my professional name when my husband's death obliged me to return to the operatic stage."

"Allow me to offer you my arm, Miss Adler," urged the detective. "Let us walk a bit apart. I must know how you come to be here. I was just telling my friend Teddy that there are only two things I miss: Miss Irene Adler and a good mystery."

"In that order, Mr. Holmes?"

"Indeed," insisted the detective.

Irene Adler laughed gaily at the lie. Then they picked out a design in the carpet to use as a path and walked together toward the big window. "I'm from the Diva series of dolls," she explained, "each a replica of a prima donna of a European opera house. The museum has us displayed on the stage of a Victorian doll opera house.

"Well, last year there was that terrible business when the alligators swarmed in on us right at the start of the Christmas Hour, shouting their vile sewer language. If it hadn't been for Captain Rataplan and his thin red line of soldiers which bestrode the aisle and Punch who backed them up with his club no one would have had time to find high ground. The rest of the Victorian Christmas people sought refuge up on the hassock. But in the excitement Lady Gwendolyn, the mistress of the doll-house, fell over the edge into the midst of the alligators and was swallowed up in a single gulp."

Holmes and the woman had reached the window. They stood in silence, contemplating the darkness beyond the glass and watching the wind swirl the snow beneath the streetlights. Then Irene Adler said, "So here I am. I was chosen to take Lady Gwendolyn's place. Personally, I found the Diva Christmas Hours oppressive, with all the ladies trying to upstage each other. I have always preferred the company of men." Then she said, "But come, tell me how you come to be here?"

But before the detective could answer, Teddy came up behind them. "My dear Holmes," he said in a voice which had become progressively more British since he'd learned of his ancestry, "there's been a terrible thing. Judy's been murdered."

Judy was quite dead. There was evidence of a severe contusion under her hooked chin. But death had come another way.

Concealed within the folds of the voluminous smock hand puppets wear was the handle of the ice pick which had found her heart.

Holmes rose from his examination of the corpse and surveyed the horrified toys who stood around it, including a newcomer, a young man in a cap with bells and a particolored suit. This would be Jack. His box stood wide open and empty.

Irene Adler was pale. "Are we toys capable of murder?" she asked.

"And of seeing that justice is done, as I assure you it will," nodded Holmes grimly. "Now, what happened here?"

Gretta said, "Judy came running up to Jack's box, giggling like a goose and squeaking something about olives. Next thing you know it's whacko!"

"I guess she was leaning over the box when I popped out and the lid caught her under the chin," said Jack. "A nasty rap, Mr. Holmes. And it knocked her out. But she wasn't dead. I sent Gretta for a wet cloth." Here the young man broke down and buried his face in his hands. "Oh Judy, Judy, Judy," he sobbed.

"When Punch and I ran back with the wet cloth Captain Rataplan here was bending over her," said the ballerina. "Then he jumped up quick and started an argument with Jack."

"I thought the scoundrel'd hit her, Mr. Holmes," said the hussar. "I accused him of striking a woman. Not that it surprised me. The man's an utter coward. He proved that last year, lurking in his box when there were alligators to be driven off. I lost my temper and tried to throttle him, I admit it. But Punch leaped up from taking care of Judy and pulled me off."

"The cloth fell from Judy's head," said Gretta. "I leaned over to put it back on and that's when I saw the ice pick. That's when your stuffed friend came running up."

"I was on the hassock getting some tables and chairs from the house for the ladies," said Teddy. "You know me. Anything to help the festivities along. I saw the fight from up there and came on the double."

"Any chance it was an accident?" asked Punch. "We'd all warned the dumb old hoss not to carry the ice pick around in her pocket."

"This was no accident," said Holmes. Then he paused for a

thoughtful moment. "Gretta," he asked, "did you examine Judy before you ran off for the cloth?" When the ballerina shook her head he added, "So she might have been dead already?"

The young woman shrugged.

"And you, Captain Rataplan," asked Holmes, "could you swear Judy was alive when you bent over her?"

"I didn't look further than the mark on her chin and flew off the handle," admitted the fierce hussar. "This Jack fellow's an upstart."

"You can say that again," mused Holmes.

Rataplan did and added, "This fellow whose trouser legs aren't even the same color had the brass to have his eye on Lady Gwendolyn, who lived in the big house on the hassock. Last year I slew three alligators and left them as dead as luggage. And only the brave deserve the fair. But I would never, never have aspired to the hand of so fine a lady."

Rataplan paused to clear his throat. "Of course my heart is elsewhere," he said. Here, like many brave men he was overcome by an attack of shyness and averted his eyes. Holmes was quick to observe that it was the ballerina's unsympathetic gaze he was avoiding. The emotional lives of toys with only an hour of life each year lay close to the surface, like those of young people in wartime.

Holmes looked at Punch. "Landlord, was Judy alive or dead when you put the cloth on her forehead?"

"Search me, guv," said the hunchback "I mean, the fracas broke out right away."

"And yet you were certainly attached to Judy."

"A strictly professional relationship," insisted Punch. "I mean, did you ever see the snoot on her?"

"You're rather well endowed in that department yourself," observed Holmes.

"But I don't have to look at me, you see," said Punch quickly. "And while we're on the subject, you've got something of a beak yourself."

Holmes turned to confront Jack. "And just what was your relationship with the deceased?" he demanded.

"We all need someone, Mr. Holmes," said Jack.

"But why do you in particular need someone?"

Jack turned white. He lay a hand on the detective's arm and murmured, "Could I have a word in private, Mr. Holmes?"

"If you'll be more straightforward than you have been up to now," replied Holmes.

The bells on Jack's cap jingled as he swore he would be. When they had moved off a bit from the others Jack said, "I'm sure you realize that I can't trigger my lid latch from the inside."

"I am quite familiar with the Wunderbar jack-in-the-box mechanism," said the detective.

"But the others aren't, you see," said Jack. "My lid latch is defective. Traffic can trigger it and out I pop. 'Surprise!' They think I do it myself, but I can't. When the Christmas Hour comes I can't even get out of my box myself. That's a humiliating situation for a grown toy. That's my dark secret. My first Hour here in the Victorian Christmas exhibit I was lucky. A passing subway train triggered my latch. But I couldn't depend on that. I had to tell my secret to someone. I chose Lady Gwendolyn because she was so kind and good. Every Christmas Hour after that she'd slip over here first thing and let me out.

"But last year the alligators attacked and she fell to her death. In fact, I'd still be in the damned box if Rataplan hadn't come storming over after the alligators turned tail. He called me a coward and beat on the lid with his bloody saber until he accidentally triggered the latch. But what about next year? Well, Judy'd always been a bit soft on me so I took the chance of explaining things to her. She was the one who thought up the olive business. Rataplan's martooni was always the first drink of the night. She'd tell Punch she was keeping the olives in my icebox."

"Your secret has cost the lives of two people," said the detective. "I cannot believe that to be a coincidence. Come, let us settle this matter."

They returned to the waiting circle of toys where Holmes said, "Ladies and gentlemen, Judy's murderer is a very resourceful and decisive person who has committed a perfect crime."

"Come now, Holmes," protested Teddy, "don't tell us you are baffled."

"Consider my dilemma," said Holmes. "There are four suspects: Jack, Captain Rataplan, Punch, and Gretta. All had the opportunity to kill her. There is no clue to tell us which one did. Ergo, a perfect crime."

"And so justice will not be done, Mr. Holmes," said Irene Adler.

"Ah, but it will be, Miss Adler," said Holmes. "It will be indeed. Our murderer's mistake was in committing two perfect crimes. You see, you all believed Lady Gwendolyn's tragic death an accident. But in fact she was murdered. Someone pushed her to her death. That was a perfect crime and the murderer would have escaped discovery except for killing again.

"Judy's murder, perfect though the crime was, points the unerring finger of guilt at Lady Gwendolyn's killer. Rataplan and Punch were fighting the alligators. Jack was in his box. Of the three toys on the hassock two are dead. Clearly the murderer is—" Holmes was about to point an accusing finger when a corgi coughed.

The Christmas-tree angel fell silent and the toys froze in their places. The figure of an owlish, self-satisfied-looking young man loomed on the other side of the window glass.

Under his breath Teddy whispered, "It's the second assistant curator from the toy museum, Holmes. Met him once. Something of a royal stuffed shirt, don't you know? Miss Ivy Tinker has spoken of him most severely to me."

"He looks invincibly square, old fellow," whispered Holmes, venturing a glance. "I'd say she's got her work cut out for her." After what seemed an interminable period of time, the human outside the window was led away and Holmes's accusing finger pointed.

But as quick as a cat, Gretta snatched the astonished Rataplan's saber away from him and knocked him to the floor with the flat of it. Punch made a grab for her but she wounded him in the arm. Jack turned pale and popped down in his box, pulling the lid shut after him.

"There are soldiers at all the exits. You can't escape, you know," said Holmes calmly.

"We'll see about that," said the ballerina, holding them at bay with the saber and moving slowly backward in the direction of the Christmas tree. Leaving Irene Adler to tend to the wounded, Holmes and Teddy kept pace as close as Gretta would allow.

"I killed them both, okay?" she boasted. "When fate brought Jack and me together I swore to myself I'd kill anyone who came between us."

"It wasn't fate," insisted Teddy. "It was the second assistant curator."

Gretta didn't hear him. "I knew Jack had something going with Lady Gwendolyn," she said. "I saw them whispering and he'd always pop out of his box the minute she came to visit. I waited for my chance. When the alligators broke in, I took it." She was directly under the tree now. She looked around her and then continued. "But right away he took up with Judy. Judy—can you imagine that? Tonight when she came waltzing over to the box, I saw red and applied my foot to the small of her back. It knocked her over the lid just as Jack popped out. I'd only meant to warn her off. But later when I saw I could get away with it, I said what the hell and slipped in the ice pick."

"And now the game's up, Gretta," said Holmes.

With a contemptuous laugh the woman put the saber between her teeth, leaped up into the tree, and disappeared from sight.

"But surely she doesn't think she can get away, Holmes?" said the amazed bear.

"There's only one way to find out, old fellow," answered the detective, clambering up the tree trunk.

"Onwards and upwards, then," said Teddy, who was stuffed with excelsior.

But pursuit wasn't easy. As Gretta fled up the tree, she cut the strings on the wooden ornaments and sent them crashing down on her pursuers, obliging them to seek frequent shelter. And the dancer's excellent physical condition enabled her to leap from branch to branch like a monkey. She soon left them far behind.

"Adios, okay, Mr. Holmes?" she shouted triumphantly.

"I've been a blind fool, Teddy," said the detective, ducking to avoid a falling ornament. "She's going to hijack the angel and make it fly her to the Cuban Mission to the United Nations."

"Political asylum?" puffed Teddy.

"More than that, you dumb animal!" shouted Gretta, who was now at the top of the tree with the blade of the saber across the angel's throat. "Before the clock strikes one tonight, the rats in the basement of the Cuban Mission will know of Rataplan's great fear because I will tell them. When you all come to life next Christmas Hour, an army of alligators with rat riders will be there to greet you. Hell hath no fury like a scorned toy!"

With this cry, she vaulted onto the angel's back and slapped the creature's thigh with the flat of the saber. The angel flapped its wings and launched them both into space. It circled the top of the tree in a wide arc and then executed a barrel roll Amelia Earhart would have been proud of. Gretta fell head first the long distance to the floor.

The Victorian Christmas exhibit has been returned to the museum, where it continues to attract crowds. A Bo Peep with a velvet bow on her crook was Metcalfe's replacement for the broken music-box ballerina he passed on to Mr. Jacoby for repairs. "Listen, Metcalfe," said the overworked Mr. Jacoby, laying the doll in a small cardboard box and fastening the lid with a stout elastic band, "this goes on the shelf in the closet. If I get to it in twenty years it'll be lucky."

A new, less timid Judy has been found. They say it gives Punch as good as it gets. And sitting in the wing chair wearing the whole regalia of a Knight of the Garter is Teddy. A card nearby informs the world that it is in the presence of a rare Bear of the Realm on loan to the museum from Miss Ivy Tinker.

And here's how this dramatic change came about. When Metcalfe arrived at the museum that Christmas morning, the night watchman claimed more alligator sightings. The second assistant curator used an arch laugh he had developed to heap scorn on things. But since the man's breath passed muster he took a turn around the museum to see for himself.

In each wing of the museum Metcalfe experienced the uncanny feeling that he was interrupting a celebration. Worse than that, out in the corridors every shadow along the wall took on an amphibian shape and every night sound the building made became a vile mutter. Metcalfe was happy to let Owen Glendower lead him home. In spite of the late hour, he was so unsettled he had to read himself to sleep, choosing an old monograph on stuffed toys he'd picked up in a second-hand bookshop.

Later that day when he arrived at McTammany's for his confrontation with Miss Tinker, his indignation vanished when he noticed Teddy's English nightingale stitching and glass Homard et Fils eyes. Excited, he begged her to loan the priceless antique to the museum. She did not agree at once. They were obliged to return to the subject over several dinners and during numerous events about town. Metcalfe was also required to listen to her views on the dangers of extremism on matters of authenticity. To illustrate what she meant, one night she told him that in spite of when they were made, there was something about the Diva doll and the Sherlock Holmes doll that made them go together wonderfully. Metcalfe made the mistake of heaping scorn on this idea with that laugh of his. As a result, she swore she would not loan Teddy to the museum or set eyes on Metcalfe again until the Holmes doll had been rescued from the McTammany stockroom and was standing beside the Irene Adler doll in the Victorian Christmas exhibit.

Of course, Miss Tinker retained visiting rights to Teddy. Sometimes when she and Metcalfe would come to the museum in the evenings when it was closed, they would bring Owen Glendower along. The corgi rather liked her. The young woman hadn't knocked off all Metcalfe's corners yet but she was well on the way. And sometimes all three of them would stop in on the late-working Mr. Jacoby. In the middle of one of their discussions, Mr. Jacoby set his teacup down on the workbench, stroked his cat, and said, "Speaking of authentic, Metcalfe, how about this: suppose I make the broken Judy doll into a Victorian Christmas-tree angel?"

"Great," said Metcalfe, making an admiring gesture with his pipe. "Honestly, Mr. Jacoby, I don't know where you come up with your ideas."

Here Mr. Jacoby lowered his eyes modestly. But the cat and Owen Glendower were obliged to exchange glances.

The Ultimate Crime

by

Isaac Asimov

The collection would not be complete without a scholarly story. Although Ronald Mason looks and acts nothing at all like me, he was inspired by me in a sense. When I joined the Baker Street Irregulars, I thought it would be easy to write a Sherlockian article, and I suffered the same miseries Mason did, till I worked out the true intentions of the infamous Moriarty.

The Ultimate Crime

by Isaac Asimov

"The Baker Street Irregulars," said Roger Halsted, "is an organization of Sherlock Holmes enthusiasts. If you don't know that, you don't know anything."

He grinned over his drink at Thomas Trumbull with an air of the only kind of superiority there is—insufferable.

The level of conversation during the cocktail hour that preceded the monthly Black Widowers' banquet had remained at the level of a civilized murmur, but Trumbull, scowling, raised his voice at this point and restored matters to the more usual unseemliness that characterized such occasions.

He said, "When I was an adolescent I read Sherlock Holmes stories with a certain primitive enjoyment, but I'm not an adolescent anymore. The same, I perceive, cannot be said for everyone."

Emmanuel Rubin, staring owlishly through his thick glasses, shook his head. "There's no adolescence to it, Tom. The Sherlock Holmes stories marked the occasion on which the mystery story came to be recognized as a major branch of literature. It took what had until then been something that *had* been confined to adolescents and their dime novels and made of it adult entertainment."

339

Geoffrey Avalon, looking down austerely from his seventy-four inches to Rubin's sixty-four, said, "Actually, Sir Arthur Conan Doyle was not, in my opinion, an exceedingly good mystery writer. Agatha Christie is far better."

"That's a matter of opinion," said Rubin, who, as a mystery writer himself, was far less opinionated and didactic in that one field than in all the other myriad branches of human endeavor in which he considered himself an authority. "Christie had the advantage of reading Doyle and learning from him. Don't forget, too, that Christie's early works were pretty awful. Then, too"—he was warming up now—"Agatha Christie never got over her conservative, xenophobic prejudices. Her Americans are ridiculous. They were all named Hiram and all spoke a variety of English unknown to mankind. She was openly anti-Semitic and through the mouths of her characters unceasingly cast her doubts on anyone who was foreign."

Halsted said, "Yet her detective was a Belgian."

"Don't get me wrong," said Rubin. "I love Hercule Poirot. I think he's worth a dozen Sherlock Holmeses. I'm just pointing out that we can pick flaws in anyone. In fact, all the English mystery writers of the twenties and thirties were conservatives and upper-class oriented. You can tell from the type of puzzles they presented—baronets stabbed in the libraries of their manor houses—landed estates—independent wealth. Even the detectives were often gentlemen—Peter Wimsey, Roderick Alleyn, Albert Campion—"

"In that case," said Mario Gonzalo, who had just arrived and had been listening from the stairs, "the mystery story has developed in the direction of democracy. Now we deal with ordinary cops, and drunken private eyes and pimps and floozies and all the other leading lights of modern society." He helped himself to a drink and said, "Thanks, Henry. How did they get started on this?"

Henry said, "Sherlock Holmes was mentioned, sir."

"In connection with you, Henry?" Gonzalo looked pleased.

"No, sir. In connection with the Baker Street Irregulars."

Gonzalo looked blank. "What are—"

Halsted said, "Let me introduce you to my guest of the evening, Mario. He'll tell you. Ronald Mason, Mario Gonzalo.

Ronald's a member of BSI, and so am I, for that matter. Go ahead, Ron, tell him about it."

Ronald Mason was a fat man, distinctly fat, with a glistening bald head and a bushy black mustache. He said, "The Baker Street Irregulars is a group of Sherlock Holmes enthusiasts. They meet once a year in January, on a Friday near the great man's birthday, and through the rest of the year engage in other Sherlockian activities."

"Like what?"

"Well, they—"

Henry announced dinner, and Mason hesitated. "Is there some special seat I'm supposed to take?"

"No, no," said Gonzalo. "Sit next to me and we can talk."

"Fine." Mason's broad face split in a wide smile. "That's exactly what I'm here for. Rog Halsted said that you guys would come up with something for me."

"In connection with what?"

"Sherlockian activities." Mason tore a roll in two and buttered it with strenuous strokes of his knife. "You see, the thing is that Conan Doyle wrote numerous Sherlock Holmes stories as quickly as he could because he hated them—"

"He did? In that case, why—"

"Why did he write them? Money, that's why. From the very first story, 'A Study in Scarlet,' the world caught on fire with Sherlock Holmes. He became a world-renowned figure and there is no telling how many people the world over thought he really lived. Innumerable letters were addressed to him at his address in 221B Baker Street, and thousands came to him with problems to be solved.

"Conan Doyle was surprised, as no doubt anyone would be under the circumstances. He wrote additional stories and the prices they commanded rose steadily. He was not pleased. He fancied himself as a writer of great historical romances and to have himself become world-famous as a mystery writer was displeasing—particularly when the fictional detective was far the more famous of the two. After six years of it he wrote 'The Final Problem,' in which he deliberately killed Holmes. There was a world outcry at this and after several more years Doyle was forced to reason out a method for resuscitating the detective, and then went on writing further stories.

"Aside from the value of the sales as mysteries, and from the fascinating character of Sherlock Holmes himself, the stories are a diversified picture of Great Britain in the late Victorian era. To immerse oneself in the sacred writings is to live in a world where it is always 1895."

Gonzalo said, "And what's a Sherlockian activity?"

"Oh well. I told you that Doyle didn't particularly like writing about Holmes. When he did write the various stories, he wrote them quickly and he troubled himself very little about mutual consistency. There are many odd points, therefore, unknotted threads, small holes, and so on, and the game is never to admit that anything is just a mistake or error. In fact, to a true Sherlockian, Doyle scarcely exists—it was Dr. John H. Watson who wrote the stories."

James Drake, who had been quietly listening from the other side of Mason, said, "I know what you mean. I once met a Holmes fan—he may even have been a Baker Street Irregular— who told me he was working on a paper that would prove that both Sherlock Holmes and Dr. Watson were fervent Catholics and I said, 'Well, wasn't Doyle himself a Catholic?' which he was, of course. My friend turned a very cold eye on me and said, 'What has *that* to do with it?' "

"Exactly," said Mason, "exactly. The most highly regarded of all Sherlockian activities is to prove your point by quotations from the stories and by careful reasoning. People have written articles, for instance, that are supposed to prove that Watson was a woman, or that Sherlock Holmes had an affair with his landlady. Or else they try to work out details concerning Holmes's early life, or exactly where Watson received his war wound, and so on.

"Ideally, every member of the Baker Street Irregulars should write a Sherlockian article as a condition of membership, but that's clung to in only a slipshod fashion. I haven't written such an article yet, though I'd like to." Mason looked a bit wistful. "I can't really consider myself a true Irregular till I do."

Trumbull leaned over from across the table. He said, "I've been trying to catch what you've been saying over Rubin's monologue here. You mentioned 221B Baker Street."

"Yes," said Mason, "that's where Holmes lived."

"And is that why the club is the Baker Street Irregulars?"

Mason said, "That was the name Holmes gave to a group of street urchins who acted as spies and sources of information. They were his irregular troops as distinguished from the police."

"Oh well," said Trumbull, "I suppose it's all harmless."

"And it gives us great pleasure," said Mason seriously. "Except that right now it's inflicting agony on me."

It was at this point, shortly after Henry had brought in the veal cordon bleu, that Rubin's voice rose a notch. "Of course," he said, "there's no way of denying that Sherlock Holmes was derivative. The whole Holmesian technique of detection was invented by Edgar Allan Poe; and his detective, Auguste Dupin, is the original Sherlock. However, Poe only wrote three stories about Dupin and it was Holmes who really caught the imagination of the world.

"In fact, my own feeling is that Sherlock Holmes performed the remarkable feat of being the first human being, either real or fictional, ever to become a world idol entirely because of his character as a reasoning being. It was not his military victories, his political charisma, his spiritual leadership—but simply his cold brain power. There was nothing mystical about Holmes. He gathered facts and deduced from them. His deductions weren't always fair; Doyle consistently stacked the deck in his favor, but every mystery writer does that. I do it myself."

Trumbull said, "What you do proves nothing."

Rubin was not to be distracted. "He was also the first believable super hero in modern literature. He was always described as thin and aesthetic, but the fact that he achieved his triumphs through the use of brain power mustn't mask the fact that he is also described as being of virtually super-human strength. When a visitor, in an implicit threat to Holmes, bends a poker to demonstrate his strength, Holmes casually straightens it again—the more difficult task. Then, too—"

Mason nodded his head in Rubin's direction and said to Gonzalo, "Mr. Rubin sounds like a Baker Street Irregular himself—"

Gonzalo said, "I don't think so. He just knows everything—but don't tell him I said so."

"Maybe he can give me some Sherlockian pointers, then."

"Maybe, but if you're in trouble, the real person to help you is Henry."

"Henry?" Mason's eye wandered around the table as though trying to recall first names.

"Our waiter," said Gonzalo. "He's *our* Sherlock Holmes."

"I don't think—" began Mason doubtfully.

"Wait till dinner is over. You'll see."

Halsted tapped his water glass and said, "Gentlemen, we're going to try something different this evening. Mr. Mason has a problem that involves the preparation of a Sherlockian article, and that means he would like to present us with a purely literary puzzle, one that has no connection with real life at all.—Ron, explain."

Mason scooped up some of the melted ice cream in his dessert plate with his teaspoon, put it in his mouth as though in a final farewell to the dinner, then said, "I've got to prepare this paper because it's a matter of self-respect. I love being a Baker Street Irregular, but it's difficult to hold my head up when every person there knows more about the canon than I do and when thirteen-year-old boys write papers that meet with applause for their ingenuity.

"The trouble is that I don't have much in the way of imagination, or the kind of whimsy needed for the task. But I know what I want to do. I want to do a paper on Dr. Moriarty."

"Ah, yes," said Avalon. "The villain in the case."

Mason nodded. "He doesn't appear in many of the tales, but he is the counterpart of Holmes. He is the Napoleon of crime, the intellectual rival of Holmes and the great detective's most dangerous antagonist. Just as Holmes is the popular prototype of the fictional detective, so is Moriarty the popular prototype of the master villain. In fact, it was Moriarty who killed Holmes, and was killed himself, in the final struggle in 'The Final Problem.' Moriarty was not brought back to life."

Avalon said, "And on what aspect of Moriarty did you wish to do a paper?" He sipped thoughtfully at his brandy.

Mason waited for Henry to refill his cup and said, "Well, it's his role as a mathematician that intrigues me. You see, it is only Moriarty's diseased moral sense that makes him a master criminal. He delights in manipulating human lives and in serving as the agent for destruction. If he wished to bend his great talent to legitimate issues, however, he could be world famous—indeed, he *was* world famous, in the Sherlockian world—as a mathematician.

"Only two of his mathematical feats are specifically mentioned in the canon. He was the author of an extension of the binomial theorem, for one thing. Then, in the novel *The Valley of Fear*, Holmes mentions that Moriarty had written a thesis entitled *The Dynamics of an Asteroid*, which was filled with mathematics so rarefied that there wasn't a scientist in Europe capable of debating the matter."

"As it happened," said Rubin, "one of the greatest mathematicians alive at the time was an American, Josiah Willard Gibbs, who—"

"That doesn't matter," said Mason hastily. "In the Sherlockian world only Europe counts when it comes to matters of science. The point is this, nothing is said about the contents of *The Dynamics of an Asteroid;* nothing at all; and no Sherlockian has ever written an article taking up the matter. I've checked into it and I know that."

Drake said, "And *you* want to do such an article?"

"I want to very much," said Mason, "but I'm not up to it. I have a layman's knowledge of astronomy. I know what an asteroid is. It's one of the small bodies that circles the Sun between the orbits of Mars and Jupiter. I know what dynamics is; it's the study of the motion of a body and of the changes in its motion when forces are applied. But that doesn't get me anywhere. What is *The Dynamics of an Asteroid* about?"

Drake said thoughtfully, "Is that all you have to go by, Mason? Just the title? Isn't there any passing reference to anything that is in the paper itself?"

"Not one reference anywhere. There's just the title, plus the indication that it is a matter of a highly advanced mathematics."

Gonzalo put his sketch of a jolly, smiling Mason—with the face drawn as a geometrically perfect circle—on the wall next to the others and said, "If you're going to write about how planets move, you need a lot of fancy math, I should think."

"No, you don't," said Drake abruptly. "Let me handle this, Mario. I may be only a lowly organic chemist, but I know something about astronomy too. The fact of the matter is that all the mathematics needed to handle the dynamics of the asteroids was worked out in the 1680s by Isaac Newton.

"An asteroid's motion depends entirely upon the gravitational influences to which it is subjected and Newton's equation makes it possible to calculate the strength of that influence between any two bodies if the mass of each body is known and if the distance between them is also known. Of course, when many bodies are involved and when the distances among them are constantly changing, then the mathematics gets tedious—not difficult, just tedious.

"The chief gravitational influence on any asteroid is that originating in the Sun, of course. Each asteroid moves around the Sun in an elliptical orbit, and if the Sun and asteroid were all that existed, the orbit could be calculated, exactly, by Newton's equation. Since other bodies also exist, their gravitational influences, much smaller than that of the Sun, must be taken into account as producing much smaller effects. In general, we get very close to the truth if we just consider the Sun."

Avalon said, "I think you're oversimplifying, Jim. To duplicate your humility, I may be only a lowly patent lawyer, and I won't pretend to know any astronomy at all, but haven't I heard that there's no way of solving the gravitational equation for more than two bodies?"

"That's right," said Drake, "if you mean by that, a general solution for all cases involving more than two bodies. There just isn't one. Newton worked out the general solution for the two-body problem but no one, to this day, has succeeded in working out one for the three-body problem, let alone for more bodies than that. The point is, though, that only theoreticians are interested in the three-body problem. Astronomers work out the motion of a body by first calculating the dominant gravitational influence, then correcting it one step at a time with the introduction of other lesser gravitational influences. It works well enough." He sat back and looked smug.

Gonzalo said, "Well, if only theoreticians are interested in the three-body problem and if Moriarty was a high-powered mathematician, then that must be just what the treatise is about."

Drake lit a new cigarette and paused to cough over it. Then he said, "It could have been the love life of giraffes, if you like, but we've got to go by the title. If Moriarty had solved the three-body problem, he would have called the treatise something like, *An Analysis of the Three-Body Problem,* or *The Generalization of the Law of Universal Gravitation.* He would *not* have called it *The Dynamics of an Asteroid.*"

Halsted said, "What about the planetary effects? I've heard something about that. Aren't there gaps in space where there aren't any asteroids?"

"Oh, sure," said Drake. "We can find the dates in the Columbia Encyclopedia, if Henry will bring it over."

"Never mind," said Halsted. "You just tell us what you know about it and we can check the dates later, if we have to."

Drake said, "Let's see now." He was visibly enjoying his domination of the proceedings. His insignificant gray mustache twitched and his eyes, nested in finely wrinkled skin, seemed to sparkle.

He said, "There was an American astronomer named Kirkwood and I think Daniel was his first name. Sometime around the middle 1800s he pointed out that the asteroids' orbits seemed to cluster in groups. There were a couple of dozen known by then, all between the orbits of Mars and Jupiter, but they weren't spread out evenly, as Kirkwood pointed out. He showed there were gaps in which no asteroids circled.

"By 1866 or thereabouts—I'm pretty sure it was 1866—he worked out the reason. Any asteroid that would have had its orbit in those gaps would have circled the Sun in a period equal to a simple fraction of that of Jupiter."

"If there's no asteroid there," said Gonzalo, "how can you tell how long it would take it to go around the Sun?"

"Actually, it's very simple. Kepler worked that out in 1619 and it's called Kepler's Third Law. May I continue?"

"That's just syllables," said Gonzalo. "What's Kepler's Third Law?"

But Avalon said, "Let's take Jim's word for it, Mario. I can't quote it either, but I'm sure astronomers have it down cold. Go ahead, Jim."

Drake said, "An asteroid in a gap might have an orbital period of six years or four years, let us say, where Jupiter has a period of twelve years. That means an asteroid, every two or three revolutions, passes Jupiter under the same relative conditions of position. Jupiter's pull is in some particular direction each time, always the same, either forward or backward, and the effect mounts up.

"If the pull is backward, the asteroidal motion is gradually slowed so that the asteroid drops in closer toward the Sun and moves out of the gap. If the pull is forward, the asteroidal motion is quickened and the asteroid swings away from the Sun, again moving out of the gap. Either way nothing stays in the gaps, which are now called 'Kirkwood gaps.' You get the same effect in Saturn's rings. There are gaps there too."

Trumbull said, "You say Kirkwood did this in 1866?"

"Yes."

"And when did Moriarty write his thesis, supposedly?"

Mason interposed. "About 1875, if we work out the internal consistency of the Sherlockian canon."

Trumbull said, "Maybe Doyle was inspired by the news of the Kirkwood gaps, and thought of the title because of it. In which case, we can imagine Moriarty playing the role of Kirkwood and you can write an article on the Moriarty gaps."

Mason said uneasily, "Would that be enough? How important was Kirkwood's work? How difficult?"

Drake shugged. "It was a respectable contribution, but it was just an application of Newtonian physics. Good second-class work; not first class."

Mason shook his head. "For Moriarty, it would have to be first class."

"Wait, wait!" Rubin's sparse beard quivered with growing excitement. "Maybe Moriarty got away from Newton altogether. Maybe he got onto Einstein. Einstein revised the theory of gravity."

"He extended it," said Drake, "in the General Theory of Relativity in 1916."

"Right. Forty years after Moriarty's paper. That's got to be it. Suppose Moriarty had anticipated Einstein—"

Drake said, "In 1875? That would be before the Michelson-Morley experiment. I don't think it could have been done."

"Sure it could," said Rubin, "if Moriarty were bright enough—and he was."

Mason said, "Oh yes. In the Sherlockian universe, Professor Moriarty was brilliant enough for anything. Sure he would anticipate Einstein. The only thing is that, if he had done so, would he not have changed scientific history all around?"

"Not if the paper were suppressed," said Rubin, almost chattering with excitement. "It all fits in. The paper was suppressed and the great advance was lost till Einstein rediscovered it."

"What makes you say the paper was suppressed?" demanded Gonzalo.

"It doesn't exist, does it?" said Rubin. "If we go along with the Baker Street Irregular view of the universe, then Professor Moriarty *did* exist and the treatise *was* written, and it *did* anticipate General Relativity. Yet we can't find it anywhere in the scientific literature and there is no sign of the relativistic view penetrating scientific thought prior to Einstein's time. The only explanation is that the treatise was suppressed because of Moriarty's evil character."

Drake snickered. "There'd be a lot of scientific papers suppressed if evil character were cause enough. But your suggestion is out anyway, Manny. The treatise couldn't possibly involve General Relativity; not with that title."

"Why not?" demanded Rubin.

"Because revising the gravitational calculations in order to take relativity into account wouldn't do much as far as asteroidal dynamics are concerned," said Drake. "In fact, there was only one item known to astronomers in 1875 that could be considered, in any way, a gravitational puzzle."

"Uh-oh," said Rubin, "I'm beginning to see your point."

"Well, I don't," said Avalon. "Keep on going, Jim. What was the puzzle?"

Drake said, "It involved the planet Mercury, which revolves about the Sun in a pretty lopsided orbit. At one point in its orbit it is at its closest to the Sun (closer than any other planet, of course, since it is nearer to the Sun in general than the others are) and that point is the 'perihelion'. Each time Mercury completes a revolution about the Sun, that perihelion has shifted very slightly forward.

"The reason for the shift is to be found in the small gravitational effects, or perturbations, of the other planets on

Mercury. But after all the known gravitational effects are taken into account, the perihelion shift isn't completely explained. This was discovered in 1843. There is a very tiny residual shift forward that can't be explained by gravitational theory. It isn't much—only about forty-three seconds of arc per century, which means the perihelion would move an unexplained distance equal to the diameter of the full Moon in about forty-two hundred years, or make a complete circle of the sky"—he did some mental calculations—"in about three million years.

"It's not much of a motion, but it was enough to threaten Newton's theory. Some astronomers felt that there must be an unknown planet on the other side of Mercury, very close to the Sun. Its pull was not taken into account, since it was unknown, but it was possible to calculate how large a planet would have to exist, and what kind of an orbit it must have, to account for the anomalous motion of Mercury's perihelion. The only trouble was that they could never find that planet.

"Then Einstein modified Newton's theory of gravitation, made it more general, and showed that when the new, modified equations were used the motion of Mercury's perihelion was exactly accounted for. It also did a few other things, but never mind that."

Gonzalo said, "Why couldn't Moriarty have figured that out?"

Drake said, "Because then he would have called his treatise, *On the Dynamics of Mercury.* He couldn't possibly have discovered something that solved this prime astronomical paradox that had been puzzling astronomers for thirty years and have called it anything else."

Mason looked dissatisfied. "Then what you're saying is that there isn't anything that Moriarty could have written that would have had the title *On the Dynamics of an Asteriod* and still have represented a first-class piece of mathematical work?"

Drake blew a smoke ring. "I guess that's what I'm saying. What I'm also saying, I suppose, is that Sir Arthur Conan Doyle didn't know enough astronomy to stuff a pig's ear, and that he didn't know what he was saying when he invented the title. But I suppose that sort of thing is not permitted to be said."

"No," said Mason, his round face sunk in misery. "Not in the Sherlockian universe. There goes my paper, then."

"Pardon me," said Henry, from his post at the sideboard. "May I ask a question?"

Drake said, "You know you can, Henry. Don't tell me you're an astronomer."

"No, sir. At least, not beyond the average knowledge of an educated American. Still, am I correct in supposing that there are a large number of asteroids known?"

"Over seventeen hundred have had their orbits calculated, Henry," said Drake.

"And there were a number known in Professor Moriarty's time, too, weren't there?"

"Sure. Several dozen."

"In that case, sir," said Henry, "why does the title of the treatise read *The Dynamics of an Asteroid*? Why *an* asteroid?"

Drake thought a moment, then said, "That's a good point. I don't know—unless it's another indication that Doyle didn't know enough—"

"Don't say that," said Mason.

"Well—leave it at I don't know, then."

Gonzalo said, "Maybe Moriarty just worked it out for one asteroid, and that's all."

Drake said, "Then he would have named it *The Dynamics of Ceres* or whatever asteroid he worked on."

Gonzalo said stubbornly, "No, that's not what I mean. I don't mean he worked it out for one particular asteroid. I mean he picked an asteroid at random, or just an ideal asteroid, maybe not one that really exists. Then he worked out its dynamics."

Drake said, "That's not a bad notion, Mario. The only trouble is that if Moriarty worked out the dynamics of an asteroid, the basic mathematical system, it would hold for all of them, and the title of the paper would be *The Dynamics of Asteroids*. And besides, whatever he worked out in that respect would be only Newtonian and not of prime value."

"Do you mean to say," said Gonzalo, reluctant to let go, "that not one of the asteroids had something special about its orbit?"

"None known in 1875 did," said Drake. "They all had orbits between those of Mars and Jupiter and they all followed gravitational theory with considerable exactness. We know some asteroids with unusual orbits *now*. The first unusual asteroid to be discovered was Eros, which has an orbit that takes it closer to the Sun than Mars ever goes and brings it, on occasion, to within fourteen million miles of Earth, closer to Earth than any other body its size or larger, except for the Moon.

"That, however, wasn't discovered till 1898. Then, in 1906, Achilles was discovered. It was the first of the Trojan asteroids and they are unusual because they move around the Sun in Jupiter's orbit though well before or behind that planet."

Gonzalo said, "Couldn't Moriarty have anticipated those discoveries, and worked out the unusual orbits?"

"Even if he had anticipated them, the orbits are unusual only in their position, not in their dynamics. The Trojan asteroids did offer some interesting theoretical aspects, but that had already been worked out by Lagrange a century before."

There was a short silence and then Henry said, "The title is, however, so definite, sir. If we accept the Sherlockian premise that it must make sense, can it possibly have referred to some time when there was only a single body orbiting between Mars and Jupiter?"

Drake grinned. "Don't try to act ignorant, Henry. You're talking about the explosion theory of the origin of the asteroids."

For a moment, it seemed as though Henry might smile. If the impulse existed, he conquered it, however, and said, "I have come across, in my reading, the suggestion that there had once been a planet between Mars and Jupiter and that it had exploded."

Drake said, "That's not a popular theory anymore, but it certainly had its day. In 1801, when the first asteroid, Ceres, was discovered, it turned out to be only about four hundred fifty miles across, astonishingly small. What was far more astonishing, though, was that over the next three years three other asteroids were discovered, with very similar orbits. The notion of an exploded planet was brought up at once."

Henry said, "Couldn't Professor Moriarty have been referring to that planet before its explosion, when speaking of *an* asteroid?"

Drake said, "I suppose he could have, but why not call it a planet?"

"Would it have been a large planet?"

"No, Henry. If all the asteroids are lumped together, they would make up a planet scarcely a thousand miles in diameter."

"Might it not be closer to what we now consider an asteroid, then, rather than to what we consider a planet? Mightn't that have been even more true in 1875 when fewer asteroids were known and the original body would have seemed smaller still?"

Drake said, "Maybe. But why not call it *the* asteroid, then?"

"Perhaps Professor Moriarty felt that to call the paper *The Dynamics of the Asteroid* was too definite. Perhaps he felt the explosion theory was not certain enough to make it possible to speak of anything more than *an* asteroid. However unscrupulous Professor Moriarty might have been in the world outside science, we must suppose that he was a most careful and rigidly precise mathematician."

Mason was smiling again. "I like that, Henry. It's a great idea." He said to Gonzalo, "You were right."

"I told you," said Gonzalo.

Drake said, "Hold on, let's see where it takes us. Moriarty can't be just talking about the dynamics of the original asteroid as a world orbiting about the Sun, because it would be following gravitational theory just as all its descendants are.

"He would have to be talking about the explosion. He would have to be analyzing the forces in planetary structure that would make an explosion conceivable. He would have to discuss the consequences of the explosion, and all that would not lie within the bounds of gravitational theory. He would have to calculate the events in such a way that the explosive forces would give way to gravitational effects and leave the asteroidal fragments in the orbits they have today."

Drake considered, then nodded, and went on. "That would not be bad. It would be a mathematical problem worthy of Moriarty's brain, and we might consider it to have represented the first attempt of any mathematician to take up so complicated an astronomical problem. Yes, I like it."

Mason said, "I like it too. If I can remember everything you've all said, I have my article. Good Lord, this is wonderful."

Henry said, "As a matter of fact, gentlemen, I think this hypothesis is even better than Dr. Drake has made it sound. I believe that Mr. Rubin said earlier that we must assume that

Professor Moriarty's treatise was suppressed, since it cannot be located in the scientific annals. Well, it seems to me that if our theory can also explain that suppression, it becomes much more forceful."

"Quite so," said Avalon, "but can it?"

"Consider," said Henry, and a trace of warmth entered his quiet voice, "that over and above the difficulty of the problem, and of the credit therefore to be gained in solving it, there is a peculiar appeal in the problem to Professor Moriarty in view of his known character.

"After all, we are dealing with the destruction of a world. To a master criminal such as Professor Moriarty, whose diseased genius strove to produce chaos on Earth, to disrupt and corrupt the world's economy and society, there must have been something utterly fascinating in the vision of the actual *physical* destruction of a world.

"Might not Moriarty have imagined that on that original asteroid another like himself had existed, one who had not only tapped the vicious currents of the human soul but had even tampered with the dangerous forces of a planet's interior? Moriarty might have imagined that this super-Moriarty of the original asteroid had deliberately destroyed his world, and all life on it, including his own, out of sheer joy in malignancy, leaving the asteroids that now exist as the various tombstones that commemorate the action.

"Could Moriarty even have envied the deed and tried to work out the necessary action that would have done the same on Earth? Might not those few European mathematicians who could catch even a glimpse of what Moriarty was saying in his treatise have understood that what it described was not only a mathematical description of the origin of the asteroids but the beginning of a recipe for the ultimate crime—that of the destruction of Earth itself, of all life, and of the creation of a much larger asteroid belt?

"It is no wonder, if that were so, that a horrified scientific community suppressed the work."

And when Henry was done, there was a moment of silence and then Drake applauded. The others quickly joined in.

Henry reddened. "I'm sorry," he murmured when the applause died. "I'm afraid I allowed myself to be carried away."

"Not at all," said Avalon. "It was a surprising burst of poetry that I was glad to have heard."

Halsted said, "Frankly, I think that's perfect. It's exactly what Moriarty would do and it explains everything. Wouldn't you say so, Ron?"

"I will say so," said Mason, "as soon as I get over being speechless. I ask nothing better than to prepare a Sherlockian paper based on Henry's analysis. How can I square it with my conscience, however, to appropriate his ideas?"

Henry said, "It is yours, Mr. Mason, my free gift, for initiating a very gratifying session. You see, I have been a devotee of Sherlock Holmes for many years, myself."